For Kristy,
I hope you
enjoy the mystery!
♡ Andrea

A Curious Spring Fever

By Andrea Mina Savar

This book is dedicated to my parents, for believing in the unseen and protecting me from the monsters that go bump in the night. The early years were rough but I am forever grateful!

Chapter 1

Spring fever had come early to Port Townsend the year my daughter Wilhelmina Winship turned sixteen. It was late February and already the cherry trees were beginning to blossom and the primroses were unfolding their colorful skirts after a short winter of intense snow. I, Charlotte Winship, felt uneasy at the premature celebrations of spring as children forgot their jackets and became fiery in their temperaments. The bees were buzzing in and out of the Winship house each time I opened the door, signaling a new arrival to our quiet town.

As Wilhelmina's birthday approached, my husband James said teasingly that I was just feeling the pain that all mothers have when their daughters are nearly grown. But something more ominous lurked in the back of my mind as I swept out the winter dust from the mudroom and opened all the windows to let the house breathe. The dreams had begun a week before arriving with the wisp of warm winds and the smell of lilacs. It was the same dream each night that often ended in my sitting up in bed screaming, waking James with a fright.

Two little girls came to me as the house settled into its midnight repose, their dresses of crumpled taffeta swishing as they walked up the stairs side by side, whispering to each other to keep quiet. Eventually, they snuck into our bedroom as we slept and stood next to my side of the bed. The older girl touched my face with hot, burning hands. Her tiny voice whispered in the dark hush of the room, "Mommy, help me. I have a fever," and that was when I screamed myself awake.

I had been experiencing ghostly visits for almost forty years, my special gift in a family who all had curious talents. I could see and communicate with the lingering dead. But each time I awoke with my heart pounding, expecting the little girls to be standing there, they were gone, leaving me clueless about what they needed from me. And while their presence was fleeting, the place where they touched me burned for hours, their feverish fingers leaving their mark on my cool skin.

After their visit, I went down the hall to my eight-year-old son Felix's room to make sure he was sound asleep. Next I climbed the third stairwell to check on Wilhelmina. As a child, the turret bedroom had been my safe haven whenever I stayed in the Winship house with my grandmother, Margot. It was comforting to know that my daughter was now in that sacred space. Margot had moved out of the Winship house a year after James and I returned to Port Townsend after several years of living in Seattle.

The first year we all lived together while James designed a new home for Margot on Annie Christy's old land, which the Winships had inherited after her death. James had opened his own architecture business in Port Townsend, which was desperate for someone with his talent and passion for restoring the old Victorian homes that had long been abandoned. His first project was Margot's new home. He preserved Annie's cactus garden and the original fence while turning the crumbling log cabin into a two-story home with a willow tree at its center, along with a greenhouse for all her roses. Shortly after Margot moved into her new home, Wilhelmina was born and the Winship house added a new generation to its long list of women with gifts.

It would take several years to understand Wilhelmina's gift, but it slowly began to emerge. She would cry uncontrollably when other children hurt themselves or an animal was injured. When she was five years old, a baby bird became trapped in one of the many chimneys in the Winship house. James had been too late to save it. She was inconsolable for days as she tried to explain with her young vocabulary that she had felt trapped and couldn't breathe. Eventually her Great Uncle, Morgan, came by the house to speak with her and he revealed to us that she was empathic. She felt the emotions as well as the mental and physical pain of others around her. This was a gift that could easily become a burden, so from then on we tried to shelter her as best we could so she would have a safe place to come home to and rest with as little emotional upheaval as possible.

Surprisingly, she had not grown into a meek young woman, overwhelmed by the feelings of others; rather, Willa had a sweet, but fiery, personality that made people want to stand next to her. By the age of nine she was a leader among her peers, and James' pride and joy as he took her to softball practice and drama club and other activities that inspired her. Wherever she went, the other children her age wanted to follow; now at just a few weeks shy of sixteen, she was vibrant and enchanting with her long auburn hair and dark eyes. Most of all she was strong-willed although not without deep compassion for others and she had a creative side that amazed even the most jaded residents in town.

Felix was born eight years after Willa on a dreary November 2, sharing his birthday with his Great Uncle Morgan. When we found out we were having a boy, James was so smitten he could barely contain his excitement and wore a circle into the hardwood floors in the kitchen from pacing. I, on the other hand, was filled with fear that not only would I be the mother of a male Winship, which was generally accompanied by much worry over the extent of their gifts, but also that the due date just happened to be on the same day that Morgan was born, which felt like a bad omen. In the weeks leading up to his birth I became obsessively superstitious; and harassed my friend, Bee, for protection charms, while insisting that both Deidre and Margot hold my hands during the birth. When the fated day finally arrived, Felix was born in less than an hour with no complications; all my worry and dread washed from me the instant I held him in my arms.

When the doctor handed him to me I froze, waiting to feel the sensation of looming darkness I'd dreaded, but instead I felt a wave of joy dance over me. Felix stared up at me with calm, deep eyes and a small sigh of relief escaped my lips. I knew he was untouched by evil forces. Felix was like Margot; his element was water. Whenever he fussed or seemed restless, I would walk him over to Chetzemoka Park where the swings overlooked the ocean and we would rock back and forth with the sound of waves crashing nearby. Felix's gift was revealed as soon as he began to speak. One afternoon he was perched in his high chair near the old wood stove as I was juggling a cherry pie, talking on the phone and kindling the flames. He kept wiggling in his chair to get my attention and as I slid the pie into the oven he began to cry hysterically. Thinking he had burnt himself on the wood stove, I dropped the phone and ran over to inspect his limbs, but he was unscathed. He kept crying "Pie crash, Daddy crash." Not knowing what he was trying to tell me, I eventually calmed him down and managed to put him down for a nap.

An hour later as the pie was ready to come out of the oven, I reached in to remove it and was shocked by a horrific screeching of tires outside of our house. As the pie crashed to the floor, my heart sank at the sounds of crumpling metal followed by a sickening bang that ricocheted through the street. I ran out the door and watched as James pulled himself from the twisted metal that had been our car; a logging truck lay overturned nearby, hanging precariously over the cliffs. It was a miracle James was unharmed. I sank to my knees when I saw the passenger side of the car crushed by a massive log that had fallen from the truck. James had been picking up Willa on his way home from work; by all reason she was meant to be in the car with him. Stunned, I watched as he ran from the car and called the police on his cell phone. The bell tower began ringing on its own; the town ghosts often responded to my emotions of fear or danger by sounding their own alarms.

As James ran to the porch, blood pooling above his eye, he collapsed next to me on the old floorboards and grasped me tightly in his arms. His body shook with adrenaline. I finally choked the word "Willa" from my deadened lips, fearing the worst. As if lightening had shot through James' body, he grabbed my shoulders and looking me in the eyes, spoke slowly so I could comprehend through the shock:

"Morgan picked her up early," he said. "She is at the cider mill."

As his words finally made sense, the fire trucks and police cars arrived in a flurry of blinking lights and sirens. I clung to James with desperate relief. Later, when all traces of the accident were removed from our usually sleepy street, I noticed the cherry pie splattered across the kitchen floor. The cherries were a horrific reminder of the blood and disaster that had been outside only hours before and that was when Felix's words shot through my mind. As he learned more words, his premonitions became more precise and we began to write them down in a large, leather-bound book. At the age of six he was keeping his own journals of premonitions and though he kept many to himself, there were times when he would whisper little glimpses of the future into our ears.

Now, as the cherry trees began to show signs of early pink buds and the ghost girls were creeping into our bedroom at night, Felix finally came to me with a premonition that had been bothering him. He tiptoed into the Winship library, which had become my jewelry workroom. I still made adornments for stores in Seattle as well as Deidre's store, which I had taken over several years earlier. In stocking feet and his favorite pajamas, he climbed into my lap before heading to bed. Unlike Willa's bubbly personality, Felix was shy and introspective, but I had noticed he had been quieter than usual in recent days.

"Tomorrow is a special day, right?" he asked me as I set down my pliers and breathed in the smell of his freshly shampooed hair.

"Well," I said, turning to look at the small calendar on the big oak desk. This year was a leap year so tomorrow would be February 29. "It is a special day. It's leap year so we get one extra day in February," I said, as he slowly nodded his head, seeming none too happy about my confirming words.

"Is something going to happen tomorrow?" I asked, not wanting to push him if he didn't want to talk about it. He slowly nodded his head, curling himself into my arms. I slowly rocked him and then carefully asked:

"Do you want to talk about it?"

He silently pondered my offer as James' footsteps sounded in the hallway coming towards the library. He poked his head around the corner and smiled when he saw us.

"Almost bedtime, Buddy," he said, tapping his watch before heading back down the hall.

Slowly, Felix climbed out of my lap and, with his head hanging, walked towards the hallway. When he reached the door, he stopped and turned towards me, leaning on the doorframe. I could tell he was working out the best way to tell me what was bothering him. Finally he looked me in the eyes and in a whispered voice said:

"The vampires are coming, Mom. They will be here tomorrow.

I just keep seeing the color red," he said in a rush of frightened words.

A cold chill ran down my back and the hair stood up on my arms. Felix looked at me with frightened eyes. What had he seen in his premonition?

"What do you mean by vampires?" I asked in an even tone, not wanting to scare my small boy any more than he already was.

"I don't know," he said, shyly looking at his feet.

He looked back down the hall. We heard James whistling his favorite song of the moment. Felix ran to me quickly and gave me a fierce hug, then was down the hall in a flash where James was waiting to tuck him in.

Later, as quiet filled the Winship house and I slowly drifted to sleep, I sent out a silent prayer for my family and my town to be safe from whatever darkness Felix knew was coming. When I thought of the word 'vampire' it instantly conjured images from old silent films and Gothic classics, but I had never known these things to exist outside of Hollywood. Was this the ominous feeling I had been having for the past few weeks as the town was thrown into an early spring? As I slipped into sleep, I thought I heard the old bell tower's muffled clanging through the warm night air.

CHAPTER 2

The town was in a panic the next morning. We awoke to a red tide so true to its name, it looked as if a massacre had occurred somewhere off shore. The waves rolled in, leaving the rocks covered in a red sheen and the water was so thick it looked like blood beginning to congeal. I immediately thought of Felix's words about vampires and thought this must be what he had seen in his mind's eye. A red tide was not all that uncommon on the coast, although usually it was less literal and consisted of high levels of bacteria that caused the shellfish to be unfit for human consumption. But the red tide of February 29 was of a more extreme nature. Scientists rushed to our quiet town to take samples of the algae bloom erupting in the waters, likely due to the early spring heat.

Willa and Felix left for school that morning looking fatigued from restless nights, though for very different reasons. For Willa, I was sure she had tossed and turned about the upcoming St. Patrick's Day dance, an enduring high school tradition. She wasn't sure who she was going with. All the teenagers in town obsessed about this event for months. Though Willa was popular with her peers, she was also a Winship, and while our family was now more accepted than it had been in my youth, our name still carried the stigma of being different. Tonight, I'd try to talk to her about dresses while expertly slipping in ancient Winship tricks for finding the right dance partner.

As James and I sipped our morning coffee at the large kitchen table, I kept a close eye on Felix. He had dark circles under his eyes and was more quiet than usual. As he reached for his lunch, I touched his forehead to check for fever, but his skin was strangely cool. His words about vampires lingered in my mind and I tried to convince myself his premonition had to do with the red tide and not with the possible arrival of mythical creatures. One by one everyone left the house. I finished up the last of the coffee pot's rich brew and began packing my basket of pieces to work with while at the shop in what was now my store The Curious Crow.

When Samir retired from years of working as an ER doctor, both he and my mother, Deidre, were ready for a change of scenery. For years, Deidre had taken flying lessons while working her way towards earning a pilot's license. Eventually her dream of taking to the air like her bird companions came true. They invested in a small plane and began creating an itinerary that left us all excited and worried for them at the same time. Deidre had always wanted to explore the South Pacific and conduct her own Winship research on the energy surrounding the islands. In less than six months their bags were packed, their houses rented, and Deidre handed me the key to The Curious Crow and all its contents for the symbolic amount of one dollar. Though it pained us to have them leave, the excitement in both of their faces at the prospect of adventure was contagious as we waved them off on their trip. Postcards poured in from all their stops, and both Willa and Felix had a Grandma Deidre and Grandpa Samir wall of cards and trinkets in their rooms.

It was almost two years since they had left on their voyage, but every day I thought of them as I stepped into the store of curiosities and gazed upon several of Deidre's paintings. Today was no different. The shop was built on piers and once inside with the lights turned on, the color of the water just outside the French windows that faced the bay had a startling impact on me. The waves were calm as the bright sun beat down on the sands, but the shocking red of the water felt like a bad omen.

Throughout the day people came in and out; the premature spring weather had lured tourists to town, although the red tide was more than most had expected. Everything glowed an eerie crimson as the sun reflected the color of the algae on the old brick buildings that made up downtown's Water Street. There was a sense of confusion in the air; people were clumsily tripping along the sidewalks. Sadly, a rare piece of reliquary shattered when a well-meaning client reached up to examine it closer only to fumble the framed pieces of saintly bone and flesh.

After two hours of watching people trip, bump, and stumble their way through town, I decided to call my grandmother, Margot.

She was tied to water in a curious way and would know what was happening. The phone rang several times until I heard her familiar voice, scratchy with age, answer in her formal manner:

"Margot Winship residence, who, may I ask, is calling?" she croaked into the receiver and waited patiently for a response.

"It's Charlotte," I said, trying to figure out how to bring up the odd phenomenon in case she hadn't turned on the local news.

"Are you calling about the tide?" she asked, mischievousness in her voice; she knew I'd be calling her sooner or later. I let out a sigh of both relief and exasperation.

"Yeeeess," I said, drawing out the word a bit longer than normal. "It's probably nothing, but I've had a peculiar feeling that something unnatural was about to occur ever since this early spring weather began; then this gruesome tide shows up."

"Why would you think it was nothing?" she asked in a stern tone. She had been telling me for years to listen to my instincts and for some stubborn reason I was always denying what I felt. "This morning Morgan and I went to the beach to gather driftwood to repair the fence, and there were at least eight great white sharks that had beached themselves on the shore. That, my dear, is a bad omen!"

Her words sank in as I envisioned Margot and Morgan looking out over the blood red waves and the carcasses of the huge fish scattered over North Beach. The Straights of Juan de Fuca were home to many creatures including orca whales, seals, sea lions, and, of course, sharks. The thought of that many great white sharks in our waters this early in the year was odd enough, but to have them beached as well was even more unusual.

"Were they still alive?" I asked, not really wanting to know the answer.

"There was nothing we could do for them. Two were still struggling, but their size alone was enough to keep us from being able to get them back in the water. I've never seen anything like it. At first I thought the blood-colored water may have attracted them too close to shore, but Morgan thought otherwise. He said he could feel a presence moving towards town and that we needed to keep our eyes open for something seeking blood."

I suddenly felt queasy as her words rang in my ears along with the feeling of dread I'd been having since the appearance of the feverish ghost girls and Felix's revelation.

"Felix had a premonition," I whispered, just as the bell on the shop door clinked announcing a customer. "He said vampires are coming." I quickly added as a family of three came in and began to examine a basket of old skeleton keys.

"Vampires?" she said with an air of surprise. "Call me tonight when you get home and the house is quiet. Put up the usual protection stones and make sure the children have holy water by their windows."

Her words made me feel ill at ease. I hung up quickly so as not to ignore my customers, but my uneasiness mounted by the second. When the shop clocks struck closing time, the light outside was fading fast and the red glow from the setting sun on the even redder water was more than unsettling. As I began locking the front door, a loud rumbling noise ricocheted off the huge old buildings downtown. Even the boards beneath my feet began to vibrate and I wondered if an earthquake was shaking the region. Then two huge, black shadows came rolling down the street just as the sun dipped beneath the horizon. I made out the familiar words that read "U-Move" on the sides of the huge trucks barreling down the narrow street. They shook the pavement with their grinding gears, leaving a trail of black smoke behind them. Shop owners stood motionless in the street watching as these monstrous contraptions shook their way into our small town.

Slowly the rumble faded and the two trucks headed steadily up the small road towards the cliffs and came to a halt in front of the Bell Tower House. From below, I had a perfect view of the home that had been empty for over ten years. Local lore claimed numerous poltergeists and other noisy spirits kept residence there, but now it seemed the Bell Tower House finally had human inhabitants; which meant a new family had arrived....on the day of the red tide.

AUTEL D'OR DES PARFUMS

CR 14 SO

By the time I closed the shop and made my way home, the sky was completely dark. Pulling into the driveway, I felt a sense of relief the moment I passed through the old iron gates. The glow of light from the kitchen of the Winship house felt like a beacon of safety. James' car was absent from the carriage house which meant the kids were already home waiting for me, while most likely rummaging around the cupboards for sustenance. As I walked up the old stairs to the front door, the lock clicked before I could put my key in the hole. It slyly creaked open a few inches. Then, from the edge of the door, I noticed two small hands wrapped along its edge. A tiny face peered around to greet me. It was Felix, sporting a peevish grin along with a mess of jam around his mouth.

"Hi Mom, Grandma Margot is here," he said with obvious glee.

I was sure that Willa's and Felix's appetites had been thoroughly ruined for the chicken and broccoli I was about to prepare. Despite that minor detail, I felt a sense of relief. She was most certainly here to talk about the red tide and Felix's premonition once the children were doing their homework in another room. Setting down my basket, I followed Felix as he ran and then slid his way along the hardwood floors. Margot was sitting at the kitchen table with Willa, whispering conspiratorially.

"Well hello, ladies," I said as I flopped down in my favorite wooden chair nearest the wood stove. "I hope I'm not interrupting anything."

Willa smiled at me as Margot began covering another piece of her homemade bread with blackberry jam.

"I just popped over for a quick visit and found these two famished," she said in a teasing tone. If I hadn't known better, it might have seemed Margot was the old witch fattening up two hapless children before cooking them into a minced meat pie. Thankfully she wasn't that kind of witch. There was still a glimmer in her eye, though, that betrayed a quick mind despite her advanced age. Although her hands were gnarled and her hair was wisps of white, she retained her knowledge of all things otherworldly. In the past few years, the storms that had once plagued the coast began to wane in their ferocity as Margot's emotional state mellowed with time. I knew she was here tonight to make sure her descendants were all under a powerful protection spell.

Willa was first to head up to her room and Felix followed, thumping loudly on the stairs for such a small boy. Margot quickly cleaned away the remnants of breadcrumbs and drops of jam on the old wooden table. The vibrant red of the errant blackberry jam drops looked eerily like blood. I quickly pushed the thought from my mind as a slight wave of nausea rolled over me. As she buzzed around the kitchen that had for so many years been her own, I also realized there was a huge bouquet of lilacs overflowing on the countertop. The smell had become so omnipresent in town the past week, with the unexpected heat and subsequent early blooming of flowers, that their perfume hadn't registered.

"Thank you for the bouquet," I said, motioning to the flowers.

"I have so many in bloom; the branches are full to breaking," replied Margot. "You know what they are, don't you?"

I hadn't the slightest idea what she was hinting at. I just shrugged, hoping she would let me in on some of her mystical knowledge. She clicked the oven on to 450 degrees, knowing I would be putting the chicken in to roast for dinner when James arrived. Margot carefully settled into her chair across from me and made herself comfortable before speaking.

"My mother, Elsiba, always said that lilacs were far more powerful in warding off vampires than garlic. The problem is they only bloom for a short time, so garlic is much easier to procure," Margot paused and watched as I took in her words. "Her favorite perfume was lilac."

"I had no idea," I whispered, then gulped, thinking of the moving trucks that had rumbled up the street earlier that evening. "There is a new family that arrived tonight. I saw the moving trucks at sunset. They stopped at the house by the Bell Tower. Do you think...?"

I couldn't finish my sentence, but Margot jumped in for me.

"That they are Felix's vampires?" she said with a gloominess that I rarely saw in her. "I think they may be, but we will have to wait and see. One thing is for sure: the lilacs bloomed nearly five weeks early this year and that cannot be just a coincidence. That, with the red tide, bothered me, but along with Felix's premonition, I am convinced something unholy is about to set up housekeeping in town."

With that, she reached over and set her garden basket on the table and began to remove protective items for the Winship house. She lined up five vials of holy water in a neat row on the tabletop, followed by two wreathes of garlic. A small pouch of iron nails made a loud thud on the table as one slid from the bag. Finally she revealed a tiny hand-blown perfume bottle that I immediately recognized as being from Annie Christie's old cabinet of treasures. It was decorated with finely-painted winding purple flowers over opaque lapis blue glass with hints of green leaves. Carefully, Margot loosened the delicate glass stopper and let me breathe in the heady aroma of lilacs with a hint of lemon. She dabbed a few drops behind my ears and, with a wrinkled smile, put her now-empty basket back on the floor. Looking down at the table, Margot seemed pleased with the array of items she had set before me.

"The holy water is for the front and back doors of this house as well as the doorways to Felix, Willa and your bedrooms," Margot explained. "The garlic is also to hang directly on the outside of both doors of the house." She paused, reading my thoughts and finally asked, "Do you really care what the neighbors think?"

"No," I grudgingly admitted, but I knew that James cared and that we would most likely be having a long discussion tonight before bed. "What about the nails?"

"They are iron. More importantly, they are from Annie's collection of objects. I think they may be old coffin nails, but I can't be sure. I do know they are more effective than silver and that each of you should wear one at all times. I'm sure you can figure out a way to make them wearable."

I already had several ideas flitting through my head that combined linen and a few strikes with my jeweler's hammer to make the nails into small coils. Even though I knew the perfume bottle had been in Annie's possession, I waited to hear what Margot would say about it. She sat quietly for a moment, caressing the raised designs on its edge that formed miniature lilacs across the small vessel.

"This was my mother's," she said in a quiet voice, "and I have made this perfume each spring according to her instructions should the day come when vampires returned to our town."

As the meaning of her words began to sink in, I felt a chill run through my body as if someone had suddenly opened a window and a cool wind had blown through the room.

"When were they here before?" I asked, trying to hide the anxiety in my voice.

"It was before I was born. My mother never spoke much about those days in front of me. I know that every year when the lilacs bloomed she made this perfume with their flowers and a special mix of other herbs. She always made enough to last the entire year, with some to spare. This is the fragrance that most conjures Elsiba's memory to me."

She reached into the pocket of her linen apron dress and handed me a folded paper. I carefully opened it and read the list of ingredients written in Margot's intricate script. It included the proper method of concoction and, as I read through the steps, I imagined Margot in her modern kitchen re-enacting this ancient process each year. It felt odd that I'd never seen her do this and that she had kept this a secret all these years. I would have to ask my mother if she remembered Margot making this perfume, but our weekly phone call wasn't scheduled for another two days. She and Samir were often unreachable since they headed in and out of the remotest of islands on their research trips. The vast area where they flew was a cellular dead zone, so we had to plan specific times for our weekly calls.

"I want you to wear this perfume every day without exception. If you can, try to get Willa to wear it as well, although I know she can be particular. Also, slip a bit into the laundry as it dries so Felix and James will have a bit on their clothes; I doubt the boys will want to wear perfume," she said with a grin. I thought it was funny that in her eyes, Felix and James were both "boys." Actually, anyone under the age of seventy was considered a child. I had to admit that she had her reasons for feeling superior to most folks in terms of life experience.

"Should I make more?" I asked, wondering if that was why she had taken pains to write down the process for me.

"No, I have enough for all of us for at least a year. But this needs to go in your own grimoire," she said, while looking directly into my eyes. "You know I won't be here forever to watch over everyone."

My throat immediately tightened at the idea of Margot no longer being on this earth. I quickly banished the thought and folded the paper back into a perfect square, as if my own stubborn refusal of the notion could make her immortal. A loud bang sounded from outside as James arrived home and closed the carriage house doors for the night. Margot had the chicken in the oven before I even had time to stand up from my chair. Soon the kitchen was in a state of commotion as James entered the house through the kitchen door and Willa and Felix came clamoring downstairs. James stacked papers on the table and draped his jacket over a nearby chair and greeted Margot with a hug and me with a kiss.

"So the weirdest thing happened tonight," were the first words from his mouth. "As I was getting ready to leave the office my phone rang. Normally I would have let the machine get it but I felt compelled to answer." He paused for a moment, settling himself next to us as Willa and Felix meandered around the old wood stove for warmth. "Anyway, it was a man by the name of Mr. Renard. Apparently he and his wife and son just bought the old Bell Tower House and the Cliffside Chapel. They want to use my firm to do the restorations."

He seemed almost giddy as he spoke. From the first day that James set foot in Port Townsend, he had vowed to one day restore both of those structures. The Bell Tower House was built with some of the most unique materials on the Peninsula, including peach woods and other exotic designs. Over the years it had begun a slow decay as residents were few and far between. The damp winters and the sea salt had withered away the former glory of the once magnificent dwelling. The mansion would be stunning once the exterior repairs were undertaken. I had heard the interior was still furnished with the original Victorian furniture.

The Cliffside Chapel was only a few blocks east of the Bell Tower. It was true to its name as it was perched precariously on the cliff's edge with only the blackberry brambles holding the foundation in place. It was used as a temporary church until the larger batistes were completed in uptown in the early 1900s. The Cliffside Chapel was a simple two-story whitewashed building with a steeple and one room perched on top of a small basement. It had been empty for the last twenty years with a faded "For Sale" sign hung dutifully in the window.

Margot and I said nothing as James told us about the new family that had just taken up residence in our town. His excitement at finally being able to work on saving two of his favorite buildings was almost contagious. He explained that the Renard family had been living on the East Coast, but decided to move West after a long-time friend raved about our little town. They were ready for a change and planned to use the Chapel as an office or meeting place of sorts for their business. James would be starting on the project tomorrow as Mr. and Mrs. Renard wanted the house to be in pristine condition as quickly as possible.

"This is a wonderful opportunity," James continued. "Oh and Willa, they have a sixteen year old son starting at the high school tomorrow. He should be in your class, so maybe help him out a bit?"

I felt the same cold breeze from earlier rush through the house with James' words. Even though I had no way of being sure this new family was anything more than just a normal new arrival in town, my instincts screamed danger. There was no way I could tell James not to take this job. He had been waiting for this opportunity for nearly seventeen years. So I smiled as he continued on with almost childlike glee. Eventually, I helped Margot to the car with her basket as James, Willa, and Felix set the table for what would certainly be anything but a dull dinner.

"Keep an eye on them," Margot said as she shut her car door and pulled slowly out of the Winship driveway to make her way home for the night. As I walked down the gravel drive to perform the nightly ritual of closing the large iron gates for the evening, the smell of lilacs floated on the cool breeze. The intriguing aroma was also wafting off of my skin from Margot's perfume as it became heated by my body temperature. As I closed the two ten-foot tall gates that enclosed the Winship house and its gardens, I wondered if there really were such things as vampires. Would something as simple as a flower concoction and a few nails really protect us? I had the sinking feeling we'd soon find out.

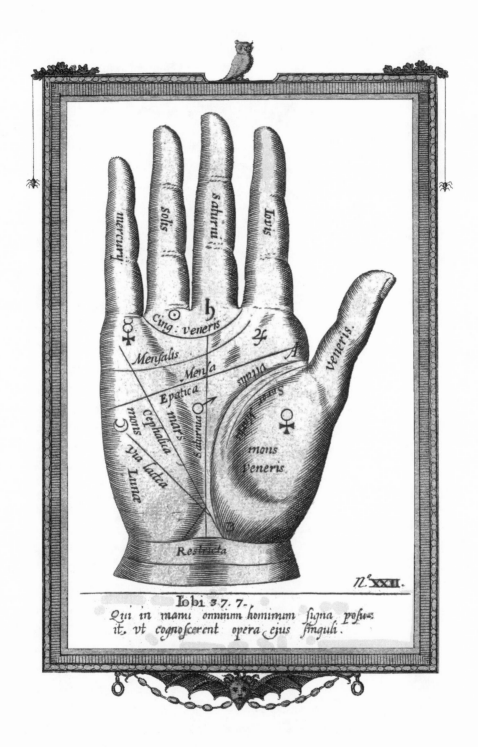

Iobi 37. 7.
Qui in manu omnium hominum signa posu-
it, vt cognoscerent opera ejus singuli.

N.º XXII.

CHAPTER 4

The dreams came the moment I fell into bed after what felt like one of the longest days I'd experienced in years. After hearing the click of the light switch, James climbed in beside me and the next thing I remember was the rustle of skirts and small feet moving along the hallway. The little ghost girls were back again. Standing at my bedside, I heard them whispering in tiny voices to each other.

"Eva, you have to wake her up and tell her about your fever. Mommy will make it better." The younger girl spoke with a nervous tone as she urged her older sister to wake me. The older girl, who I assumed was Eva, held her hand just above my shoulder, frozen in place with apprehension. Her blond curls danced above my nose, tickling my face as she leaned closer to me.

"Shush, Colette," the older girl whispered, "Mommy is sleeping. She looks just like my dolly with her hair pulled back." Both girls had matching white bows tied neatly to the top of their golden hair and identical pearl necklaces. Their perfect white taffeta dresses had puffed sleeves and edges of trimmed lace. With innocent porcelain doll faces, it made their presence all the more dreadful at the thought they'd died so very young.

"Tell her we had our picture taken today," Colette squeaked with excitement. "Tell Mommy that Daddy had the barber take our picture with your dolly." I could feel the small ghost's excitement. Little bursts of electricity sparked around her as she hopped up and down next to my bed. Eva gave her another stern look and then slowly reached out to touch my hand with her own. The moment her tiny spirit fingers landed on my skin I shot straight up in bed as the heat surged through my body. There was a sweeping sound as they fled the room. I saw them escaping from our bedroom, blond ringlets flying behind them. My hand continued to burn as if I had been touched by a hot ember, though there was no visible mark.

James turned abruptly, but remained deep in sleep. Feeling

suddenly restless with the pain in my hand and the image of the two ghost children seared into my mind's eye, I quietly left our bed and tiptoed down the hall to check on Felix and Willa. It had become a habit the past week to check on my children after the ghostly visits from the two little girls. There is something about motherhood that brings one's anxieties of mortality to an even more intense level of worry. The thought of my own children falling victim to a sickness, an accident, or another person's malice had become an ever present torment in my mind. Carefully pushing open the slightly ajar door to Felix's room, I noticed that all was quiet. He was cocooned in his favorite quilt, a patchwork of cotton shapes that formed red tulips and green leaves on a soft white background. Margot had made it while pregnant with Deidre and Morgan more than sixty years earlier and yet it looked as if it hadn't aged a day. Margot's bottle of holy water sat dutifully on a small table next to his door and I could also smell the sweetness of lilac in the air.

I continued up to the third floor to check on Willa and also found her door slightly open. As I made my way closer, an odd sensation shot through me and I immediately felt something was wrong. There was a ticking noise coming from somewhere inside the bedroom. I noticed that she was in a deep sleep, unmoving in her four-poster bed, but the ticking continued. I quietly came into her room careful not to wake her and began searching for the source of the noise.

Willa had painted her room a deep violet shade the past summer and in the dark it took on a hue closer to the blue of a midnight sky. One of the other changes she had insisted on was removing the Victorian dresser set that had been mine, and replacing it with a 1920s vanity that had belonged to Elsiba. It was situated next to the door on the wall that faced the window and boasted a large round mirror with etched swallows along its edge. There was a small stool covered with violet and blue satin embroidered with birds that matched the mirror. They frolicked on the material as if bound in an enchanted garden. As I watched her sleep, an odd shimmer passed across the mirror drawing me to it with a sudden visceral instinct to protect my young and vulnerable child. The ticking became more persistent and I saw two red eyes flickering across the mirror.

It took me several minutes before I realized that the eyes were reflected from outside the window directly across the room. Perched on the edge of the sill, looking straight at me with shocking crimson eyes was a solitary night heron tapping its beak on the window. These strange birds with a cap of dark plumage on their heads had odd lanky bodies much like their heron cousins, except they hunted at night. As I inched closer to the window to look at the unwelcomed night messenger, he let out a caw that sounded almost as shrill as a crow. Then with a final tap, he snapped his beak on a fat cricket that was lingering on the window's edge and flew away with what seemed like a haughty sneer. Quietly, I made my way to leave the room having found the source of the ticking, but the bird's departure had in no way eased the anxiety that perched in my heart. As I crossed to the threshold of the room, I noticed the bottle of holy water by Willa's door lying on its side, its contents spilled across the old wood floor. I would clean it tomorrow so as not to wake her, but in my heart the uneasiness grew as the odd omens began to accumulate with each passing hour.

I also realized that I had not yet spoken to Willa about taking a trip to Seattle to find her a dress for the St. Patrick's Day dance. Tomorrow I would have to make time for her as both her sixteenth birthday and the dreaded ritual of the Spring dance loomed closer. But for now, I asked her guardian angels to watch over her as she slept and whispered a quiet protection spell as I crept back to our bedroom. Despite my worry, I quickly fell into such a deep sleep that the next thing I knew our alarms were sounding and it was time to face the first day of March.

March had never been my favorite time of the year. To me, it felt capricious and rife with miscommunication. Coupled with the increasingly odd omens and the arrival of a new family, I could only hope that it would pass quickly into April without incident. After everyone was off to school and work, I made my way to my shop. I was shocked to find the color of the water downtown had returned to normal overnight. It glistened its usual blue green in the sunlight. It was as if the red tide had never happened and all was well and normal on the streets of town. In addition to the sudden reversal of the tide, the streets were bustling with twice as many tourists than was normal for

March. There were long strings of cars patiently inching their way down the central two-lane street that made up the shopping district. Considering that winter had been tragically slow for the local businesses, the new influx of visitors inspired giddiness in the merchants.

Henry Gunn was outside George's old grocery and café sweeping manically with a huge grin from ear to ear. As George's great nephew, he had taken over the business when George was left with no other choice than to live out the remainder of his days in the local retirement home. Old age had crept up on him seemingly overnight in the form of a stroke, which made it impossible for him to do his daily routine of running the store. Margot visited him once a week with gifts of caramels, oranges and other delicacies that he cherished. I tried to get to see him at least once a month with all the downtown gossip and happenings. Henry was just a few years younger than I and we had become fast friends when he moved back from Seattle to keep George's business running. Today he looked out of his mind with the idea of having a busy day after experiencing his first off season winter.

Once I was settled into my usual routine of getting everything lit and opened, I began to examine the small nails that Margot had given me the night before. After everyone left the house that morning, I had hammered them into tiny coils that looked almost like miniature snakes wrapping in on themselves. I then began to braid red and white striped cotton string into a delicate cord. I planned to attach the coiled nails not only to my children's wrists, but also my own and James'. I knew the children would be an easy sell, but James might take a bit more convincing, so I had fashioned his into something he could put inside his wallet instead. Just as I was tying my own amulet onto my left wrist a tinkle from the bell on the door announced a customer.

Looking up, I met a man and woman in their early forties dressed so impeccably that it struck me as unnatural. Tourists wore shorts and flip flops while the locals donned casual attire fine-tuned to the necessities of daily life in a town that could still be rugged. The man was clean-shaven with a crisp button down shirt perfectly tucked into stylish dress pants. His hair fell in a clean wave of tamed curls to each side of his smooth temples and his sculpted jaw was without blemish. The woman was tall and thin with a meticulously styled chignon of wheat blond hair. She wore a beige shift cut out of stunningly simple yet elegant raw silk. She ran her fingers over lampshades and tabletops with a nonchalance that whispered of money to spare. As her heels clicked across the wood floors, I suddenly felt out of place in my own store. My favorite black skirt and top felt too provincial in the face of such elegance. The antique objects became more lustrous as she pointed to each, while commenting to the man in quick French phrases. After perusing in this manner for a bit, they approached the counter. In a polite yet cool demeanor, they asked to purchase six of my hand-blown glass lamps as well as two matching walnut bedside tables.

"We just purchased the Bell Tower House," the woman said while holding out her hand to shake my own. "I am Sophie Renard and this is my husband Thomas." There was only a slight hint of an accent that lingered beneath her otherwise perfect English. I shook her hand which was surprisingly cool to the touch considering the overly warm day.

"I believe you just hired my husband to oversee restorations to your new home," I said with as much conviviality as I could manage. I wondered if there hadn't been so many negative omens prior to their arrival if I'd have warmed more to them. It was hard to know; but their presence made me nervous. I quickly began wrapping their lamps in tissue paper while anxiously chatting about the town history and other pleasantries. They did not seem to notice my discomfort at their presence, but rather remained cool and collected as I fumbled their purchases into bags and arranged to deliver the two tables in the evening.

In the middle of their transaction, Pat Savage burst through my shop door with an arm full of lavender bundles and his usual warm smile. Pat was the owner of the Beltane Lavender Farm located on the outskirts of town. He had started the farm when James and I settled in Port Townsend and we were the first to befriend both Pat and his wife, Diana. The rest of town was slow to accept them as they came with not only their own young family, but a small compound of six husbands and wives who all lived together in a massive farmhouse. They worked the land together and created a sustainable farm that boasted not only the most fragrant lavender for miles around, but also all varieties of herbs — both common and rare. Under normal circumstances farmers were usually welcomed to the community with open arms, but with Pat there came the rumor that they were more than just a farm but rather a coven of witches. This was entirely true, but many of the people in town had fantastic notions of what that really meant. Though many in town avoided or ignored the members of the Beltane Lavender Farm/Coven, we opened our arms to them. Naturally they felt drawn to the Winships with our natural gifts and traditions. Though I didn't feel the need to practice with others outside of my family, I understood and accepted their desire to do so in a safe environment.

So with each season Pat brought me the freshest of his crops and I sold them in my store. The lavender bunches had always been my favorite, although much like the lilacs, it was unusual to have any this early in spring. As Pat heaved his large basket of bunched lavender onto the counter he noticed the Renards. His demeanor immediately shifted from his usual gregarious manner to a guarded and tense stance. He nervously began scratching his short beard while examining the newcomers. It was as if his senses were suddenly alert and he was very ill at ease. His eyes darted to the Renards and back to me with near panic as I quietly introduced them as the new family in town. Thomas Renard moved fluidly over to us and held out his hand to Pat. I was shocked when, instead of returning the gesture, Pat backed away towards the door refusing to shake Thomas' hand or look him directly in the eye. Before making his quick escape from the shop, he looked at me with an intensity that I wasn't used to and said "Charlotte, please come to the farm to drop off a check for the lavender this week." I nodded and said I would, although I was taken aback by his odd retreat and uncouth manners. Had the coven been experiencing odd omens in the same way I had been the past few weeks? Whatever it was, it certainly didn't make me feel any better about the Renards.

The atmosphere in the shop at this point was best described as painfully awkward. The Renards lingered for a few more minutes and finally handed me perfectly pressed hundred dollar bills in payment for their items. They tossed the money on the counter with complete apathy as though such things had little importance. I assured them the tables would be brought to their home within the day and planned to send over one of the local boys for the delivery. They waved goodbye while walking out the door and as they passed one of the antique mirrors, I saw an odd reflection; a fleeting image. It was a misshapen reflection that didn't match the individuals who were just in my shop. Something unnatural had taken their place in the looking glass; two twisted doppelgangers in fine clothing, but imposters' none-the-less. Whatever the something in the mirror was, it made my skin crawl. I couldn't quite put my finger on what I'd seen, but a feeling of loathing stayed with me the remainder of the day.

In all honesty, there was nothing they'd done to make me feel as anxious as I did in their presence. It was simply a feeling that something was wrong, although nothing in their appearance could prove my apprehensions were founded on anything other than anxiety. When closing time arrived, James met me at the door just as I was turning the key in the lock. I could tell he had much to share with me about his new projects. While I wanted to feel joy at the prospect of his working on two of his favorite buildings, my own unease was hard to ignore. He lifted my basket from my tired hands and put his arm around me as we walked a few blocks to our favorite pub. We ate there with Kat and Gavin at least once a week. James chattered on about the changes he would be making to the structures as we strolled down Water Street and finally up several flights to the eatery and pub "Sirens." Kat and Gavin were already seated at our usual table and, as I slid into the booth across from them, I tried to clear my mind for the next hour. Even though I knew Felix and Willa were safe at Margot's house this evening, I still felt a nagging in the back of my mind that something dreadful was about to happen in my beloved town.

CHAPTER 5

Port Townsend had never lacked for local watering holes. In the days of prohibition, it seemed the local thirst for whiskey and other libations only increased exponentially. This led to a local tradition of moonshining that produced everything from deadly gin to mild beers. Along with this practice came an ornery group of otherwise law-abiding men and women perfecting their craft. One of these men was Mario Cabral, an otherwise gentle soul with a hand skillfully trained in the art of tattooing. He spent his days dotting sailors' and lumberjacks' skin with wispy-haired mermaids and American eagles. At night he tended to his well-hidden moonshine stills. Tonight, I spied his grey figure on the waterfront docks looking out over the vast sea. He had passed over sometime in the 1960s and was survived by a large family that I knew well and loved. I would have to ask him what he was waiting for in that deep sea.

But for the moment I contented myself with my other two favorite moonshiners. I peered across the table at my oldest friends who were also well-known local drink alchemists. Gavin and Kat were now sitting in the one bar we frequented other than their own. It was impossible for us to sit all together and have a night out in their bar, the Waterside Brewery, so we made a point of coming to Sirens at least once a week, if not more. It was up two flights of stairs, tucked away in one of the monumental Victorian buildings that faced the water. Tonight the sun was just setting and candles were glowing on the tables, along with a robust fire in the old fireplace. A small group of white-bearded men sat in a circle in the main room. After tuning their fiddles and cleaning their drums, they began playing Irish jigs and sea songs, as was the custom each Friday night. Kat was fidgeting with an amulet bracelet I had made for her several weeks ago to protect her from darkness. She had married and divorced what had turned out to be an abusive man and in the middle she had given birth to what I liked to call her angel baby. Lily was four months older than Willa and the two had been friends from the crib. But every once in a while, the creeping darkness of her ex-husband would flicker through town leaving Kat nervous and terrified that he would try to steal Lily away. So I took it upon myself to give her all my protective magic in the hopes that he would simply disappear back into the swirl of darkness that was the outside world. It had worked so far, but I could tell that Kat's thoughts were elsewhere tonight as she twisted the red cord and the magically charged medals and stones in her long fingers. Over the years she had gone from pink hair to blond and her hair was now a fiery red hue that seemed to match her current temperament. There was a passion in her that was both infectious and sometimes dangerous, but it was why I loved her so much.

Gavin, on the other hand, was sitting back observing the room while James excitedly talked to us about the upcoming plans that had been set in motion with the arrival of the Renard family. Kat listened to him with her full attention as she, too, had always loved those two buildings, but Gavin seemed to be away in his mind somewhere. He was still my reclusive friend, the one who spent more nights reading into the wee hours after closing the bar than interacting with other people. Women had come and gone in his life, but overall he was a solitary man. In a way Kat, James, and I kept him tethered to the daily ins and outs of the world; left to his own devices, I'd worry about him getting buried under a pile of books. He would joke that when he died he would most likely be eaten by wild dogs before anyone figured out he was missing. Sadly he was only half joking about this, and if it hadn't been for us, it may have proven true in the end. So we made it a point to drag him outside into the sunlight as much as possible.

"They came in the shop today," I said, since we were still on the topic of the Renards. Chances were at least half the town was having similar conversations at the same moment. Gavin's attention turned back to the table. "In fact they were the one and only sale of the day and it was not a little sale at that." I went on to explain that they had bought lamps and two tables.

"Are they really French? What were they like?" asked Kat. She had always had a longing to leave Port Townsend and live for a year in France but the business had proven too successful to justify her departure. Someday she would have to pack it up and just go, but for now she spent her time reading and dreaming about walks along the Seine.

"Well, polished I guess. But there was something a little strange about them. I thought I saw something in the mirror when they were leaving the store. I'm not sure what it was but it struck me as unnatural." The room became suddenly quiet. It was as if everyone heard my words and was contemplating them. Gavin's brow furrowed and James seemed agitated in his silence. "It's probably nothing," I quickly added and the room again began to bustle with noise.

We ordered our meal, a combination of local salmon mixed with various greens from the surrounding areas. Much like the sudden lilac blooms, the local asparagus was growing almost more quickly than it could be harvested. Even the fishermen had come home early with nets full. Spring had arrived with an early abundance. But in my mind it felt like the earth's reaction to something sinister coming to our region. It could not be a coincidence that the lilacs, a powerful vampire repellent, had all bloomed so early for no explainable reason.

"So James, when is the actual knock down, tear out walls thing going to start on the Cliffside Chapel?" asked Kat.

"Tomorrow," James replied with obvious excitement. "The contractor has a crew starting at 7:00 a.m. There really isn't too much to do to the interior. There's just one wall with water damage that needs to be torn down. Then we'll be designing a new entryway that will remain in the style of the time period." He began sketching on a nearby napkin with an enthusiasm I hadn't witnessed in years.

"So I got a text from Lily after she got home from school and apparently the new boy, Daniel Renard, is gorgeous," Kat said, imitating her daughter's voice. "And he had an eye on Willa all day. He even asked to sit by them on the back stairs at lunch." Her eyebrows lifted in a teasing way. Suddenly my heart was fluttering. I felt a moment of panic thinking back to my night-time visit to Willa's room with the night heron at her window and the holy water spilled on the floor. James seemed to think this information was amusing, but I suddenly felt very protective of my daughter.

For the first time in my life, I wished I was as technologically literate as Kat and could text Willa for more information on her day. Kat and Lily were more like sisters than mother and daughter. I wondered if I had made a mistake in removing myself so much from the latest technology. Even Deidre and Samir were more interested in phones and all things high tech than I was. Samir would stand in line for hours when a new phone came out, then hand me or Willa his old one. James had to have his phone and computer for work, but I intentionally cut myself off from these things. I always felt as if these electronic apparatuses interfered with my own energetic awareness. It felt as if they fed off of me in a way that seemed parasitic and so I avoided them as much as possible. But in this instant, I felt almost jealous of Kat's and Lily's additional form of communication. I would have to ask Willa about this new boy when I got home.

The rest of the dinner we talked about business, the new plans for a second ferry into town, and the beer festival that Gavin was planning for later in the summer. As the night wore on, the pub became more and more crowded with people of all ages. There were the old-timers playing music near the front of the bar. The younger crowd was hovering in the back around the pool tables. And there was the same group of sailors sitting stubbornly on the balcony outside, rain or shine, as if defying the waves below. Soon it was time to return home. I was oddly relieved to say goodbye to Kat and Gavin so I could get home as quickly as we could to check in with both Willa and Felix. Gavin gave me one of his pick-up hugs, which always made me feel like a small child, while Kat and I did our usual parting dance of hugs and giggles. I was the shortest of the four of us, although I usually countered by saying I had the biggest personality.

James pulled into the driveway to drop me off. He would be working late at his office on the drawings for the Renard projects. I gave him a long kiss feeling the scruff from his beard scratch my cheeks as I pulled away. My fingers caressed his chin as he smiled and I sent him little purple sparks of energy from my fingertips. There were ways that Winship women entangled their husbands in long-lasting love stories. One of them was a special magic that seemed to emanate from our fingers straight to their heart strings. I smiled while slipping out of the car. Before shutting the door, I warned him not to stay out too late or I would have to go back to the bar and take a lonely lumberjack to my bed. He looked a little panicked as I shut the door and walked back to the house, with a teasing twist and whip of my long black hair over my shoulders.

The house was aglow with lights in every room as I came up the walk. I opened the back door into the kitchen and was greeted by a lingering fragrance of lilacs. Margot sat by the fireplace with Willa at her side, books open and spread across the table. The dishes were washed and drying in the rack by the sink which told me they'd all been fed. I set down my basket of work projects and immediately brought out the bracelets I'd made for Willa and Felix that afternoon with Annie's iron nails.

"I have a little something for you," I said to Willa, hoping she would indulge me. "Can you hold out your arm?" Jewelry wasn't something that my friends or family members lacked. Willa held out her arm without looking up from her chemistry book. I quickly tied it to her wrist before she could argue with me. Margot gave me a lopsided grin of approval.

"Really, Mom?" she said, looking at the braided strings and the little coiled charm as if it was the most hideous thing she had ever seen. Granted it wasn't one of my most elegant designs, but its main purpose was to protect, not to adorn. "This is really ugly." I grinned to myself. Recently, I'd noticed that Willa wasn't one to hold back her opinion to spare my feelings.

"Just wear it please," I tried to say with good humor. "How was school?"

"It was OK. There's a new boy stalking me," she said in a deadpan tone. "He sat by me in all our classes and Lily kept texting me about how cute he was. I don't know, though, he's kind of quiet."

Margot shot me a dark look, but didn't say a word. She was sitting in her chair, observing. But I knew her mind was rapidly processing everything she saw. There was a thump on the stairs and then a scamper of feet running along the floorboards in the hallway. Felix hopped over the bottom step as I used to do when I was a child. He slid into the kitchen in his stocking feet with an exuberance reserved for a boy of eight. He slid into me and wrapped his small arms around my waist.

"Hold out your hand, little man," I said and quickly tied his amulet to his thin wrist.

"Cool," was his response as he examined the nail. "It looks like a snake" he said with a little hiss.

Margot rose slowly from her spot beside the fire and began to gather her things. With each movement I smelled a mixture of lilac and rose petals that floated around her. She gave the children long hugs and made her way to the back door to her car. Even though Margot was approaching her eightieth year she seemed ageless. She walked slowly, but she still drove. But most importantly, her mind was still as sharp as it had been when I was a child. As she carefully gripped the banister making her way down the back steps, she glanced up at me with a worried look.

"Watch her closely," was all she said. I knew she was speaking of Willa and my heart dropped to my stomach. I watched as she backed out the long driveway and through the metal gates, her headlights illuminating the garden in bloom. As I turned to go back inside, a snap of a branch alerted me to movement in the willow tree. I carefully walked along the stone pathway that circled the house with the willow at its center. In the branches nearest Willa's bedroom window was the night heron. His red eyes peered down at me as if daring me to climb into the tree and shake him loose. In the twilight, I saw he'd begun building a nest of twigs and moss, wrapped into a swirl of green. With a caw, the odd bird broke a branch off the massive tree. It defiantly tucked it into the nest, his red eyes fixed on me. With an ever-growing sense of worry, I made my way back inside to find the kitchen empty, an eerie silence hovering around the old house.

CHAPTER 6

I locked all the doors before heading upstairs to check on Felix and Willa. The hush that had fallen over the house reminded me of the silence earlier in the evening at Sirens. I heard my heart pounding in my ears and swiftly ran up the stairs. On the first floor landing stood the old grandfather clock that chimed the hour announcing the passing of time. It was silent. I noticed the pendulum was no longer swinging back and forth as it had for over a hundred years. The only time the clocks were stopped in the Winship house was when a member of the family died. As I walked down the darkened hallway towards Felix's room, I noticed an odd shimmer in the full-length mirror that stood at the end of the hall. It had flashed behind me. I turned frantically around expecting someone to be standing near me, but there was nothing but an open window at the opposite end of the hallway near the library.

In a panic, I shoved open the door to Felix's room with an urgency that left me breathless. The instant the door opened, all the sound came back with a rush of air as if the house itself had exhaled. Felix was sitting cross-legged on his bed with his journal in his hands scribbling what I assumed were his premonitions. His hair was standing on end in the back giving him the look of a mad scientist.

"Hey there," I said, "Everything OK?"

"Um hm," he replied, and then looked at me with a big grin. "Thank you for the amulet." Having grown up with me as his mom, he knew all about amulets and talismans and had immediately recognized it as such.

"It's to keep the vampires away," I said in a soft voice hoping this didn't scare him.

"Oh, I know," he said with another grin and then went back to writing in his journal. I left his door open and made my way back down the hallway, closing the window that had mysteriously been opened. Walking back to the stairwell, I noticed the clock was again ticking, its pendulum back in motion counting the moments of our day. I made my way up the stairs to the turret bedroom and knocked softly on the old wooden door. Gently, I pushed the door open to find Willa lying on her stomach across her bed with her books spread around her. Her telephone was her main focus as she furiously pushed the keys with her thumbs.

"I had an idea today for a dress for the St. Patrick's Day dance," I said, immediately capturing her attention. She set the phone down and peered at me with a glimmer of excitement in her hazel eyes.

"Really?" she replied, allowing her enthusiasm to show through her usually impervious fifteen-year-old cool veneer.

"I know how much you like Elsiba's things and I remembered that in the attic there is a trunk filled with some of her dresses from the 1920s and 1930s. They are sort of flapper style with intricate beadwork. Do you want to take a look and see if anything catches your eye?"

She was off the bed in less than two seconds and I took this as an affirmative response to my query. Willa rushed past me and was at the attic door before I could start down the hallway. The old attic door was somewhat fickle when it came to opening. I had taken to asking it politely to allow entrance before even touching the knob. As I started to speak to the door I heard the lock click and Willa gave a little hop of joy before bolting through it.

The Winship house attic was filled to overflowing with a variety of relics from nearly every member of the family dating back to when the house was first built in 1856. From Victorian prams to boxes of antique photographs, it was a testament to all the people who had lived inside its walls. I remembered having last seen the box of Elsiba's clothes tucked in the far corner in a gigantic steamer trunk. How anyone had been able to move it up all the stairs to the attic, was beyond me and yet here it had sat for the past 80-odd years. Willa and I tugged open the large lid to reveal tissue paper delicately folded around each article of clothing. Immediately, the room filled with lilac and lemon scent that wafted up from the contents of the trunk. How Elsiba's clothes had retained her smell after so many years was a mystery, but we both swooned from the headiness of the fragrance. It was intoxicating in a way I couldn't make sense of but knew in my very bones to be magic.

The first delicate package held a gorgeous silk Kimono-style wrap dress with embroidered umbrellas along the sleeves and back. The next package held a silk floral A-line dress with violets scattered across the fabric like a miniature garden. There were fans, gloves and lace camisoles woven in between the plush garments that looked as if they'd rarely been worn. Nearing the bottom of the trunk, Willa found a delicate flapper dress in a celadon green with tiny white beads that were expertly arranged into roses. She held it up to herself and let out a sigh. It was perfect. The green made her auburn hair all the more vibrant and the white beads enhanced her creamy skin perfectly.

"I'm going to try it on," she said, running from the attic back to her bedroom with the dress clutched to her chest. Carefully, I wrapped the clothes back into their original paper. One by one I set them inside the trunk exactly as they had been before opening it. As I began to close the lid, a little piece of paper tucked into the lining slipped out and fell directly onto my lap. It was an antique postcard with a photograph on the front. The back had the name "Dennis Morrison Photography, Port Townsend, Wash., 1912"in scrolled letters across the top. Turning it over, my mouth went suddenly dry. It was a picture of Eva and Colette as I had seen them the night before in my bedroom. The two girls stood on either side of an antique pram with a porcelain doll tucked daintily inside. They wore the same white dresses as their ghostly forms with matching bows and strands of pearls.

I heard Willa call to me from her room and quickly closed the trunk, grasping the photograph firmly. Closing the attic door behind me, the lock clicked shut of its own accord. When I walked into Willa's bedroom, she was standing in front of the vanity mirror in Elsiba's dress. She looked stunning with her hair hanging in long waves down her back. The dress fit her perfectly.

"What do you think?" she asked, scrunching up her nose while craning her neck to look over her shoulder into the mirror to see the back of the dress. In this peculiar position she looked like a swan primping her feathers with a regal twist.

"I think you look beautiful," I said, feeling proud and protective all at the same time. "And it's green so you won't get pinched." She gave me a stern look as if no one in their right mind pinched anyone anymore. In my day, the Saint Patrick's Day dance was a pinch-a-thon if you forgot to wear even the smallest hint of emerald. Her look made me think that times had changed.

"Thanks, Mom," she said, and then immediately picked up her phone and began texting to, I assumed, Lily.

"OK, then. I'll be downstairs if you need me and maybe we can look at some jewelry tomorrow?" She nodded in agreement without looking up and I gently shut her door. With the antique photo still grasped tightly in my hand, I made my way down to my workroom, which doubled as the Winship library. I turned on the overhead lights and started my laptop, which was my one link with the world beyond Port Townsend. I still sold my jewelry to stores in Seattle and managed everything through emails and phone calls, but tonight I wanted to know more about this photograph.

If there was one place to look for information about the town's rich history, it was the Jefferson County Historical Society's website. They had accumulated a vast archive on the outskirts of town for over fifty years and recently had begun to enter digital copies of their information into an impressive database. It included over 20,000 photographs as well as letters, deeds, and other paper trails from early settlers. Typing in "Dennis Morrison 1912" proved interesting as it showed a lease agreement for a shop space on Water Street next door to where my shop was now situated. There were also several photographs of the man himself who was quite dapper in his suit of the times. There was also a link to an article written in the Port Townsend Reader that had the headline "New Photographer Sets Up Studio on Water Street" but when I clicked on it I only got an error message claiming no such article existed. I then typed in Eva and Colette, but nothing popped up. Having only their first names would prove tricky so I tried "1912 Eva and Colette Fever" and got a link to an article with the title "Spring Fever Takes its First Two Victims in Eva and Colette Duprey," with the date of March 25, 1912. It was exactly one hundred years ago this month! I clicked on the article's link to read further, but received an error message that no article existed, which proved to be quite frustrating.

I heard the door slam downstairs, accompanied by James' familiar footsteps on the wood floors below. It would soon be time to make sure that Felix was in bed and Willa had all her electronics turned off for the evening. I turned off the computer but decided to set my alarm early to head to the archives and look for the original newspaper articles that had eluded me online. Tomorrow was Saturday, which meant James would be home helping the children with whatever needed to be done as I ran my store downtown on what was usually my busiest day. I would have to get up early if I wanted to make it to the archives and back in time to open my shop.

I could hear the familiar rumblings of my husband's domestic routine downstairs. The faucet turned on and then off in the kitchen. Eventually I heard James flop onto the couch in the front parlor and click on the television to watch the late night news. Vaguely, I heard the words "tide" and "peculiar" echo up the stairs as the news reporters voiced excited concern over the strange happenings on the coast. Slipping into our bedroom, I set the alarm and quickly sprayed a few drops of clove and flower essence on James' pillow. It was an old trick that my friend Bee taught me to awaken a man's senses. Though I was tired, I planned on working a bit of my magic on James before turning the lights off for the night.

CHAPTER 7

The turn into the Historical Society Research Center's driveway was a tricky one. With speeding logging trucks rumbling around the bend in the road, it was best to turn in further down the highway and double back. But today I was in a hurry. I had expected to dream of Eva and Colette once I put my tired cheek on my pillow last night, but instead everything remained eerily calm. No ghost children came to me talking of fevers; no tapping on windows by birds or any other oddities, which for some reason felt strange. My intuition told me I needed to find out what had happened to Eva and Colette because, in some way, it was connected to the odd omens occurring in the present.

I sped down the highway that led out of town, past the paper mill and into long stretches of untamed forest. This particular section of road always made me think of fairytales where lost travelers succumbed to the trees and found enchanted castles to take them in during a storm. As I made the hairpin turn into the long driveway, the building that housed all evidence of local history was anything but a castle in appearance. It was a modern warehouse. The back section was only open to the archive workers. A small welcome desk and study for visitors sat in the front. And while the outside appearance held no immediate charm, it was what it contained that was precious far beyond the finery of any fairyland mansion. Inside those metal walls were all the newspapers dating back to the first editions, along with photographs, old letters, deeds, maps, and a variety of other scraps of ephemera that together created the patchwork of Port Townsend's collective history.

I wound my way up the gravel drive and parked near the entrance. Inside I was greeted by Evelyn Pettygrove, whose grey hair was expertly pinned into a twisted bun. If she had loosened it a bit, it would have been a perfect Gibson girl coif. Her eyes were lined with fine wrinkles that told of many hours spent squinting into books categorizing the crinkled papers and photos that came into her hands over the years. But behind the obvious signs of age, her eyes twinkled bright, a crisp blue, which evoked the workings of an ever-inquisitive mind. Evelyn was from one of the founding families, and with that came the indescribable feeling of belonging to this land in a way that newcomers would never entirely understand. She and Margot had a checkered history of being on-again, off-again friends. The usual source of their disputes generally was attached to Margot not wanting our family pictures and documents available to the world at large through the historical society. Margot was protective of them, while Evelyn had the view that their lives were part of the town and should be shared. I had to admit I was more inclined to agree with Evelyn, but Margot's wishes trumped my own inclinations to give them a massive donation of artifacts the likes of which would take years to sort.

"Hello Charlotte; what a surprise to see you here!" said Evelyn in a giddy voice. I had a feeling she thought I was here to drop off some of the Winship archives. I hoped she wouldn't be too disappointed by the real purpose of my trip.

"Hi, Evelyn, I was hoping you could help me find something?" I asked, seeing a slight slump in her shoulders. I had been right about her initial excitement at seeing me.

"Of course. What are you after?" she replied in her usual helpful way.

"I looked up a few articles last night in your online archive from 1912 but couldn't pull up the originals. Maybe you can help me find them?" I asked feeling a sudden dizziness envelop me.

"Are you ok, dear?" she said as I swooned slightly. I hadn't eaten this morning and had simply grabbed my coffee to go. The room was suddenly spinning and I felt my energy drain from me. Evelyn was at my side before I realized that I was about to collapse on the floor. She maneuvered me to one of the chairs around a large reading desk just as my knees were about to buckle. I slipped into the chair, putting my elbows on the desk and my head in my hands. Evelyn sat next to me and when the room righted itself again, I noticed that her forehead worry-lines were creased into tight ripples.

"I'm not sure what that was," I said with a smile, trying to ease her worry. "I was in such a hurry to get here before opening the shop that I forgot to eat anything." She still looked concerned.

"Well how about if I pull up the 1912 articles on the microfiche files for you since the digital ones are being troublesome and you just sit here for a moment." She brought me a cup of water from the dispenser and then bustled over to one of the microfiche viewers that lined the walls of the study. The center of the room was filled with tables and chairs much like a library. Carpets lined the floors making the room warm and inviting. Other historical society volunteers worked on nearby computers, scanning in pictures and pages one at a time. The whir of the images being scanned into the machines was a constant hum in the well-lit room. Evelyn rushed back to my table, still with a look of worry on her face.

"It's the strangest thing," she recounted, "1912 seems to be missing from the files." There was a lilt to her voice that revealed a touch of confusion. "I'll be back in a second. We have all the original papers in the back, bound into tomes, so I'll get you those instead. Just wait here." She rushed into the back with a tenseness that betrayed a bit of anxiety brewing. These documents were under her care and she took her role as guardian seriously. A few minutes later, she arrived back in the main room empty-handed and began to whisper to another of the volunteer members in a hushed but hurried voice. She made her way back to me quickly. With a look of deep regret, Evelyn explained to me that the original newspapers also seemed to have gone missing from the archives.

"They must be misplaced," she said, trying to convince herself that the missing documents were still somewhere in the building, although grossly misfiled. The thought of them being missing entirely was too much for her to bear. I thanked her and lifted myself slowly from the chair to avoid further dizziness. I could tell that her mind was working furiously to figure out where these documents had vanished. I felt slightly guilty for being the cause of such worry so early in the morning. As I thanked her and made my way back to the door, she stopped me just as I was almost over the threshold.

"Charlotte, you may want to ask Tom Caldwell if he has any of the 1912 newspapers," she said in a voice louder than what was normally acceptable for the study room. I nodded and headed out to my car. The cool morning air made me feel instantly better as I breathed in the scent of pine trees and the underlying perfume of lilacs. I would make a point of calling Tom later in the day to see if he had any of the old articles in his vast collection. Tom's archive was almost as coveted as the Winships'. He had been one of the most prolific local journalists of his time. Now, at over eighty years old, he was a goldmine of local lore and history. After retiring, he became a local historian with two books to his name and the materials for at least ten in his writing studio.

In his days as a journalist, he had covered everything from the events at the State Fair to the more tragic accidents of drunk drivers speeding on Discovery Road. Now in his elderly years, he was devoted to the untold stories of the first settlers. The ones that inspired him were of those who had lacked the means of the founding families, and had instead felled their trees and built their log cabins with their own two hands. An evening with Tom was usually filled with tales of moonshiners, shipwrecks and opium smuggling. He and my grandfather, George, had been friends through their entire lives and also rather rebellious in their day. Not quite as rebellious as Elsiba or Annie Christy who were a generation older, but they still held a certain place in the community as rebel rousers.

Now, with a brood of children and grandchildren gathered on his porch on hot summer days and the love of his life, Emmalina, sitting close by, he would tell his stories. He knew of my ability to communicate with the dead and, even though I could tell he was curious about their forgotten tales, he never pushed me to reveal their secrets. Instead, he wove together tales from the past that left me feeling connected to the town in spite of the way many of the townspeople still avoided me. He had always been the champion of the underdog or the outcast, so the Winship women didn't scare him the way we did others.

The first time he told me one of his true stories about the town is forever fresh in my memory. Once, when I was a child, I had wandered over to Chetzemoka Park with my pail and shovel with the hope of catching my first gooey duck. This is a large clam, native to the coast, and extremely elusive for the average clam digger. Samir had attempted to "catch" one the first time we had taken him to the famous park that boasted an impressive low tide. He had dug a three-foot-deep hole in the sand after a gooey duck squirted him in the face. It was, of course, long gone by the time his shovel reached the sand's surface, but we had let him dig like a madman anyway, hiding our mirth as best as we could. But by the time I was seven, I was an accomplished clam digger, although the gooey duck was still my "Moby Dick" to be found and conquered. I was out in the tide pools with my overalls rolled up and my saltwater sandals strapped to my tiny feet. The beach was deserted as it was a Monday and though my mom knew I had gone to the park, I had failed to mention that my plan was to clam.

As I concentrated on my ever-growing pile of clams, a geyser-like squirt of water burst up in front of me. This was a sure sign of a gooey duck in shallow sand. I made a leap for it and furiously began to dig. It took about twenty minutes of tunneling before I gave up, but what I hadn't noticed was the tide had begun to race back towards land. In my haste to catch the near mythical beast, I had become surrounded by waist high water that left me on a little island in the middle of very strong currents. How I had ended up so far out on a sand flat with at least twenty feet of water between me and the beach is still a mystery, but there I was — stuck. I had begun taking swimming lessons earlier that summer and still felt a bit of panic around water. My element was earth, so water always felt dangerous and unpredictable to me. Now I had to choose between putting rocks in my pockets and wading back to shore through the currents, or face a worse fate: being swept out to sea.

Just as I was about to head into the freezing cold waters with only my seven-old-year old body to anchor me to land, I heard a little shout from behind me. It was Tom Caldwell in his rowboat only a few feet away. He pushed his boat up onto the little sand island that had formed as the tide came in. Tom lifted me into its safety along with my pail and shovel. This was the first time that Tom had saved my life, but it would not be the last. As we rowed on the current, I began to shiver. The adrenaline that had flooded my body only moments before was still telling me to sink or swim. I couldn't speak for my chattering lips. That was when Tom began to tell me a story. It was about two local boys who had found a treasure on the same beach eighty years before. He wove the tale of the two children and their skiff into a golden thread that made me forget the fear I'd felt only moments before. Eventually, he had me back on land and made me promise not to go clamming by myself anymore.

Reflecting on my protectors from the past, my energy slowly returned as I headed into town to open my store. If anyone had a copy of the 1912 newspapers, it would be Tom. Also, I could openly tell him the reason I was so interested in that year as he wouldn't bat an eye at my mention of ghost children and vampires. He knew better than to think these things were myths, having lived in a town that often boasted a curious arrangement of people and happenings. It was with these memories swirling in my mind that I wove along the forest road without the information I'd come for, but not deterred from digging deeper into the sands of times past.

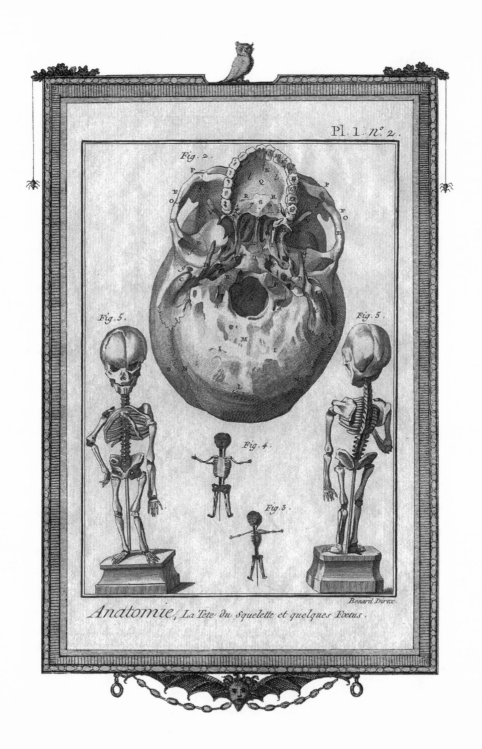

Pl. 1. n.° 2.

Fig. 2.

Fig. 5.

Fig. 5.

Fig. 4.

Fig. 3.

Benard Direx.

Anatomie, La Tête du Squelette et quelques Fœtus.

CHAPTER 8

Back at my store, I opened the doors to let in the warm air from outside. I made a quick call to Tom hoping he would have information about 1912. He promised to look in his archives for me and we agreed I'd stop by his house that evening on my way home. Saturday mornings were by far the busiest day at The Curious Crow. The crowds would come in from the arriving ferries and swamp local stores in search of souvenirs or odd artifacts from our town. Thankfully, Henry Gunn was kind enough to bring me a cup of coffee and a sandwich in the afternoon, much as his great-uncle, Tobias, had done for years before him. Since the dizzy spell earlier that morning, I had been feeling a bit ill. The beginnings of a headache hiding just behind my eyes were kept at bay by caffeine, although the light was bothering me more than usual.

In the early afternoon I stepped onto the small porch in front of the store, hoping a bit of air would help me. That's when I first saw them together. Being a few months older than Willa, Lily already had her driver's license. Kat had given Lily the 1964 Volkswagen Beetle that she had driven when we were in high school. It was a convertible which made Lily one of the most envied girls in town, despite the fact that it was rarely possible to have the top down because of all the rain on the coast. As I rested my back against the old porch railing, I spotted Lily cruising down Water Street with her boyfriend Aaron next to her and Willa in the back seat. Sitting close at Willa's side was a boy I had never seen before and I immediately knew he was the Renard boy. He had dark brown hair and an average sixteen-year-old physique. The way he looked at Willa with a predatory intensity made my skin crawl. I saw her pointing to buildings. I imagined they were giving him a tour of the town. He didn't seem interested in the old brick buildings in the slightest, but was instead examining Willa's every movement with a singular focus that spelled only one thing: Trouble!

As they drove out of my view, the dizziness again came over

me and I rushed inside to sit down. There was no real reason for me not to want Willa to be friends with this new boy and yet I felt a visceral reaction to his family that defied common sense. I tried to tell myself that he was just another sixteen-year-old and nothing more. But I knew in my gut that there was more to this family. Felix's words of vampires and all the omens weren't just a coincidence.

As I wrapped up old photographs, various pieces of my jewelry and several rare reliquary pieces for clients, my mind became set on finding out as much as I could about the Renard family. Just as I picked up the phone to call James, intent on grilling him about his new clients, Sophie Renard walked into the shop as if summoned by my persistent thoughts. I produced the tense smile reserved for my least favorite clients. Her shoes scraped across the wooden floors like fingernails on a chalkboard. She was perfectly groomed in a beautiful peach colored wrap dress. The large diamond solitaire on her left hand flashed in the sunlight casting miniature rainbows along the walls. She made her way over to the counter where I stood and gave me a smile that seemed genuine.

"I just wanted to say that we love the new lamps and tables we purchased from you," she said with her slight accent lifting the end of each syllable.

"I'm very glad they work in your new home," was all I could muster with a forced grin.

"And also I wanted to thank you for allowing your daughter to make our son Daniel feel so welcome," she said, followed by a small laugh that seemed airy even though her eyes revealed a coldness that gave me a shiver. "They were up until past 2:00 a.m. last night texting!"

Again I faked a smile but my throat had gone completely dry. I had assumed Willa had been texting Lily, but she had been texting Daniel all along. Suddenly my face felt hot with embarrassment at not being aware of what had been happening under my own roof. Sophie Renard ran her long fingers over an antique crucifix sitting on the counter. Her perfectly manicured nails matched her dress in tone. Part of me expected to see wisps of steam rise from her skin as in old vampire movies. Nothing happened. In fact, she simply moved along to the next item and perused a bit longer before purchasing an antique locket.

My fingers shook slightly as I wrapped the gold locket in tissue paper and tucked it into a small box. Again, she tossed cash onto the counter as if it were impolite to touch anything as dirty as hundred dollar bills. I thanked her for her purchase with a cool reserve as she walked to the door. She made her way across the threshold just as a cloud moved in front of the sun. In that moment, she was standing directly in front of the long, antique mirror by the door. Although her reflection was complete, there was something terribly wrong with it. Immediately the word "dead" popped into my mind. It was as if the image in the mirror was nothing more than an animated corpse completely devoid of life and soul. The perfectly manicured hands that had just been touching myriad objects had visible signs of decay in the reflection. The outline of a hollowed-out cheek with bone protruding from her jaw was evident. I tried to hide my shock but I must have gone a whole new shade of pale. The cloud passed and as the sun blazed back into the shop, the reflection returned to normal. Her rosy cheeks once again appeared where the skeletal reflection had been, though the image was unshakeable from my mind's eye.

"You and your husband will have to come over for dinner once we are settled in," she said without acknowledging the horrified look on my face, "especially if our children are to be such close friends." Her last words, seemingly innocuous, sounded like a threat in my ears.

"We shall see," was all I could manage, but it came out far more defiant than I'd intended. She smiled and with a flip of her shoulder length hair she waltzed out of my shop. As soon as she left, my stubbornness was replaced by exhaustion. The dizziness was back and the room began to spin as it had earlier that day. I laid my head on the cool countertop and gathered the earth's energy to me through my feet. This was no dizzy spell from lack of sugar; this was a psychic attack. I was being drained of energy! I called on my family, the town ghosts and a host of Saints that were dear to me. With a rush of wind, Mario Cabral was standing in the corner of my shop, a grey guardian. He was the ghost from the old piers, a friendly bootlegger with a sad history of love and loss. But today he was a protector. I had expected my loyal guardian ghost, Fox, to come to my side as he always had before. Still I was grateful for this obviously protective tattooed man who had immediately come to my aid. He didn't speak but I could tell he was acting like a sort of shield, allowing me to regain my strength. The lightheaded feeling began to pass, and I sat up and gathered energy to me from various objects in the store, in addition to the ground beneath me. One of the ways I'd learned early in my life to bolster my strength was to pull it from my element. Margot drew power from water, Deidre from air, Uncle Morgan from fire, and I from the very soil beneath my feet.

Soon my strength had returned and Mario faded back into the wall with a polite nod in my direction. I thanked him just as a small group of people entered the store. The rest of the day went by quickly. It seemed every time I was about to call my family, another client would come in making it impossible. I wanted to call Willa first and foremost, and yet I knew I had to tread carefully. I didn't want to make Daniel into forbidden fruit. I, too, had been sixteen once and anything that my mother had warned me not to do immediately became more desirable. Tonight, I would have to talk to James. But of one thing I was certain: Sophie Renard was definitely a vampire.

CHAPTER 9

A quick call to James as I headed to Tom's house made me feel slightly better. He assured me that Felix and Willa were both at home under his watchful eye. The light was fading as I drove down Discovery Road on my way to Tom's house. He hadn't called me at the shop, so I hoped that was a good sign and he'd have piles of dusty papers for me to sort through. As the sun went down over the rows of ancient trees and shimmering water, I felt a shiver pass through my body. The day had been warm and I had my car window down as I wound past the graveyard and up into the back hills. Swarms of crows were flying in the fading light, creating intriguing shadows in the sky.

Ahead, I saw Tom's house perched on the hill that overlooked the west side of town. The Caldwell home was built in 1854. Over the years, dormers had been added, along with a vast front porch. It was bright yellow with white detailing that made it look like a lemon meringue pie on a pastry dish. The lights were all on in the front room when I pulled into the driveway. I stepped onto the front porch just as the sun vanished behind the mountains. Emmalina had insisted on having a real doorbell installed instead of the traditional old knocker. I pressed it and heard the odd chime resonate through the house.

It took several minutes for Tom to finally open the door and invite me in. I noticed the rich smell of whiskey on his breath. Tom came from one of the old moonshining families and it was said that whiskey pumped through their veins just as surely as blood. He joked that in his youth the only way he finished his newspaper articles on time while raising a family was to keep himself fueled on a steady diet of coffee and liquor, in equal measure. He invited me in with a sweep of his arm and I followed him to his study at the back of the house.

The room was lined with floor-to-ceiling shelves full of beautiful books of bound newspapers. Dates were embossed on the bindings of the antique leather covers. At a glance, I estimated at least a hundred years' worth of local history on one wall. In addition to the newspapers, he had books on all kinds of genealogy. Scattered on the shelves were antique cameras. Black and white photographs of friends and family were tucked into the few, empty spaces.

He motioned me to a nearby chair. I fell into it with relief and he immediately began pouring himself a drink in a cut crystal tumbler. Without asking, he handed me a glass that was nearly half-full. I chuckled, but took it from him all the same.

"What?" he said, trying to sound innocent. "You look pale. A drink will do you some good. It'll get your blood flowing."

"If you say so," I said in a teasing tone. "Were you able to find the newspapers from 1912?" I asked, hoping he had loads of information for me. Instead he got very quiet as he sank into his leather wing-backed chair.

"It's the strangest thing," he said and my heart immediately sank. "I have everything organized chronologically and yet 1912 is the one volume that seems to be missing," he said motioning to the wall. Looking up, I saw the books for 1911 and 1913 next to one another. Before I could ask if he knew where he might find it, he stopped me and said, "But I remember a bit about that year from writing my first book."

I leaned forward waiting for him to elaborate, not wanting to make a noise in case it stopped his train of thought. Even though Tom was in his eighties, he had a laser sharp mind and a memory to match. Maybe homemade whiskey was the true fountain of youth? He leaned back in his chair and swirled the amber liquid in the beautifully cut glass.

"In 1912, the first ghost ships came to town, if I remember correctly. There were cases of meningitis spreading across the Seattle area causing many people to flee the sickness. It was approaching epidemic proportions. But then something much worse hit the local shores," he paused for effect and leaned in, "ships with only the dead to man them. The boats carried a deadly cargo: hundreds of rats that would scamper into the wooden walls or hide in the crates. The first case of bubonic plague came to Port Townsend in the spring of 1912."

His words sank in as he continued to tell me what he remembered of the newspaper accounts of the time. There was a ship that drifted into dock with over 40 dead sailors and thousands of dead rats strewn across the vessel. The local authorities burned the ships in the bay to avoid contaminating the town. The local Native American tribes had suffered near extinction from smallpox several years earlier, and this new threat of plague would have wiped everyone out if not for the precautions.

"What about a photographer? Do you remember a man named Dennis Morrison? He had a studio in the building where my shop is." He closed his eyes as if trying to conjure the newspaper articles in his mind.

"That name sounds familiar, but I can't place it," he said, sounding a bit frustrated with himself.

"What about Eva and Colette Duprey? They were children who died in 1912, possibly from a fever," I said, hoping this would bring forth a memory from Tom's vast amount of research.

"I remember there was a fever that struck down many of the local children that spring. It was right after the ghost ships arrived and many thought it was the plague that had somehow made its way into town. There was even a rat scare. But the names don't ring a bell." He was up again re-filling his tumbler. I slipped my hand over the rim of mine preventing him from adding more of his whiskey elixir to my already full glass.

"Tom, do you know where I might find more information about that time period since it seems everything has gone missing?" I asked, feeling another wave of disappointment at not finding any answers to assuage my ever-growing unease.

"I'll call around to a few of collectors I know and see if I come up with anything," he said, slipping back into his chair with a quiet fatigue. I knew he would write well into the night, but I had a feeling I was cutting into his usual dinnertime. I finished my glass with one gulp and stifled a cough. It was by far the strongest whiskey I had ever tasted, and that was saying something considering my two best friends owned a bar. He gave me a little smirk and then rose to follow me to the front door. As I stood on the porch smelling the white lilacs that lined the sides of his property, I decided to ask him one more question regardless of how crazy he might think it sounded.

"Tom, did you ever read anything about vampires being part of the town history?" I said, hoping that he would have an amazing story that would explain the events of the last few days.

"You mean Bella Lugosi?" he asked with a chuckle.

"Never mind, if you find any of the 1912 documents, let me know! And thanks for the lighter fluid," I said, walking back to my car. We had a habit of teasing each other that went back to my youth. He was the one person in town who I could count on for a sarcastic comeback. His humor had become a saving grace for me because it made me feel normal, as everyone else was always a bit more careful around the Winship women. He raised his hand to wave goodnight before returning to his lemon meringue house.

As I made my way back home, my mind kept returning to the vision of Sophie's reflection in the shop mirror. I knew what I had seen and it was obvious she wasn't part of the natural ways of the world. My knowledge of these creatures was limited to everything I had seen on television or in the movies. If anyone would know more about vampires, it would be Morgan. Tomorrow my shop was closed, so a trip to my Uncle Morgan's cider mill was in order. After barely escaping with his life during an exorcism of a dark entity many years before, he had rebuilt his life on the outskirts of town. He'd been long settled into his new home and had built his cider and fruit wine production up over the years. People came from all over the region to taste his blackberry and dandelion wines. Every autumn, a cider festival was held at Kat and Gavin's bar featuring Morgan's potions that he'd concocted over the year. He would still tell people their future on the occasional dark winter night, but most of his evenings were occupied with his girlfriend, Astrid.

Astrid had moved to town a few years after the dramatic events of his renewal of spirit. She was in her late forties and was originally from the Black Forests of Germany. Her heart had been broken by a cruel man and she had fled to the farthest corner of the earth to try to mend her soul again. It was here that she met Morgan. He had been riding his bicycle along the road to North Beach after a storm. Astrid was speeding along the highway in the other direction. With tears streaming down her face after a nasty phone call from her ex; she didn't see Morgan until it was too late. She nipped his back tire and in a panic nearly ran her car into a nearby tree. Morgan was thrown into a well-placed hay roll that just happened to be on the side of the road in a local farmer's field. Astrid was out of her car running to his aid expecting to find his broken and crumpled body. Instead, she found Morgan dusting the hay from his usual uniform of black clothing with irritated brushing movements.

"Are you ok?" she asked in a thick, yet charming, German accent.

"It wasn't exactly the best roll in the hay I've ever had," he quipped with a smirk. Morgan hadn't yet looked up to see his aggressor. When he lifted his head and saw Astrid with her long golden locks and lithe stance, he felt immediate embarrassment at his retort. Thankfully, one of Astrid's best qualities was her sense of humor and they both began to laugh nervously as she helped him back to his bike. From that day forward they had been inseparable. He later told us that he knew when he saw her standing there they had been with each other over many lifetimes. It was obvious from the way they looked at each other, as well as the comfort with which they moved. They were like orbiting planets. Always in sync and with a gravitational force that kept them both balanced. Fortunately, Margot and Deidre took a liking to Astrid immediately and now, after more than fifteen years of being a couple, we considered her part of the family.

Turning into the Winship driveway, I quickly closed the iron gates behind me before driving the full length of the lane. I wanted my home and my family to be protected. I was only a few feet from slamming it shut when a rustle of feathers rushed through the opening with a loud "caw" that made me jump. It was the night heron that had nested in the willow tree. It had slipped in before I shut the gate. I felt as if it was mocking my attempts to keep unwelcomed creatures out. Tomorrow I would go to the cider mill with the hope that Morgan might know more about what a real vampire consisted of in this day and age. Bella Lugosi or not, there was something very wrong with Sophie Renard and I was determined to get to the bottom of it before her son got any closer to Willa.

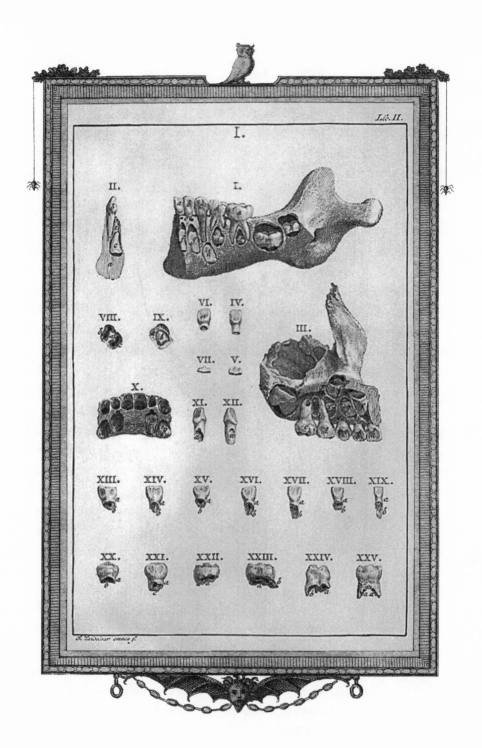

Lib.II.

CB 64 BO

Chapter 10

My dizzy spells lasted through the night between fits of restless sleep, but as the sun burst into our bedroom the next morning, I felt like myself again. No ghost children visited during my slumber. The house felt peaceful as I lay under the white quilt on our bed. I heard James and the children downstairs clambering about in the kitchen. Once we'd moved to Port Townsend and my days revolved around my shop, James began to wake up earlier than I to sketch drafts and later, to help with early-rising babies. I loved to sleep later in the morning, safe in the glow of light that snuck through the linen curtains, unlike the nighttime hours which had always been rife with ghostly visitors. There was a sacred calm to the dawn, and the several hours that followed, that made me feel as if all was right in the world.

This morning I tried to keep the feeling for as long as I could, but soon my thoughts were back to the odd happenings in town and what the Renard family might or might not have to do with them. The window was open and the curtains were blowing slightly. I pulled myself from bed and put on my favorite sundress, adding a soft sweater to keep my arms warm. There was still a nip in the morning air, though it was considerably warmer than any March I could ever remember in the Pacific Northwest. As I made my way down to the kitchen, worry that our old grandfather clock had stopped again nudged at me. I was relieved to hear its familiar ticking, the beating heart of our house.

Felix sat on the countertop with his legs crossed and a bowl of cereal in his tiny hands. I was sure at one point he had used a spoon to fish out the last wheat o's that were soggy with milk but was now drinking directly from the bowl. We were not a formal family. In fact, he looked like a miniature version of James with his sandy blond hair sticking up slightly and a drip of milk escaping from the rim of the breakfast bowl. Willa was thumbing through a French fashion magazine while sipping a colossal cup of black coffee. She took after me in this way. I could always be found with a cup of black coffee either steaming from a cracked mug or brewing somewhere. It had been so from an early age, so I couldn't imagine telling her not to drink the very elixir that had fueled me through late night studying. It was my one vice.

"Good morning," I said, pouring myself a cup of the waiting liquid gold. My family greeted me, in unison, with a distracted, "Good morning."

"So Felix and Willa, do you want to come with me to see Morgan in about an hour?" I said, knowing that they both loved going to the cider mill. It was a mysterious place filled with a power that was almost palpable. It was hard not to feel recharged after visiting the sanctuary that Morgan and Astrid had built together on hallowed land. This time of year they would be harvesting dandelions for a summer wine and the cabin would have a green scent in every corner.

"I want to go!" said Felix with an excitement that I hoped would be contagious so Willa would come along as well.

"I can't," she said, and I felt a needle of disappointment. "I'm going to Seattle with Kat and Lily to shop for shoes and things for the dance." This was the first I'd heard of it but James gave me a confirming look, which meant he had already given her permission. I tried to convince myself that her being away from Port Townsend for the day under the watchful eye of my best friend would be better than having her here with the Renard boy in close proximity. Her phone made a sound of little rings indicating she had received a text. She glanced at it and then folded her magazine, put her cup in the sink and was down the front hall before I'd sat down at the table.

"They're waiting for me outside!" she shouted down the hallway while struggling to put on her shoes while unbolting the door. "See you tonight!" Before I could get the words "Be careful!" out of my mouth, the door had closed behind her. I must have had a look of rejection on my face, because James immediately pulled me out of my chair and into one of his bear hugs.

"Kat said she would have them home by 8:00 unless they miss the ferry," he said, caressing my head with one hand and holding his own coffee cup with the other. I tucked myself into his tall body, feeling safe. That was the one thing about being married that I loved most. The feel of a man's presence in the home, while at times tedious in the quotidian aspects, was also a grounding energy. He acted as a shield in ways that I would never entirely understand and yet it was so. I breathed in his familiar scent, a mix of cloves and a muskier odor that lingered on his shirt collars. I pulled away reluctantly to fix myself some toast for a quick breakfast. Felix was out of the kitchen and up to his room to get dressed for our outing together. There was nothing he enjoyed more than an afternoon with his great-uncle Morgan. If Deidre and Samir had still lived in town, they would be in close competition, but their recent absence made Morgan his "go-to" family member for stories of magic and long-forgotten lore.

Soon we were in the car heading out of town. Felix was in a bright mood as we headed down the long stretch of road that led to North Beach. Morgan's cider mill had been built in the early 1900s and had once been owned by my great-grandmother, Elsiba. Felix was wearing his favorite rock t-shirt that Willa had picked up for him on her last shopping trip with Lily and Kat in Seattle. She went to various vintage clothing stores I had frequented in my twenties. We chatted about his teachers and other happenings that were important in his eight-year-old life, the most intense of which was the addition of swim classes to the school curriculum. Felix was connected to water much in the way that Margot was, in that it was his commanding element. Unlike me, he felt at home in water and was not in any way nervous around rising tides or gigantic waves. He had begun to swim when he was just a baby with James, so he was well acquainted with water activities but apparently the swim coach was trying to get him to compete and competition was simply not in his nature.

As we talked about different ideas for getting him out of the swim class, the subject of vampires emerged. Felix had been having dreams the past two nights about vampire-like creatures trying to climb the iron gates. I listened carefully as he began to tell me his dreams.

"There were eight of them and they had no hair and were dressed in torn clothes as if they had come up from out of their graves," he explained. "And they were trying to climb over the iron gates but because everything was locked they were struggling to get over the spikes on the top."

"Why were they trying to get in?" I asked, wanting to know every detail of the first dream before he told me the next one.

"Because they were so hungry and they wanted to eat all these children who were hiding inside of our house," he said, and I could tell that saying the words out loud was making him uncomfortable.

"Who were the kids? Was it you and Willa or other kids?" I asked, hoping that what he had to tell me might be a clue to the odd happenings in town.

"Well, they wanted to get us, but more than that, they really wanted all these other kids who were hiding in the closets, the attic, the basement, and all these weird places where no one goes in the house."

"What did the kids look like?" I was concentrating on the road, but I wanted to hear every detail.

"They were all wearing old fashioned clothes. There were two little girls with blond hair and white dresses who were crying in the closet in your bedroom and lots of other kids trying to hide. Willa and I were in her room and we couldn't get her window closed and we were afraid they would climb the willow to get inside," he said with a shudder despite the warm day.

"What happened? Did they get over the fence?" I asked, hoping his answer would be that they had not made it over the iron balustrade.

"I woke up just as the first one climbed over and hit the ground running towards the back door," he said in a shaky voice. I could tell this dream had frightened him as it would any child of eight. It frightened me, and I was over forty!

"What about your dream last night?" I asked, hoping it was a bit on the lighter side, although I doubted it.

"I was in my bedroom and something kept hitting my window. So I got up and looked outside and there was a man sitting on the garden table near the red rose bushes. He was very pale and he had no hair like the vampires in the dream before. He was throwing little pebbles at the window, but when I looked on the sill they were actually teeth. People teeth. Scattered all along the edge." He paused and I could tell that he was picturing the molars and canines strewn on the window's ledge.

"Then what happened?" I asked, almost not wanting to know.

"Well, he was just sitting on the table playing a guitar and singing a lullaby. And there were rats swarming everywhere in the garden. Almost like they were drawn to him, but he was looking at me. In his song he said 'One hundred and thirty children, ever so many teeth, a rat is more than an omen, it brings the town to weep.' But he was smiling like it was all a big joke." As he said this, I realized he was explaining what it was to look upon true evil. I had experienced looking into the face of a demon when I, along with Margot and Deidre, had removed the entity that had haunted Morgan for over four decades. This gave me the same feeling in the pit of my stomach.

"What happened then?" I asked in a careful tone so as not to let any sign of worry betray me.

"I turned to leave and there were the two little ghost girls, standing in the doorway of my bedroom. They were afraid and ran under my bed. Then I woke up," he said with a sigh of relief. I knew what it was like to have vivid dreams and it was definitely a mixed bag. The dreams of flying or being in other places in the world were magnificent, but the dark visitations were never something I looked forward to when I closed my eyes each night. I would have to get him a dream catcher from the Native American shop a few doors down from my store.

Soon the familiar driveway leading to Morgan's house appeared on the left hand side of the road. It now boasted a new wooden sign with the words "Winship Cider Mill" in scrolled letters. We pulled in and parked in front of the cabin. Crocuses bloomed in vibrant purple waves along the front and sides of the log cabin's porch. Astrid had even decorated the banister with flower boxes filled with primroses and other spring perennials. The log cabin had been built after Morgan had been released from the curse that had tortured him for the better part of his life. The original cabin had burned to the ground many years before. This new and improved structure was now his home. Although he had built it before he met Astrid, the cabin had a Bavarian feel to it by design. If I hadn't known better, I would have thought we'd stepped into the Black Forests and this was the home of a woodsman. There were black bears carved out of hundred-year-old wood logs that framed the stairs that led to the front door and covered porch. The porch was decorated with willow furniture, including two large chairs and a long table that held a bowl of apples. Everywhere were planters and fancy ceramic pots filled to overflowing with brightly blooming flowers.

Felix ran up the stairs and rapped on the massive wood door before I was even out of the car. As with every Winship home, there were chimes lining the entryways to frighten away any hungry spirits. The chimes on Morgan's front porch clanged as the old glass medicine bottles clinked together in the breeze. Felix paced on the porch impatiently waiting for Morgan to answer the door. The house seemed unusually quiet for a Sunday, and I wondered if maybe they had gone to the beach.

"Hey there little man, don't knock my door down," said a voice from the walkway that led to the back yard. Morgan had been in their garden. He walked over to the car where I was standing and gave me a quick hug. He was just over six feet tall, which was shorter than James, but still tall for a Winship. The women in my family barely made it past 5 feet 4 inches, but I had hopes for Willa considering James was so tall and lanky. Morgan's black hair was now streaked with grey. He also wore black-rimmed glasses that reminded me of something the "mod" kids I knew when I lived in Seattle would have worn to look hip. He was dressed in his usual uniform of all black clothing and smirk, to match. Felix jumped off the porch and ran to Morgan giving him a hug around his waist before taking off into the back yard.

"Come to talk about ghouls and goblins?" he asked with a knowing tilt of his head, implying that he was well aware of what had been happening in town.

"Have you heard about the new family that moved into the Bell Tower House?" I asked, knowing he would have felt the energy shift, but might not have been aware of the comings and goings.

"Oh, I know. Things have been humming for weeks. And then Margot told me about them. Come to the back and see what we've been up to. We can sit and talk there."

I followed him along the stepping stones that led around the log cabin. Felix was already through the gate. I had a feeling Morgan was going to show me more than just his handiwork in the garden. There was a glint in his eye that betrayed both his intelligence, and the underlying hint of a welcome challenge. I felt a glimmer of excitement wanting to know what Morgan thought of recent events, then a frisson of fear as the unpleasant images from Felix's dreams ran through my mind. It had not escaped my notice that Felix had had these dreams on the two nights that Eva and Colette, the ghost girls, had allowed me to sleep soundly.

Turpin P.

Lambert F. sculp.

DIGITALE.

Chapter 11

Nearly everyone in Port Townsend had a garden. There were people like Margot, who grew roses to perfection, pampering them in the summers and protecting them through harsh winter winds. Then there were others, like Deidre, who grew vegetables. When Deidre had still lived in Port Townsend, her labors began in Spring with the first strawberries and went through autumn when she would harvest her prize-winning pumpkins in time for Halloween. She once told me her secret. She whispered stories to the plants as she weeded and watered to keep them interested in the act of life. Each day, the story from the day before would continue its next chapter. The plants shook in anticipation when she opened the gate each morning. At the end of the harvest season she would put them to bed telling them the final outcome. She promised to revive their children in the spring with new stories of love and adventure.

Morgan's garden was a labyrinth of herbs, flowers, vegetables, and berries growing together in specific combinations. It was vast and led up to the apple orchard on one side and the old cemetery on the other. As I rounded the corner of the cabin, I was greeted by the astonishing sight of blossoms and budding vegetables tangled together. The fragrance made me giddy. There was rosemary to the side of the gate as well as at the entrance to the back door of the cabin. White, purple and pink lilacs created a hedge on the far side of the property and were full with open blossoms. The garden was in the form of concentric circles of tall trellises, one inside of the other, with stone pathways in between the thirteen wheel shapes. There was everything from edibles such as raspberries, mint, marigolds, and the beginnings of tomatoes to more dubious plants like belladonna, foxglove, elderberry, and poison parsnips. To venture into the circles in search of sustenance could be deadly if you didn't know your way around Morgan's garden. In addition to plants, Astrid had a chicken coop and a rabbit hutch near the back entrance to the cabin.

Felix ran straight to the rabbit hutch, unlocking the little latch to take out his favorite hoppy friend, a beige rabbit named Esther. Together they sat in the grass near the lilacs. Morgan offered me a chair at the outdoor table on the small patio behind the cabin. The iron trellises to each side and overhead dripped with a canopy of wisteria. I heard Astrid inside on the phone speaking German, chatting with someone from her previous home.

"So, what do you think of my schizophrenic garden this year?" Morgan asked with a grin. "It's pure madness that everything has come out of the earth so early and with no hope of sustaining its usual vigor."

"I thought it was just the lilacs, but this is really bizarre." The sheer combination of plants growing all at once instead of step by step as the seasons advanced was quite unsettling. Though beautiful, it was unnatural.

"Margot told me she gave you Elsiba's recipe for the special repellant," he said, glancing in Felix's direction to see if he was within earshot. Felix was in his own little world feeding Esther a carrot out of the rabbit food bin, gently stroking her fur. I seized the moment to fill Morgan in on everything that had transpired from Sophie Renard's frightening reflection to Felix's terrifying dreams. His brow furrowed as he listened, although I did not get the impression that he was at all surprised.

"So I'm guessing that the guy in the backyard throwing teeth at Felix's window probably isn't the tooth fairy," he said with his usual sarcasm. I gave him a quick shake of my head, but couldn't bring myself to say any more on the subject. I felt that speaking about Felix's dream might conjure the darkness to us further. At that moment, Astrid strolled out of the back door with a tray of three coffee cups and a full French press.

"I thought I saw you out here with Felix," she said in a sweet voice. She poured me a cup of black coffee that smelled of cinnamon. Astrid always put a pinch in her ground coffee to lessen the acidity. It was enchanting and reminded me of Christmas. As Astrid poured herself and Morgan a cup as well, I felt a welcome sense of relief to be here after so many days of strange happenings.

"So the lilacs and all kinds of other plants bloom early and then there is a historic red tide that washes up sharks. At the same time, two ghost girls are visiting you, talking about fevers. Felix has a premonition that vampires are coming and the next day the Renards roll into town at sundown and move into the Bell Tower House of all places. Then there are the weird reflections, the missing newspaper tomes, and now Felix's scary-ass dreams." Morgan had summed it all up in a quick breakdown of events with no sugar coating.

"Pretty much," was all I had to add, while Astrid listened to us intently. She liked to sit back and examine things before joining in, then when she did, she had a sharp mind and often saw the flip sides of arguments.

"Well, I think we have a problem," said Morgan, stating what was beginning to feel more and more obvious.

"There is something else," I said, hesitating because I was going on a gut feeling, "I think Willa and the Renard boy are interested in each other." Saying the words out loud made me squirm inside. Willa obviously didn't want me to know she had been texting him past her curfew nor showing him the town with Lily. It made me feel like I was spying on her and I had never felt the need to do so before this moment.

"Oh, that's not good at all," said Morgan. "You can't tell her not to see him," he said with a look of worry on his face.

"I know. He becomes the forbidden fruit that a teenage girl will gobble up with twice the gusto if I tell her he's bad for her," I said knowing because I, too, had been sixteen, once upon a time.

"Is she using Margot's protective charms?" Morgan asked and I nodded a yes. "Hopefully that will be enough for the time being, but we need to find out more about these people and what they want here. As for the dreams, the song reminds me of something I can't quite put my finger on. What were the words again?"

"I think it was something like 'one hundred and thirty children, ever so many teeth, a rat is more than an omen, it brings the town to weep' although I may be a bit off." Just as I finished my phrase a clatter of porcelain hitting the stone patio brought my attention to Astrid. Her coffee cup had slipped from her hand leaving a pool of dark liquid on the ground and shards of white china strewn at her feet. Her face had gone from her usual rosy color to an ashen grey.

"I'm so clumsy," she said, quickly picking up the broken cup before rushing back into the house to get a towel. Something about the song had frightened her. Morgan rose quickly and followed her into the house. I heard them speaking quietly but couldn't make out the words as they had switched from English to German. Morgan spoke several languages, but when he and Astrid began living together his language of choice had become her native tongue. After a few minutes they both came out and Morgan began clearing away the broken cup as Astrid sat in a chair that provided the most sun. As Morgan left us to fetch a new cup, she began to tell me what had given her such a jolt.

"Charlotte, that song is more than just a part of Felix's dream. It comes from a real German folk song," she said in a soft voice with an underlying tremble. "Do you know the story of the Pied Piper?" I nodded a yes. It was a story that my mom had read to me from a Grimm's fairytale book when I was young. I remembered the moral was to pay a person their due, but it had always struck me as having a truly frightening array of imagery with its stolen children and hypnotized rats.

"Well, the fairy story is from a real event that happened in Hamelin, Germany in the eleventh century," she said with a sudden fervor. I knew that she and Morgan spent many evenings talking about magic and philosophy, but Astrid was a history teacher by trade. Up until a few years ago, she had taught history at the Port Angeles Community College until the work at the cider mill took too much of her time. I leaned forward in my chair and she continued on, glancing over my shoulder to make sure that Felix was still happily playing in the garden with the rabbits.

"There is a story about a man who came to town during the plagues that were killing so many at the time. The rats were the problem and while people did not know this in a scientific way like they do now, it was their intuition that told them that the rats were bringing the disease. He claimed that he knew how to get rid of the rats, but most of all how to get rid of the fevers and the disease that were decimating the countryside. The town had to give him one hundred and thirty of their children for him to take back to his home in Transylvania. The population there were so few that it was becoming almost impossible to marry outside of family. The inbreeding was causing disease in the bloodlines — primarily mental disease. So he promised to free the city of rats, and hence plague, in exchange for these children. He promised they would be healthy for much longer than any normal children in plague-ridden cities could hope for. The people were so desperate they agreed to the man's request and within a fortnight the town was the only place for miles around which was miraculously free of rats. Soon the town was also unburdened of the former pestilence. When he came to collect his pay in the form of seventy girls and sixty boys under the age of ten, the town refused. They hung him in the town square, fearful of allowing him to leave in case he would rain the black plague down upon them. The people knew that he was a powerful sorcerer of some type and condemned him to death rather than hand their children over to him.

"It wasn't until the following spring that people began to see the familiar form of the strange man on the roads leading out of town. He was said to be alive and playing a musical instrument that made people feel dizzy or hypnotized. Soon there was a panic. The woods, still devoid of all rats, were searched for the presumed dead traveler. Nothing was found. Then on the Ides of March, in the middle of the night, one hundred and thirty children disappeared from their beds. The adults spoke of an odd feeling that came over them, accompanied by the faint sound of music on the wind. It had put them to sleep and when they awoke all that was left of their children was a pile of bloody teeth resting on their pillows. The parents searched everywhere, pulling their hair and wailing their mournful cries, but the children had vanished. There are stories that these were the first vampire children who later populated the Carpathians, brought from Hamlin by a dark conjurer. Whatever happened in reality, the song was passed down for hundreds of years as a warning not to make deals that you know you will not uphold. It could be a deal with the devil, and he always gets his due."

As she spoke I felt the hair rise on the back of my neck and arms. I quickly turned to make sure that Felix was within my sight. He was still playing with Esther the rabbit far enough from us that he had not heard Astrid's telling of the disturbing Pied Piper legend. Her words were ringing in my ears. Morgan brought her a clean cup and poured her a fresh cup of coffee. Her hands shook as she raised the porcelain to her lips. It was hard not to feel terrified after listening to her story, especially considering that the song that had triggered her to tell me this legend had come from my eight-year-old son's dream. My protective instincts were kicking in, although I had no real evidence that the Renard family was planning anything dubious.

"So what do we do?" I asked, looking from Morgan back to Astrid.

"We can only protect ourselves and the family for the moment, but we will keep trying to find ways to expose them. In the meantime, keep a close eye on Felix and Willa. If you can, ask the ghost girls to tell you more of their message. Maybe that will help us figure out why the vampires have decided to come here again," he said, reminding me that Margot had said the same thing.

"Again?" I asked hoping he would enlighten me about what had happened when they were here before. Margot had been vague at best.

"Elsiba had an experience with vampires but she was reluctant to talk about such things further than to say we needed to wear her repellent if they ever came to town again. She seemed to think that they wouldn't be able to stay away forever. I'll try to find out more, but in the meantime, keep the children close," Morgan said with a protective glance at his great-nephew.

We finished the rest of the morning examining the odd combinations of plants that had twisted themselves together in a burst of fertility. Astrid cut us rhubarb which was one of my favorite vegetables for making tarts. Morgan and Felix collected fresh eggs for us and eventually we said our goodbyes at the garden gate. I cannot say that our trip had me feeling any less anxious about all the things that were occurring since the early spring had bloomed in Port Townsend. However, with each confirmation that something unnatural was afoot, I felt as if I was getting one step closer to unveiling the dark side of what was transpiring. I would keep my children close, although in my heart I knew that trying to confine Willa would only make her want to break free even more. If this was to be a balancing act, then I would have to gather my strength for the coming storm. At least I had exceptional allies in Morgan and Astrid, although the look on Astrid's face as we left gave me a sinking feeling. I could tell she was holding something back and it was troubling her, but she had been so shaken, I didn't want to push her. Hopefully, if there was more to the story of the Pied Piper of Hamelin, she would tell me before it was too late. In the meantime, we waved goodbye as Felix and I headed back to the Winship house with baskets of fresh delicacies and my mind swirling with fairy stories and feelings of trepidation.

Pflanzen als Insectenfänger.
Nach der Natur aufgenommen von E. Schmidt.

CHAPTER 12

Arriving home I noticed a note from James saying he'd be at his office working on the plans for the Renard projects. He wanted to set them into motion beginning the following morning. Felix took off to play video games with his best friend Cody who lived down the street. With Willa in Seattle with Kat and Lily, I had the whole house all to myself; a rare luxury. It was intensely quiet. The only noise was the ticking of the grandfather clock on the second floor and the usual creaking boards. Under normal circumstances, I would have treasured this moment by cloistering myself in the library/workroom to create a one-of-a-kind piece of jewelry. I had multitudes of ideas. Some had been hovering on the periphery of my creative thoughts for months. But today I felt preoccupied with the new information I'd been gathering about the unusual occurrences in town with the arrival of the Renard family. So instead of enjoying my day of solitude, I decided to call Gavin.

Gavin and I had been best friends, along with our mutual friend, Kat, from childhood to the present day. I liked to joke that Gavin would waste away without us, but secretly, I wondered if the same wasn't true of me. In a way, he was an anchor, having kept me grounded on several occasions when I was ready to run away and join a convent. When I was on the edge of throwing in the towel on life, he had helped put things into perspective by doing what all good friends do: listen. Also, he was the one person I knew outside of my family that read with a voracity that seemed almost unhealthy. He nourished himself on the written word. Often times he kept his body fueled on peanut butter and jelly sandwiches and beer, but his soul was fed by the elegance of letters combined into symmetric phrases. This was one of the other reasons I wanted to call Gavin. Maybe he could give me a little more of a historical background on all things related to vampires. He picked up his phone on the first ring and was soon on his way over to the house.

I left the front door open while I started a pot of coffee. I heard a car pull up and a few seconds later Gavin's deep voice echoed down the hallway.

"Charlotte?" he called out, "It's me. Are you decent?"

"I'm in the kitchen," I yelled back and heard him shut the front door. He made his way to the kitchen as I set out coffee cups and homemade banana bread on a tray to take into the garden. Gavin had aged with grace and now, well over forty, he still held himself like a young man. He was tall with sandy blond hair and striking blue eyes and often the women in town followed him around like lovesick cats. To me, he was the big brother I'd always wanted and was lucky enough to find just down the road from my house when I was a kid. This afternoon he came bearing an odd gift in his outstretched hands. It was a peculiar looking plant.

"I got this for Felix," he said, setting the strange botanical on the kitchen table.

"What in the world is that?" I asked, leaning in to inspect the odd looking plant. It had seven stems shooting from the base and on the end of each was a little green taco-shaped leaf with spiny ends along the edge that looked like teeth. The inside of each little mouth was vibrant magenta. There were delicate tendrils curled along the bright green stems.

"It's a Venus flytrap," he said with a certain amount of pride. "I had one when I was his age and thought it was pretty much the coolest thing ever. So when I saw one at the nursery the other day I had to pick it up for Felix. I didn't think Willa would want one." He smirked at his inside joke. Willa refused to work in the garden. She insisted that she would be the one Winship without a green thumb if she had anything to do with it. I knew that as soon as she finished high school and was off to college it would not be anywhere nearby but rather as far from this town as she could get. She hungered for the city and even Seattle felt too small for her. Her eye was set on New York or even more appealing were cities like London or Paris. I knew that whatever she put her mind to would manifest, but it hurt me to think of her so very far away. Thankfully, I still had a few years before any of those options became a reality.

"Felix is going to go nuts when he sees this thing." I said, knowing he'd put it on the windowsill in his bedroom. This was the kind of thing that would fascinate his young mind. Hopefully he would be able to find a book or two in the Winship library that talked about carnivorous plants. We made our way out into the rose garden near the willow tree. There was a Victorian cast iron garden set of a table and chairs that had been in the same place for the past one hundred and fifty odd years. We brushed off the table and settled ourselves into the old chairs that had woven metal roses on the legs.

"So how are you enjoying this very unusual spring?" he asked, and I could see in the corner of his eye a twitch that betrayed a bit of worry just under his calm surface.

"Not very much to be honest," I said, and then told him everything that had transpired. I included the most recent clues that Astrid had shared with me earlier that morning.

"So you think they are really vampires?" he asked, and I could hear the disbelief in his voice.

"I have no idea, Gavin. I just feel something isn't right. And now this boy is hovering around Willa, which makes me really nervous and protective," I said, hoping he wouldn't think I was some crazy, overbearing mother.

"Well, everything I've ever read about vampires I always assumed was fiction. Let me think," he paused, making a mental list and then began, "They can't walk in the sunlight, they don't like holy water or crucifixes, they don't like garlic; they are the undead and need blood or some other energy source to sustain them; they are against all things in the natural order; they are possessive of their prey and often stalk them first; they are obsessive compulsive..." I interrupted before he could go on with his list.

"What do you mean they're obsessive compulsive? That is absurd!" I said with a laugh, thinking Gavin was just teasing me.

"No really," he said with a serious frown, "that's one of the ways to escape from one. There are tons of folk stories of maidens escaping the grips of a vampire by spilling seeds or rice on the ground. The vampire absolutely has to stop and pick up all the grains out of his obsessive need for order. It's said they'll keep picking up the grains even if it means perishing in the sunlight. They simply cannot walk away like a normally adjusted individual. I think it may even be one of the reasons we throw rice at weddings."

My mind immediately created an image of a ridiculous vampire clad in a cape with protruding fangs frantically picking up rice grains as the sun came over the horizon. No death by stake for this guy, but death by tidiness instead. Gavin kept rattling on about vampire legend and I admired the amount of information he provided.

"What about mirrors?" I asked, thinking back on the odd shimmers and reflections I'd seen recently in my shop. "I can still see the image of the reflection that Sophie cast when she was in my store yesterday. There was no doubt about it; she looked dead; like protruding bones and rotted way of being dead."

"All I know is that vampires in literature do not cast a reflection in a mirror or a shadow." He thought for a moment and then continued, "But I know the Victorians used to say that a mirror reflects a person's soul. I wonder if that was what happened with Sophie? The soul of a vampire is in a state of decay trapped inside a dead body. I know dark spirits travel through mirrors to steal souls, which is why people used to cover all the mirrors in the house when a family member passed away."

The last part I knew as well; we still did such things when a family member died in the house. Mirrors were covered with black cloth and clocks were stopped to mark the moment of death. Then another thought occurred to me regarding souls.

"Do you remember Betsy Ford?" I asked, hoping he knew who I was talking about.

"That sounds vaguely familiar," he replied, waiting for me to continue.

"We learned about her in school. She was the last of the Quilcene tribe and died here in the early 1900s. The Quileutes slaughtered her tribe as retribution for gambling gone awry. She had her picture taken by one of the local photographers when she was well over a hundred although she swore from that moment on the photographer had stolen her soul. She died not long after and every time I see that picture of her hanging on the wall at the City Hall it gives me the creeps. It reminded me of the ghost girls that keep visiting and their picture that I discovered in Elsiba's trunk. I have no idea what this has to do with the Renards, but I feel there is a connection or I wouldn't be having these ghostly visitations at this moment in time. Ghosts always choose their moments carefully. And then Felix's vampire dreams with the ghost children as well — not to mention his premonition."

"I don't think any of this is coincidence, but I still find it hard to believe that there are blood-sucking ghouls living in the Bell Tower House. What do you know about them besides their name and that they are French?" Gavin asked, while leaning in to stuff a piece of banana bread into his mouth.

"They are, by all guesses, on the wealthy side. Sophie has exquisite taste in antiques. The husband seemed rather cold, but I only met him briefly. Their son, Daniel, stared at Willa in a way that made my skin crawl. That's about all," I said, realizing how very little I knew about the family.

"Does James say anything about what it's like to work for them?" he asked.

"James is so over the moon about the project I think he could be fixing those houses for Mussolini and he wouldn't have noticed. It's all about the work and the beauty of the structures. He's had his eye on both of those buildings for years now and finally has a chance to save them," I said, although in my heart I hoped that James would let me in on a bit more history of who these newcomers were.

"I get it. James has been gawking at those buildings for years now," Gavin said with a grin. "I'll let you know if I hear anything at the bar when the workers come in after they start construction. Their tongues always loosen after a few shots on the house."

The sky was beginning to darken. I knew Felix would soon be home wanting dinner as would James and, hopefully, Willa. The clouds were a vibrant orange as the sun began to make its way behind the hills and everything glowed with a tangerine light. Even the willow tree had taken on a surreal hue. Gavin helped me bring the cups and plates inside as the sun faded and the birds returned to their nests. I hoped he wasn't going to go home to an empty house and decided to invite him to stay for dinner if he didn't already have plans.

"Normally I would, but Kat is waiting for me at the brewery. She's been doing the books and payroll all day. I promised her I'd get there tonight. We need to look over orders to get out by tomorrow morning," he said casually. He had no idea what a bombshell he had just dropped on me. If Kat was in her office working today, then who had taken Willa to Seattle?

"Are you ok, Charlotte?" Gavin asked, as a look of worry flashed across his face.

"Willa said she was going to Seattle with Kat and Lily all day and would be home by 8:00 p.m. James checked, how is that possible? Did she and Lily go alone?" I asked, visions of them both lying in a ditch somewhere floating through my mind.

"I doubt that Kat would let Lily go to Seattle alone with Willa. She just got her license a few months ago," he said, and I could see that my worry had become contagious.

"I'll call her," he said, pulling his cellphone from his pocket. Every ring took what seemed like forever until I heard Kat's voice on the other line. Gavin explained the situation and he hung up quickly before I could talk to her.

"She had planned to go but then the paperwork kind of overwhelmed her. So Sophie Renard offered to take the girls along with her son Daniel. Apparently she had to go to Seattle for the day to pick out new curtains, or something, and dropped them off in Fremont for the afternoon. Lily just called and they should be home soon," he said although neither of us had what would be a normal reaction to this news. I had almost wished that Willa had taken off with Lily for the day without telling me because then I could have grounded her for the rest of eternity. But this was with permission from Kat and supervision of another parent. I could not legitimately get angry with her for going to Seattle with a vampire and a half. And yet I felt angry. I felt as if I was being kept in the dark and I was the only one who could see the impending danger that this family represented not only to the town, but to my own immediate family. I knew I had to be very careful how I reacted so I didn't give Willa more reasons to keep things from me. In a word, this was torture.

Gavin gave me a bear hug as he made his way to the door. Before leaving, he kissed the top of my head, a long-standing tradition, and then headed off into the night. I washed the cups and then sat in the front parlor with two white candles lit on my altar to the Virgin Mary. In my mind I asked her to watch over my children and protect them from any lurking darkness. The glow of the candlelight created little shadows against the walls as I let the silence and the darkness wash over me. When I was a child, the dark left me fearful until my Uncle Morgan explained that it can also cloak us from the things that go bump in the night. We can sneak up on them as easily as they can us, but inherently the darkness was ours to use to our benefit. I kept repeating in my mind the tricks Gavin had spoken of to recognize a vampire and wondered if next time Sophie came into the shop I could put them to the test. As I concocted ridiculous ideas in my mind, two headlights flashed across the living room wall. A black Mercedes pulled up in front of the Winship house and Willa stepped out of the car with several shopping bags. She waved to the car as it pulled away from the curb and came bouncing up the front stairs in a light-hearted manner. As the door creaked open, I switched on a small lamp next to my reading chair, startling Willa.

"Mom! You scared me! What are you doing sitting in the dark?" she asked, as if I was a complete freak.

"Oh just enjoying the quiet. Felix is at Cody's house and your dad should be home soon. Did you find anything cool?" I asked, trying to change the subject. She took off her shoes and flopped down in the old reading chair across from me. One by one she pulled her vintage finds from the bags. She had an eye for fashion and could find the one stellar piece any store had and somehow get it for a bargain.

"Tomorrow we should try to find a necklace to go with the dress for the Saint Patrick's Day dance," I said, and she smiled with excitement. "Do you know who you are going with?" I asked dreading the answer.

"Well, I was just going to tag along with Lily and Aaron but since Daniel asked me I said I would go with him," she said trying to be nonchalant about being asked by the new boy in town. If I had been sixteen and a handsome new boy came to town who knew nothing about the Winships, and was flirting with me obsessively, I would have been ecstatic. This false casual attitude had my mom-radar screaming danger. Yet there was nothing I could reasonably say to her that wouldn't sound like me trying to stifle her social life. So I decided to simply observe for the moment, but not without putting my own power into action. I would protect my family on an energetic level and make this house a sanctuary for them.

I listened as she talked about her day trip to the city. James and I had lived in Fremont so we knew the neighborhood well. It was nice to hear that things were the same but also hear about the inevitable changes. The Lenin statue was still looking for a buyer and many of the vintage clothing stores had been replaced by more upscale boutiques. But there were still treasures to be unearthed, especially at the Sunday flea market, which they had visited that afternoon.

I still found it odd that she didn't mention much in the way of details about Daniel. It was as if he'd been a ghost following her and Lily around the whole day. I would have expected a boy his age to have visited record shops that boasted collections of rare vinyl and up-and-coming bands. But apparently he'd just shadowed the two girls everywhere, taking in all they said and did without comment. Or maybe she was just keeping it from me.

Soon the front door clicked open and in came Felix with James following behind. Felix loved his Venus flytrap and immediately installed it on the windowsill in his room. I made him promise to write a thank you card to Gavin as Margot had always taught me. With the family back home, James and I began to prepare dinner together as he talked about all the amazing plans that would soon be under way for the Renards. Willa listened intently as he spoke about the inside of the two structures, especially when James began to describe the interior of the Bell Tower House. Strangely, it had one entire room with floor-to-ceiling mirrors that was original to the structure. The room was not to be touched even though the mirrors were scratched and faded. As we talked and then ate together, I listened with only half my attention; the other half was busy reciting numerous protection spells in my mind. The act of sitting together around the wooden table created a protective circle and in doing so I was able to cast a light around my family to keep them safe. Tomorrow I would have the whole day to myself and decided to spend it unearthing as much information as I could on the Renard family. I hoped to finally figure out exactly what kind of vampires they were. And if indeed they were vampires, then how to banish them in the process. But for tonight, my thoughts were on protection of my own and the calm before the storm.

CHAPTER 13

Calm settled over the house once everyone was tucked into their beds. I made a quick trip down the hallway to peek in on Felix and saw that all was well, his new plant keeping guard on the windowsill. Next, it was up to the turret room to check on Willa. I was relieved to see her door slightly opened and all the lights off. There was no need to wrestle her phone from her or insist that she get to sleep. In my own bedroom, I found James softly snoring. I had a feeling this would be the norm for the next few weeks until the brunt of the restoration work was finished. He told me that because the Renards had insisted on an impossible deadline for the work, the company had to hire three extra crews from neighboring towns. Thankfully, everyone was free and needing work so the construction crews from Chimacum, Irondale, and Port Angeles were glad to throw in together to have everything completed in two weeks. It was a colossal project, but I knew if anyone could do it, it would be James. His love for the buildings meant the work would be done well, even if the deadline was insane. However, this probably meant I would listen to his tired body snore the nights away.

I always went to bed well after midnight. My creativity ignited when the sun went down and the night owls came out. It was my moment of tranquility when I knew my family was safe in the house. I could focus on whatever gemstone or rock had been calling to me throughout the day. Tonight, I intended to make a necklace in the shape of a dragonfly. The body, I formed out of an old crucifix, the wings were hammered copper that I oxidized into an intense green, and the necklace was a combination of emeralds and little pebbles that I had found on the beach. Why this little insect had asked to be created I didn't know, but I allowed my fingers to twist and file until it was complete. A last minute addition was a tiny mirror that dangled like a diamond teardrop from the dragonfly's tail. With all these thoughts of vampires and mirrors waltzing through my head, it seemed appropriate that this necklace be adorned with a reflective power.

I slipped under the covers next to James. The bed was cool despite the hot day. Temperatures always dropped drastically on the coast after nightfall. I tried to calm my mind as I listened to his melodic breathing and light snores. Snuggled under the cotton quilt with my head on my pillow, I felt a sense of peace come over me in spite of all the unsettling information I had gathered today. I sent out one last protection spell over the house and my family in the hopes that it would keep Felix safe from any nightmares and Willa from being spied on by the creepy night heron. Soon I was adrift in sleep and with it the two ghost girls reappeared after their two-night respite.

Again, the rustling of their dresses betrayed their presence in our bedroom. Eva moved to my side in a quick swish of crinkled fabric. She motioned to Colette to stand next to her and then put a tiny finger up to her lips, wordlessly telling her sister to be silent. The little ghost then leaned over and began to whisper in my ear.

"Be careful of the rats, Momma. They made us so sick and the lady with the red masque at the ball promised to make it all better, but she only made the fever worse. We can't leave here until the fever is gone," she said with a sadness in her little voice that broke my heart. If a ghost was stuck it was usually for one of several reasons: unfinished business, ignorance of their own death, a binding that keeps them in a certain place, or a warning. I couldn't quite put my finger on what it was, but with Eva's words I wondered if someone had bound her to this place, and why. In my mind, I began asking her questions, hoping it wouldn't scare her and Colette away.

"Did someone trap you here?" I asked.

"The lady in the red masque said we could leave when the fever broke. But I still feel so hot. And Colette's fever is worse and worse. And the man with the rats is looking for us again." Her voice raised into a worried pitch at the mention of the man. Could this be the same man that Felix had seen in his dream?

"Let me show you," she said, taking my hand and pulling me from my bed. This time I kept calm even though the touch of her hand on my own was scalding. Her ghostly fingers were like holding a hot coal in my palm. She pulled me towards the bedroom window and

Colette followed hiding behind my legs, much as Willa and Felix had done when they were her age. I felt protective of these two ghost children. If they had come to me it was not to scare or intrude, it was because they needed me. For what reason, I still wasn't sure, but I was becoming more convinced by the day that their appearance was linked to the arrival of vampires in our unusual town.

As I reached the window, Eva pointed to the garden below. Our bedroom overlooked Margot's ever-lush rose garden that included climbing vines that reached up to the sill. My eye followed her finger to the center of the garden where a man and woman were standing side by side. The roses around them were wilted and hung limply on dried branches, lifeless. The man was tall and thin and wore a black three-piece suit typical of the turn of the last century. He held a pocket watch in his hand and sported a bowler hat on his head. His mustache was curled on the edges and he was looking at his feet, which made it hard for me to distinguish his facial features. The woman was dressed in an exquisite gown of red-and-black-striped silk draped from the waist down in ripples of fabric that shimmered with red beads. The beads looked like little droplets of blood hanging precariously from the fabric; the bodice was a corset-style, laced in the back with elegant puffed sleeves. Around her neck hung multiple strands of red glass teardrops from a choker all the way to an opera length strand. Her hair was an intricate cascade of curls with majestic red ostrich feathers creatively fashioned on top. All I could see of her face were her brilliant red lips, since the rest was hidden by a hand-held masque.

The two figures stood frozen in time. I was sure the ghost girls were conjuring this image for me from their memories. That was when I noticed the ground beneath them was undulating. I had been so transfixed by the beauty of these two creatures I'd failed to notice that at their feet were thousands of rats frantically squirming and crawling over one another. I shrank back from the window feeling a wave of nausea. Colette and Eva hugged the edge of my nightgown. The heat coming off of their small ghostly bodies was stifling, but I wanted them close and away from the darkness that lurked on the other side of the window. As I took a step back towards the glass to see if the figures were still there, a loud thud hit the window. It was the night heron slamming itself into the glass. I must have screamed both within the dream and without, because I was suddenly aware of James standing next to me.

He shook my shoulders and as I emerged from the dream, I found myself standing in front of the window. James was looking down at me with a panicked expression. I glanced behind me to see if Colette and Eva were still in the room, but they had gone in a rush of wind. James was moving his lips, but no sound was coming from them. Immediately, all the noise swept back into the room and I heard James' voice echoing off our bedroom walls.

"Charlotte, are you ok?" he kept asking, firmly holding onto my shoulders.

"I'm ok," I whispered, "I was dreaming and..." my voice trailed off as I revisited the images that had haunted me only moments before. It had been years since I'd had a dream where I physically left my bed. The image the ghost girls had shown me was important and I needed to commit every detail to memory before it faded away. I closed my eyes and buried myself in James' bare chest, my ear carefully placed over his beating heart. It was racing. I must have woken him from a deep sleep. He held me in his arms with one hand protectively placed on my head.

"Come on, let's get back in bed," he whispered. I followed him to the safety of our blankets and pillows. I snuggled close to him as he welcomed my invitation for affection. There was more than one way to warm up a cold bed, though I wished it hadn't been preceded by such a disturbing nightmare.

Eventually James fell back into a deep sleep. I was tucked into the crook of his arm against the warmth of his body. The clock was glowing a bright 3:00 a.m. on the bedside table. Even with the fatigue that had settled over me, my thoughts were still with Eva and Colette. My hand was still burning where she had touched me almost an hour later and the feeling of fever began to fill my own senses. I wondered if I wasn't falling ill. I was disoriented; the room tilted slightly. The heat in my hand began to spread through my body. I rolled over to feel the coolness of my pillow and after a few moments fell into a fitful sleep of feverish dreams.

When the morning light came into our bedroom, I woke to find myself twisted in the sheets, a sheen of cold sweat over my forehead. James was already in the shower and the clock read 7:00 a.m. Usually I would have made my way to the kitchen to make sure the children were fed and off to school, but I couldn't seem to move. Exhaustion and the remnants of fever had settled over me. As James came back into the bedroom dressed and ready for work, he took one look at me and worry spread across his usually calm features.

"Oh, wow, you are sick," he said, without even asking how I felt. I must have looked really bad. I could feel my long hair in tangles around me; I felt hot and cold on my skin and through my bones. He sat next to me on the bed feeling my forehead with the back of his hand.

"I'm just going to rest all day," I said, feeling a weakness in my body the likes of which I hadn't experienced in years. With all of Margot's herbal teas, I rarely got sick, although this felt less like actual illness and more like the residue of a psychic attack. I had been feeling on the verge of being ill since my dizzy spells at the store. Over the years, I had honed my abilities but even so when there was a tremendous amount of spiritual energy flowing into my space, it took its toll. This was especially so since I was trying to protect my own family, as well as myself.

"I'll make sure the kids are off to school. Just rest and I'll check in on you later today," he said with concern. James wasn't used to seeing me bed-ridden and, on the rare occasions that I was ill, it tapped into his fears of mortality. He kissed my forehead before leaving the room. The rest of the morning I spent drifting in and out of sleep until eventually my growling stomach forced me up and into the shower. With wet hair and the most comfortable pair of yoga pants and t-shirt that I owned, I made my way to the kitchen. This was not how I had planned to spend my day off from the shop. The effort it took to put bread in the toaster and water in the kettle for tea felt like climbing a mountain. My head was buzzing and when I looked in the mirror in the hallway, my face was shockingly pale.

Sitting at the large kitchen table I kept picturing the two figures from last night's dreams. The man seemed familiar, yet was no one I had ever met. The woman was elegant to the point of being almost grotesque with the blood red of her clothes and jewels. Who were these figures that Eva and Colette were so fearful of? As I nibbled on my toast with a mix of revulsion and hunger, I was startled by a loud knock at the front door. I walked slowly down the long hallway that ran from the kitchen to the front of the house. I used my right arm to periodically lean on the wall to stop the hall from spinning. There was the outline of a large figure on the other side of the stained glass window of the front door. I opened it a crack and saw the familiar form of Kyle Monroe.

Kyle and I had gone all the way through school together. Even though we had not run in the same crowd, he had always been a friendly acquaintance. In high school he had been one of the football players while I had been the loner art-obsessed girl who everyone called "Graves." Our paths rarely crossed, but I knew he was part of one of the crews that James had hired to work on the Renard projects. I felt a sudden wave of worry that something had happened to James on one of the sites.

"Hi Kyle, is everything ok with James?" I asked, sounding more worried than I had intended. He gave me a warm smile and then motioned to a huge box at his feet.

"James is fine, he sent me over to give you these. Where should I put them?" he asked and I slowly stepped onto the porch to peer into the cardboard box. It was stacked with old Port Townsend newspapers dated 1912!

"Where did you find these?" I asked, shocked to see what must have been a whole year's worth of chronicles in the box at my feet.

"We could barely believe it either. When we tore out the water damaged wall in the Cliffside Chapel these were stuffed in between the beams. It's a miracle they weren't completely water-logged. That wall was soaked but these are dry as a bone. Just a little dusty and musty, but I bet if you air them out a little they will be in fine shape. Anyway, James said you were looking for these so he had me rush them over. Figured it would keep you resting if you had something to read through," he said with a smile.

My excitement must have been obvious. I had Kyle carry the

box up to my workroom in the Winship library. He scanned the room with a look of awe and fascination at the combination of books mixed together with jars of all my beads and stones.

"I've never seen the inside of this house before," he said, sounding like a small child. "It's amazing."

"You and Jenny will have to come over for dinner sometime," I offered in the hopes of being cordial. He nodded a yes, although I could sense a bit of fear lingering under the surface. The Winship family, though respected, was still feared by many in town. Our gifts defied common logic and we simply couldn't hide ourselves in such an insular community. Most people knew we had no intention of harming anyone, but there was still a wariness that was understandable. I thanked Kyle and showed him to the door without offering him anything to eat or drink. Even though it was somewhat rude of me, I was burning with desire to start sorting through the newspapers. I had a gut feeling there would be answers in those musty old papers and the coincidence that they were found in the walls of the Renard family's new acquisition was not lost on me. I climbed the stairs feeling a shudder of weakness but determined to unearth a link to the ghost girls and the present day happenings. I could only hope that hidden within those dusty pages were the answers needed to protect my family from impending danger.

Fig. 93

CHAPTER 14

Half way up the stairs the phone began to ring. In a perfect world, I could have ignored it, but now that I had children no ringing phone was ever left unanswered. As quickly as I could, I rushed back to the kitchen and picked it up just before it went to voicemail. It was Tom Caldwell on the other line.

"Hello, Charlotte?" he asked in his raspy whiskey voice.

"Tom? I can't believe you called right this minute, you aren't going to believe what just showed up on my doorstep," I said, breathless from the run downstairs.

"Before you tell me, I thought of something after you left the other night. I couldn't quite put my finger on it when you were at the house, but it kept me up half the night," he said, grasping my attention.

"I'm intrigued; do tell," I said, sitting down on the kitchen floor with my legs crossed. The coolness of the wood felt welcoming on my still feverish body.

"It was the mention of the word vampires," he said in a quiet voice. I wondered if he didn't want his wife to hear him talking about something so foreign to normal conversation. I held my breath as he went on. "I remembered there was something around the turn of the century that lasted up until the 1920s in Port Townsend. A tradition of planting lilac bushes on the gravesites when any death by mysterious means came about. There were all kinds of illnesses that ravaged the region, and some claimed that the source of the sickness was supernatural. The word vampire wasn't used casually at the time, but there was talk and subsequent folklore. Anyway, people claimed that planting lilacs on the recently deceased's grave would keep them from returning as the undead."

"I remember seeing an unusual amount of lilacs in the graveyard, but I never knew why so many had been planted directly on the graves," I said. I had spent an uncommon amount of time playing in the town's oldest cemetery, Laurel Grove, since my grandfather, George, had been the volunteer groundskeeper. While he mowed and trimmed back overgrown trees, I flitted through the graves saying hello to all the residents and making sure the children's graves were weeded and cleaned of lichen. This was where I had acquired the town nickname "Graves." The lilacs all bloomed at the same time each year and many had grown so big they threatened to crack the old tombstones with their roots. There were all shades of purple and an abundance of white lilacs on the children's tombs. That was when it struck me that I should go see if I could find Eva's and Colette's burial place. If they died in 1912, then they most surely would be buried in Laurel Grove. Maybe I'd find a clue in the graveyard as had proven true in the past.

"So, what was waiting on your doorstep?" he asked; I had all but forgotten he was on the line.

"Newspapers from 1912," I said, my voice shaking with barely contained excitement. "They were hidden behind a wall in the Cliffside Chapel. James is working on the restoration and the construction crew found them this morning and brought them over to my house." Tom gasped and I could tell he was as intrigued as I. "Don't worry, when I'm done with them you can have a look and then we'll give them to Evelyn Pettygrove. You know if we keep these from her she'll never forgive us," I said with a laugh.

"I don't know about you but I would rather not be on Evelyn's bad side," Tom said with a chuckle. "If you find anything interesting, let me know. You have piqued my interest." After hanging up with Tom I made a mental note to visit the graveyard and see if I could find my ghost girls' graves.

It was also in that moment that I realized I had forgotten to put on Elsiba's lilac potion for not just today but the past several days as well. I had paid special attention to put it on Willa's, Felix's and James' laundered clothing, but I had forgotten to put it on myself. I rushed up to my bedroom feeling dizzy on the stairs as the feverish feelings threatened to overwhelm me. It was on my hands and knees that I finally made it into my bathroom. Sitting on the white penny tiles, I reached up and grabbed the bottle off the sink and quickly dabbed several drops on my neck and my wrists. The effect was immediate. In an instant the fever I had been feeling vanished. My mind cleared and the sickness that had begun to splinter through my body evaporated. I had to give it to Elsiba for creating such a potent counter spell in the form of this potion. Never again would I imagine it to be just a charming perfume. This concoction held power and with it I felt a greater sense of protection.

Feeling renewed after such a horrible night and morning, I immediately made myself a huge pot of coffee to take with me into my workroom. Slowly I began sorting through the box of Port Townsend Reader's beginning with January. One by one, I organized the hundred-year-old ephemera in chronological order and amazingly it was all there. Every single week for the entire year of 1912 had been hidden in the Cliffside Chapel's wall. There were a few water stains and I had to open the windows in the room to keep from choking on the musty smell, but it didn't diminish the astonishment I felt at seeing all of these articles spread before me. Then it hit me how much time it would take to read through them all. A few days at best and more likely weeks if I had to read them at night after my motherly work was finished or in-between clients at my shop. I decided to try my luck and skip to March 1912 in the hopes that this strange spring was a parallel to one in the past.

My intuition proved right. Though there were no articles with headlines about vampires, there was a large column on the arrival of ghost ships.

Ghost Ship Burns

On this day of March 1 our bay has acquired a ship of peculiar origin and intent of voyage. It was first spotted by a local man known by the name 'Spades' who spied it in the early morning hours after leaving the 'Good Time' saloon. At first he thought the vision of the unmanned ship was a trick played upon him by cheap whiskey. It was only when he ventured closer to the docks that the smell of an enormous number of rotting, dead rats cured him of any doubt about the vessel's place in reality. He summoned the sheriff who had to think twice before following the inebriated man, but upon arrival to the downtown shore was equally as shocked by the putrid smell that rose from the empty vessel. The Sheriff gathered a crew of locals to man a small skiff in order to inspect the ship for survivors or more importantly precious cargo in the hold. Upon approach it proved impossible to board for the boat was a floating tomb. From a distance one of the sailors reported seeing the common flag flying from the Captain's quarters that indicated plague. It was immediately decided that the ship should be burned, as reports of a severe outbreak of meningitis had been rumored to have struck much of Seattle in past months. After setting the ship ablaze, the town residents gathered on the cliffs and along the waterfront to watch as the most impressive explosions short of the Fourth of July erupted from the burning boat. We can only hope that no rat left alive made its way to shore, for surely the beasts were the cause of this seafaring massacre.

I continued to thumb through the thin pages hoping stories that contained a link to the ghost girls would catch my eye. I was repeatedly caught up in the absurdity of some of the advertising. The quack medical remedies soon became my favorites to read. There was everything from concoctions to boost the strength of one's blood to laxatives that claimed to stave off appendicitis. It was fascinating. There were also many articles relating to the rougher side of life on the waterfront. The gentleman and ladies of town stayed in the uptown area for the most part, as the downtown streets were lined with unsavory saloons and numerous brothels. The downtown was frequented by sailors, common folk, laborers, and gentlemen looking for everything from opium to a soiled dove's affections. It was definitely a very different world from the downtown of today. To think that my store stood directly across the street from one of the most popular brothels of the time always surprised me. There were many mornings when I opened up shop that the Palace, now a beautiful hotel, had a majestic ghost looking out of the second story corner window. It had been Madame Marie's room and she was one of the more scrupulous brothel owners of the time. I had a feeling she had loved her work so much that when the light came to take her she preferred to stay and look out onto the changing downtown streets.

Not all the brothels were as civilized as hers, as was attested to in the many articles claiming certain girls committed suicide, when in many cases murder was most likely the cause of their demise. One thing was certain; the downtown activities were a dark contrast to the uptown civility. While downtown girls as young as thirteen were living in the sailors' houses working as prostitutes, the uptown ladies were organizing luncheons or balls. Whether they chose to ignore what went on downtown because they could not change it or because they simply didn't care, would forever remain a mystery to me.

One thing was certain; the uptown events took on an even more lavish tone in the spring of 1912. There were countless articles about the new ladies' club called "The Herons" that had opened its doors in the Cliffside Chapel that March. It was the ladies' version of the men's secret society, "The Owls," which had opened its doors in January of the same year. These two clubs were in direct competition with the Masonic order that had long been the most popular lodge in town. One article in particular caught my eye:

Owls Hoot and The Herons Nest

The gracious ladies of the new order of "Herons" invite all of upstanding virtue to attend their first annual St. Patrick's Day Masquerade Ball. The theme is the French aristocracy and all should be in attire suited for a royal court. The doors of the Cliffside Chapel, new nest for the Herons, will open at nightfall and merriment will then ensue as champagne and hors d'oeuvres will be in abundance. We ask that all in attendance are careful not to lose their heads.

I couldn't help but chuckle when reading the last line, but it seemed like more than a coincidence that last night Eva and Colette had shown me a man and women clothed for a masquerade ball. Now I found that the site of said ball was the Cliffside Chapel where these very papers had been discovered this morning. I began to photocopy each article that caught my eye as being somehow unusual. Soon I had a stack of pages and I began to feel suddenly overwhelmed with information.

Sifting through a year's worth of events was becoming more laborious than I had first imagined. It brought to mind all the hours that Tom Caldwell had spent laboring over the words and images of the past to create his books — and this was after a lifetime of creating more articles documenting the daily activities of Port Townsend than any other journalist in the town's history. His was a labor of love and devotion. If I had been his wife, I would have been jealous of the attention given to his typewriter.

As I continued into the month of March there was a sudden shift right after the date of the Masquerade Ball. It seemed that the first cases of illness began to appear in Port Townsend and the words "fever" and "plague" began to fill the yellowing pages with a frequency that was disconcerting. By the second week in March, almost the entire newspaper was nothing but news of children suffering from a mysterious fever. The original article recounting that the first victims of the fever were Eva and Colette Duprey.

Spring Fever takes its first two victims
in Eva and Colette Duprey

The Duprey family is mourning today as both of their angels have succumbed to the strange illness that has befallen our town. The two young cherubim first fell ill less than one week before today and though all efforts were made by local doctors, nothing could be done to keep the darling Eva, age 7, and Colette, age 3, from the grips of the merciless Grim Reaper. Like other children, the first symptoms were weakness followed by dizzy spells. This quickly developed into high fevers which then led to delirium and finally a swift death. Their bodies will be laid to rest this coming Friday in Laurel Grove while their souls are most undoubtedly being looked after in heaven. The family asks only for prayers.

I felt a lump rise in my throat while reading this article. I felt not only a pinching sense of loss for the unlived possibilities of my ghost girls but also grief for their mother and father. Now that I was a mother, the thought of parents outliving their children felt all the more horrific. It was not in the natural order of the wheel of life, and I doubted no loss was more painful than that of one's child.

As if on cue I heard the back door open and the familiar thud of Felix's backpack on the kitchen table. This was followed by the opening of the refrigerator and the search for his favorite glass in the dishwasher. I set the article aside feeling a sudden need to be in the same room with my child, followed by a twist in my stomach that Willa was not yet home. I would continue reading tonight, but for the moment I stepped back into the present in order to thank the heavens that my child was alive and clunking around in the kitchen. I said a silent prayer to all the Winships who had gone before me to watch over their descendants and keep them safe from whatever plague I was sure was soon to befall Port Townsend.

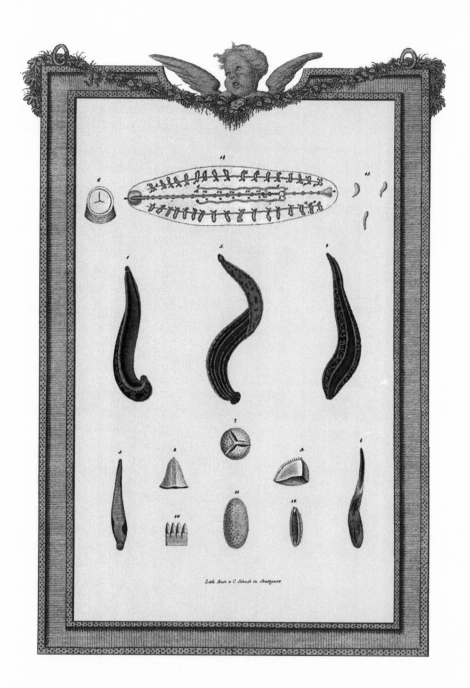

Chapter 15

There are certain boundaries of which I had always tried to be mindful of when it came to being Felix and Willa's mother. My mother had always respected my space as a separate individual even though we were bound tightly together through our hereditary gifts and our love for one another. I didn't want to stifle my children. And yet, when I made my way downstairs to greet Felix, all I wanted was to keep him in the house where he would be safe. I hugged him a little longer than normal as thoughts of Eva and Colette's young demise spun inside my mind. The article I had just read was burned into my memory much as their feverish hands had burned my skin each time they touched me.

We sat together at the table and ate cheese sandwiches. I didn't want to pry into his premonitions but I wondered if he had sensed anything since his initial vision of vampires. As we sat, me drinking coffee and Felix a glass of juice, I carefully asked him if he'd had any strange dreams the night before or if all had been quiet. He sat pensively for a moment. I wasn't sure if he was trying to form words or simply trying to wade back through murky memories of dreams from the previous night. His nose scrunched a bit and he scratched his head with one hand. In that moment he looked exactly like James when he was deep in thought at his drafting table.

"Well," he began, "I don't think I dreamt anything last night. But I keep thinking about the man in the garden. And rats. I saw a huge one today on my way home from school and it made me think of the nightmare."

"Where did you see a rat?" I asked, feeling a bit surprised. It wasn't common in our town to see them during the day. Usually they were out in the evenings, especially by the docks.

"By the school," he said with a little shiver. "It kind of seemed like it was watching me and Cody when we walked out the back gate." I felt my hackles rise and without restraint I jumped in to ask if he had felt anything else unusual.

"Have you had any more visions about the vampires?" I asked even though saying the words out loud sounded intrusive. Felix didn't seem to think it was out of the ordinary.

"A few things, but they don't really make sense to me," he said, piquing my curiosity even more.

"Like what?" I pried, feeling like an overbearing mother in the process, but I felt the intense need to know and get to the bottom of things.

"Well, I had a vision a few days ago about a bunch of kids stuck inside all these mirrors and everything smelled like peaches. It made me hungry," he said with a little giggle. I smiled and waited for him to go on. "Then there were the bad dreams, but also I dreamt about Willa and she was so sick. She looked really pale and couldn't get out of bed and she had all these things on her arms...you know...um," he searched for the word as I threw out all kinds of wrong guesses of everything from bracelets to pimples until he found the word, "Leeches!" My body shuddered as I imagined my vibrant daughter struck ill in the turret room with parasites drinking her dry.

"Anything else?" I asked, hoping I wasn't being too pushy.

"Not really. But Mom can I go to Cody's house? We have a project at school and his Mom said I could come over today if it was ok with you." In a way, I was a bit relieved because ever since I had begun to feel better with the lilac potion, I had one thing on my mind and that was going to the cemetery to see the ghost girls' graves.

"OK, give me a few minutes and I'll drop you off on my way to run errands," I said. He hummed while finishing his sandwich. Soon we were out the door and I was waving to him as he trudged up Cody's walkway. I saw him safely in the front door standing behind Sheila, Cody's mother. He would be fine there until I could get home from my quick trip to Laurel Grove Cemetery. It was already four o'clock and James would soon be home, as would Willa, which would give me just enough time to search my old haunt.

The old iron archway that had once held the words "Laurel Grove Cemetery," in beautiful curled metal letters, had finally fallen only a month ago in a winter storm. Now there were only two brick pillars on either side of the gravel road that led into the oldest graveyard in town. There was talk of restoring the rusted sign to its former glory but the donations process was just getting underway, which meant it could take months or possibly years to see any real repairs. I parked across the street in one of the few empty parking spots that lined Discovery Road. The sun was blazing at an angle that created shadows and odd reflections off the familiar tombstones. I made my way to the right following the pathway up to the oldest section of the cemetery. The first thing I noticed was the intense fragrance of lilacs in the air. As I looked more closely at each tomb hoping to find the Dupreys, it became more evident that nearly all of the headstones dated around 1912 to even as late as 1930 had lilac bushes planted directly behind them. Some of the lilacs had grown all the way around the edges of the graves, almost like protective hedges marking the inhabitant's space.

I heard music somewhere on the wind and I wasn't sure if it was ghostly or just an echo from someone's far off radio. I climbed the gravel path reading the familiar names of some of the families who still had living descendants in the town. I soon noticed an odd rainbow reflection near the children's graves that were nestled in the far hilltop corner. These precious tombs were often sectioned off with little white fences that were reminiscent of a crib. Some of the graves had crushed white shells covering the surface of the small resting places as if an alabaster blanket was forever keeping the little souls warm. As I moved closer, I noticed the reflection was coming from one of these little graves in particular. I made my way to its edge and was only half surprised to see both Eva and Colette's names side by side on the two small white picketed crib graves. The reflection was coming off of two little mirrors that had been embedded into the tombstones under their dates of birth and death.

I immediately thought of what Felix had said about kids stuck in mirrors as well as the deathly reflection that Sophie had cast in my shop. I kneeled before the two graves and began to whisper little prayers that their souls would be allowed to go free. Nothing happened. Not even a rustle of air. This was odd for several reasons. Usually the resting place of a person's remains is one of the most powerful spots from which to call their spirit. It is like a marker for them that is easy to find in the ethers. This is not to say that graveyards are filled with wandering ghosts because surprisingly, they are rather peaceful. Rather, they are sacred places where the remains are hallowed and thus it's easier to make a magical connection to a specific person. The other reason that I found the stillness so odd was that I knew for a fact that both of these girls were bound to the earth plane and so calling them should have been even simpler since they had been making contact with me so easily. Were they bound somewhere and couldn't get back to this sacred place? Why was it that they could come to the Winship house almost nightly and yet they could not or would not be summoned to their resting place? These questions buzzed through my mind as I sat in front of Colette and Eva's graves.

Again, the sounds of music floated on the wind in my direction. It was closer than it had been earlier and with it came the familiar sound of a girl's airy giggle. Dusting off my jeans, I decided to follow these whispers on the breeze. The haunting sounds seemed to be coming from near the Winship family mausoleum. All of our family members, including Annie Christie who was an honorary Winship, were laid to rest inside the marble structure. As I wove my way across the bumpy mounds past overloaded lilac bushes, I could hear the music getting louder. Pushing aside the branches of a white lilac tree, I froze on the spot. The origin of the music was a cellphone and the giggle had come from none other than my own daughter, Willa.

She was leaning against the column that read "Winship" in letters carved into the white stone. The sun was shining down on her, giving her hair a brighter red hue than her usual auburn. She looked luminous as she held her cellphone casually in her hand as the music emanated from the small device filling the lonely graveyard with sound. Lounging at her side was Daniel Renard. His dark hair was perfectly unkempt in a way that I knew would attract most living and breathing teenage girls. The best way to describe him was catlike, in that he looked unbothered by anything, including the fact that he was lounging on the graves of a family of very powerful witches. I could hear his deep voice whispering to Willa and her unbridled laugh that followed. Soon he was inching his way closer to her with a slink that made me think of a snake inching towards its prey. He reached a hand up to her perfect cheek and in that instant it was as if little shadows from his fingers detached and scurried across her skin. The shadows looked exactly like leeches. I stifled a scream and yet I felt frozen. Part of me wanted to rush through the bushes and grab Willa by the arm and drag her home. And yet another part of me simply couldn't humiliate her in that way. As he leaned closer to her it became obvious he was going to kiss her. It was also in that moment I noticed her shadow falling across the white marble from the sunlight overhead. It was her perfect double. Daniel's shadow should have overlapped her own, given how they were sitting; yet there was nothing. There were only the living shadows that had squirmed from his fingers a moment earlier and into Willa's being. He cast no natural shadow.

Just as his lips were mere centimeters from hers, I inadvertently knocked over a loose tombstone from its pedestal. Many of the oldest headstones were unattached to the ground and a clumsy movement could send them crashing down. The horrible sound of stone hitting the granite below echoed so loudly that it startled both Daniel and Willa and in doing so averted his kiss. I quickly hid behind the lilac bush feeling mortified that I was not only spying on my sixteen year old daughter's first kiss, but also that I had just broken a century old grave marker in the process. I quickly sprinted in the other direction and followed the path back to my car. I was sure they hadn't seen me as the far side of cemetery was lined with willows and lilacs. I sat in my car for a moment with the windows rolled down trying to put into perspective the things I had just witnessed.

I couldn't get the images of those leechlike shadows out of my mind. No trick of the sun could have caused what I saw. Also the fact that Felix had just mentioned his dream about Willa being ill with leeches on her seemed far too similar to be a coincidence. Then, Gavin's ways to recognize a vampire also came to mind and not casting a shadow was on his list. The whole being out in the sun part didn't fit but maybe not all the legends were spot on. I felt suddenly ill again. My thoughts were rushing between worry and making connections that would explain what I had just seen. One thing was for certain, Willa was far more attached to Daniel than she had let on and they were most definitely on their way to being a couple. Her sixteenth birthday was three and a half weeks away and yet I was still picturing her as a four-year-old little girl. She was becoming a woman and I had to accept that, but this was not what I had in mind.

Once I had my nerves settled as much as possible, considering the circumstances, I began to drive back down Discovery Road. The light was beginning to fade from the sky, leaving a vibrant orange and pink watercolor spread across the clear clouds. I should have headed straight home, but I felt restless. As I wove back down the hill towards town, I made a sudden jerk to the left and instinctively headed in the direction of North Beach. With Deidre so far from home, the one person I knew I could talk to about everything related to motherhood was Margot. She wouldn't mind my showing up on her doorstep unannounced. More than anything, I needed guidance from the one person in town who, I hoped, would have more insight into the Renards and all the strange occurrences that had happened in just the last twenty-four hours. Also I knew that she would help to put things into perspective regarding Willa. Her mother, Elsiba, had been one of the wildest women in town in her day, so nothing shocked Margot.

I sped down the deserted country road past the old lagoons and into the forest. The smell of lilacs was still in my nostrils and I wondered if it was the potion gaining more potency as my body heat increased due to stress. I zipped past Morgan's cider mill and farther up the road until I saw the familiar old iron talisman gate. It had stood in the same place for over a hundred years. Every time I came to visit Margot in her new house I still expected to see Annie's old log cabin whenever I made the turn into the driveway. But instead of the rustic abode that Annie had built, there stood a sleek modern construction that James had designed and built over fifteen years ago. This was where Margot had chosen to live out her old age. I breathed a sigh of relief when I saw her car in the driveway. I felt desperate to see her and for some odd reason tears began to threaten as I pulled in next to her car and turned off the engine. Last night's illness and this afternoon's interlude in the cemetery had overwhelmed me physically and emotionally. As I made my way up to the front porch, after unlatching the complex old gate, I felt a wave of safety wash over me. I was again under Margot Winship's wing of protection and could only hope that her guidance would lift my heart from this moment of confusion and despair.

Lorichon Sculpsit.

CHAPTER 16

Margot's home reminded me of a giant birdhouse with its steeply pointed roof reaching into the tall trees that surrounded it. She and James had spent countless hours around the Winship house kitchen table discussing her desires for what would later be her new roost. She had lived in the Winship house her entire life and though the idea of leaving after more than seventy years of residence was frightening, the prospect of having a house built to her liking was seductive.

The one thing that was non-negotiable was that Annie's fence and garden were to be kept intact. The log cabin was disintegrating. And though Annie had done her best to keep it patched together, time had worn it down to rotting timbers. All Annie's carefully preserved treasures were stored to later be installed in curio cabinets that lined the walls of the new living room. The most surprising aspect was that in the very center of the house was a small courtyard with a willow tree at its heart. From the front it was impossible to guess that there was a secret garden tucked away in the middle of the home, but it was glassed in and opened to the heavens above. It could be seen from the kitchen, living room and study. I sat on one of Margot's cream-colored couches looking out at the flowing branches from the willow in the courtyard. As always, Margot's roses were in full bloom. One side of the courtyard had a wooden wall with a trellis. Her climbing roses were a tangle of vines and multicolored blossoms that reached up to her bedroom window above.

Margot was in her modern kitchen putting a pot of her herbal tea to infuse on the countertop. Soon she was sitting across from me with a concerned look on her wizened features. The combination of the lilac potion and her natural smell of roses was delightfully overpowering. It felt indescribably like home. She poured a cup of rosehip and hibiscus tea for me and then leaned back on the couch across from me with her own cup in hand.

"I'm worried about Willa," I finally said, although the words felt stuck somewhere underneath my tongue. I told her about all that had transpired from the articles to this afternoon's cemetery interlude. She looked at the loose leaves in the bottom of her cup while listening.

"You should be worried," she said with a grave tone when I had finished. "He has picked his prey. Once a vampire has an eye for someone he becomes extremely possessive of them."

"Margot, what do you know about these beings? Are you telling me that they are like the monsters in bad B movies? What are these people?" I asked, feeling a rising panic. I had seen many unusual things in my life. I knew that ghosts were real, as were demons and other creatures in-between, but for whatever deluded reason, vampires still felt fictional to me.

"I don't know if the type that we see in the movies really exist in nature, but there is a version of it that is far more insidious. There are real vampires walking among us. I didn't want to frighten you when you first called about all the strange omens and Felix's premonition, but I know more than I first let on. As you know, my mother, Elsiba, was a very powerful conjurer and worker of potions in her day. One of the reasons she was so motivated to perfect her gift was because of the tragedy that had befallen the Winships not long before she was born. She had an older sister who died in 1912, a victim of the strange plague that your ghost girls also suffered. Magdalene Winship was only seven years old when she was taken from this world by the fever. Elsiba was born a year later and her mother Cecilia was still mourning the loss of Magdalene. Magdalene's spirit haunted her very much in the same way that the little girls' ghosts come to you. Cecilia knew that Magdalene was magically trapped and yet she was unable to figure out how to free her.

Elsiba made it part of her life's mission to find out exactly what had happened in the years before her own birth so she could set wrongs to right. One hundred and thirty children died in the spring of 1912 and then the fever disappeared as quickly as it had come. Her explanation of what vampires really are was terrifying. They move in small groups, usually a husband and wife with several children. They do not age the way that we do because their existence is one that defies natural order. Instead, their bodies are preserved through the continual theft of energy from unwilling hosts. The easiest prey is a child, as their energy is pure and not as protected as that of adults. Many adults unconsciously establish energetic boundaries in their day-to-day life, but children are more open in their nature and tend to let the good and the bad into their auras in equal measure. Some people do this unintentionally; you have felt those people in your shop? The ones who leave you feeling exhausted as they tell you all their turmoil. They leave energized and you are left drained. This is actually part of the natural order in the sense that they do this unintentionally and you allow them to take your energy because they are in desperate need of it. But the real vampires are the ones that know how to do this intentionally and in a ritualistic fashion. Also, real vampires keep their victims' soul forever bound to them after their death. It is part of the way they continue to survive. They can live many lifetimes longer than a normal human without aging. Their sole purpose is to keep this artificial youth and each group has its own fetishized way of recreating soul stealing rituals to insure their lives continue. They are parasites, immoral and driven to survive regardless of the cost to others.

"Elsiba said there were two families at that time that left town quickly after the deaths of the children. By the time she pieced together who they were, they were long gone. One was a photographer; he and his wife did not have children. The only reason he was someone that Elsiba suspected was because the local tribes accused him of stealing their souls with his photographs. He and his wife disappeared without a trace after the last child died. The other was a high society family that had several children and, more importantly, began two local lodges. The thing that caught her attention about them was that they were one of the only families that did not lose a child during the fever. They left in the middle of the night immediately after the 130th child died, which was not common at the time. You didn't just pick up and leave the way that people do now. It was more arduous, especially after they had invested so much of their time and money into the local lodges. They had become an integral part of the community.

It was Elsiba who insisted, when she was old enough to begin her research, that the town continued to plant lilacs with each new addition of a house. People knew instinctively that it was best to listen to her even if she inspired more fear in many than the thought of vampires. She made the potion each year and taught me to do the same when I was just a small girl. There was a time before I was born when she left Port Townsend to search for the missing families. She refused to talk about this part of her life much as she refused to talk about the later disappearance of my father Louis. It was all a great mystery and Elsiba gave nothing up unless she wanted to. But she always insisted that one day the vampires would come back to this town. She was sure of it."

Margot paused and continued to examine her tea leaves. The light in the interior garden was fading and I thought that I saw a shadow move from behind the willow tree. Looking closer it seemed that it had simply been a trick of the light. A branch must have moved in an odd direction in the breeze although the hair on my arms was standing on end.

"Margot, how do I stop Willa from seeing him?" I asked, feeling completely overwhelmed.

"You can't stop her. He has his hooks in and it will only make it worse. But we can work from the outside to break the connection. I will see if I can find Elsiba's grimoire. When I moved it disappeared. I know it was in a box with my own, but when I went to unpack it was gone. I still haven't found it so I am just going from memory with the exception of the potion; that I added to my own book of spells many years ago."

I glanced at the clock and saw that it was far later than I had first thought. I gave James a quick call to tell him I would be home soon and was relieved when he said that Willa and Felix were both in their rooms. Slowly putting the pieces of Margot's story into place with all the information I already had, a dark patchwork began to immerge. Could it be possible that the Renards were really the same vampires who had come to Port Townsend one hundred years earlier to steal the souls of children? It seemed it might be so and yet impossible all the same.

"Did she ever say what one had to do to stop them?" I asked.

"She had a few theories, but because she never was able to find the original vampires she said there was nothing that could be done." Margot's head dropped as she set her teacup on the coffee table before us. As both of us rose, I gave Margot a long hug. She was not a naturally affectionate person and always felt stiff whenever I would impulsively hug her, but tonight she felt tired in my arms. I wished in that moment I could have stayed and talked with her into the night. I missed my time with Margot and though she showed no signs of illness, at her age it was only a matter of time before she left us for the other side. If not for a waiting husband and children, I would have camped out on her couch just to be near her as I had when I was a child.

Sadly, for tonight it was not to be. As she turned to lead me out, I glanced at the inside of her teacup. She had been staring at it intently throughout our conversation and I was itching with curiosity to see what had grabbed her attention. I quickly leaned over to steal a peek while grabbing my purse off the table. I was shocked to see the leaves inside the white porcelain vessel had formed themselves into the perfect silhouette of a rat.

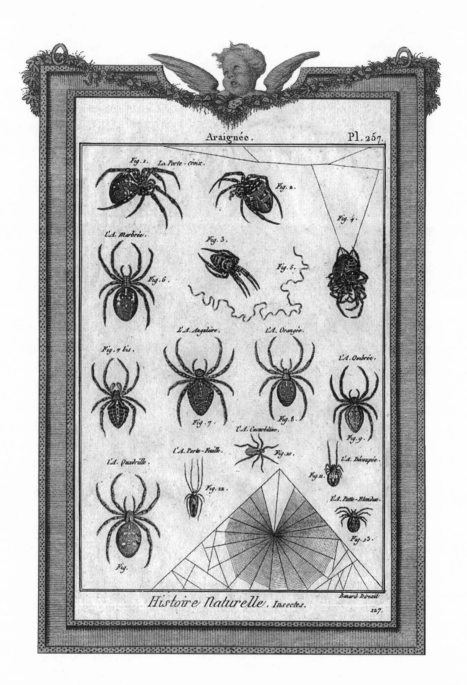

Fig. 1.   La Porte - croix.

Fig. 2.

Fig. 4.

L'A. Marbrée.

Fig. 3.

Fig. 5.

Fig. 6.

L'A. Angulaire.

L'A. Orangée.

L'A. Ombrée.

Fig. 7 bis.

L'A. Cucurbitaine.

Fig. 7.

Fig. 8.

Fig. 9.

L'A. Quadrille.

L'A. Porte - Feuille.

Fig. 10.

L'A. Découpée.

Fig. 11.

Fig. 12.

L'A. Patte - Blendue.

Fig.

Fig. 13.

Histoire Naturelle, Insectes.

Renard Direxit.

127.

Chapter 17

As I pulled into my driveway, the Winship house glowed in the early evening light. The air was scented with roses and lilacs as I walked past the garden and up the front stairs. It felt as if Margot was walking beside me. I usually went into the house through the kitchen, but I noticed the mailbox arm was up. James must have forgotten to bring in the mail when he came home from the office. It had been one of the first things James and I replaced when we took up residence in the Winship house after Margot signed over the deed to me. Now it was wind-battered and weathered but I couldn't bear to take it down. It had marked the beginning of the chapter in my life of being a mother.

I pulled open the lid, expecting a pile of mail; instead there was only one envelope. It was a deep red and felt like suede on my fingers. The paper was exquisite and addressed in perfect calligraphy. Across the front of the envelope was "James Gallagher and Charlotte Winship." There was no stamp or return address which meant it had been hand delivered. I carefully slid my finger under the flap and did my best to open it without tearing the paper. Just as I had it nearly undone, I felt a tiny pinch on my knuckle as the edge of the paper sliced a clean cut on my finger. Instinctively I slipped my knuckle into my mouth, to ease the sting and catch any errant droplets of blood.

With one last defiant tug, I tore open the envelope and removed the card inside. It was a stunningly beautiful invitation, the likes of which I had never seen before. It was a combination of black, red and gold stripes reminiscent of a Victorian circus poster. The outside of the card read "You are cordially invited..." and as I opened it the inside revealed a black masquerade style mask on a deep red background. Gold letters announced that the Renard family was throwing a masquerade ball on the same night as the Saint Patrick's Day dance. It would be to amuse the adults in their own night of revelry. It was to be held in the newly-remodeled Bell Tower House.

My hands shook as I looked over every last inch of the invitation. Little droplets of my blood had smeared into a dark brown stain across the red envelope giving it a gory addition. The mask on the invitation immediately evoked the dream images of the man and woman my ghost girls had shown me. This, combined with the recent articles and Margot's divulging the link between the vampires of old and the Renards, made my blood run cold. They were setting a plan into motion that followed the same pattern as what had occurred one hundred years ago. Would there be ghost ships carrying plague next? There was already a blood tide that defied all reason. I carefully slipped the card back into the envelope and made my way through the door into the house.

James was sitting at the kitchen table with papers piled high around him, holding a steaming cup of coffee. He looked up as I walked into my favorite room of the house and smiled. I pushed my way close to him in his chair so I could sit on his lap. His arms moved instinctively around my waist as I gave him a kiss. Up close, I could tell he was fatigued. There were dark circles around his eyes. I spied a few new grey hairs in his beard. He put his hand on my head to feel for signs of fever. I just smiled and shook my head.

"All gone," I said, reassuring him I felt a million times better than earlier this morning. "Thank you for the newspapers," I added and he grinned, looking extremely pleased with himself for having found them and thought of me.

"Strange that the year you were looking for was hidden in the wall of the project I just started," he said with a tilt to his head. Peculiar happenings had become more commonplace for James since he'd joined my family. He still wasn't sure what to make of some coincidences and preferred to find rational explanations for them.

"The kids have eaten?" I asked and he assured me they had stuffed themselves and were in their rooms doing homework. "And you?"

"I'll be up late working on this," he said, motioning to the table covered with paperwork and architectural blueprints. I heard a growing anxiety in his voice as he explained all there was still to do before the fast-approaching deadline. "The Renards certainly know what they want and how they want it done."

"This was in the mailbox when I came home," I said, slipping the red envelope out of my purse and handing it to him. I got up and poured myself a cup of coffee as well and made myself a peanut butter and jelly sandwich while he examined the card. He tried to brush the blood smear from the front of the paper and then promptly gave himself a paper cut on the same crisp edge. He swore as he sucked on his finger. He then impatiently threw the envelope on the table to open the card. A look of panic flashed across his face as he read the date of the party. By sending out these invitations, to what I assumed was more than a handful of the town's oldest families, the Renards had effectively put a non-negotiable completion date on the construction being done at their home. While I knew that James had every intention of having everything finished by the promised date, there were always elements out of his control.

"This was in the mailbox?" the surprise in his voice, coupled with his weary look, made my heart sink. I nodded as I sat across from him eating my less–than–healthy dinner. He shook his head while re-examining the invitation. "I checked it when I got home. There is a pile of bills and things that I put on your desk."

"The arm of the mailbox was up so I assumed you had forgotten to look," I said, feeling another wave of dread wash over me. Sometime in the half hour since he'd come home and I'd returned, one of the Renards had slipped this invitation into our mailbox. Why they hadn't just rung the door bell and given it directly to James seemed odd. If it had been any other family, I would have assumed they didn't want to disturb us during dinner, but coupled with all the other unusual omens, this felt like yet another unwelcomed harbinger of doom.

"I don't want to go," I said, feeling hopeful that he, too, would want to refrain after working at that house day and night.

"I think we have to," he said. Even though I knew that he was right, I felt suddenly rebellious.

"I would prefer not to go." I said with a hint of stubbornness that made the politeness of my phrase sting a little in my mouth.

"Charlotte..." my name trailed off his tongue with a softness that made me love him and hate him all at the same time. I knew we had to go because his work would be showcased and it would be important for his firm. But to walk right into the monsters' den made me feel unreasonably vulnerable. I would have to figure out a way to make it a fact-finding mission with a suitable amount of protection for both of us.

"Fine," I said, putting up less of a fight than I had initially intended. "But you give them the RSVP. I have other things to tend to," I said, feeling angry at him even though I knew perfectly well that none of this was his fault. I finished my sandwich and listened as he told me all that was underway with both structures.

Soon he was back working and I slipped upstairs to check on Felix and Willa. At first I expected to find Felix in his room, but instead, found him on one of the window seats in the library. He was reading a botanical book. I decided he was probably finding out more about the plant Gavin had given him. He was looking at the pages with an intensity that reminded me of Gavin when he was the same age. He always had his nose in a book to escape into whatever world the pages promised. He smiled at me as I cleared my throat while leaning on the door frame.

"Is it any good?" I asked.

"Fascinating," he said, with an enthusiasm that lacked any hint of irony. It felt good to see him so enthralled. I left him to read in peace and made my way up the stairs to check on Willa. My heart pounded as I approached her room. I felt guilty for having spied on her. I was overwhelmed with the feeling of being a helpless bystander watching the fateful elements of a collision before it happened. But I had no idea how to stop any of it. If Margot was right and Daniel Renard had already chosen Willa as his prey, then there was nothing I could do without causing more damage.

I knocked on her closed door hoping to hear her bright voice invite me in. But there was no response. I turned the knob and poked my head around the edge of the door not wanting to disturb her. She was sitting in a chair by the open window with her telephone in hand. Her profile was lit by the moon, which had risen high into the clear night sky, casting a beautiful shadow of her across the bedroom wall.

There was only her bedside lamp lighting the space. At first she didn't notice me until the wood floor cracked slightly alerting her to my presence.

"Mom, you scared me!" she shrieked, in a tone that belied her irritation with me. "You have to stop creeping around like that!" She went back to looking at her phone as her thumbs rapidly typed in secret messages to who I now assumed was Daniel instead of Lily.

"Have you finished your homework?" I asked, lamely unable to form a more interesting question. I still had the images of her and Daniel in the graveyard burned in my mind.

"Um, hm," she answered evasively without bothering to look up.

"I think it's time to turn off your phone for the night." I said, although it was still an hour before her electronics curfew. She gave me a withering look.

"I know you want me to be Amish but really, Mom, I still have an hour and I plan to use it. Besides, I'm texting Daniel and Lily about a group project we're working on for Bio," she said, proud of what I was sure was a bold-faced lie.

"Willa, look at me." I said, and she slowly turned her face towards me. With the window open beside her and the eerie light from the moon outside filtering in, I could see something in her face had changed. Like James, she had dark circles under her eyes and her skin had a sickly pallor that it had not had earlier in the day. She looked at me and I could see a shadow hanging over her usually vibrant aura. Just as I was about to tell her that I had seen her that afternoon, a loud flutter of wings followed by a caw made my heart leap in my chest. The night heron had landed on the window sill of her open window. It was staring at me with its red eye. Willa hadn't moved a muscle despite the racket the bird caused in its sudden appearance.

"What?" she asked sounding annoyed with me again.

"The bird, don't let it inside," I said rushing to the window, slamming it down in a hurry. Willa scooted her chair back, startled with my sudden intrusion. For a quick moment, her usual sparkle returned and then it quickly faded again as she flopped onto her bed and began texting again while ignoring me.

"It's a harmless bird, Mom. Don't be so superstitious," she said with a sigh of exasperation. "Daniel says that small towns are rife with silly folk tales that are just the product of ignorance."

Her words cut straight to my heart. I knew our ways were often thought of as backwards in the modern world, but it didn't change the fact that our practices were based on ancient truths. To hear these words from her lips made me feel like I was losing her to something far more dangerous than a city boy. If our traditions weren't taken seriously they would be lost to time, and with them, Willa's personal power would also be diminished.

"Is that so," I said with a coolness that caught her attention. "Maybe you should tell that to your Great Uncle Morgan or your Great Grandmother Margot." She suddenly looked mortified. In that moment she knew she had gone too far and the invocation of those two names reminded her of who she was and where she came from.

"I was just saying," her voice trailed off as she saw how the hurt of her words had transformed my face to stone. I cut her off before she could finish.

"I want that phone turned off in exactly one hour. And do not let that bird in this house," I said with a finality that made her look forlorn yet resigned. I turned and left her door open on purpose as I made my way back downstairs. Tonight I wanted to keep searching the newspapers for more clues about what had happened to Eva and Colette and how it correlated to what was happening now. I had a feeling that somewhere in those dusty pages something was waiting for me. Before going back to my workroom, I made a quick stop in our bedroom and dabbed the lilac potion on my neck and wrists. If I was going to protect my family from the encroaching darkness I was going to need all my strength. One thing was certain, my ire was up. In many ways I felt more than willing to welcome a fight.

Tab. XIX

Ulula Kirch Eule

Ulula Unel.   Kulu eule   Ulula

Aluco Waldeur   Noctua

Strix   Saxatils   Noctua   Kaualein   Ulula alia
                        Noctua   Steinkaus

CHAPTER 18

As the night wore on, I continued reading through the old newspapers. They littered every surface of my workroom, but I felt increasingly distracted as the hours rolled by. The day's events still had me reeling. While I wanted to concentrate on learning more about the plague that had struck our town 100 years ago, my mind simply wouldn't focus. It was Monday night and the children and James had long gone to bed. I picked up the phone and called Gavin. It was well past midnight, stretching into Tuesday morning but he was always up late after closing the bar. I knew it wouldn't bother him if I called. He picked up after only two rings which meant he was definitely awake.

"Let me guess, it's Charlotte?" was how he answered the phone, which made me grin. I had always been a night owl.

"It's me," I said with a chuckle. "I can't sleep and I can't seem to concentrate on anything either so I thought I would call and bug you."

"You can bug me. I can't sleep either. It was a long day at the bar with an unexpected brawl midway through the evening. Our big event of the day." Without his telling me I figured out that it was between two people we had known our whole lives. One was sleeping with the other's wife and even though the whole town knew about it, the cuckolded man had only just found out.

"Poor guy, he really didn't know?" I asked, thinking it was all but impossible in a town as small as Port Townsend not to know that his wife was cheating on him and with his best friend.

"Not a clue. He's been pretty busy drinking at the bar, though, so maybe that was part of the problem. Anyway, any more information on the vampires?" he asked without a hint of mockery. I told him everything I'd discovered, including having spied on Willa and Daniel and subsequently how conflicted I felt about it.

"Have you told James any of this?" he asked carefully. Gavin knew that from the very first part of my relationship with James I had always been wary of sharing too much about the Winships' gifts. It wasn't anything he had ever experienced in his world. He preferred things to have a rational explanation. He was used to a certain amount of strange happenings over the span of our marriage, but such things were still foreign to him. He believed in my ability to see ghosts, although he tried to downplay it by avoiding hearing any of the details. James knew Felix had a unique gift with his premonitions, but left it to me and my side of the family to coach him. He and Willa had always been close, but I felt that part of that was Willa's own empathic abilities sensing when and how to make her father feel most at ease with all things paranormal. That was why it was always a relief to be able to tell everything to Gavin. He knew me and my family as a town member, but also as a brother. He believed me when I told him strange things were afoot and he was always ready to listen and try to help.

"No, he's up to his eyeballs in work on their buildings and I can't heave this on him right now. It would make it really hard on James to go to work in the morning, which isn't fair to him. But I am worried about Willa. You should see the way Daniel Renard looks at her," I could hear my voice rise a pitch "and the shadows that moved over her skin like leeches. Also when I went into her room tonight she looked so tired. Like the light had been sucked out of her." I could hardly go on. My chest tightened with pain just thinking about it.

"I know you hate to go to this masquerade thing, but maybe think of it as reconnaissance," Gavin said, trying to change the subject from Willa, as he had no answers for that particular dilemma. "Check James' drawings of those buildings for anything odd. I bet if this is the same family that was here a hundred years ago then those two buildings probably mean something to them. It can't be just a coincidence."

I hadn't really thought about that part of the puzzle yet and I knew immediately that Gavin was on to something. The blueprints to both of their homes were sitting on my kitchen table. If there was something unusual in those houses, maybe I could find it on the original drawings. I had all day tomorrow to run errands and be home as my shop was run by my only employee, Jasmine. I would take the time to look things over as James left blueprint copies at home.

"I'll look through them in the morning. I have to drive to Pat's farm to give him a check, but after that I'm free all day," I said, feeling buoyed by having a task other than sorting through endless piles of old papers. Margot's story about how this town had first suffered vampires had terrified me and I felt adrift in a sea of odd facts and folklore. The blueprints were at least something concrete to examine. "Have you heard anything at the bar from any of the construction workers?" I asked in the hopes some interesting tidbit might help piece things together.

"The only thing I've heard was that, in addition to the discovery of your newspapers, the walls at both houses were filled with dead rats. They have been tearing down the worst of the enclosures, but most of them have to stay because of the deadlines, even though the rat skeletons were actually pouring out. I know that rats and squirrels get stuck in walls over the years but apparently this was an unusually large number of carcasses. Most of the guys on the crew took extra care to wash their hands at the bar which isn't always the case," he said with a slight air of disgust in his voice.

"That sounds really heinous," I said, as I remembered Felix's words about the rat he had seen outside of school. "Gav, just so you know, Felix loves the plant that you gave him. He was reading about it tonight in a book from our library. Probably one of George's old books on botanicals." I said, remembering my grandfather with a little twinge of sadness. All these years later, I still missed him.

"I'm glad," he said with a hint of pride in his tone, "Now get to sleep," he said like an annoyed older brother. Before we hung up I promised to call him if I found anything unusual in the blueprints. Feeling centered again, I started to thumb through the old newspapers in search of a headline that somehow tied into the situation at hand. There were numerous articles about local murders that had happened primarily on the waterfront and were generally in combination with whiskey and women. There were ads for products that promised all kinds of remedies, my favorite of which assured that newly married women would retain their healthy glow after the burden of housekeeping began to take its toll. It was an eye cream the likes of which was probably still promoted today.

As I thumbed through the pages examining each day carefully so I didn't miss any hidden clues, I eventually drifted to sleep. It was well past 2:00 a.m. when I'd finished talking to Gavin and instead of going to bed, I had stubbornly continued to work. Once sleep overtook me, I began to dream. It was a lucid dream where I was in the library looking through the newspapers, but finding nothing. A movement caught my eye by the curtains across the room. I turned to see what had shifted and noticed a tiny pair of shoes peeking out from under the edge of the material. An outline of a small body made a bump behind the fabric. I rose from my desk and made my way towards the hidden form. The shoes didn't move as I inched closer, my heart rate speeding up. With one hand I slowly moved the curtain to the side, bracing myself to find something horrible staring back at me. Instead there was a small raven-haired girl in a simple black dress looking down at her feet. Her clothing was suitable for the 1912 time period and I immediately knew that she was like Eva and Colette.

"Don't be afraid," I said to the dark-haired ghost girl, "I won't hurt you." She slowly raised her head so that her eyes met mine. Tears poured down her pale cheeks, although she was silent. I held the curtain back expecting her not to move, but in a flash she was sitting at my desk where I had been moments before. I followed to see what she was looking at so intently. She had her hands on a book that looked familiar, though it wasn't what I'd been reading. She opened the old book to a page with hand-written words and symbols etched into every corner. She put her finger on a word that I couldn't make out from where I was standing.

"What is your name?" I asked tentatively, and as I did her eyes again shot up to meet mine. This child was different from Eva and Colette. She looked to be around seven or eight years old and had all the appearances of a regular child ghost, but power was coming off of her in waves. Her silence was not timidity, but rather felt as if it was her own, frustrated energy. She looked at me and right through me at the same time. As I stepped closer to the table she shot up and was immediately standing in the doorway. Again I asked her what her name was with added focus and force. A little smile slowly crept across her face and she whispered in a cool tone, one word.

"Winship," and then she was gone in a flash.

"Magdalene?" I shouted after her, and in doing so woke myself from the dream. I was again sitting at my desk where I had put my head down and dozed. I frantically pushed the papers in front of me to the right and left hoping the book the ghost child had been examining was somewhere amid the newspapers. It was not. The desk was a mess of paper. The room had grown extremely cold, despite the warm evening outside and a chill ran through my bones as I saw her odd smile in my mind. It was Elsiba's sister come to visit and she had seemed none too pleased. I knew it was time for me to head to bed, but just as I was rising to leave my desk an article caught my eye.

Winship Child Third to Perish

The Winship house has suffered the loss of their own Magdalene, aged 7, of the plague that is sweeping our homes. It has thus far claimed three of our town daughters with a mercilessness that can only prove more lives will undoubtedly soon be lost. Many are blaming the rat infestation that has overtaken the sewers and the secret tunnels used to bootleg moonshiner's whiskey and smuggle unwitting sailors onto ill-famed vessels. If these unholy business dealings are leading to the deaths of our most innocent citizens then all must be sealed and every rat exterminated. The mayor is offering a reward for every rat corpse brought to the waterfront to be burned in the days and weeks to come. This is no consolation to Johannes and Cecilia Winship in their time of sorrow. May Magdalene's soul be whisked to the Summerland on the wings of swallows on this the saddest of March months to date.

If Magdalene was the third child who perished, and on today's date, then I wondered if one-by-one the children would all pay me visits as the one hundred-year anniversary of their death occurred. At first I wondered if Magdalene had left this for me to see because it mentioned her death, but as I read on I had the sensation that she wanted me to see something else. The tunnels stuck in my mind. There were many secret tunnels built and used from the late 1800s through the 1920s when prohibition buckled down on booze across the country. I had heard of a tunnel leading from the Cliffside Chapel in uptown to the Haller Fountain which was at the foot of the cliffs in downtown. I thought the tunnels had been sealed off years before. There was one way to find out; go look through the blueprints downstairs. I would have to be quiet; I didn't want to awaken James, but there was no way I would sleep until my suspicions were quieted. As I tiptoed down the stairs, I felt I wasn't alone. Out of the corner of my eye I saw Magdalene slip out of Felix's room and disappear into the hallway mirror. In a flash she was gone into the looking glass like Alice, but I had a feeling she would be back in the nights to follow.

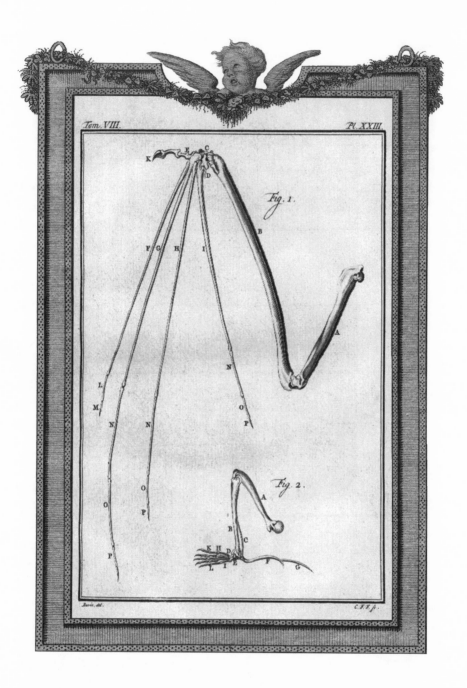

Fig. 1.

Fig. 2.

CHAPTER 19

I left the lights off as I made my way downstairs to the kitchen. I had every turn and loose board memorized after years of walking through this aging house. The darkness felt safe as I slinked down the long hallway. The only sound was the ticking of the grandfather clock on the second floor landing. In the kitchen, I turned on the small wall sconce by the table as not to illuminate the entire downstairs. As I suspected, James had left the blueprints strewn across the table. Carefully I sifted through each one hoping to find evidence of a tunnel. Near the bottom of the stack, a note written by James in pencil on the side of the blueprint caught my eye. It read "tunnels to be left accessible for historical preservation." My heart sped up as his familiar script confirmed my suspicions.

With the tips of my fingers I pulled the document to the top of the pile to examine it more closely. Being married to an architect meant I had seen hundreds of these drawings over the years and in so doing had a general idea of what I was looking at. Doors, walls and windows all had their special markings that promised the creation or transformation of a space. In this case there was a special notation marked "tunnel" on the first drawing. It showed an opening in the lower level of the Cliffside Chapel that led down through the hill and out a small door near the Haller Fountain. I knew this tunnel had at one time existed and was therefore not entirely surprised to find it. I was shocked; however, to see a second tunnel I'd never heard mentioned. It had the same entrance in the Cliffside Chapel but instead of heading left towards downtown it went up the hill along the edge of the cliffs. The exit was in the Bell Tower House, though in what room I wasn't sure. The spaces in that structure looked much like a labyrinth. Wrapping hallways with cloisters inside of rooms and all manner of stairwells and dormers created an odd organization of space. The house was vast and contained hidden passageways from two of the bedrooms into the third floor attic. While all of this caught my attention, it was the discovery of the second tunnel that made my heart thump in my chest. Instinctively I thought this second tunnel might be important, though I didn't know why.

There was a sudden creaking of floorboards above my head coming from our bedroom. The familiar thump of James' feet sounded in the hallway. I quickly, and as soundlessly as possible, put the blueprints back in order and feigned getting a drink of water. Soon he was downstairs clad only in his pajama bottoms. His body looked paler than it had only a day before. He yawned and scratched the back of his head and he made his way to the fridge next to me.

"Come to bed," he said with a sleepiness that was endearing. He stood with the refrigerator door open as he drank three glasses of water.

"Thirsty?" I asked with a touch of sarcasm, although as he lifted the glass to his lips I thought I spied a subtle change in his musculature. His usually rounded shoulders looked slimmer and there was even the hint of his collarbone protruding. "I know these projects are stressful, but you look like you're losing weight. Have you been stopping for lunch?"

"Haven't had time," he answered between gulps of water. "It seems like every time I sit down to eat, Sophie Renard calls with another idea or precision on the house."

"Take the time James, please, you're looking ragged. Just let the phone ring if she's harassing you." I expected him to agree with me, but instead his whole body suddenly tensed in what seemed like irritation. "I just don't want you to get worn down," I added, hoping to soften his sudden shift in mood.

"It's work Charlotte," he said while slamming the fridge door shut behind him. "I'm going back to bed. You should get some sleep, too, even if you don't have to be in your shop tomorrow." Usually he would take me in his arms and lead me to bed. Instead he put his glass in the sink and left the room without a backwards glance. I wasn't used to James acting so bristly with me and wondered if the Renards weren't getting their hooks into him as Daniel had with Willa. Whatever it was, I felt hurt and tiptoed back upstairs to my workroom. There was no way I was going to be able to sleep now.

It was too late to call Gavin back so I sent him an email letting him know about the tunnels I'd found on the blueprints. Somehow I would have to ask James about them in a way that hopefully didn't annoy him. Just as I was about to shut down my computer and grudgingly make my way to bed, an email appeared in my inbox. It was from Tom Caldwell and the subject heading was "Morrison Photographs."

Tom always joked that he disliked sleeping because it felt too much like death. He stayed up even later than me which was pretty rare in a town that boasted a large population of early birds. I quickly clicked it open and began to read:

Charlotte-A collector friend just unearthed some old photos that happen to be by the man we talked about, Dennis Morrison. Come by the house and you can take a look. Also found out some more info about him, strange character! You may be on to something with the vampire thing…talk tomorrow. -T

I scrolled down wishing he'd attached the images. Sadly, there was only the message, which made me anxious for more information. What did he mean about Dennis Morrison being a strange character? Also, the mention of vampires in conjunction with him had my full attention. I would call him first thing in the morning. My eyes were beginning to blur as I shut down the computer for the night. It was time I headed to bed, regardless of James being short with me.

I turned off the workroom light and began my way down the hall to our bedroom. The house was completely dark and the only light came from the moon outside. It had been shining in on Willa earlier in the evening as she sat by her open window. A wave of worry washed over my body as I thought of my daughter. As I reached the end of the hallway, I glanced into the mirror that reflected the length of the second floor. The opposite end of the hall had a large window that overlooked the staircase. In the reflection stood Magdalene Winship with her back to me. She was peering out at the moon. Her silhouette was that of a diminutive child of seven despite the fact that her soul carried power the likes of which I had rarely encountered. I turned hoping to catch her presence, but the hall was completely empty. There was no child ghost lingering in the house that I could see. I turned back to the mirror and the reflection was as it should be. There was something about her that made me nervous despite the fact that she was a Winship and in all likelihood was here to protect her own.

I climbed into bed with a swirl of information in my mind. It was winding itself into a hurricane of thoughts that proved more and more difficult to order into any logical sense. James was silent next to me, peacefully sleeping, while I tossed and turned until I finally fell into an exhausted repose. Tonight, instead of visits from ghost children, I dreamt of Willa. When she was four years old she had told my mother that she wanted to fly. Deidre, being exceptionally creative, fashioned her a pair of paper wings. Samir had made a metal framework and Deidre cut and painted thousands of paper feathers attaching them one by one until they made a perfect pair of wings. Willa wore them everywhere, perched on her tiny shoulders. If we had let her, she would have taken them with her to bed each night, convinced they would help her fly to other worlds.

In my dream, she was her four-year-old self playing in the garden. Her favorite pastime had been to take large clam shells and create flower offerings to the tree fairies. With a pinch of dirt in the bottom, a delicate arrangement of several blades of grass, marigold petals and a rose bud she would leave her offering at the base of the willow tree. It was her friend and she was convinced there were little people living inside. Who was I to tell her that little people didn't exist?

In the dream, she was arranging her shell offerings in a delicate row by her sacred tree. Her paper wings flapped in the gentle spring breeze. The sunlight glinted off of her auburn hair turning it into a fiery red. She was barefoot, in her favorite white cotton summer dress with a scalloped ruffle of eyelets on the skirt's edge. In this moment she was the perfect picture of innocence; safe under her willow tree. My Willa, my daughter, my blood, a piece of my soul: these were the thoughts that ran through my mind. Then the dream sun slipped behind a menacing cloud. The light shifted to darkness as Willa transformed into her present-day self. She stood with her hand on the tree trunk, pale with her wings broken at her feet. The night heron was crouched, pulling at the paper with its greedy beak. It wanted her feathers for its nest. Like a thieving parasite, it tore and twisted each hand-painted plume that had promised her flight.

The images were flashing quickly through my sleeping mind. Willa's white dress covered in blood. Her wings torn and left broken on the ground. Her offerings overturned like vulgar food before uninterested Gods. The smell of peaches was everywhere; nauseating in their sweetness as it mingled with the odor of blood. And then the rats came, scampering up from the ground to converge on her, filthy with plague.

I screamed myself awake. It took me several minutes to realize that it had only been a dream. It was a mother's worst nightmare, complete with the all-encompassing feeling that only a premonition leaves in its wake. This was a dream of foreboding the likes of which I had experienced at different critical moments in my life. I had already devoted myself to protecting my children from all harm. Now I knew I wasn't doing enough. Willa would become another of their victims if I didn't do more to stop them.

The house was silent despite the blood-curdling scream that had just echoed off the walls in my bedroom. I glanced at the clock and it read 10:00 a.m. James hadn't set the alarm knowing I'd come to bed late. In a way, I wished he had and I could have avoided the sinking feeling that comes with such dreams. Because of the hour, the children were at school and James was at work. My store opened at 11 a.m. and my employee would be running it for me today. I had orders piled up on my workbench and a stack of paperwork that wasn't growing any smaller as the days passed. None of it mattered. I had to find out more about the vampires. I had to figure out a way to stop them before they got to my children and then my town. I knew it would sound like madness if I shared too much of this with people outside of my close friends and family. This meant I also had to be very careful in how I moved forward with things. My endeavors would have to be a balancing act of maintaining an air of normalcy, while unearthing as much information as possible. To some it would sound like paranoia, but I knew there was absolutely nothing I wouldn't do to keep my children safe. With these thoughts in mind, I quickly dressed in jeans and an old black t-shirt. My hair was a nest of dark tangles, but I didn't care. My first order of business was to call Tom and find out more about the man behind the photograph of Eva and Colette Duprey and his connection to the vampires of 1912. From this moment on I would hunt them. I would destroy them before they had a chance to harm my own. Margot had always joked that it was never wise to make an enemy of a Winship. In this moment, I was determined to prove her right.

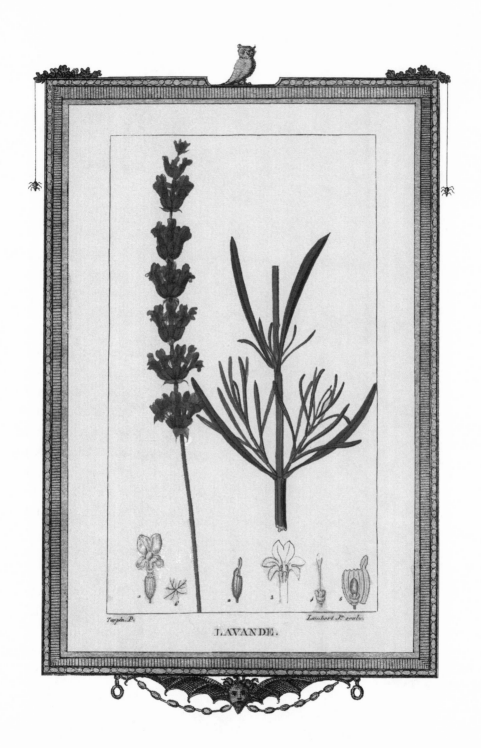

LAVANDE.

CHAPTER 20

My call to Tom Caldwell proved I'd overslept; he'd already left for an all-day fishing trip with his best friend, Bud. His wife, Emmalina, passed along the message that he'd come by my shop tomorrow and bring me the pictures he'd found. She heard the disappointment in my voice as I thanked her. Thinking it would help, she added that Tom had also found some hot, one hundred-year-old gossip for me. This actually made it worse, because I would have to wait until the following day for the information I so desperately desired. I hung up feeling I was miles away from finding out anything new as I paced back and forth in my kitchen.

Feeling restless, I wrote out a check to Pat and decided to make my way out to The Beltane Lavender Farm to deliver his payment. The drive would help clear my mind and I could claim that I did something work-related in case anyone cared to ask. With the windows down, I sped along the road leading out of town. It was another unseasonably warm day and the sun reflected off the ocean waves like tiny mirrors. The bright sunshine compared to the darkness I felt brewing was an unnerving juxtaposition of element to emotion. I felt storm clouds should be thick overhead instead of blue skies and the smell of flowers wafting on the air. If my gift had been like Margot's, the town would be bracing itself for a tornado right now. My mind was a raging jumble of terrifying images and what seemed like bits and pieces of disconnected information.

Driving helped me focus. As the road curved to the left, I saw the lavender fields in the distance. Pat's farm stretched over several acres of exposed fields and ecologically friendly hot houses. On a small hill sat a sprawling Victorian house. Several additions built over the years had created their commune. I took the right turn up to the main entrance to the farm, enjoying the rolling purple fields that stretched into fragrant rows on all sides.

The gravel crunched under my tires as I pulled in, alerting the house of my arrival. Soon a clan of children and several dogs swarmed joyously around my car. Pat stood by the gate as I maneuvered my way through giggly hugs and raucous barks of the youngest members of the coven. Usually Pat wore a lopsided grin on his bearded face, but today he looked pensive. A crease lined his forehead adding ten years to his usually youthful countenance.

"I brought your check; sorry I didn't get out here sooner," I shouted over the noise around me as I made my way to the gate, one small child attached to my leg.

"Lilith, let go of Charlotte," Pat softly scolded the little girl who had wrapped her arms and legs around my thigh like an ivy vine. She let go and everyone scampered into the gated gardens with me following behind.

"I'm glad you came; there are things we need to talk about," Pat said in an uncharacteristically serious tone. "Follow me; the others are in the back."

The Beltane Lavender Farm was run with precision; although, it seemed each member knew intuitively what their work was without the need of orders. They worked as a collective with each individual's strengths put first to create harmony. Pat was a natural leader and had a mind for numbers; he ran the financial aspects, which insured that the farm prospered and all members were rewarded equal shares. His wife, Diana, was an herbal healer of extraordinary talent. She had her own greenhouse where she grew everything from innocuous mints to more deadly nightshades to create her remedies. In addition to lavender bouquets, I also sold Diana's artisanal bath salts and other tinctures to excited tourists and more open-minded locals. Usually when I visited, everyone would be hard at work in different parts of the vast farm either taking care of the plants, livestock or packaging Diana's concoctions.

I was surprised as I rounded the corner with Pat and found the entire coven of twelve adults gathered around a large bonfire surrounded by iron fence stakes. Several of the men were running them through the cleansing fire while a group of women were sewing what looked like stretched hides. The acrid smell of burning metal and wood made my nose itch and my eyes water. Pat offered me a chair farthest from the black smoke. Everyone greeted me with warmth, but quickly went back to working on their task without lingering on conversational niceties.

"What is all this?" I asked, fascinated by the way they were all working with such focus. I knew they took their rituals seriously, but this felt somber and in many ways matched my mood of the past few weeks.

"It's about the new family in town. They are not who they say they are," Pat said slowly as if gauging his every word. "I don't really know how to say this without you thinking that we're completely off our rockers, so I'm just going to come out with it: they are vampires." He let out a small sigh as he said it. Even though I knew what he was saying was true, I could understand why he had a hard time speaking the words out loud. It sounded ludicrous.

"I know," I said, a lilt in my voice that betrayed a slight hint of uncertainty. "At least I think I know what you mean."

"We've seen this before, Charlotte, when we lived in California. It is one of the reasons we moved here. These beings will cause mortal harm and we are going to protect our own. The iron stakes will be installed around our land; we're creating protective spells to keep them out. You should do the same," he continued in a tone so grave I couldn't help but focus on his every word. "In the coming months, we will not leave the farm and neither will our children. It isn't safe. Just last night we had a rat infestation in the back barn. It took all day to eradicate them. They are the stewards of the vampires; the carriers of disease and desperation."

"How do you know all of this?" I asked, feeling suddenly lacking in paranormal knowledge.

"We've seen it before. These are different vampires, but it's the same situation. They've come back to their nest to reclaim souls from the past to ensure their unnatural existence continues. Think twice next time you see a flu outbreak or salmonella poisoning. How many children are taken and how many times are there other factors that are overlooked? You'll find that a new family or organization recruits members just before the sickness begins and then they make a fast escape right after. Charlotte, this is going to happen here and there will be losses. All we can do is protect our own."

"Can't we stop them?" I asked, my panic rising as I looked into Pat's dark eyes and his unflinching face. If anyone else had overheard us talking we would have sounded like two mentally unstable individuals evoking paranoid delusions to justify our actions.

"We're working on something, but it's too soon to know if it will be enough. Until then I can only promise that if you and your family need safe haven, the farm is open to you. But do not come after dark, we will not let you in. Stay away from the Renards and whatever you do, be careful not to make a pact with them. They will try to reel you in."

"Pat, I think they have Willa and James," I said, stifling a sob as I finally admitted to someone that my family was in danger. "Willa and the Renard boy are constantly together and he's turned her against me. James is working on their houses day and night. And I worry that Felix is going to be next." I told Pat all that I knew as he listened intently to my every word. When I finished telling him, he looked at the ground avoiding my eyes. He just shook his head slowly.

"I can't tell you what to do, Charlotte, but if you and Felix want to come here, you are welcome, but James and Willa have been contaminated. They're marked." Pat's words shook me to my core. Was he saying that I had to abandon my husband and daughter to save my child and myself? That was simply not an option for me.

"So you're just going to wait here until they do what they will with the rest of the town?" I asked, anger rising toward him and the rest of the coven. They seemed cowardly in their attempts to cordon off their land and leave the rest of us to suffer an unknown fate.

"We don't have a choice Charlotte. There is nothing we can do at this moment," he said, with an obvious look of regret as well as finality.

"What about the spell you were talking about? What will it do?" I asked, feeling a sudden wave of anger that they weren't trying hard enough.

"I can't tell you until I think it will work. It's a long shot, but as soon as I know I will tell you. I promise you, Charlotte, if I thought we could stop them then we would do everything in our power. Until then, we won't be leaving the farm." He said this with a finality that marked the end of my welcome. I followed Pat back to the front gate feeling devastated. The rest of the coven was careful to avoid my eyes as they worked on their task with desperate concentration.

As I stepped outside the gate and walked back to my car, Pat stopped at the edge of his land. He looked at me with obvious regret and yet not enough to risk sacrificing his family. I got in my car without speaking a word of parting. I had no words at this moment. My throat felt dry and only words of anger would have burst forth if I had let them. As I drove back towards the main road, I gave one last glance in my rear view mirror and saw Pat with his hand raised in a farewell. In a way, I could understand his wanting to protect his own, but I felt differently about my town. Despite the difficulties, in many ways they felt like family. We were one, regardless of squabbles or gossip. In that oneness, I would do my best to find a way to keep us all safe. Not just my family, but everyone's family.

The noon air was heavy with heat. There was a thunderstorm on the horizon. The only comfort I could take from Pat's words was that I was not alone in sensing there were dark energies afoot. At least the Winships weren't the only ones who sensed these things, although the coven's actions left me mystified. I had little knowledge as to what they were planning in the way of protection. Margot had given me all the tools she knew of, yet it hadn't kept the Renards from worming their way into Willa and James' good graces. There had to be more I could do. I sped down the two-lane highway back to town with the smell of iron in my nostrils. Just as I crossed the welcome sign, a loud rumble of thunder sounded off the bay. Normally this would have left me on edge but instead I felt an odd sensation of calm wash over me. The thought of rain was a welcome one. I sped into town just as the first drops began to hit the pavement.

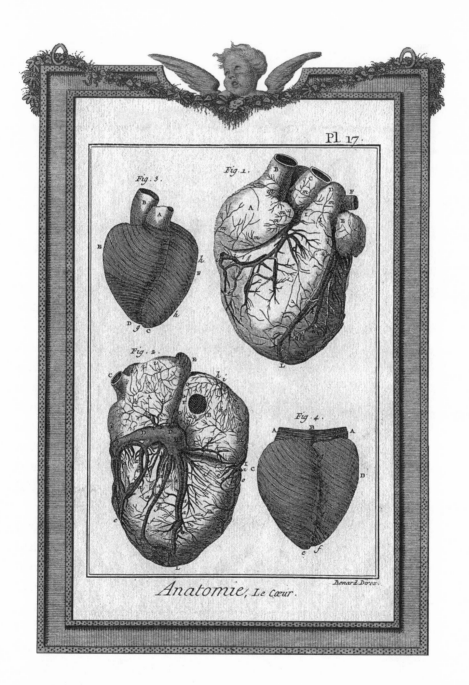

Pl. 17.

Fig. 3.

Fig. 1.

Fig. 2.

Fig. 4.

Anatomie, Le Cœur.

Benard Direx.

Chapter 21

As I pushed open the door to the Gunn Grocery and Deli, another rumble of thunder bounced off the old brick building. Henry greeted me with a welcoming smile from behind the counter. He was busy making espressos for a couple of sleepy tourists. I stood patiently in line, re-reading the sandwich menu even though I knew it by heart. It hadn't changed since the day that Tobias Gunn had opened the café almost 60 years ago.

'What can I get you, Charlotte?" he asked, after placing two steaming espressos in front of the couple.

I mulled over the choices then settled on my usual turkey on sourdough. I quickly added a pastrami on black rye to the order, feeling the sudden urge to surprise James with his favorite for lunch.

"Can you pack them to go Henry? I'm going to surprise James with lunch," I said, hoping this would make amends for my comment from last night. I also wanted to make sure James wasn't forgetting to eat in the name of work; or more accurately, in the name of vampires getting their hooks into him without his noticing. Henry packed the two sandwiches in a bag, along with sparkling juices and his homemade potato chips that James loved. The rain had turned torrential, so I made a dash to the car, clutching our lunch to my chest to keep it as dry as possible.

James' office was located uptown between the movie theatre and the town co-op. When we first moved back to town his family had given him just enough money to put a down payment on a rundown three-bedroom Victorian house. It took him six months, doing much of the work himself, to transform it into his office. We did all the painting, even though I was six months pregnant. It was a fond memory. He had kept the walls of his office the original color, refusing to change, because it reminded him of the old days. It was a charming space that had grown in size over the years as business increased with his good reputation. In addition to his own expansion, other professional offices had followed his lead over the years. A chiropractor, law office and realtor now shared the same block uptown. They, too, chose to update Victorian houses and turn them into welcoming offices that were far more inviting than any modern edifice. I parked in front and made a mad dash for the porch. I managed to make it to the door without being completely drenched.

His secretary was having lunch at the front desk. She smiled sweetly when I walked in. I motioned to James' door, but she shook her head furiously. Since her mouth was full, I took it that she simply couldn't respond. I pushed open the door to his office hoping he was inside. James was examining paperwork on the desk in front of him, a look of profound concentration on his face. He hadn't even heard the door open. Sitting on the edge of the desk was Sophie Renard.

She was leaning over James looking at the drawings, her blouse slightly open, revealing cleavage. Her too-short skirt was hitched up, showing off slim legs. The edge of a lace, thigh-high stocking showed as she precariously shifted her weight, leaning closer to James. I pushed the door open hard striking the wall behind it, alerting them both to my presence. James looked up, startled, as his eyes focused on mine. He looked exhausted. I could tell he'd forgotten to eat this morning. Sophie turned, with what looked like a genuine smile, casually smoothing her skirt as she stood to greet me.

"Charlotte, what are you doing here?" James asked, with no hint of malice; yet the question sounded like a reproach to my ears. I handed him the bag with our lunches.

"I brought you your favorite sandwich from Gunn's café, in case you didn't have time to get something," I said, ignoring Sophie. "I know how hard you've been working to make this project perfect," I added, camouflaging my irritability at finding Sophie in my husband's office, obviously flirting with him.

"Thank you, but I have so much to do, I'll eat it later," he said, setting the bag behind him on the windowsill. I felt a moment of disappointment. A few weeks ago if I'd come by with sandwiches James would have insisted we walk to the park and eat them outside. Even in the rain, he would have wanted to sit under the gazebo and have an impromptu picnic. But that was not the case today. Not since the Renards had arrived with their projects.

"Speaking of food," Sophie chimed in smoothly, "I would like to invite you and James to join us for dinner tomorrow night." Her smile looked inviting, but there was a coolness in her voice that felt calculated. She must have sensed my hesitation because she continued trying to convince me. "Now that the kitchen and dining room are complete and all the work is on the other side of the house, I would love to make you a French meal. We love to entertain. It would be an honor if you were the first guests in our newly-restored home."

I was trapped. If I said no, James would be furious. It would drive him further away from me. I didn't want her to get any closer to him than she already was. If that meant suffering through dinner with her and her husband then I would agree to go. It would be a fact-finding mission. It was time I knew my enemy.

"We'd love to," I answered, taking satisfaction in her obvious surprise at my response. "Can we bring anything?" I added, just to annoy her with my politeness.

"No, no, just come at 7:00 p.m." she stammered. With a quick glance at James, she reached for her jacket and purse on the nearby chair. "Well, I should be going. Daniel is asking about the dance and what he should wear. I promised we would do some shopping later," she said nervously, and rushed from the office. I despised her. I had to figure out a way to stop whatever she had planned for my husband.

"I'm going to take my sandwich and go if you need to work," I said, moving to the window behind him to pull my lunch from the bag. He smiled as I leaned in to give him a kiss on his cheek. I handed him the sandwich I had brought for him.

'Just a bite?" I asked, with a teasing smile. It felt like I was playing the airplane game with Felix when he was a stubborn baby unwilling to eat carrots. James leaned back in his chair and unfolded the waxed paper. He devoured the first half in three bites. The color immediately came back into his face as the sustenance entered his fatigued body.

"I brought you some of Henry's homemade chips, too," I said on my way to the door. He tore into the bag with a chuckle that revealed a hint of his usual demeanor. "I'll see you tonight at the house. I'll call Margot and see if she can watch Felix tomorrow night," I said, as he inhaled his food. "And you definitely owe me one." Hopefully he would remember how to eat in public when we were at the Renards for dinner; not that I really cared. I left his office feeling I had the upper hand with Sophie — for today. But tomorrow night, I would be walking into their nest. As I ran to my car, that thought left me feeling queasy. It was time to plan.

CHAPTER 22

The pounding rain continued throughout the night and into the next morning. March was back to its normal, stormy self for Port Townsend. Usually we weren't blessed with sunshine and heat until well into June — if we were lucky. The grey skies, mist and rain were usually constant companions through most of the Spring. I had gotten used to the smells of summer and the sight of blooming flowers in all the gardens. Tonight, instead of the fiery sunsets of the past few weeks, there were rumbling thunder clouds overhead.

The evening had been uneventful, despite my constant feeling of worry and foreboding. I helped Willa choose one of my necklaces to go with her dress; the Saint Patrick's Day dance was a little over a week away. Her sixteenth birthday followed the week after. She sat on my bed, and we looked through my jewelry box which contained my own creations and family heirlooms. She had chosen one of Elsiba's necklaces. It was a lariat style with a moonstone and a teardrop peridot that matched her dress perfectly. I felt a moment of reassurance that she would be wearing something that Elsiba had held dear to her heart. Touching it, I felt the familiar jolt of power that resided in all of Elsiba's things. She had been a powerful woman in her day. I had a feeling this would keep Willa safe on the night of the dance. She had gone to her room wearing the necklace. She was almost back to her light-hearted self again. Then the familiar buzz of her phone signaled she was receiving a text message; the door shut behind her and she was lost again to the constant communication that had become her evening ritual with Daniel.

Felix had been quiet all evening. He said the rain made him feel a little sad although he didn't know why. I checked on him before turning off the hallway lights. He was reading the old book from the Winship library with a voracity that reminded me of his carnivorous plant. More than anything, I felt relieved that he looked luminous in a way that James and Willa did not. I had more than enough to worry about with the two of them. I did not want Felix to fall victim to the allure of the Renards as well. Thankfully, for the moment, he seemed as immune to them as I was. I had to imagine it was, in part, due to his premonitions.

By the time James and I were in bed, the rain was roaring outside our window with thunder growling in the distance. James had fallen into a deep sleep the moment his head hit the pillow, but I lay on my back, watching the shadows flicker across the ceiling. The streaming raindrops created a beautiful pattern across the walls when the headlights from a passing car flashed by the house. I thought about Pat and the coven as I lay there, wondering how they were preparing for the worst. What the worst was, I still wasn't entirely sure, but if it was anything like the plague of 1912, it could be devastating to our community.

I closed my eyes and thought back to the articles I'd read in my workroom after dinner. The plague was a nameless one; some called it bubonic, though there was no proof of that. If it had been, then it would have claimed more than just the lives of children. The mysterious illness spread like a wave over Port Townsend, sweeping away the young in a feverish undertow they weren't strong enough to survive. After Eva, Colette and Magdalene's deaths, the losses grew exponentially. There wasn't enough room in the newspaper for each child to have an article of his or her own. Instead, the paper began to list the names of the dead with their ages and the times for the burials. In the first week alone, after Magdalene's article, there were over thirty children lost to the fever. Sometimes families lost all their children. The Cabral's lost seven of their little ones, which merited an article dedicated just to them. I wondered if that was why Mario could still be seen walking the pier as a ghost. Was he waiting until his seven children were set free before he moved on? If Willa or Felix were held behind and I had a choice, I don't think I could rest peacefully until they, too, were waiting on the other side.

By the end of March, one hundred and thirty children had perished. All of them from the same symptoms of high fever, malaise and finally death. Interspersed through the newspapers were articles about rat infestations being the likely cause of the illness. There was also talk that local tribes had cursed the founding families for their land theft. I searched page by page hoping to find the name of the family who had lived in the old Bell Tower house, though I had my doubts that the Renards would have kept the same name all these years. I found nothing but society articles about the masquerade ball and the good works the lodges did to help the grieving families.

An article about Dennis Morrison and his wife, Anita, caught my eye. It claimed that while Dennis had taken over the barber shop giving haircuts to paying customers, his hobby was photography. He had invited the town to come in and sit for free photographs so he could perfect his art and give families an "eternal glimpse into the soul" of their loved ones. The wording seemed odd. The language of the time was quite flowery, but this struck a chord, considering what Margot had told me about soul stealing as a means for vampires to exist. Had Dennis Morrison been a vampire? Had he and his wife, who came to town at the same time as the other family, been in league together? Eva and Colette had mentioned having their picture taken by the barber on one of their ghostly dream visits. Also the fact that their photo was in Elsiba's trunk of clothing had to be more than just happenstance. There was something to the barber's involvement that felt nefarious. With the articles waltzing through my mind, I eventually drifted to sleep. The constant tapping of rain created an unusual lullaby.

By morning the downpour showed no signs of slowing. The lilacs and other blossoming trees had been battered overnight; yards were littered with broken limbs and purple blooms as the rain had thrashed the flowers. The earth, with its early warm weather, had given all it could in terms of natural protection for the town. But it was being defeated by the heavens' unrelenting rain. Thankfully, Margot had made a huge batch of the lilac potion before the blossoms perished. Thinking the heat would continue, I had put off making my own, assuming the flowers would be there by the weekend. The storm had decided otherwise.

James and the children were gone when I awoke in the morning. I had slept in later than usual; fatigue had settled into my heart. The first thing I did after getting out of bed was to douse myself with the lilac potion to ensure I was wearing a proper amount of vampire repellant. Everything I owned wore the powerful aroma. James found it enticing. Last night I made a point of putting several drops of the potion on a small hand towel before tossing it into the dryer with the week's laundry. Now, everyone in my family had the perfume lingering on them; it was a better alternative to garlic.

I made my coffee and packed up several of the newspapers hoping I could read a bit in between customers at my store. I was anxiously anticipating Tom's visit to give me more information about Dennis Morrison. His cryptic email had me on edge. Also, tonight was our dinner at the Renard house. While I had haughtily agreed yesterday, I was now feeling a deep unease at willingly entering their home. It felt like I was walking into the lion's den, which was not something I would generally do. There would be just enough time to close my shop and return home to change before going to the Renards. I planned to douse myself with Elsiba's potion as my sole means of protection. I would try to find a way to splash a bit on James as well. In the meantime, it was time to make my way through the rain and open my shop for the day.

Once inside The Curious Crow my daily routine began as clients drifted in and out in a steady flow. When the clock struck noon, a clink of the bell on the door announced the arrival of Tom Caldwell. He was grinning from ear-to-ear as he set a small box on my counter. The postmark was from Boston. I waited for him to speak, though it was obvious he was enjoying dragging out the suspense.

"Well?" I asked, trying not to lose patience while adoring his sense of mystery. "What's in the box?"

"Ok, I called around to some of my collector friends who have bought or sold Pacific Northwest ephemera over the years. One of them gave me an unbelievable lead!" he said with excitement. "He had been in a shop in Boston years ago and had seen an entire collection of one man's portraiture work from Port Townsend. He only collects landscape images so he had passed on the lot. He gave me the name of the shop and on a whim I called and guess what, it was your man, Dennis Morrison."

"Did they still have the photos?" I asked, hoping that was what was in the box.

"They did and not only did they have the photos, but also a story. The owner is old enough to be my brother. He came into possession of the photographs from his father who owned the store before him. They sell old papers, books, newspapers, photos, postcards and such. Anyway, back when his father first opened the store, he remembered a man named Dennis Morrison and his wife Anita. They lived a few blocks from the shop. Apparently Dennis was fascinated with photography; he insisted it was a way to help free the soul. But what he remembered most was that Dennis had a tendency to talk about things that upset the upper social circles. He was obsessed with all things related to vampire mythology and frequented the man's shop in search of items on the topic. That is, he did so regularly until he and his wife moved suddenly to Port Townsend. He set up shop as a barber doing photography on the side. Now this is where it gets odd." Tom paused for effect as he leaned in to tell me the next juicy tidbit. "In the spring of the year that Dennis moved, he sent a box to the man's father at the book store in Boston. It contained one hundred and thirty portraits of children from the town and with them a letter."

Tom pried open the box. With knobby fingers withered with age, he carefully lifted the stack of photographs, fanning them out on my countertop. The sight of the first photo took my breath away; it was a haunting image of Magdalene Winship. Her eyes stared straight at the camera in defiance. I felt her spirit staring out of the photograph at me. She wasn't smiling, but rather, had her hands folded demurely on her lap with her chin held high. It was without a doubt the same little girl who was now walking the halls of the Winship house.

With a delicacy that reminded me of someone touching a holy archive, Tom unfolded a paper yellowed with age in Dennis Morrison's handwriting. It read:

> Dear Mr. Holcombe,
> I am entrusting these photographs to you as I must take my leave of my new home in Port Townsend with unexpected haste. I hope to see you in several months as I make my way back to Boston with Anita but if for some reason I never return to claim these I only

ask that they must remain together as a group. Do not split them to send them asunder! It would have grave consequences the likes of which I cannot write in enough detail to make clear with the short time that I have. Please do this for me as your loyal friend and patron. Guard these in your safekeeping until I can return or someone of a worthy heart asks for them as a whole. I also have one more request in case of my disappearance, if you must one day part with them make sure that they go forth as a group to someone who has lived in Port Townsend for a Full Lifetime. Under no other circumstances should they be released from you or your descendants care. I am forever grateful and hope to see you when the autumn trees are ablaze in fiery red.

Your loyal friend,
Dennis Morrison

I read the letter twice as Tom watched me with a proud grin. I had no idea how to begin processing what this meant in relation to current happenings.

"He sold them to me for a song," Tom said with an air of delight. "It seems he'd almost given up finding someone who filled the criteria of the letter. He's giving the bookstore to his son in the coming months and felt it was time to whittle down his stock. This was the one thing his father had made him promise to look after. It turned out that I fit the bill, a lifetime in Port Townsend and a willingness to keep the photographs together. Although when he checked the box, one picture was missing. There are only 129 images."

"Can I borrow these for a few days and give them back later?" I wanted to be able to really take my time looking them over for clues.

"I don't collect portraits, so why don't you hang onto them and when you're done, give them to Evelyn Pettygrove. It will get her and the historical society off our backs for a while," he added with a chuckle. "Now promise me if you find out there really were vampires in this town I'll be the first to know."

I gave a nervous laugh but avoided the promise, hoping that he was joking. But I could tell his curiosity was piqued. As Tom turned to leave, I thanked him again. He just waved his hand in return as he stepped out into the rain, his old umbrella raised in a vain effort to keep him dry. I spent the rest of the afternoon examining the black and white images of the children, knowing instinctively that all had succumbed to the 1912 fever. But I still didn't know what Dennis Morrison's role in their deaths had been. Was he trying to find a new way to capture souls for his own vampiric consumption or was he trying to protect the souls of would be victims? And how had the missing photograph of the two little girls ended up in my attic? Whatever it was, I now had in front of me the images of children who I was sure would visit me on the anniversary of each of their deaths. With a sinking feeling, I knew I was about to have very full house.

Turpin Pinx.ᵗ

PÊCHER.

Lambert F. Sculp.ᵗ

CHAPTER 23

The driveway leading to the Bell Tower House was lined with peach trees in full blossom, though last night's storm had left a carpet of pink petals covering the ground. The rain had finally tapered off near the end of the day, leaving the sky a vibrant purple. As James drove down the winding gravel drive, the petals fell in a constant flurry. It was like driving in slow motion through a blizzard of pink tissue paper blossoms.

My stomach was in knots. I had no desire to dine with Sophie and Thomas Renard, but here I was at their front door with a bottle of wine in my hand. The outside of the house had areas covered in plastic and there was a large commercial dumpster on the far side. Construction was well underway and began early each morning and lasted until sunset every day. James had picked me up from our house after work, giving me just enough time to change. He had enthusiastically explained how the work was progressing with almost supernatural speed. I shot him a raised eyebrow at his choice of words. He thought nothing of it and kept chattering about new sheetrock and exceptionally fast drying time.

The porch lights of the mansion gave the pink petals that floated everywhere, eerie little shadows. As James and I headed up the stairs, the door opened just as we reached the porch. Thomas stood on the threshold, a forced smile on his face. James cordially shook his hand as he invited us both in, leading the way through the main hallway into the sitting room. The hall was a mess of plastic drop sheets and toolboxes, but once we passed into the sitting room the ambience became formal.

"Please, have a seat while I bring some 'amuses-bouches'," he said, motioning for us to have a seat on one of two blue velvet settees at the center of the room.

"We brought this wine; it's a local specialty," I said, handing him one of Morgan's dandelion wines. This was part of my plan. If they were really as well-mannered as I hoped, then it would be rude not to serve my wine with the first course. Thomas eyed it with uncertainty.

"Why thank you. We are always curious about provincial recipes," he said with a subtle upturn of his nose. This was one local recipe he wouldn't forget. It had peculiar effects on those who imbibed it. And like all of Morgan's concoctions, there was an underlying magical influence. His dandelion wine would bring forth thoughts of the past and the desire to reveal one's motives. It gave me the sensation of being rooted to my town and my family. I had seen others spin off into conversations about long-forgotten family feuds and broken fences. My hope was it would catch them off guard and loosen their tongues.

He left the room going towards what I assumed was the kitchen. James and I settled side by side on the blue velvet settee. A moment later, Thomas was back in the room with four glasses and our opened bottle in hand. Sophie followed behind him with a tray of delicacies. I had hoped the food would be absolutely horrible. But I had to give them one begrudged compliment; they had excellent taste. There were little dates delicately wrapped in prosciutto, baked to warm perfection. The cold dandelion wine felt refreshing in combination with the richness of the dates. Thomas even commented on it as such.

"Charming, this libation," which was a decidedly old-fashioned way of speaking. My ears perked up. "It reminds me of something that I cannot quite identify," he added, puzzled as he finished off his glass and immediately poured himself another. Sophie had not touched her own and was eyeing her husband with a look that could have frozen ice. She excused herself to see to dinner as Thomas became more absorbed with the wine.

"So, how are you liking the town?" I asked in an upbeat way. James look relieved. I had promised to be amiable, though he knew I wasn't keen on the Renard family, despite them being his employers.

"It is much as I remember it," he said in a carefree way. In the one time I'd met him he seemed reserved and severe, but tonight the wine was certainly giving him wings. Sophie returned to remove the platter and replaced it with a second that held small canapés of foie gras dusted with sea salt.

"So you have been here before?" I asked, leaning forward with interest.

"Yes, of course," interrupted Sophie as Thomas was about to respond. "We came several years ago as tourists and fell in love with Port Townsend. There is so much character in such a tiny town. The buildings are what seduced us." She said the last part with a glance at James and then added to Thomas with a tilt of her head "Right, cheri?"

"Exactly," he said, picking up the bottle to examine the homemade label that Morgan used on all his wines. It had a black and white drawing of a bear picking berries in a field of dandelions. Astrid had designed it for him years ago and he treasured it. There was also a list of ingredients that included the flowers, alcohol and the last of which was the word "magic."

"Magic?" he asked with interest.

"Oh, well, my family has its way of doing things. Some people call it magic, but it is really just tradition," I said, completely downplaying the word hoping that he would keep drinking and start revealing things about himself. James sipped his own as did I. Sophie was flitting in and out of the room with various hors d'oeuvres that Thomas and James inhaled as fast as she could replace them.

"There is talk in town that you are a family of witches," Thomas said followed by a hearty chuckle. "Imagine — talk of ghosts and witches in this day and age! Although we did live in Boston once and the folks in Salem were quite superstitious." He leaned back and finished off his glass of wine in one long gulp then poured himself another. Sophie returned to announce that dinner was ready. She ignored her glass of wine.

"Shall we bring these with us?" I asked, motioning to the coffee table where they sat glimmering with the dandelion nectar. She gave me an odd look that implied suspicion and then grudgingly nodded a yes. Thomas was bringing the rest of the bottle with him and I smiled at the thought that it was definitely working on his sensibilities.

The dining room was painted powder grey with a row of long windows on the far end that overlooked the cliffs. The other three walls had an elegant arrangement of various antique mirrors, large and small, clustered together. Some of them had etched images decorating the edges. Others had the tell-tale signs of age with flakes of aluminum peeling off the backs. Under normal circumstances, I would have found it quite elegant. But with the flickering candlelight and the reflections of the floating blossoms moving in the wind outside, I felt uncomfortable. Sophie motioned us to our seats. James had been in and out of this room for the past few days working on the details of the space and he couldn't help but inspect the corners.

Wall sconces lit the edges of the room and there was a crystal chandelier, which was original to the house, hanging over the long dining table. A row of candles lined the table with short bouquets of peach blossoms in small vases in between. The room smelled overwhelmingly of peaches. I almost expected to see a bowl of the ripened fruit sitting on the table, but there was nothing other than the flowers and candles. I took my seat. The mirrors cast reflections that created the illusion the room was larger than it was. This altered space felt cold with the various shades of grey and the petals swirling outside.

"So, Thomas," I asked, putting on my most charming of smiles, "What exactly are your plans for the Cliffside Chapel? I'm intrigued."

"Sophie and I will be using it as a place to hold meetings for our motivational group, "Aspire." Our hope is to create a new place for the town to hold community events and to encourage better business practices with life and career coaching."

"Fascinating," I said, although my first thought was that they were probably starting their own cult. Sophie sat down with us. She served asparagus soup in delicate bone china bowls. The smell of the green, spiced soup mixed with the aroma of peaches was overpowering. I took a sip of the dandelion wine to find my center and listened as Sophie began to speak about "Aspire."

"We have been very privileged in our lives to push the boundaries of our own potential," she said in a seductive whisper. "It is so sad to watch people lose themselves in the mundane tasks of daily life when they could rise above and be truly successful instead of living off things that have been handed down to them."

I felt the last part of her sentence was undoubtedly directed at me. I filed it away in the ever-growing mental list of why I despised her. James didn't seem to notice and was entranced by the flavors in his bowl of soup. I had always found it fascinating how men rarely picked up on the malicious, catty quips women flung at each other. I let it slide — for now — because there were bigger problems to contend with than a few snotty remarks. This woman and her husband were vampires and I needed to know all there was about them if I wanted to find their weakness.

"Yes, it is our mission to teach people how to fulfill their dreams in this short life," added Thomas as he shot an odd look at Sophie. "We will be holding our first open meeting soon after the Masquerade Ball. We hope you and James will join us."

Of course the answer to that was "not in a million years," but I simply smiled instead. Thankfully, James had his mouth full. I had to attend the Masquerade Ball for James' sake but there was no way I would be joining their cultish 'success' forum.

"How long have you been doing this type of thing?" I asked, and Thomas' face lit up with a wolfish grin.

"Oh, forever, right Sophie?" he said, while drinking the last of the wine. "We have taken our model all over the world and have blessed so many with our path to success."

"Thomas, can you help me bring out the main course?" Sophie asked. She still had not touched her glass. I had hoped she'd at least take a sip. I wanted a glimpse into the darkness that was just beneath her polished exterior; a slip of the tongue much as Thomas was demonstrating. There were so many tidbits that could be whittled out with just a sip of the dandelion wine, but I had a feeling she was not going to take my bait.

Soon, they were arranging a roast duck in the center of the table. The smell of honey and peaches mixed with the familiar scent of the game wafted through the room. Thomas sliced a piece of duck breast for me and covered it with a sauce of sautéed peaches with honey glaze. Sophie was pouring us all glasses from a bottle of French red wine as she began to clear away the remnants of Morgan's dandelion potion. She saw me cast a glance at her untouched glass.

"White wine gives me a headache," she said slyly as she removed the offending bottle from the table. James had been particularly silent; the food garnered all of his attention. He seemed spellbound by it. I felt slightly ill from the sickly sweet odor of fruit and the iron scent of blood. The duck was rare, and left a red pool under the slices on my plate, turning the scalloped potatoes a light pink. James made a toast to our hosts, adding a compliment to the chef. Sophie was more than pleased with herself as she drank deeply from her glass of red wine. Her tongue even flicked a little drop from the edge of the glass. I shivered at the sight; in the candlelight it looked like she was lapping up droplets of blood.

Slowly, the conversation turned to the work being done on the two buildings. As everyone ate, with Thomas and James serving themselves second helpings, I felt suddenly out of sorts. I took a sip of the red wine and my head immediately began to spin. The combination of the duck and the wine left a bitter taste of iron in my mouth. There was something wrong with this food!

The light in the room gradually shifted from grey to dark steel as the sun faded from the sky. With the flickering candles lighting the room and the glow from the wall sconces, shadows jumped from mirror to mirror. A sense of panic rose in me and I knew I had to get out of the room and away from the Renards.

"Charlotte?" I heard James ask, but his voice came from somewhere in the distance. I tried to bring myself back to the room and was greeted by the three of them staring at me.

"May I use your powder room?" I asked weakly. Sophie immediately explained where it was — down the hall and to the left. As soon as I started down the darkened hallway, I felt as if I could breathe again. A feeling of suffocation had come over me the instant I had tasted the red wine. Could it be that she had her own magic potions? Slowly I walked the narrow hallway stepping over plastic until I reached what I thought was the door to the bathroom. I opened it to find a vast ballroom with floor to ceiling mirrors. It was the famous mirrored room I had heard so much about over the years. It was dark inside, but the ceilings reached two stories up to skylights above and a balcony lined with archways to look into the main room. The floor was made of large slabs of white marble that shimmered in the mirrors.

The nearly full moon illuminated the room from above. I stood in the center taking it all in. The mirrors were in their original condition and glowed silver. Out of the corner of my eye I saw movement in one of the mirrors followed by the sound of feet scuffling on the marble floors. I turned quickly but saw only my own reflection multiplied around me. The scuffling was soon followed by child-like giggles. I turned again towards the sound and this time I caught the reflection of two little boys running in the balcony. These were undoubtedly ghosts, but there was something different about them. They seemed more tangible than the normal ghosts that came to visit me on a regular basis. Again a scuffle alerted me, but this time it was right behind me. I turned and came face to face with at least ten children standing in the center of the room.

They were all dressed in clothing typical of the turn of the last century. It was a mixed group of girls and boys ranging in age from a toddler to a boy of Willa's age. They stood frozen in time before me. I was sure that if I reached out to them I would find flesh and blood instead of ether. A little girl, who was most likely close to Felix's age, stepped tentatively closer to me and whispered:

"My skin is so hot, can you make it better?" she pleaded in a tiny voice.

"I'm going to try," I said, inching towards them with my hand out. I stopped immediately when a loud boom resonated behind me. The children let out one, combined scream that ricocheted off the walls in a high-pitched wail. My hands flew to my ears as the children turned and ran into the mirror on the far side of the room. They disappeared into the silver reflection, but their screams still echoed in the empty space. Turning to the source of the noise, I was startled to see a dark shadow by the door. It was Thomas. His cordial manner from earlier in the evening had been replaced with a look of drunken anger. I suddenly felt I couldn't breathe again. My body wobbled and before I knew it my legs gave out beneath me. The last thing I remember was crumbling to the floor as Thomas entered the room. Before I lost consciousness, I saw his reflection change from a man in his forties to that of a corpse as a cloud passed over the light of the moon. His face in the mirrors was riddled with worm holes and his hands nothing more than skeletal remains as he made his way towards me in a confident gait.

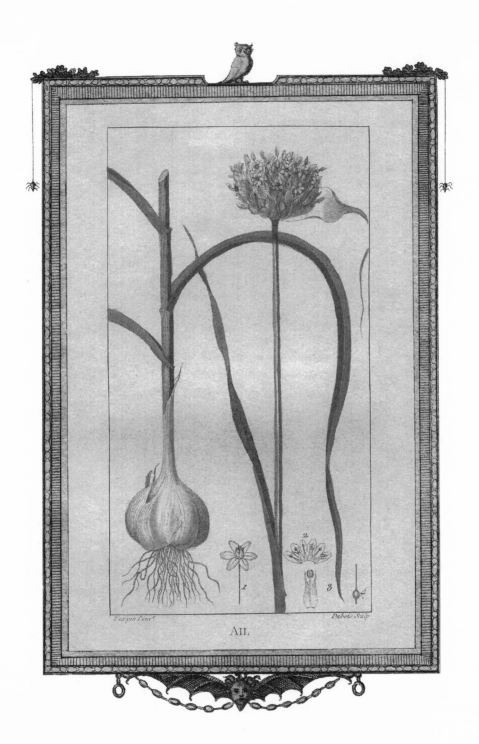

AIL.

CHAPTER 24

The blood was pounding in my ears as I regained consciousness. James was holding me in his arms on the floor. I focused my eyes on his concerned face rather than looking at Sophie and Thomas who were standing overhead. I was terrified that I would see their true image in the mirrors again. It would be unwise to run screaming from their house like a mad woman, though I could barely trust myself not to do just that. I had seen many things over the years that others couldn't, but this was different. I was having a difficult time fighting off their darkness. I felt embarrassed by the fact that I'd fainted, but part of me knew it was a psychic attack by Thomas. While I thought I was holding my own at dinner, in all honesty I hadn't been prepared for this in the least.

"I came in the wrong door and then I felt really dizzy," I said to James.

"This is not the powder room," Thomas said in a tone filled with contempt.

"I opened the wrong door and found myself in here," I answered in a soft voice so as not to anger him further. He was standing between me and the only exit. "This room is so beautiful," I added lamely, hoping the compliment would lighten his mood. Thomas turned and abruptly left the room as James helped me to my wobbly legs. Sophie gave me a slight sneer when James wasn't looking, then her features smoothed into a fake smile as she offered to get me a glass of water. As I walked back to the door, with James holding my elbow and Sophie leading the way, I glanced behind me. On the opposite side of the room stood Magdalene Winship looking at me from the inside of one of the many mirrors. Her eyes found mine for a mere second and she motioned to the corner of the mirrored panel. I had no idea what she wanted to show me but I memorized the room and where her mirror was. I knew I would be back here soon enough for the Masquerade Ball when I could hopefully get a better look.

We followed Sophie back to the dining room and I sat dutifully in my chair. Being here felt unbearable. Sophie brought me a glass of ice cool water. I drank it down with unladylike gulps hoping it would help get my equilibrium back. There was no way I was going to touch the wine again tonight. Slowly my head cleared as everyone finished their food. I had barely touched the duck and nibbled a few bites of the potatoes hoping that would mask how little I'd been able to swallow. Thomas kept filling his glass and with each wetting of his lips his bravado expanded. I listened as he bragged about all the places they had lived and how much their knowledge had helped shape the world. Maybe part of the reason I couldn't eat was because the conversation was making me nauseous. James listened and politely asked questions although I could tell he was concerned about how I was feeling.

After the main course came a platter of perfectly arranged cheeses served with bread. I allowed myself to enjoy the familiar tastes and the soothing effect that the bread had on my stomach. When we reached the dessert course, Thomas was so drunk his cheeks were a vibrant red and he was barely able to speak without a slur. Sophie chose not to notice and instead brought out a warm peach pie. Again the sweet fruit smell made the room begin to shift. Shadows flashed in the various mirrors on the walls, revealing the children I had seen in the ballroom reflected in glimpses.

"So Charlotte, tell me more about you and your family of witches?" Thomas burst out with a condescending chuckle.

"We have traditions in my family, that's all," I said, wanting to be as vague as possible.

"That is not what Willa told Daniel," Sophie chimed in as she handed out small dessert dishes and clean forks. "He told us that you all have special gifts, although Willa said they must have skipped her."

"Our gifts give us a slightly different perspective on this world, but they have more to do with our way of doing things." I felt furious that she was implying that either Willa was fabricating stories or I was not being honest. If she expected me to come out and tell her to her desiccated vampire face that we were a family of witches, then she was going to be very disappointed. In my gut I would have liked to have flung a zinger at her, a hex of the sort that would have left her reeling, but I had my doubts it would work. It would most likely just backfire and leave me feeling worse than I already did.

"And what kind of quaint traditions do you practice?" she asked, preparing to cut the pie into slices.

"We watch out for our own," was all I could manage. As she slipped the knife into the center of the pie I stifled a gasp as the pastry oozed what looked to be blood. I had no idea what kind of peaches she had used but the inside of the pie was a bubbling mess of coagulating gore. The smell was again stifling and I had to refuse my piece. I made up a ridiculous excuse about watching my sugar intake, even though James knew perfectly well that I was known to munch on an apple fritter most afternoons.

"So what is your gift?" she asked as she began to nibble on a slice of peach. James and Thomas had finished theirs and were on to seconds. I had rarely seen James eat so much in one sitting. If I hadn't known better I would have thought he was starving the way he devoured everything on his plate.

"I communicate with people who are stuck in-between worlds," I finally said, feeling fed up. All she had to do was ask around town and she would know this, although my children's gifts had been kept to the family and a few close friends. No one knew that Willa was empathic or that Felix had premonitions unless they were part of the family or were an honorary Winship. She gave me a feline smile and in that moment I knew she had already asked around town about me.

"How odd that you think you can talk to the dead. I don't believe in that sort of thing," she said with such nonchalance that even James was taken slightly aback.

"I have to say that I, too, was a skeptic until I met Charlotte and her family. While I'm still outside of that circle, I know they have abilities that defy explanation," James said coming to my defense.

"Thomas and I think that believing in superstitions only holds a person back from finding their own success. If a person is always looking for fate or destiny to decide things for them, they never take what they want to get ahead," she said, eating the last of her bloody pie.

"I think we see the purpose of life in a very different way," I said, hoping I could get out of this house in the next few minutes. My head was throbbing and the dizziness was becoming a serious problem again. "I don't think this world is a playground with children grabbing for the best toys. We have lessons to learn and a purpose to serve and much of that includes being aware of the little signs that lead us to people and places. It is a journey of the soul, not just the senses."

"I guess we will have to agree to disagree on this one, although I would love to test your little gifts one day," she said, in a condescending tone. I wanted to throw the rest of the pie at her. Instead I slipped my hand onto James' knee and gave him a look of despair which was not in any way feigned.

"Thomas, Sophie, we should probably head home and make sure that Felix is in bed and Willa is home as well," he said, knowing that time was up.

"Yes, I believe that Willa, Daniel, Lily and Aaron all went to the movies tonight," Thomas said in a voice that was louder than usual. It would have been comical if I wasn't so deeply disturbed by both of them. We made sure to give them a tedious amount of thanks and compliments for the meal. I could hardly wait to get out of the house. It felt as if the walls of the hallway to the front door were closing in on me. I had never suffered from claustrophobia before, but I kept feeling as if I was about to be buried alive. I kept my composure, for James' sake, but the moment we were out the front door it took all of my strength not to run for the car.

We thanked them again and I was to my side of the car so fast that I had to wait for James to walk the ten feet to the circular driveway to open my door. In the moonlight, Thomas and Sophie stood side by side on the front porch. There was a rumble of thunder that sounded from above. I thought for a moment that I caught a glimpse of them looking up nervously at the sky before heading inside.

Once in the car, my body began to tremble uncontrollably. My head felt like someone was hammering nails into it. I leaned back in my seat and James began to caress my head. It was obvious that I was having a physical reaction to being in the Renards' home, but I didn't know how to explain it to him.

"James, I'm going to be sick. Let's get home fast, ok?" I said in a weak voice. He started the engine and sped down the long driveway with an urgency I had rarely seen. The peach blossoms were still snowing down. Another rumble was heard in the sky and soon a torrent of raindrops fell from above. With each drop the petals fell and began to stick to the windshield.

The next thing I knew James was carrying me inside of our house. I awoke when he laid me on our bed, but moments later I was on my knees in the bathroom vomiting the little food I'd managed to swallow. I shivered with fever as currents of hot and cold shot through my body. The smell of peaches was still everywhere. I reached up and splashed some of Elsiba's lilac potion on my neck but it wasn't enough to counterbalance what I'd ingested in the vampires' lair. James ran a cold bath for me hoping to break the heat coming off of my skin in waves. I heard Felix's worried voice in the hall as James promised to come sit with him and read before bed as soon as he finished helping me. Willa wasn't home yet and while my worry for her was beyond anything for myself, I simply could not pull myself off of the cool bathroom floor tiles.

The bath only left me with chattering teeth. James carried me to bed and in my feverish delirium I made him promise to find Willa and bring her home. Somewhere on the edge of the fever I was beginning to ramble. The sickness had taken hold and before I knew it, I was telling James that the Renards were vampires. I tried desperately to put the words into the right order but it became a jumble of ravings that James would never take seriously. Eventually exhaustion took over and I fell into a feverish sleep. James slept in the guest room to give me the whole bed. I shook and vomited through the night as the rain pounded against our bedroom windows. Sometime in the early morning hours I was sure that at least fifteen children were standing in my bedroom watching over me. Eve and Colette whispered about the fever never taking adults but with worry in their voices none the less.

By morning, I could not move an inch of my body without pain slicing through my head. James called my employee Jasmine and she happily agreed to open and close my store the next day. One day turned into a week. Margot came to care for me during the day as James was working late into the evenings on the Renard projects. She wiped my forehead with cool towels and made sure the children were fed and off to school. I told her all I could recall of the night at the Renard house. She took the information in bit by bit, but insisted that I rest. Gavin came by in the afternoons before heading to work.

He sat on the end of the bed telling me all the local gossip about the Renards. Sadly, none of it was groundbreaking. He tried to cheer me up by telling me all the ways to kill a vampire. I asked if death by peach pie attack was a possibility and he said we should give it try. I didn't tell him that the first night I had been sick I had vomited whole peach pits even though I hadn't even touched her cursed pie. Or was that just part of the fever?

Willa and Felix peeked in on me before and after school but Margot herded them out of the room. The worst of the fever broke on the third day when the doctor made a house call and set up a drip IV. I was severely dehydrated. I was still in the throes of the fever and imagined that he was getting ready to bleed me. I was sure he was about to set leeches up my arms and legs to clean my blood. Had they done this to Magdalene when she fell ill? Maybe even in this very room? When James came home at night his face looked drawn and weary. He was worried and exhausted from my being ill and his own work. He kissed my head and held me as he told me about the progress he was making. I wanted to hear as much as I could about the Renards but he seemed reluctant to encourage any of what he assumed were my feverish fantasies.

One the fourth day, Morgan and Astrid brought me the remedy that would set things right. While the fever had waned, I was still completely incapacitated. Morgan was at my side with a tea to drink while Astrid washed my feet with a poultice made from specific herbs and flowers. The smell of peaches began to fade as they worked on me. Morgan spoke words aloud in a language I didn't recognize. He set up amulets at the four corners of the bed and tied a blood red ribbon onto my wrist without the IV. As Morgan cast his spell, I thought I spied Felix peeking around the corner of the bedroom door. He was a curious little boy. But he was gone before I could call to him. Morgan's spell and Astrid's herbs did the trick. By the sixth day I was sitting up in bed talking to Kat on the phone and helping Felix with his math homework. I was still too weak to be at my store or out of bed more than a few minutes at a time, but my mind was clear again. The nightmarish feeling of fever was gone and I was sure that whatever Morgan had done it had worked miraculously.

By the seventh day I was able to walk downstairs and fix myself meals. Margot was still coming over every day to make sure that I rested. The thing that shocked me the most was that during my illness, Willa had changed drastically. It was as if overnight she had become suddenly withdrawn in a way she had never been before. She rarely left her room. Her eyes had dark circles under them and I doubted it was from sleepless nights worrying about me. Her skin had become almost translucent it was so pale. And worst of all, she was with Daniel constantly. I saw them sitting in the garden under the willow tree talking until the light faded from the sky. The weather was vacillating between heat and pouring rain. When the sky clouded over they sat together in the front parlor. She rarely saw Lily anymore despite the fact that Kat had told me Lily had invited her over for dinner three times during the week.

Daniel and Willa had become inseparable. If she was laughing and smiling then I would have had less reason to worry, but instead she looked drained. Her body was losing its color and her grades had started to suffer. She stopped going to her afterschool activities and instead spent time with him. I saw him watching her movements, as if memorizing every detail. It was as if she could barely move without him being only a step away. James was too busy with work to notice, but Margot had done her best to put a wedge between them every chance she got.

The Saint Patrick's Dance was only a few days away and I felt a deep dread every time I thought of Willa being there with Daniel. Would they sneak off to North Beach to park so he could latch on to her in an even more insidious way? Even though Lily and Aaron were picking them up and they were going to the dance together, I knew that Willa was in terrible danger. The night heron's nest was getting bigger each day and I heard its wings flapping in the night by my window. I was almost back to myself now that the fever had drifted away and I felt my protective amulets buzzing around me. The one thing that terrified me about the Renards was not that they had been powerful enough to land me in bed for a week but rather that they could succeed in destroying my daughter Willa. She was my joy, my light, and to see her fading into a shadow made me even more determined to protect her. It was time to get myself up and back into fighting shape. The Renards had knocked me down, but they hadn't even come close to knocking me out.

LE LOUP ET L'AGNEAU . Fable X .

CHAPTER 25

My first day back at work after being ill was exhausting. It's amazing how little things pile up in such a short amount of time. There were phone calls to return, orders to ship, bills to pay and of course new customers to wait on. By the end of the day I could barely drag myself home. James was working late again as construction was wrapping up on the Bell Tower House. The St. Patrick's Day Dance and the Renards' Masquerade Ball were only two days away. James was putting the finishing touches on the inside of the house. Restoration to the outside would continue throughout the summer. My skin crawled at the thought of him inside of that building alone with the Renards. Thinking of them brought the overpowering smell of peaches into the room, making me gag. I locked the front door of my shop and headed to my car.

The days had been fluctuating between stifling heat under grey skies to downpours that rumbled into town on thunder clouds. Today it had been unusually humid, making me feel my fatigue more acutely. As I pulled into the driveway I noticed the parlor light was on, which meant that Willa was home and Daniel was most likely with her. He was always with her now. When they finally parted company in the evening, she would proceed to text him the rest of the night. The odd thing was that at first he had seemed quite dull to my eyes. He was around 5'10", had a strong jaw and high cheek bones. His blue eyes were a striking contrast to his dark hair and yet there seemed to be very little behind them. He was without a doubt a handsome young man, but the spark that made Willa so irresistible to others was nowhere to be found in him. That is until about a week ago.

I began to notice that as Willa started to fade Daniel became more lustrous. She was becoming more reclusive and he began to have a bit of a shine to his usually dull aura. As I walked in the front door I found them both on the sofa in the parlor. Daniel had his head on Willa's lap as she caressed his hair with one hand and looked at her phone with the other. He had his boots hanging over the edge of the sofa which instantly irritated me. Despite the formal manner in which his parents conducted themselves, Daniel seemed to be as informal as any teenager I knew. He made no attempts to charm either James or myself and instead made himself very comfortable in our house; far too comfortable for my taste.

The front door slammed shut behind me as a bit of wind caught it. Daniel barely moved an inch. Willa slowly tore her eyes away from her phone to look over at me. Her hair was in a long braid that fell delicately over her shoulder. The wisps of loose hair that framed her face proved that she had most likely slept in the braid and gone to school without bothering to do her hair. A few weeks earlier it would have been unthinkable for her to do such a thing. She wasn't prissy but had always been particular about her clothing and appearance. Her skin was pale and there were dark bruise like shadows under her eyes. She also looked thinner in her favorite jeans. In my eyes she was a little lamb pinned in place by a salivating wolf. I took this all in as I was taking off my shoes by the front door. It was only six o'clock but I wanted to find an excuse to get him out of my house and away from Willa immediately.

"Hello Daniel, I think it is time for you to get home. Willa and I need to discuss a few family issues," I said, thinking this was enough to get him to leave. It was after all my house. He looked me dead in the eye and then glanced up at Willa waiting for her to respond. It was an odd gesture to not even make a motion to leave but to instead look to Willa to deal with the situation. She flinched slightly when he looked at her, as if he'd struck her, though he hadn't moved a muscle.

"Oh, well we had some homework to do together," she said weakly. I knew it was a lie.

"It will have to wait until tomorrow, Willa. Daniel it is time for you to leave," I said firmly, standing my ground. He made no effort to respond to me and continued to look up at Willa, his head still on her lap. She fidgeted nervously with her phone while chewing on the side of her pale lip.

"Mom, I really need Daniel to stay and help me with this math homework I'm having trouble with," she said in a tone slightly higher than normal.

"Daniel, get up please," I said making my way into the parlor. "I need you to leave. Willa will see you at school tomorrow. Your Great Uncle Morgan is coming over and he will help you with your math." Willa looked horrified and exhausted all in the same moment. I could feel the anger welling up inside of me. My fingers were itching with electricity as I began to gather energy into my core. Daniel casually swung his legs off the end of the couch. He smoothed his hands through his hair taking his time to stand. He was still looking at Willa while ignoring me entirely. That was when I noticed that Willa looked not only exhausted but also frightened. Was she frightened of him, I wondered? I began to envision him encased in metal. It was a trick that my mother had taught me ages ago when there was a dark presence I wanted out of my personal space.

The moment I began to mentally wrap the metal around him, binding his energy inward, his eyes shot up to meet mine. In that second of connection he gave me a tiny sneer that made him appear even more the part of the wolf. If Willa hadn't been there I would have sneered right back at him. Instead I gave him a cool look while making a sweeping gesture towards the front door. He stood up stretching his arms into the air in an effort to make himself both imposing as well as imply his unhurried manner. I would have liked to pull the rug out from under him and in doing so wipe the superior look off of his face. Instead, I watched as he took Willa in his arms and whispered something in her ear before kissing her on the mouth. I shuddered at his closeness to her. She looked so frail next to him and as he released her arm I also noticed dark shadows on her skin. They were bruises in the exact shape of his fingers. He brushed past me and let himself out the front door.

Willa collapsed back onto the couch. She looked completely drained of energy. I moved into the room and sat in the large armchair next to her. I didn't know where to start, but it was time she knew what Daniel was and how to protect herself. It wasn't every day I had to tell my child her boyfriend was a vampire. This was definitely not a subject covered in any parenting handbook I'd ever read! She curled up into a little ball, her cream colored cotton shirt made her look all the more like a lamb. The thought of the lamb brought to slaughter flashed through my mind. I shook the image away and leaned over to smooth the wisps of her hair from her pale forehead. This was a gesture I had repeated from the time she was just a toddler with her wild auburn ringlets always in disarray.

"Willa, I'm worried you're spending too much time with Daniel," I said, hoping she would listen before rushing to his defense. "You never seem to want to see Lily any more, and your schoolwork is sliding. Is there anything I can do to help?"

"Mom, just leave us alone," she said with a sigh as she rested her head on a throw pillow. "I like spending time with Daniel and he needs me. He hates going home because his Dad is always screaming at him to make something of himself and his Mom is so superficial. Without me, he says he'll just fade away." I couldn't disagree that the Renards were insufferable, but that didn't mean I wanted him spending so much time with Willa.

"I know it must be hard for him, but you need to have time to do the things that are important to you," I said, hoping that my calm tone wouldn't irritate her. She squirmed a bit but didn't put up a fight. "There is something else I need to tell you about Daniel and his family." My voice trailed off a bit as I tried to find the right words.
"I don't know if you've noticed some of the strange things that have been happening around town since they moved here, but there is something unnatural about them." Willa raised her eyes to me revealing her curiosity at my choice of words.

"Like what?" she asked with a hint of skepticism.

"I think they may be some sort of vampire." The moment the words left my lips I could hear how crazy they sounded. She looked at me with an incredulous stare followed by a huff that proved I had gone too far, too fast in trying to explain. "I know it sounds bizarre but I have my reasons for thinking this is true. Please trust me, Willa, when I tell you that the Renards are in this town for unscrupulous reasons. I don't want you to become one of their victims."

"Mom, did your fever come back or something?" She asked in a sarcastic tone. She was sitting up on the couch with an irritated stance. "That is absurd!"

"Please, Willa, trust that I have my reasons for thinking this and it is just a matter of time before things start getting dangerous for people in town. I cannot let you get hurt," I pleaded, trying to explain. But each time she cut me off before I could start.

"Look Mom, I know you're convinced that you can see and talk to ghosts and that Margot can control the weather and that Felix has premonitions, but this is just taking everything too far. There is no such thing as vampires and my boyfriend and his family have nothing supernatural about them. Stop trying to control me!"

A lump had formed in my throat. She had gone straight to the heart of my insecurities. I knew that the Winship gifts were more than just folklore or superstition, but to think my own daughter doubted these things made me feel vulnerable to the extreme. Her own gift was a subtle one unlike mine or Felix's, but it was a powerful gift none the less. She could take on the emotions of one person or a whole room if she needed to, but in this moment her emotions and Daniel's had merged into one. Could she make out her own feelings from his? What must it feel like for an empathic to be in the presence of a person who has no soul? I had a feeling she couldn't discern her feelings from his void. It was overwhelming for her as he sucked her dry of every ounce of her light. Just as I was about to tell her in detail about the discoveries I had made, a small drop of blood appeared under her nose. A few seconds later it began to gush from her right nostril. She quickly lay down with the throw pillow under her neck as I ran to the bathroom to find a box of tissues.

There had been many times as a small child when her emotional strain translated itself into a physical ailment. It was often a nosebleed that would prove she was overwhelmed. But she had grown out of it over the years as she learned to control her gift instinctively and with coaching from Morgan. The shock of seeing the blood pouring from her fragile body again left me feeling panicked.

The blood was streaming down her face into her cupped hand by the time I came back with the tissues. I sat on the floor positioning myself next to her head to wipe the blood away as she closed her eyes. She was so frail, her vitality oozing from her in vibrant red. Willa's face was a pale grey by the time the bleeding stopped twenty minutes later.

While I wanted to continue our conversation, I knew that now was not the time. She slowly made her way up to her turret bedroom after allowing me to give her a one-sided hug. Each footstep sounded as if she was dragging her way upstairs. My heart sunk to the bottom of my stomach.

I sat on the floor unable to move for what seemed like an eternity, the pile of blood-stained tissues next to me. This was her blood, but it felt like my own in a way so visceral that it was beyond explanation. Willa was my child and this was our connection. This was her precious life's blood being drained from her by a man who was no more human than a black hole. The dark marks on her arms were reminders of her blood coming to the surface of her skin through violence; be it psychic or physical. Just as I was about to let myself sob with frustration and anger at feeling unable to protect her, a firm knock sounded on the front door three times.

It was Morgan's familiar rap-tap-tap that always felt touched with a hint of sarcasm. A chirpy knock from such a surly character made me feel a sudden surge of hope. I scrambled from the floor and headed straight for the door. Seeing his familiar outline behind the stained glass window reminded me in an instant that I was not alone fighting this darkness. I might not be a vampire, but I was most certainly part of a powerful family of witches and if anyone could stop the Renards, it would be the Winships.

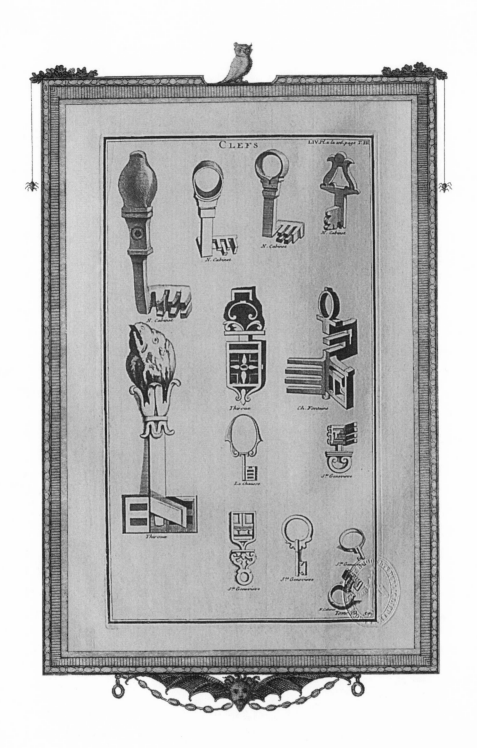

CLEFS

CHAPTER 26

Morgan sat in the parlor with a grim look on his face as I told him about my worries for Willa. The light was fading outside, casting the final rays of sun across the dusty room. As he listened to my every word, I noticed the little flecks of dust that glittered with a red illumination cast by the setting sun. Morgan leaned in as I finished with the most recent episode of Willa's nosebleed. I imagined the gears clicking in his mind as he put all the pieces into place in the hope that a solution would present itself. I held my breath waiting for him to speak hoping he would have a miraculous idea of how to stop the Renards.

"It's almost softball season, right?" he asked and I released my breath with a huff of exasperation. These were not the words I'd been anticipating.

"I guess?" I said feeling more than a bit annoyed.

"Doesn't Willa start next week?" he said, I nodded my head that she did.

"Well, that's one of the ways we can keep him from her," he said although we both knew it wouldn't be enough.

"It's a few hours a day for practice and she'll be busy with games on most weekends." We both knew this would be only a small respite from Daniel's presence. "But it isn't enough to sever whatever connection he has made with her," I said.

"I know," he said in a matter-of-fact voice and then added to my horror, "She has fallen in love with him." My throat tightened. I could see it happening but I didn't want to admit it. Those feelings of first love can be all-consuming, whether they are with a vampire or not. Mine had been with James and I had never fully recovered from that first euphoria. I knew well enough that at fifteen the feelings were even more intense with the raw emotion of adolescence.

"What else can I do?" I croaked.

"What about Lily? Is she coming over at all? Are they having their own time together or is he always there?" he asked, although I think he already knew the answer to his question.

"Maybe Kat and I can plan some things for Willa and Lily to do together with us. I've never known her to turn down a shopping trip to Seattle," I said with a limp smile.

"It will be a start until we can figure out how to cast the Renards out of town," he said, leaning back in the leather chair as the last glimmer of sun fell from the sky. A far off rumble sounded in the air above and I could almost feel the dark clouds rolling back in with evening's approach. I had hoped for a magical solution. Or something that could act as a repellent to keep Daniel from getting closer to Willa. He read the disappointment on my face.

"She has free will, Charlotte. We can't force her to give him up," he said with a seriousness that made me question if his words were entirely true. If so, then how had Daniel gotten his hooks into her so deep, so fast? It wasn't just his good looks and dull personality that had won her over. Some dark magic had entangled her in its web. He was the lurking spider and she was his helpless butterfly waiting to be devoured.

"You know that isn't entirely true," I said and remembered that I wasn't talking to just another member of the family but rather the one member who had considerable expertise in dark magic. His years with his own dark entity had taken him to murky places I could not entirely comprehend. And while his life had changed considerably in the past fifteen years, he still carried the residual burden from the dark days. The entity had whispered plenty of lies in his ears, but it had peppered them with truths about how to ensnare people for his own uses. I knew that he had fought it, but there had been times when he had been tempted by the allure of power. To bind a person from doing harm is one thing, but to manipulate them to further your own ends or existence is another. Morgan sat silent for a moment. I could tell he was measuring the words he was about to speak. He was weighing their purpose before speaking to me.

"There is something that I remembered from days long gone by," he said in a near whisper. "If you really want to drain someone of their energy and use it to increase your own, there are only a few ways it will work in the long term. If the Renards are energy vampires then their energy will need a conduit so it doesn't drain or fade completely. For a dark sorcerer to do this, there needs to be some type of an effigy to hold the spell. Sort of like a reverse voodoo doll that moves the energy from the victim into the sorcerer. These effigies can hold energy for years until it's time to refill them with new victims."

His words hung in the air like the little flecks of dust that swirled around us. I heard him swallow, waiting for me to acknowledge what he had said. We rarely spoke of his darker days. He was tinged with guilt and embarrassment even though he had been a victim of the entity.

"Tell me more about this reverse voodoo doll," I said, as the room grew darker with shadows. I turned on a small table lamp now that the world outside had gone black. Even that small luminescence couldn't chase the peculiar feeling that always came when we spoke of evil. When a witch speaks of evil aloud, it attracts dark creatures. They hover in corners hoping desperately to be allowed in. They want to be given the power they seek to use for more dark deeds. I felt them near as Morgan continued in a close whisper.

"There was one book that escaped the fire of my first home," he said, fixing me with pleading eyes. "It wouldn't burn. Nothing could destroy it and every time I tried to get rid of it, it came back. I threw it in the ocean but it washed back ashore a few days later. The surf brought it right to my feet. I tried to magically destroy it but fell ill with every attempt. I eventually put it on a shelf and tried to forget about it. But today as I walked into my study, it fell off the shelf and landed at my feet with a page open to vampirism."

My eyes were as round as silver dollars as I listened to him. I loathed the scuttling darkness that crept into every inch of the room. Evil things were salivating in the corners. I felt their excitement at the words Morgan was uttering. They knew we were the beings who could make things happen if we were seduced into their world. Morgan's eyes were still on mine. I knew he sensed them as well.

"There are many ways to become a vampire. Sanguine vampires are the most loathsome to the sorcerer. It is far too base a concept for anyone who uses dark ways with any type of elegance." I knew he was speaking of himself when he said these words. He had a brilliant mind and with it came a need to make his magic refined. The Renards carried themselves with a certain panache that couldn't be ignored, which meant they were most certainly not sanguine vampires.

"I know they aren't after blood in the common sense," I said wanting him to continue.

"The blood is for the revenant. But the energy or soul of one person can have a tremendous amount of power. If a sorcerer can syphon the energy from another living being into his own person at regular or long lasting intervals, he can essentially live forever. His soul will slowly decay not having been meant to live beyond one lifetime, but the body can keep regenerating."

He sat back as I took in his words. I had nearly figured this much out already, but to have it confirmed felt both gratifying and sickening at the same time.

"So whatever effigy or doll they create holds the energy for them so they can live eternally. The souls are trapped inside of the doll?" I asked, wanting to make sure I came to the right conclusions.

"The dolls need to stay near where the bodies are buried. Then the vampires can move freely until the energy source begins to wane and they have to come back and refill the dolls with new souls. I think the Renards took 130 children's souls in Port Townsend one hundred years ago and they are back to do the same thing again before moving on." A cold chill ran through the room as the dark entities buzzed with excitement.

"What happens if *we* get the dolls?" I asked, feeling a rush of hope and dread combined into one sickening emotion.

"If we can find the dolls, we can set the souls free with a pretty simple unbinding fire and remove one of their energy sources. But I doubt this will actually kill them. If I was the Renards, I'd have different energy sources all over the world. Essentially so all my eggs weren't in one basket," he said with a dark smirk that turned quickly into a look of sadness. The mention of eggs reminded me of the night heron building its new nest in the willow tree.

"So we could get them out of town, but they would just move on to another place where they'd set up shop so long ago no one would remember them." My need to protect my family and my town was a primal one. I would start searching this very moment for the cursed dolls, but the thought of them simply leaving to repeat the process somewhere else was unacceptable.

"We need to find a way to end them," I said, a shudder shifting through the room. The dark things were backing away into the walls and out into the night. I would never give in to them or anyone who had gained at the cost of others. My first step would be to find the dolls and I had a feeling they were in one of two places: the Cliffside Chapel or the Bell Tower House. I had to find a way to keep them from harming anyone else.

"I think we both know where those dolls probably are," he said, speaking my thoughts. I nodded and he continued with his usual sarcasm "Well it's not like we can barge in there and start knocking down walls without them noticing."

"No, we can't — but James can," I said, feeling slightly smug until I saw the stern look on Morgan's face.

"He can," Morgan sighed "but will he?" I felt my cheeks redden with his words. Despite the fact that he liked James as a person, Morgan had always been somewhat opposed to my marrying someone who had no real intuitive inclinations. I had promised him that with time I would let James in on more of what it meant to be a Winship, but almost nineteen years later I still could only hint at things. It wasn't that James didn't know, it just felt too hard to explain my dreams or my ghostly visions. I kept things to myself or to those who I knew wouldn't be bothered by them. Namely: my blood family, Gavin and Kat.

"No, he won't," I said in a meek voice. "He likes the Renards. But I can get in there. They are throwing a Masquerade Ball the night of the St. Patrick's Day dance," I said, changing the subject. "I'll be able to snoop while I'm there. If we can weaken them by taking their energy source, then maybe we can find a way to bind them from doing any more harm."

Morgan agreed that this was a logical first step. I had no idea how to proceed once we found the dolls, but I hoped a solution would present itself.

"One more thing, what would this doll look like?" I asked as images of a crude voodoo doll bounced through my head.

"Well, they have to last, so cloth is out of the question. Rats and other critters would destroy them otherwise. The book mentioned certain kinds of wax, but the most powerful element to use is apparently peach wood." Morgan's words brought the sickly sweet smell of peaches into the room. His eyes widened and I knew he smelled them as well. I pictured rows of peach wood dolls. They flashed through my mind like a photograph from another time and place.

We sat in silence for a time as the house creaked with the dropping temperature of early evening. When James' headlights flashed into the driveway, Morgan rose to leave. Felix was at Cody's house overnight and Willa was up in her tower room. I gave him a quick hug and he promised to keep searching for a way to stop the Renards entirely. I watched as his dark outline glided down the front stairs into the night as James came in the back through the kitchen. The familiar sound of rolls of paper plunking on the table and the refrigerator opening reminded me that I should start dinner.

As I made my way into the kitchen, I found James drinking what looked like his second glass of water. He smiled when he saw me as I rushed over to greet him. I stood on my tiptoes to give him a kiss. We lingered that way for a moment until we heard Willa's footsteps on the stairs. Just as I was turning from him to greet her, I noticed the now repugnant smell of peaches wafting up from his shirt collar. It was all over him just as it was Willa. I ran quickly upstairs making a ridiculous excuse of needing to look at a recipe. Instead I doused myself with Elsiba's lilac potion hoping it would rub off on them before it was too late. I had tried to slip the potion into the laundry or dab little droplets on James and Willa while they were sleeping, but the scent never remained. In its place, the perfume of peaches prevailed. Felix had been a willing wearer of the potion, but James and Willa refused, making it impossible to protect them with it. Without their approval; the potion was powerless.

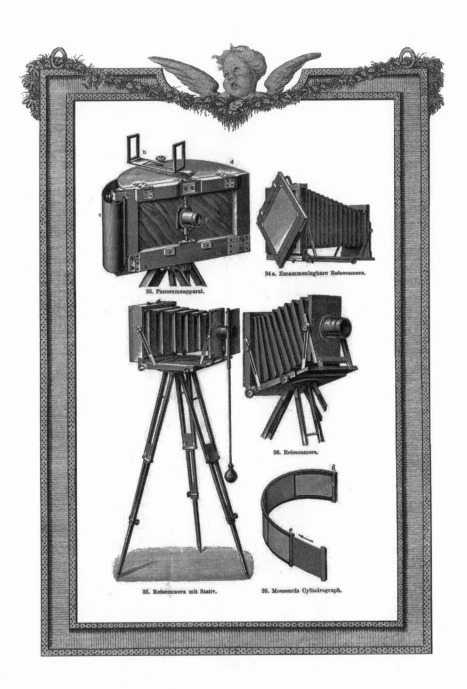

38. Panoramaapparat.

34a. Zusammenlegbare Reisecamera.

36. Reisecamera.

35. Reisecamera mit Stativ.

39. Moessards Cylindrograph.

CHAPTER 27

I spent the next hour listening to James and Willa rave about the Renards while gorging themselves on pasta. They both ate ravenously, like starving animals before a feast. I only half listened to what they were saying and instead began to think of the places I'd hide a sacred doll if I was an energy vampire. After dinner, Willa returned to her room promising to work on homework, but I knew she was texting with Daniel. James continued to work at the kitchen table. He had a hollow look about him even though he had just eaten a considerable amount of food.

Slowly I made my way up to my workroom. The newspapers were still strewn across every surface. The illness had kept me from any further reading about 1912. More children came to me in my dreams as the days passed, signaling the anniversary of their deaths. I began to sort and organize but there were papers in the box I hadn't even put into order yet. As I was shuffling them into date order, the phone gave a shrill ring. I answered, surprised to hear Tom Caldwell's raspy voice on the other end of the line.

"So you got my old journalistic curiosity revved up with this Dennis Morrison character," he said.

"Did you find out more about him?" I asked, giving him my full attention.

"I did indeed, Charlotte," he said, teasingly; he had me hooked on his every word. "I used my best genealogy searching techniques and discovered that he came to the United States from England with his wife not long after the loss of their seven-year-old son. He died of complications from fever. They left quickly thereafter and made their way to Boston."

"What else?" I asked, knowing he was just leading me along.

"Well, he was an avid photographer, as we know, but he had all kinds of strange theories about saving souls in the form of images. He even wrote an essay about it that was published in the Scientific

American magazine. He claimed we didn't understand the full impact of all these modern inventions on the body."

I immediately thought of Morgan's words about an effigy used to contain a soul. Dennis Morrison had taken pictures of the 130 children who had mysteriously died. I spread them out in front of me as Tom continued on. The faces of each child looking straight into the camera and out of the photograph directly at me gave me a sudden chill. The pictures seemed oddly alive. Had Morrison merely captured a candid moment, or had there been other, more sinister intentions behind these photographs? For all I'd heard from Tom, along with the note, Dennis Morrison had been obsessed with vampires. Had he lost his son to one? Had he been trying to become a vampire? One thing didn't fit. He'd sent the pictures away from Port Townsend. If he had wanted to use the photos to funnel energy, he would have needed to keep them near the children's graves. Something still didn't feel right, but I couldn't quite make sense of it. I tuned back in as Tom continued on with his discoveries.

"So it turns out that he and his wife left Port Townsend right as the plague ended. But here is the odd thing: he reappears a few months later in census records, but in Portland, Oregon, except there he had a teenage son and daughter listed as dependents!" he said excitedly.

"Was he still working as a photographer?" I asked, wondering if having completed his energy drain he had moved on to more victims. Or, had he discovered a way to carry souls with him in photographs and didn't need to keep dolls near the grave sites? It all seemed peculiar. The image I'd seen of him looked nothing like Thomas Renard so I wondered how they could be the same family.

"No, he opened a gentleman's club — of all things," he chuckled. "Apparently his wife was a bit of a socialite in Portland, but he catered to a seedier side of the city."

"That is just bizarre," I admitted, feeling like even more elements weren't fitting into place. "Was he in Portland long? Were there any outbreaks of plague at the same time he was there?"

"I'm still searching for more information, but Portland was a much bigger city than Port Townsend. There was a lot of sickness at that time; many people died nameless deaths." I could tell he was hooked on finding out more about this.

"Tom, while you're looking into this, can you also check out any information on the other family that left Port Townsend around the same time? They were the ones who opened The Owls Club and had lived in the Bell Tower House. I can't seem to find any mention of their name in the papers, although they are alluded to constantly." I still had a notion that Dennis Morrison, while he had a connection to this mystery, was not its main source. My gut told me that he was following something and not orchestrating the soul theft. But I needed more information to be sure. There was an eeriness to the photos that was undeniable and the thought that I might have the tools in my hands to destroy the Renards was a seductive one. But in my heart, I knew it was more complicated.

"Will do; and you let me know if you think you have the vampires pegged," he chuckled, then hung up. I had a feeling he'd be up late into the night searching computer databases and contacting old journalist friends across the country. Tom would have been an exceptional detective, but he always said he preferred writing about gore than actually coming face-to-face with it. I grabbed a piece of blank paper from my desk and began to make notes on everything I knew about Dennis Morrison, the nameless family that lived in the Bell Tower House in 1912 and the Renards. I felt they were all connected in some way, and yet nothing fit together. I needed to find out more about this other mysterious family. If Dennis Morrison had moved on to Portland, had this family moved there as well? I also wondered if they weren't both vampires using different means to capture souls. Margot had mentioned that vampires each had their own specific rituals. Could there be a stash of peach tree dolls hidden somewhere by the Renards a hundred years ago, as well as the photos from Dennis Morrison? Were they both vying for the same young victims? Or was Dennis trying to save the children in his own way by capturing a part of them first? If only he could come to me and tell me what was occurring, it would make life easier. I had tried several times to summon him, but like the children in the graveyard, all I felt was a dark void. This either meant he was still living or his soul was somewhere I couldn't reach.

As the evening wore on, and Willa and James both turned off their lights and went to sleep, I continued looking at the notes in front of me hoping an answer would magically present itself. It did not. I finally gave in and climbed into bed next to an exhausted James. He felt cold next to me, unlike the usual warm glow that emanated from his body. The dead children came to me the moment I closed my eyes. Instead of filling my room, they were all through the house now; hiding in closets and scrunching themselves into corners. Eva and Colette sat next to my side of the bed on the floor, playing cat's cradle. Their tiny fingers worked weaving the strings together with a quiet patience. Magdalene was less patient and paced at the end of the bed mumbling to herself about needing a plan. I tried asking her about Dennis Morrison but she just shook her head sadly at the mention of his name. Then I asked her where the dolls were hidden and the entire house went silent. All the ghost children were waiting for her to speak. She froze at the end of my bed as Eva and Colette looked at her with anticipation. Her mouth formed itself into a perfect 'o' but made no sound. Magdalene's hands flew to her neck as if some invisible force was choking her. The panic on her face shifted to anger and she began to scream a high-pitched wail that filled the house, leaving the other children covering their ears. I woke with a start to find the room empty and only the faint hint of Magdalene's scream hovering in the air like an echo.

It was early morning and James was still deep in sleep. His alarm wouldn't go off for another hour. I rose from bed knowing that any further rest would be impossible and headed downstairs to start a much-needed pot of coffee. The sun was beginning to rise, illuminating the rose garden that bordered the kitchen. I stood looking out at the morning dew as the coffee pot gurgled. Needless to say, I was feeling troubled and even the beauty of the morning light on the yellow climbing roses couldn't distract my dark thoughts. I decided to call Kat.

I had known her my entire life and, like Gavin, she was fiercely loyal to me, and to my family. Also, she was an early bird. Gavin and I could stay up until all hours of the night while Kat began to fade by ten o'clock. But when the first tide went out and the sun rose, Kat was awake and chirpy. This was why she took the day shift at the bar while

Gavin preferred to keep things running after she was tucked into bed. I grabbed the phone and sat next to the window with a cup of strong black coffee. Two rings and she answered with a clear voice signaling she had most likely been up for at least an hour.

"Seriously, Kat, how do you do it?" I teased, as I imagined her already showered and with a full face of makeup by 6:00 a.m.

"Lottie, what the hell are you doing up so early?" was her response. She knew I preferred the dark quiet of midnight and the early hours thereafter in contrast to garish sunlight.

"Can't sleep. Listen, I was thinking that since the girls are having their big dance tomorrow night, maybe we could spend the day with them together helping them get ready?" I said hoping she would agree.

"I think that would be great, Lottie. Lily has been feeling a bit cast aside lately with Willa spending her every waking moment with Daniel," she said with more than a hint of worry in her voice.

"Well, I can't say this isn't partially motivated by my concern for Willa's attachment to that boy. Plus, I miss seeing Lily around the house and I hate that Willa is becoming so isolated. Also, there are darker things afoot, Kat," I said, hoping not to scare her. She knew all of my secrets and my families' gifts, but I could tell that sometimes it frightened her to think of not just the beings of light, but also the darker ones that hovered under beds and around corners. I tried to shield her from all things evil, but felt it might be time to let her in on what was happening in town. I told her all that had happened from Felix's initial premonition up to Willa's recent nosebleed. I didn't go into detail about the ways in which I planned to move forward because I wanted to protect her from that aspect of the situation. She didn't need to know the mechanics of it. With every detail she gasped in horror. I knew she would be at the Masquerade Ball the following night and hoped I hadn't ruined it for her. But still, she needed to know what she was walking into when she stepped through the Renards' front door.

"Whatever I can do, Lottie, you know I have your back. Does Gavin know?" she asked, although I had a feeling she knew he did. I always went to Gavin first with these types of dilemmas because nothing ever scared him.

"He does. He's my source for pop culture vampire trivia," I couldn't help but say with a smile. Just yesterday he had emailed me another list of myths about how to kill a vampire, but it was geared towards the sanguine form. Energy vampires, it seemed, had kept a much lower profile over the years, moving in and out of communities with ease. Their best defense was blending in and then introducing an element of sickness to mask their trapping of souls. I was sure the rats were their instruments, their familiars that used disease as a cover.

"Great. So tomorrow, I'll see if Jasmine will watch the shop again. She has been thrilled with the extra days; this will send her over the edge into complete bliss if I'm not careful," I said. The truth was that any extra days I gave to Jasmine not only freed me up, but helped her fill the holes in her budget. A recent divorce had left her with little but an old car in need of fixing and a tiny one-bedroom studio in the downtown area. She worked many evenings at the Waterside Brewery waiting tables, but it still wasn't enough to get out of debt. Her heart was good and she loved our town so it was a blessing for us both.

"I like that idea, Lottie. I've missed you and I need some girl time anyway," she said in her usual sweet voice. "So let's get them ready and then we can pretty ourselves up to go kick some vampire ass at that stupid ball."

"Sounds like a plan. I'll tell Willa this morning and hopefully she won't be too snarky with me. The more ways we can find to get him away from her the better until I can do some of my magic," I said, knowing in my heart the Renards' days in our town were numbered.

"You know Lottie, I couldn't put my figure on it until now, but I've been feeling worried about Willa. The way that Daniel looks at her and watches everything she does reminds me of my ex," Kat's voice trailed off. I knew what she meant. Her ex-husband had been an extremely abusive man. He was charming at first, luring her in with a guise of devotion only to become possessive and jealous to the point of locking her in a closet when she tried to leave him the first time. Needless to say, the Winships stepped in. During the bitterest part of the divorce, when he was fighting for custody of Lily, he suddenly changed his mind and signed papers. This came on the heels of a late night visit from Morgan to his house. I don't know what Morgan said or did, but it helped set Kat free once and for all. There was only the occasional glimmer of his wanting to come back to town, which was handled swiftly in our own way.

"I know, Kat," I said, feeling the weight on my shoulders. Kat still had nightmares about her ex-husband stealing Lily. She had never even considered remarrying after they split. The damage to her trust ran so deep that for many years it was all she could do to get up in the morning and take care of her daughter. I still had my hopes for Kat. There was a soul out there waiting to find her that would treat her with love and kindness. It simply had to be the right moment in time.

"So how about tomorrow at your place around 1:00 p.m.? Maybe we can all have lunch together and then come home to primp?" she said in her usual spunky voice.

"That sounds like a plan," I said, feeling a glimmer of hope in the darkness. After we hung up, I sat at the table drinking my coffee and enjoying the sunrise. James' alarm went off followed by Willa's and soon both were bustling around the kitchen making toast and filling their coffee mugs. I told Willa about our afternoon with Lily and Kat and instead of giving me grief she actually seemed genuinely happy. I told her to let Daniel and Aaron know they could meet them here at the house at 6:00 p.m. so Lily could drive them to the dance together. My mention of Daniel's name made her smile, though my motivation was not to show any acceptance of him. I rather wanted him here to send the three of them, Lily, Willa and Aaron, off with a protection spell.

The rest of the day went by quickly as I made plans for the following afternoon. As I had hoped, Jasmine was thrilled with the prospect of working on Saturday. By the time I closed up shop my mind was spinning with things to get done. As I turned the Open sign to Closed, I got an unexpected phone call from Felix. Margot had just brought him home. His trembling voice triggered an immediate feeling of primal fear.

"Mom," he said, in a tiny eight-year-old voice, "Something really bad happened today." I could tell he was on the verge of tears.

"Are you ok?" I asked in a sudden panic.

"I'm ok. But Cody got bit by that huge rat that was watching us by the school the other day." I froze as his words began to sink in.

"What happened, tell me everything," I said, locking the front door of the shop. I could be home in a few minutes to hear it from him in person but that seemed like far too long to wait. He needed me to hear him now.

"We were leaving school and it ran at us. At first it was heading straight for me and we turned to run back inside but Cody tripped and fell. The rat bit him on his leg and then ran off. It bit through his jeans and his leg was bleeding pretty bad. His Mom took him to the hospital after the school nurse looked at him. But Mom, it stopped and looked at me after it bit him. It was like the rat was trying to decide whether to attack me or run away. That's when one of the teachers came and it took off. It was huge Mom, like the size of a cat." Felix's voice trembled. I reassured him I would be home soon. Margot was staying with him until I could make it back and she would keep him calm and safe. I called Sheila, Cody's mom, to see how he was doing before leaving for home. She said he had instantly fallen ill with fever and was in the hospital on intravenous antibiotics. The doctors could only guess what the rat may have had in its system and Cody's fever had spiked dangerously fast. Sheila's voice was strong, but I heard the worry and fear just below the surface. In my mind, I knew that the vampires had begun to cultivate their new prey. Had Felix been the initial target and Cody had simply gotten in the way? Whatever it was, a son of my town was in immediate danger. I needed to find where the old effigies were being kept before it was too late.

As I hung up with Sheila and was about to turn off the lights, a rap sounded on the shop's glass door. Standing in the fading light was Thomas Renard. He was motioning me over to let him in. My heart was beating rapidly in my chest as I began to gather energy to me. I asked the town ghosts to stand at my side. A swoosh of air sounded as Mario Cabral's grey ghost stationed himself in the corner of the room. I turned the key in the door to let the vampire in.

LE SURMULOT.

Pl. XXVII.

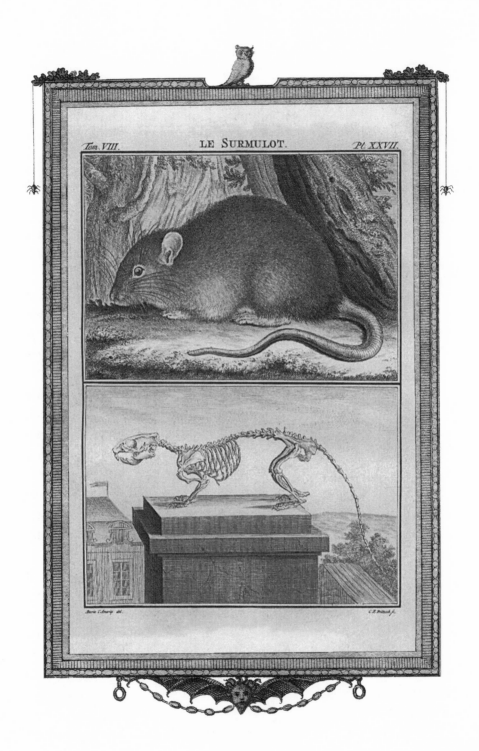

CHAPTER 28

I reluctantly opened the door for Thomas Renard. He was dressed in a casual suit that was still too dressy for our streets. Like Sophie, everything about his appearance was perfectly put together. He looked impeccable and yet, to my eyes, he was a dangerous beast disguised in a man's clothing.

"Charlotte, I'm sorry to bother you, but I couldn't make it over earlier and I would like to buy a piece of jewelry for Sophie for the Masquerade Ball tomorrow night," he said with a repulsive grin.

"I don't know that I would have anything that would be her style," I said, hoping this would dissuade him. Instead he brushed past me into the shop with a proprietary shove. Being in such close proximity to him made my flesh crawl. I just hoped that I could get him out as quickly as possible.

"I have an emergency at home, Thomas. I'm sorry, but I really need to go," I said, still holding the front door open to usher him out. He stood by my jewelry case peering in hungrily. His finger tapped the top of the glass as he pointed to a necklace I had made using a vintage cameo.

"This is the one," he said, looking satisfied with himself while waving me over. "She mentioned it and I thought it would be a nice gift. She has given up so much for me in coming here. A city life with glamorous events, I think I should at least buy her jewelry, no?" Under normal circumstances, I always found it charming when men came in to purchase a love token for their beloved, but this felt like a game. I propped the door open with a wedge as not to lock myself in the shop alone with this man. I moved quickly behind the counter and removed the necklace. It was wrapped before he could fish out his wallet. He threw four, one hundred dollar bills on the counter and told me to keep the change for the inconvenience, which only irritated me more. I gave him back exact change.

"I'm sorry, Thomas, but it is imperative that I leave right now.

There has been an accident," I said, swallowing hard as I thought of Cody in the hospital.

"Oh yes, I heard that Felix was bitten by a rat? Is he alright?" Thomas said in a smooth tone. My head shot up to meet his eyes. He had a phony look of sympathy plastered across his perfect face. It made me want to punch him in his perfect nose.

"Not Felix, his friend Cody," I said in a cool tone. Our eyes locked on one another, unblinking. He looked shifty and then glanced at the counter doing a double take. My eyes followed where he had been looking. It was to the stack of Dennis Morrison's photographs that were still sitting by the checkout stand. I had brought them with me to work to examine more carefully. There was an unmistakable glimmer of recognition in his eye.

"I am so sorry. I hope he recovers quickly," Thomas said with a quick lick of his lips as he glanced back at the photographs. Magdalene's picture was sitting on the top on the stack. "I had heard wrong. How much are these?" he asked, pointing innocently to the photographs.

"They aren't for sale. They are my private collection," I said, protectively gathering them up in my hands. He had a hungry look in his eyes that betrayed his cool demeanor. They shined in a way that made me even more leery than usual. I didn't like the way he was looking at these photographs of the children. If they had been his victims, which I was all but sure they had been, then he still took pleasure in seeing their images. I was sure he was titillated by looking upon his past conquests even in black and white. I instinctively held the photographs to my chest, keeping them close.

"Thomas, I don't mean to be rude, but I need to leave right now which means you have to leave," I said in a firm tone. It brought his eyes back to mine as he gave me a sly smile. His eyes twinkled repulsively as he held the box with the necklace in the air rattling it in one hand.

"Of course," he replied in a casual tone "see you tomorrow night at the party. I am sure Sophie will be wearing this lovely piece." I nodded as he sauntered out the front door. He lingered in the archway for a moment looking back at me and the precious photos with a longing that made me nauseous. Mario, my newest ghost protector, stepped out of the shadows, and for a moment I thought maybe Thomas could see him standing at my side. He waved as he strolled across the street with Sophie's gift in hand. As soon as he was gone, I rushed to the front door locking it quickly so he couldn't come back in. I frantically packed up my things, including the photographs and rushed home. Felix needed me. I had to get home as quickly as possible.

I pulled into the driveway and made a beeline for the back door. The light was on in the kitchen. That was where Margot and Felix always liked to sit whenever she was at the house. Inside, I found Margot making Felix a cup of her tea. He sat in his favorite chair with his elbows propped up on the table and his head in his hands. His tiny face was streaked with tears of worry and he had a slight case of the hiccups. I rushed to him, squatting next to his chair, as he fell over with his head on my shoulder like a rag doll. He had such an adult way of thinking that at times I forgot how small he really was. Eight years on earth is but the blink of an eye.

"Let's go for a walk," I said, knowing the one place that would make him feel better. I hugged Margot and we all left together. She was silent, but I felt her worry overflowing from her old bones. She held Felix in her arms, kissing him once on the top of the head before retreating to her forest home. Felix and I walked side by side in silence. The sky was slowly fading to a cool blue. I pointed up to the sky where the moon was just becoming visible. That was one of Felix's favorite oddities of the heavens, the moon making a daytime appearance. That, and rainbows.

With each step closer to Chetzamokah Park, we could hear the surf rolling back in. It would soon be high tide. The park sat on a short cliff above the beach. It was a beautiful stretch of rolling green grass with rows of swings on one side and winding pathways on the other. There was an eighty-year-old rose arbor that created a tunnel through one side of the park. A Victorian gazebo sat just on the edge of the cliff overlooking the water. The floor of the gazebo was an intricate marquetry design showing the cardinal points of the compass. James and I had said our vows on those very boards, promising to always be each other's North.

Today Felix went straight to his favorite swing. The park was completely empty as dinner time was approaching and people had made their way home. We sat side by side holding the cool chains in our hands, twirling at first. I wanted him to open up when he felt like it. Whenever Felix had been fussy as a small child I would bring him here as the sound of the waves always calmed him. It had slowly become our special place when he was upset with events in his blossoming life or premonitions that bothered his young mind. After about ten minutes of swinging as high as we could, we both let our momentum wane until we were back to twirling again.

"Mom," he said in a pensive voice, "I feel like it should have been me that got bit."

"No one should have been bitten, period," I said hoping this would settle into him as truth.

"It was looking at me, like really staring," he said with a slight tremble to his voice. "And if Cody hadn't tripped it would have got me. It wanted me. I dreamt a few nights ago that rats had dug all kinds of tunnels under the town and they were dragging children into them." Dread washed over me as he spoke. The word tunnel brought to mind the Shanghai tunnels that led from the Bell Tower House to the Cliffside Chapel and down to the Haller Fountain. This would be a perfect place for the Renards to hide the peach wood dolls for safekeeping! No one had explored those tunnels in probably a hundred years. And it was just like a rat to burrow into the dirt and create a filthy nest.

"How about we go and see Cody the day after tomorrow?" I asked, knowing Sheila had said no visitors until the doctors knew what they were dealing with. He silently nodded his head in agreement.

"I'm worried, Mom. I'm worried about Cody, but something bad is happening to Willa and Dad, too," he said, and my throat tightened. The worry in his voice made my heart hurt. He knew enough to see there was something amiss in our home. Willa was fading into nothing and James was preoccupied and distant.

"I won't let anything happen to us. Or to anyone else in town. Morgan and I were talking about it last night and we are finding ways to make everything safe again," I said, hoping I was convincing. I still had no real idea how to banish the Renards while binding their power. Felix's mention of tunnels stuck in my mind. I would find a way to get into them. A plan formed as I listened to Felix. Soon he was worn out, but I could tell he felt a small sense of relief at being able to release his worries to the wind.

"What say we head home and make some dinner for your sister and Dad?" I asked, and he nodded in agreement. "I think vegetable soup will make everyone feel better." He wrinkled his nose at my suggestion which made me laugh. I still hadn't convinced him that green things were delicious. "Pizza?" I asked, feeling like tonight was probably better spent ordering in and maybe watching a movie together. That was of course dependent on whether or not James came home at a decent hour and Willa could be detached from Daniel. It was worth a try.

As we trudged back up the hill to the Winship house the sun was just beginning to fade. Every once in a while there would be a scurrying sound from behind a bush or near a car. I heard faint squeaks coming from the gutter grates. By the time we reached our driveway we were both running for the house. I let him sprint ahead with the key to the kitchen door in his tiny hand. Just as I had stepped into the house, behind Felix, and slammed the door shut, a thud sounded loudly on the other side of the door. A huge rat reeled and then scampered down the back steps. It glared at me with red eyes, as I watched it through the upper window of the door. Felix looked shaken as he sat in his chair with a perplexed look on his face.

I tried my best to reassure him. I ordered our favorite family pizza. I called James at his office to let him know all that had happened with Cody and he promised to try to get home before Felix's bedtime. Willa was with Daniel helping to decorate the school gym for the dance and wouldn't be home until late. When the pizza came, I quickly stepped onto the front porch closing the door behind me so no surly rats could make a quick entry into the house. Finally, we settled on an old black and white movie that we had watched a million times before but that made us both feel better about life. We ate our pizza in the living room, each with our favorite blankets piled over our legs. Felix's teddy bear Max sat between us on the couch, content to watch the TV screen with his glassy bear eyes.

Eventually Felix fell asleep, exhausted from such an emotionally stressful day. I carried him upstairs along with Max. As I tucked him in, I whispered a prayer for him to be watched over by beings of light. As I was leaving his room, his tiny voice sounded sleepily in the darkness.

"Mom," he asked half asleep, "will you make me a cherry pie for dessert?"

"Of course," I whispered, thinking it was an odd request but was most likely part of a dream he was experiencing in half sleep. I heard him sigh as he settled in and I turned on his small owl nightlight.

Back downstairs my own worry set in as the night dragged on and all the unnatural events of the day played over and over in my mind. The garden seemed alive with red eyes flitting on the ground and the caw of the night heron. Tomorrow night was the St. Patrick's Day Dance and the Masquerade Ball. I had a sinking feeling that something horrible was about to happen.

CERISIER.

Chapter 29

The day of the St. Patrick's Day dance began with a whirlwind of activity in the Winship house. I got up early for the second day in a row. Feeling a growing uneasiness at the coming events, I used the early morning hours to bake a cherry pie. It was James' favorite when we were first dating. Margot canned sour red cherries every year from Annie Christy's ancient trees. I had eight jars left of the tart berries that made the sweetest pies imaginable. As everyone slept, I rolled out the pie crust the way my mother had taught me. She was a master fruit pie maker. Willa and I loved her strawberry/rhubarb pie with its bittersweet succulence. What made it especially wonderful was the fruits came from her magnificent garden.

As I pinched the edges of the dough around the porcelain dish, I felt a longing to have Deidre here with me. She was off on her adventures with Samir. I adored that she was following her dreams, but I needed her now more than ever. I hadn't been able to talk with her since the arrival of the Renards. I wanted to tell her about the vampire situation in all its complexity. For some cosmic reason, we kept missing each other's calls. Deidre and Samir had promised to make a trip home at the end of summer to check on us all. Then they would fly back to Bora Bora for another year of research. I just hoped she would find us all alive and well. I poured the dark red cherries into the crust after mixing in sugar and other secret ingredients. I then covered it with a second round of dough and cut out tiny stars to allow the steam to escape as it cooked. As it went into the oven, I sat looking out at the morning sky.

I sipped my coffee not realizing anything was amiss. It took my brain several seconds to catch up with what my eyes were seeing. Then it hit me. The lilac bushes had died overnight. There were at least twenty large holes at their roots. The flowers were in a tragic state of withered brown. I frantically pressed my hands against the window; Margot's roses were all drooping. The ground was covered with a massacre of petals and leaves. The only thing left standing tall was the willow tree. I felt panic strike me, not for the loss of the flowers, but for what it symbolized. Death had come to the living elements we used to protect ourselves with our natural magic.

I didn't notice James until he was standing right behind me. The smell of the pie baking had most likely lured him downstairs. He wrapped his arms around my waist and then froze as he, too, saw the overnight destruction of the garden.

"What happened out there?" he said in amazement as he pressed himself close to the glass. I swallowed hard, not wanting to come out and say that vampires were messing with us. There had to be a better lead-in or he would think I had lost my mind.

"I think we have a rat problem," I said, pointing to the holes. His brow furrowed as he tried to make out the placement of each of the entrance points to the large tunnels.

"It could be gophers, those look too big for rats," he said, moving away from the window to pour himself a cup of coffee.

"No, it's rats," I said emphatically, which caused him to lift an eyebrow. "I saw them last night when Felix and I came home. One tried to get in the house as we came in the back door."

"I'll put out some traps today before I go to the office," he said, as if that would be the ultimate solution to a very nasty problem. I couldn't think of any way to tell him that the tunnels were more than just a simple rodent issue. I swallowed my coffee trying to ignore the wave of dread that had come over me. My home was a sacred place to both me and my ancestors. To have it infiltrated by carriers of pestilence and evil made me feel violated. I stared at the disaster that had been my garden in disbelief.

Soon the kitchen was buzzing with noise as Willa and Felix joined us. Both James and Felix kept crouching down in front of the oven's glass door to see the progress of the cherry pie. It had been awhile since I'd taken the time to bake anything for my family. I could barely keep James from scalding his fingers when it came out of the oven to rest for fifteen minutes. It wasn't our usual breakfast meal, but for some reason it felt right to have something slightly decadent in the midst of all the turmoil. I cut everyone a slice and James ate his so fast he was already serving himself seconds before I sat down to my slice. Willa daintily slipped an errant cherry into her mouth with a sigh of delight. Felix did his happy dance by his chair before digging in and I was content to watch them all before I tasted it myself. With each bite the color came back into Willa and James. Suddenly, the light that had been fading inside of them shone brightly. Willa's cheeks had a sudden rosiness where there had been a grey pallor. James was in the throes of ecstasy as he licked the juice from his plate. Felix immediately followed his example. I had a moment of joy seeing them look themselves again, despite what was waiting outside our doorstep.

Even though the moment was fleeting, soon plates were in the sink. I felt I'd given them all a boost of much-needed energy with this small delicacy. James kissed me as he left for work. I heard him fumbling in the garage as he put out several rat traps in the hopes that would solve the problem. Margot picked up Felix for the day. They were going to help Morgan and Astrid in the garden. And Willa and I prepared to spend our day with Lily and Kat.

Our afternoon began with lunch at one of our favorite spots downtown. The restaurant "Alchemy" had its bistro tables outside in the courtyard for what was proving to be a warm day. We chose the table closest to the Haller Fountain. Kat and Lily looked thrilled to see us. Even with Willa checking her phone every five minutes, we managed to have a lovely meal together. As the day wore on, Willa looked at her phone less and less. The glow that had reappeared with the cherry pie had grown throughout the day and by evening she looked like herself again. She and Lily laughed giddily as they curled each other's hair and spun around in their dresses. Kat was rummaging through my closet looking for a gown. I had a number of formal dresses from some of my gallery events so there was plenty for her to choose from. My dress was a vintage piece of Elsiba's in vibrant purple silk from the late 1930s. We had been about the same size when she was in her late 20s and this dress flattered all my curves, including the extra bits I wanted to hide. It had a chiffon sheath that fit snugly over the silk slip dress. It was cut in an A-line that nearly touched the floor. And like most of Elsiba's outfits, it had matching purple beaded shoes. I added one of my own necklaces with a pear shaped amethyst surrounded by blue topaz and black pearls. I left my hair long in black plaits.

Kat chose a shocking red dress I'd worn years before to an Art Gala. She was a few sizes smaller; it fit her perfectly. She chose a pair of red stilettos and completed her ensemble with red lipstick that matched the color of her hair. Just as we were putting on the final touches to our outfits, the knocker thumped loudly on the front door. Before Willa and Lily could run to open it, I splashed all of us with healthy doses of Elsiba's lilac potion.

As Willa ran down the stairs in her stocking feet, shoes in hand, I had the sudden realization that her old energy had returned in full. She was filled with light, almost overflowing with it as she and Lily opened the door. Aaron was dressed in a sharp looking suit most likely borrowed from his older brother. He was carrying a gardenia corsage for Lily. She blushed as he pinned it to the strap of her dress. Behind Aaron stood Daniel, lingering in the shadows of the pillared front porch. He glided towards the open door in an exquisite formal suit. His hair was combed back into perfect black waves, which made his blue eyes all the more alluring. And yet despite his physical perfection, he looked hollow. There was no light coming off of him, only shadow. Even my grey ghosts had more presence than this boy. He shot a cool look at me as if he could hear my thoughts. In a way I wished he could, because I would have given him an earful. His eyes shifted to Willa.

She slipped on her green beaded shoes, wobbling from one foot to the other as Lily held her arm. Willa grabbed her leather jacket and slipped it casually over the pale green flapper dress looking like a starlet from two different ages. Instead of giving her a corsage, Daniel nonchalantly pulled a diamond bracelet from his pocket. Before she could say a word he had silently slipped it onto her wrist as Willa let out a gasp.

"Um, I can't top that," Aaron half-jokingly announced to Lily.

"It's beautiful," Willa shrieked, flashing her arm in the light. The stones sparkled brilliantly even in a nearly dark hallway. I must have had a sour look on my face because Kat jabbed me in the rib. To me it was nothing more than a lovely trapping; a gorgeous shackle that symbolized (to him) that she was his property. He looked smug as they prepared to leave. Once they were on the front porch I made them stop so I could take a picture of them all together. I would have liked to have kicked Daniel out of the photo. But I saw how nervous he suddenly looked. He didn't want his picture taken by me.

"Quick, into the parlor," I said ushering them all back in. "It will only take a second!" They filed back inside and stood dutifully in front of the stone hearth that symbolized the heart of the house. Daniel was increasingly fidgety, but allowed me to snap a picture of them all together. At first I felt he wouldn't appear in the image, but the digital screen proved otherwise. Still, he looked irritated and began to pull on Willa's arm complaining they'd be late.

As Kat and I stood watching them pile into Lily's bug, the same one we used to zip around town in, I was overcome with the smell of cherry pie. That moment of peace and joy we'd shared only hours before in the kitchen, was still lingering in the air. I whispered a prayer asking St. Patrick to watch over our children on this night and chase any snakes from our sacred home. And by snakes, I meant rats and vampires. As they drove down the hill towards the high school, I felt suddenly fearful. I didn't want to let them out of my sight, especially to go to a party at the Renards.

"Come on Lottie, James will be here any second. Let's lock up and get this freak show on the road," she said, looking vibrant in her red ensemble. Just as I was locking the front door, James walked up the stairs dressed in a beautiful cream-colored suit and white shirt. He had changed at his office, having worked up until the last minute. With Kat on one arm and me on the other, we walked the few blocks to the Bell Tower House. People would be coming from all over town so the cliff would be crowded with cars. The sky had grown dark as we walked. Occasionally, a rustle of vermin could be heard underfoot. The air smelled of peach blossoms. Peach trees seemed to be the only plant in town that hadn't suffered the overnight blight. As we neared the Bell Tower House the air became heavier with heat. People were walking up the driveway in their finest attire. I felt nauseous as we approached. Kat and I had found several Victorian masks in the Winship attic while searching for clothes. We both put ours on as James fastened his silly black Zorro mask from an old Halloween costume over his eyes.

"Look, it's bearded Zorro," said Kat, giving James a teasing push.

"What can I say, I'm just too handsome not to wear a mask," he chided back.

Kat's masque was covered in silver beads; powder grey ostrich feathers cascaded over the side. Mine was embellished with black beads and what looked like crow feathers. As we marched down the driveway through the towering peach trees surrounded by floating petals, I marveled at the white lights covering every surface. As we neared the door I froze in place. Standing on the porch of the Bell Tower House were Thomas and Sophie on either side of the front door. They were greeting each guest as they entered the house. It wasn't their presence that shocked me, but rather what they were wearing. It was the mirror image of the couple Eva and Colette had shown me in my dreams. The red and black striped Victorian dress fit Sophie as if it had been made for her. Thomas was in the same black suit along with the bowler hat. The only difference was that now he had a full head of hair and was clean-shaven, unlike in my dream. My feet felt stuck to the ground. James and Kat stopped to look at me as I stared intently at the two figures by the door. I gave them a weak smile then summoned my energy and prepared to enter into the vampires' den, again.

CHAPTER 30

We stepped onto the porch and stood before Sophie and Thomas Renard. They both looked overly pleased to see us. Thomas greeted Kat and I with a kiss on the hand. I instantly felt repulsed as if a rat had licked my palm. Thankfully, the mask hid my face because I was sure I must have looked horrified. It was all I could do to keep myself from immediately wiping my hand on my dress.

"Welcome to the party. Everything is in the ballroom," said Sophie, with a seductive lilt in her voice.

"You remember where that is," said Thomas, eyeing me closely "don't you, Charlotte?"

"Indeed I do," I said, in the chilled tone I reserved for those I despised most. Kat was enjoying the exchange, though I could tell James felt nervous.

"Shall we? It seems we're holding up the line," James said, as he whisked us past the Renards and into the long hallway that led to the mirrored ballroom. The walls of the hallway were lined with flowering peach branches in large vases. The sconces provided a soft glow. As we turned the corner, I heard the low roar of voices coming from the ballroom. Two French doors were open inviting us into the massive space. I gasped at the lavish site before me. Hanging from the very peak of the glass pitched skylight were hundreds of strands of tiny white lights cascading in all directions above the dance floor. It resembled a massive spider web lit with morning dew.

The balconies skirting the room's edges were filled with people leaning over the archways to spy on those below. The aging floor-to-ceiling silver mirrors made the room feel immense. There were flickers of light flashing back and forth across the silver-plated surfaces as the guests were reflected three and four times over. It made my head spin. A bar and banquet table were set up on the far side of the room. We made our way there through the mass of beautifully adorned guests. A quartet was playing in one of the balconies; the haunting waltz sifted through the room like an invisible mist. The flutter of feminine laughter and manly jest could be heard on all sides as we approached the bar.

It was obvious the Renards had spared no expense with this gathering. The bar and banquet tables were fully staffed by caterers from Seattle. Waiters were expertly weaving through the crowd, passing hors d'oeuvres and fluted glasses glimmering with champagne. Everything twinkled in the dim light. I looked up at the hundred-year-old skylight that filled the ceiling and spied the full moon overhead. Although I was pretty sure a full moon was primarily related to werewolves, it still made me a bit nervous.

With champagne glasses in hand, we accompanied James to the banquet table. It held every delicacy imaginable from caviar to fois gras on toasted canapés. There were clusters of round tables around the edges of the dance floor where people could stand while enjoying their food before returning to a languid waltz. James loaded his plate while I was content to sip my champagne. The memory of the last time I had eaten the Renards' food was still sharp in my mind. I had no intention of allowing anything on the table to pass my lips. The notion was set in stone when I noticed the whole roast pig that was the centerpiece of the banquet. Its gruesomely charred body was complete with an apple in its mouth. Kat gave me a look that confirmed what I was thinking; Lily would have passed out cold if she had seen this spectacle. A vegetarian from birth, this would have pushed her over the edge.

We gathered at one of the small round tables off to the side. James was gorging himself; he had most likely skipped lunch again. I doubted that a slice of cherry pie at breakfast had been enough for the entire day. Kat had a small plate of delicacies and she nibbled at each while sipping the champagne. Since she owned a bar, alcohol held little mystery for her, though she had always been partial to a crisp glass of champagne when occasion called for it. Scanning the room, I began to see that, unlike I had first assumed, the party was not reserved for only the descendants of the founding families. This was a relief, but it also made me wonder at the odd combination of guests. Gavin had not been invited, which suited him well, nor had Tom Caldwell. Most of the attendees were in their late 20s to mid-40s. There were at least two hundred people bustling to and fro, some in couples and others alone. Sheila, Cody's Mom, had been invited, although she had declined at the last minute because Cody was still in the hospital. That was when it struck me. We all had children. Our children ranged in age from newborns to teenagers; all of us had children under the age of eighteen. This realization left me trembling. Our children were all marked. I felt a sudden mix of fury and fear.

Taking a long look at the jovial faces around me, I saw myself standing on a table shouting the truth at the top of my lungs. Thankfully, this notion quickly passed; it was definitely not the solution to the current dilemma. Nonetheless, I felt a deepening sense of urgency to stop the impending tragedy that loomed closer. No amount of champagne or caviar could pay for what they were planning to take from us. The decadence being used to seduce us one by one was opulent yet hollow; I prayed it would all come crashing down before it was too late.

My plan tonight was to try to find the entrance to one of the tunnels while the hosts were distracted with their guests. I was waiting until James had finished helping himself to the chocolate fountain to ask where they might be located when I heard the light tapping of forks on crystal glasses. The noise went from a tinkling to a crashing sound as everyone invited the Renards to speak.

Like monarchs speaking to their court, the Renards were perched in the largest of the balconies that looked down upon the entire room. Sophie stood with her hands clasped in front of her as Thomas raised his glass to the crowd. He took a long drink of the champagne before clearing his throat. His cheeks were ruddy with color and I imagined he had already consumed a considerable amount of drink throughout the evening.

"First, I would like to thank you all for gracing our home this evening with your presence," Thomas' voice boomed through the large room signaling the musicians to stop their bows. "You are the life blood of this community. We feel honored by the warm welcome that has been given to us upon arriving in Port Townsend." There was a demure applause at his words which signaled him to continue. "It is one of the reasons we chose this town as our home. We would like to announce that we will be opening a community allegiance in a few weeks' time. It will be located in the Cliffside Chapel and will be home to our efforts of creating events that will help to further unite the people of this town. We are calling it 'Aspire' and it will be a place where as a community we can grow and serve the needs of those less fortunate while also encouraging cultural and social activities. You are all invited to become a part of the 'Aspire' family. Thank you again and please enjoy the rest of the evening. There is no curfew for us on such a glorious night." With this there was a louder round of applause and immediate chatter followed. People on all sides were whispering about what the new club would do for the town. I knew exactly what it would do, but instead of saying anything I simply watched as the guests become more frivolous. Even Kat was swirling around on the arm of one of our high school friends as the champagne took its effect. James kept his arm around my waist as we moved through the crowd while he talked to people about the restoration work on both buildings. Little beads of sweat pooled at his temple as the heat became stifling as the evening wore on. Glasses clinked loudly on all sides as the merriment continued. My glass was still half-full. I would not fall under their spell a second time.

Every attempt to bring up the tunnels with James was interrupted by a new interloper breaking into our conversation, frustratingly changing the subject. Just as I was about to excuse myself to go snooping on my own, Sophie and Thomas appeared. James thanked them as graciously as ever and spoke of upcoming additions to the structure. Sophie complained about recent leaks in the skylight and James immediately said one of the crews would look into it in the following week. Little by little I noticed that Sophie had inched her way closer to James. She took every opportunity to touch his arm with a lasciviousness that made my skin crawl.

"May I have this dance," Thomas whispered the words in my ear. I was so surprised that my hand almost slapped him as I brushed my hair aside. He reminded me of a mosquito buzzing annoyingly close to my skin. I looked at James with pleading eyes but he just raised his shoulders apologetically as Sophie pulled him onto the dance floor. I wondered if I could feign a sprained ankle to avoid having to dance with Thomas. No sooner had I thought it, he forcefully grabbed my waist and began to spin me around the room. His breath smelled of a combination of strong liquor and the ever-present aroma of peaches. His hands were burning hot and sweaty. I kept glancing at James as Sophie maneuvered her way closer to him. She would whisper in his ear and then throw back her head in graceful laughs so calculated I was appalled that he didn't pick up on it.

Little by little Thomas had twirled me to the opposite side of the room. I could no longer see James. We moved in circular motions weaving in between other couples that crowded the dance floor. The room was so oppressively hot that men had abandoned their jackets and women were down to the barest elements of their outfits. With each dizzy glimpse, the spectacle of the Masquerade Ball was becoming more grotesque. The shimmers in the mirrors were flashing with each twirl and Thomas almost grunted as he moved from side to side with his hands firmly planted around my waist. I tried to scan for Kat and found her tipping a glass of champagne back while giggling with the bartender. The airy laughs that had filled the space earlier had now become harsh cackles.

That was when I noticed people who weren't moving in the space. It was a horrible contrast when I realized that looking on as we danced and ate were the one hundred and thirty dead children from 1912. On all sides of us, trapped inside of the silver mirrors they stood motionless watching our revelry. The flurry of colorful dresses and flushed faces was a sharp reminder of life compared to their grey countenances watching us like sentinels. I felt a wave of panic flood me as I spotted Magdalene alone in one of the mirrored panels. She was trying to get my attention, pointing to the panel next to her with a sharp finger and a stern look. Then I felt a constriction in my chest. It was as if all the air had been sucked out of the room. I must have faltered because Thomas asked me if I was all right in a saccharine sweet tone.

That was when I saw them standing near Magdalene. If not for my sudden lack of air, I surely would have let out a horrific scream. In the mirror standing together were Lily, Aaron and Willa. They were wearing the same clothing as when they had left for the dance but instead of the glow of life emanating from them they were a steely grey. There were dark stains on their clothes indicating blood. I pushed Thomas away and ran through the room looking for James but he was nowhere to be found. I scanned for Kat and it seemed that she, too, had disappeared. There were only the ghosts watching as I ran for the front door.

I must have looked like a mad woman crashing down the hallway, pushing people aside as I bolted from the house. The moon was at its apex lighting the sky and my way from the property. As I ran down the petal strewn driveway everything was eerily silent compared to the rumble that had filled the Renard house only moments before. Once I had hit the pavement of Willow Street, the air rushed back into my lungs. I lifted my skirt in my hands and sprinted as fast as I could back to the Winship house. Thankfully, I had left the back door unlocked as James had our keys. I would have kicked the door in otherwise. My panic had reached dangerous proportions as I flipped on the lights and saw my cell phone resting on the kitchen table. I'd left it behind in the bustle of our leaving the house. I flipped it open and felt a rush of fear as I saw I'd missed nine calls. With a trembling hand I connected to my voice mail and heard Margot's voice shaking on the line.

"Charlotte, Lily and Willa have been in a car accident! You need to come to the hospital as soon as you get this. The hospital hasn't been able to contact you all night," she said in a fragile voice. I fell to the floor. If Margot was shaken then that meant it was really bad. I glanced at our home phone and saw the light on the machine blinking as well. I couldn't bring myself to listen to it. The smell of cherry pie filled the room; it sat on the counter, a gruesome reminder of the accident that had signaled Felix's first premonition. Willa had been saved from a sure death on that day. I could only pray, as I ran to my car, that tonight she and Lily would be protected once again.

Pl. XXII.

Fig. 2.

Fig. 1.

CHAPTER 31

I broke every rule of the road as I sped to the hospital and I still felt I was moving in slow motion. Every second that ticked by felt like an eternity. My mind was completely empty of all thoughts other than getting to my child as fast as was humanly possible. I skidded into the first parking spot I saw and ran through the sliding glass doors of the emergency room. The smell of disinfectant mixed with the overpowering odor of blood was everywhere. I almost slipped on a freshly mopped section of floor then noticed the janitor cleaning a trail of blood that led from the emergency bay door into triage. My heart sped up at the thought that it might be Willa's.

I stopped at the information desk and they sent me back to speak with a doctor. They would tell me nothing until the physician came into the emergency waiting room to see me. Having had Samir as a father, I knew they wouldn't do this if it wasn't serious. I paced back and forth for several minutes until the attending physician pushed through the doors that said "Hospital Personnel Only." She walked over to me with a brisk gate, still in her scrubs and looking weary.

"Ms. Winship?" she said, I nodded afraid to speak for fear I'd burst into sobbing hysteria.

"Your daughter Willa was in a car accident tonight and she has a concussion as well as a broken arm and collar bone." I felt the air rush back into my lungs. She was alive. "But her friend Lily has sustained more serious injuries and we haven't been able to reach her mother, Katherine Starret. You are listed as the emergency contact on Ms. Starret's information in case she is unavailable." I nodded taking it all in. All I kept thinking was that she had to be ok. It was not possible that she was in our house only hours earlier giggling and excited about the dance and now she was in this horrible place, broken.

"What happened to Lily? What can I do?" I asked, feeling helpless.

"She is in surgery. Her gallbladder burst as a result of the impact of the accident. She also sustained head trauma. We're making sure no other internal organs were injured and will know more about her prognosis in the days following the surgery. If you can get her mother here, it would be a great help." I nodded and immediately pulled out my phone to call her.

"Can I see Willa? Is Aaron alright?" I asked, feeling another wave of dread. I had seen him in the mirror as well looking dead and grey. His parents were also at the Renards' party dancing in the artificial euphoria brought on by the lavish food and drink.

"He's being treated for a broken nose and also suffered a concussion, but he'll be fine. You're welcome to go back and see Willa. Your Grandmother Margot is in the room with her. It's through the door, third room on the left," she said with a lift of her eyebrow. I was sure that Margot had interrogated this doctor on every aspect of the children's prognosis probably to the point of exhaustion.

"What about Daniel Renard? Was he in the accident? Is he with them?" I asked. Part of me wished that something irreparable had happened to him. The thought of his possible demise made me feel guilty. I had the unfortunate habit of feeling compassion even for the worst people, so the feeling of wanting him to be hurt, or worse, was an odd sensation for me.

"Ask him yourself," she said pointing to the chairs behind me. He had been sitting there the entire time like a shadow. How I had not seen him the moment I walked in was almost impossible, and yet there he was. "Please contact Lily's mother as soon as you can," she said, rushing back through the doors. I turned to look at Daniel and was greeted by a hollow stare. He had a small drop of blood on his temple but other than that he looked as he had when he came to the house earlier. His clothing was still impeccable; his skin was without a scratch. I was sure the blood wasn't his own. He looked at me with feigned innocence.

"What happened?" I asked in a tone harsher than I intended.

"Shit, I guess," was his reply, as he looked me straight in the eye and smirked. If it hadn't been for the nurses nearby, and hence witnesses, I might have strangled him right then and there. Knowing that he wasn't going to tell me anything, I turned and pushed my way through the doors to find Willa.

"Hey!" he shouted behind me, "Can I see her now?" He came rushing forward as if to follow me through.

"Family only," I growled, letting the door nearly smack him in the face as I rushed through. The hallway was lined with empty beds and beeping monitors from behind the curtains. It looked like it had been a busy night in the ER. "Sickness demons" scurried along the corridor, unseen to most, but there all the same. These entities thrived on chaos and illness and hovered in hospital corners feeding off sadness. They scattered as I made my way towards Willa's room. I called Kat at the same time but got her voicemail. I was sure she couldn't hear her phone, or had done as I had and left it at home. I tried calling James but his phone also went immediately to voicemail.

I pushed open the door to find Willa propped up in the hospital bed with Margot at her side. Aaron was sitting in one of the chairs with the beginnings of two black eyes and his swollen nose in a splint. He smiled when I walked in, though I could tell it was followed by immediate pain. Willa looked like a bird with a broken wing. Her arm was set in a pristine white cast and cotton sling. She had a few scratches on her face but she was conscious and whispering to Margot. The thought that Lily wasn't able to do the same started another wave of panic. A burst gallbladder could be deadly, but I was more concerned about the head trauma.

"Mom?" I heard Willa speak. I rushed to her side. The minute I put my arms around her she started to sob. I knew it wasn't for her injuries but rather her concern for Lily. Aaron was trying to hold in his tears but they were welling up. He and Lily had been a couple for a year, but friends since kindergarten. She was as much a part of his family as she was ours. Margot looked at me with a sternness that let me know she was none too happy I'd left my phone at home. I was still dressed in the evening gown and heels, though I'd torn off the mask before running out of the house. I held Willa until she stopped crying. She felt so small in my arms. Without her usual teenage bravado, she looked as she had when she was just a small girl.

"What happened?" I asked, dreading the answer. Had they been drinking? Had they hit anyone else? All these things rushed through my head when Aaron explained the accident.

"We were going to North Beach for the after party when Lily slammed on the brakes and swerved into a telephone pole. She said she almost hit a cat but it looked more like a huge rat to me. It ran in front of us. She was just trying to avoid hitting it but she lost control of the car. Lily hit her head hard on the steering wheel and because we only had lap belts I hit my head on the dashboard. Willa was thrown to the side during the swerve and broke her arm. I guess nothing happened to Daniel." We called 911 and Lily was talking and everything until they showed up and then she just passed out. She was complaining about pain in her side." His face was grave as he mentioned Lily. I shot a look at Margot hoping she would be able to tell me more, but she just looked at her hands folded in her lap.

"We'll know more soon about Lily. Have you been able to get through to your parents?" I asked. Vestiges of shock and injury marred his young face. He shook his head indicating that he hadn't. I knew they were most likely still at the party.

"Margot, do you think you could take Aaron home?" I asked, knowing she was exhausted, but she nodded and stood slowly, giving Willa a kiss.

"Felix is with Morgan and Astrid at my house. They came to stay with him while I came to the hospital. You really need to put Morgan's name on the paperwork, too, dear. I won't be here forever." I told her I would, though I didn't want to. It meant I was giving her permission to leave and I didn't want that to happen anytime soon. "Oh, Margot, when you leave, best go out the side door." She gave me a smirk that confirmed she knew that Daniel was still waiting in the lobby. I didn't care how he got home and I certainly didn't want Margot going out of her way to drive him anywhere. Thankfully, Aaron and Willa were too much in shock to get my meaning.

Willa drifted in and out of sleep as I tried over and over again to get ahold of Kat and James. I had all but given up when I heard a ruckus in the hallway. It was Kat as she pushed past a nurse and into the emergency area screaming that a doctor better tell her what was happening before she burned the place down. I slipped into the hall closing the door quietly behind me and ran to Kat. She collapsed on the floor when she saw me. This had been my same reaction when I'd heard Margot's message on my cell phone earlier in the evening. I knew exactly how she felt and what was rushing through her body at this moment: panic, fear, desperation. I held her and told her everything as quickly as I could while holding her hand. Her sobbing waned as she took in every syllable. I spoke in my calmest voice, sending waves of light from my core into hers. Her trembling slowly lessened as the information formed in her mind. Soon the doctor was with us in the hallway telling Kat that she could see Lily.

We were taken to ICU where Lily lay with dozens of tubes sticking out of her tiny arms. Thankfully she was breathing on her own and the doctor said that she had been conscious after she came out of the anesthesia but had fallen into an exhausted sleep. The original prognosis had been far more dire than what they found when she was rushed into surgery. Other than the gallbladder, no other organs had been injured. We were both relieved when the doctor added that her concussion was serious, but wouldn't cause any permanent damage as far as they could tell. It would take more time to know the full extent of her injuries but she was out of any immediate danger. Kat sat holding Lily's pale hand. This was such a horrific contrast to earlier in the day. Those happy moments seemed a million years ago. So much had passed between our girls' lunch and the devastation of the evening. And while I knew it could have been much worse, there was the deepening feeling that it shouldn't have happened at all. After an hour with Kat and still no news from James, I checked in on Willa, who was fast asleep. I decided to go home for a few hours. I needed to find James. It was almost 3:00 a.m. Willa was to be released in the afternoon, but it looked like Lily was going to be in the hospital much longer.

As I walked out into the humid night air, the adrenaline in my body gave way to fatigue. There was no doubt that this was not just a simple accident. I thought about my ideas for keeping Willa away from Daniel; softball and spending time with Lily. Now with a broken arm softball was out of the question. Worst of all, Lily had almost died. And Daniel had walked away from it all without a scratch. I was sure it had been a rat that ran into the road. I had seen the size of the creatures that had so recently invaded our town and they were big enough to be mistaken for household pets. Had Daniel somehow instructed it to run in front of the car? I wondered about the extent of the Renards' abilities. Could they control animals as some dark sorcerers often did? Morgan thought they could and that the rats were the harbingers of more than just disease.

I pulled into our driveway, a combination of rage and exhaustion building in my body. I felt powerless; that much had been proven tonight. While I was in the vampires' lair, I had nearly lost three children closest to my heart. I needed to find a way to act more quickly. I needed to find their weakness! Was it hidden in the tunnels or were Dennis Morrison's pictures a piece of the puzzle? I had to figure it out now! Daniel would become omnipresent with Willa housebound with her injured arm and her best friend incapacitated. I had to act quickly. I also had to tell James. I couldn't do this on my own and I couldn't risk having him fall victim to the Renards as well. We had to join together if we were going to conquer this darkness. And right now we were becoming more divided by the day.

As I pulled into the driveway, the Winship house was still dark. James had not come home yet! The sky was clouding over, hiding the full moon behind layers of grey. I heard a rumble near the ocean. As I walked to the back porch, I heard the night heron caw as if announcing my arrival. The garden was dead. My once sacred house felt defiled as I spied more rat holes near the rose garden and along the hedge. I opened the door and was quickly enveloped in darkness. All was quiet except for the ticking of the grandfather clock on the second floor. Without my family creating a bustle of energy inside, the house was just a dead shell. Was this a mirror image of what I would be without my husband and children? I refused to find out. A rattle sounded in the lock of the front door. I peeked down the hallway from the kitchen and saw James' familiar outline against the stained glass window. It was time to tell him everything and hope I could convince him to become a believer in the unimaginable.

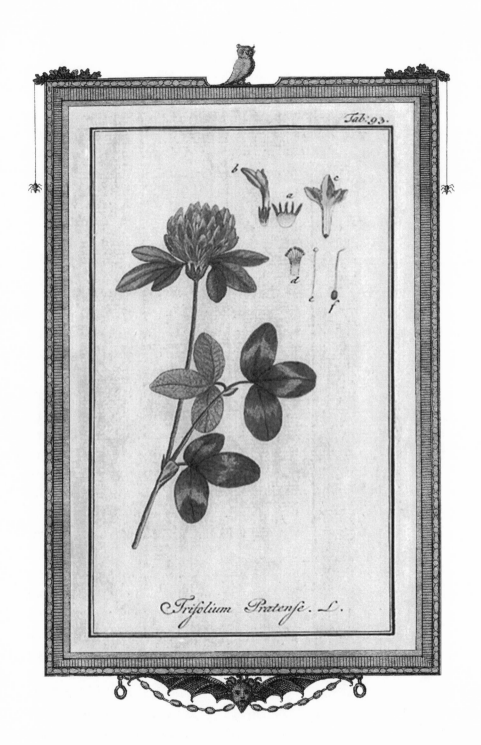

Trifolium Pratenſe. L.

CHAPTER 32

James instantly panicked the second I told him about Willa. At first he was angry with me for leaving the party without finding him first. Apparently he'd looked everywhere for me to no avail before finally coming home. I had a feeling that he'd done more than just look for me. His collar was rumpled and I'd seen the way Sophie whisked him out of sight into the decadence of the evening. It felt odd to be jealous of a monster. I wanted nothing **she** had, yet her family was scheming to devour **all** that was precious to me.

I spent the next twenty minutes telling James about the accident and Willa, Lily and Aaron's conditions. He paced back and forth in the familiar worn circle of the kitchen floorboards. As I finished, I saw the knot on his forehead furrow into a pinched crease. James wore all of his emotions on his face, even the slightest variations in his expression revealed what was brewing in his quick mind. It was time I told him what I really thought of the Renards, though I had no inkling how he'd react. I motioned for him to sit at the table as I put two cups for tea out. It was now well past 4:00 a.m., yet neither of us could possibly consider sleep. He reluctantly sat, taking off his jacket while nervously undoing the top buttons of his white shirt. I could smell the aroma of peaches as he shifted his clothing.

"James, there is something you need to know about the Renards and I don't think you're going to like it," I said, trying to think of the best lead-in. I couldn't just come out and say that we had three sociopathic vampires trying to suck the lives out of 130 children in our town without sounding like a loon. I decided to start with the obvious. "You know how sometimes I see and know things that others are not sensitive to?" He nodded. I could see the beginning of the conversation was making him uncomfortable. "Well, the day before the Renards arrived, Felix had a premonition about vampires coming to town. Then the blood tide came and the Renards arrived the same night. Since then, there have been more than just coincidences that now lead me to believe they are a type of vampire and that their purpose here is nefarious." I paused as he looked at me with wide eyes.

"Charlotte, that is insane," he said in an irritated tone "There is no such thing as vampires. Have you encouraged Felix to believe this nonsense?" His voice rose in anger. I began telling him everything about the old families, the sick children ghosts who had been visiting me and all the other elements of this ghastly puzzle. I tried my best to convince him without a trace of hysteria in my voice. He stared at me with growing disbelief.

"I know that you and your family, and this whole town for that matter, are convinced that you see the dead and that's one thing. But to accuse newcomers, who have been nothing but gracious to us, of something so absurd really worries me," he said. He reached across the table to grasp my hand. "I think you need some help with this." Sadly, the help from him I'd hoped for had now turned into him thinking I needed to see a psychiatrist. I knew this would be a delicate conversation, but I'd hoped he would at least give me the benefit of the doubt. James had experienced plenty of odd phenomena over the years by being in close proximity to me, and my family, so his response was all the more painful to me. The only thing that gave me an iota of comfort was the thought that part of this was the Renards' fault. They already had their hooks in deep.

"I'm sorry you can't be open-minded about this, but I have to do whatever it takes to keep my family and this town safe. And that includes keeping that praying mantis away from you as well," I said with a hint of venom. James looked as if I'd slapped him with my words. It was becoming harder to believe that he hadn't noticed the way Sophie tried to devour him with her sensual manipulations. "Also, you should know that Daniel is hunting our daughter like prey; draining her energy to the last drop. And if it hadn't been for Cody tripping it would be Felix in the hospital with a deadly fever. There are others who know this is happening and you would be wise to think about who you give your allegiance to." I stood up and calmly put my tea cup in the sink and made my way upstairs.

I quickly changed into my nightgown but rushed from our bedroom to my workroom to avoid James. I heard him drag his feet up the creaking stairs, wash his face and quickly settle into bed. The hurt and anger combined inside of my heart into a hard stone. I wanted to sob at being utterly abandoned yet again with my gift and yet I couldn't shed a single tear. They were all wedged into the back of my throat, burning with shame and rejection. His was the opinion that mattered most to me. I knew my family loved and accepted me unconditionally, but James was my link to the outside world. And he thought I was crazy. I knew I wasn't delusional. I needed so badly in this moment for him to believe me; to be at my side, protecting our family in the face of evil. Instead, he was being drawn into the darkness by the illusion of beauty. I now knew it would be entirely up to me to find a way to keep us all safe.

I tiptoed back downstairs and found James' key ring on the kitchen table. He had two sets of keys for the Bell Tower House and the Cliffside Chapel until the projects were completed. I slipped one of each off the ring and quietly placed it back on the table. I needed to find those tunnels. The best time to get in and out would most likely be the early evening. The crews stopped for the day when the sun went down and the Renards usually went out for the evening. Daniel was almost always at our house after school and James went back to his office to finish his work. I would sneak in to the Cliffside Chapel first since it was a smaller space to search and then carefully move on to the Bell Tower House.

I made my way back upstairs and hid the keys in a secret compartment of the large oak desk in my workroom. Dennis Morrison's photographs were sitting in a neat pile and I quickly hid them in the desk with the keys. The way Thomas had looked at them in my store immediately triggered my protective instincts. I despised the way his eyes had lingered on the pictures. There was a look of perverse pleasure on his face when he saw the images of the children whose souls he had bound. The way he'd licked his lips and swallowed louder than normal indicated his guilt and attraction. I needed to keep the photos safely away from him.

As I was about to head to bed, a little chime sounded from my computer indicating that I had a new message in my email inbox. I clicked it open to find a message from Gavin and another from Tom

Caldwell. First I read Gavin's and couldn't help but let out a much-needed chuckle. It read:

Charlotte- How was the vampire popularity party? Was it heinously gaudy? Or did you end up doing the "Monster Mash?" I bet you did didn't you...don't you usually prefer the dead to the undead? Just teasing...Needless to say the bar was pretty empty tonight although there were a few locals feeling less than happy about not being invited to the big event. Did you find out anything new? Are they obsessive compulsive about hors d'oeuvres? –G

I quickly wrote him back that the lovely evening had been cut short due to the car accident. I was sure that Kat was still at the hospital and she had probably not wanted to bother Gavin so late at night. Knowing Gavin, he would be at the hospital first thing in the morning. I gave him the room info for Lily and told him Willa would be home tomorrow. There was too much for me to delve into tonight and I needed to have him in front of me for several reasons. It was easier not to miss any of the finer points in person and also I needed to have someone look me in the eye and believe what I was saying.

The next email was from Tom Caldwell. It had been sent only a minute earlier, which was usual for Tom when he set his mind to something. He was like a bloodhound on a scent when it came to digging up answers to a mystery. The email was a long one detailing all he'd discovered about the family who had lived in the Bell Tower House in 1912. He had finally discovered their name on the register for the Owl's Club and it was listed as Mr. and Mrs. Draner. From there he had followed them back to the same club in Boston and before that London. I had expected the family to be French, but the Draners were from Romania; Transylvania to be exact. This had Tom excited for obvious reasons, although I hadn't told him Astrid's story of the Pied Piper taking the 130 children from Hamlin back to Transylvania yet. In a way, I felt a bit let down they hadn't been French. I wanted them to be the exact image of Thomas and Sophie to confirm my suspicions. The last bit of information that made me feel uneasy was that after Port Townsend, the Draners had vanished. There was no trail leading anywhere; no new towns. It had been reported they'd left with their two teenage children; a boy and a younger girl. Tom also discovered that at the same time the Draners were in those cities, Dennis Morrison and his wife Anita had also been there. And, in addition to their presence, there were also outbreaks of unknown plagues at the same time, including on the ship that gave both families passage to America. The plagues claimed mostly children, though in larger cities it wasn't as devastating as it had been to a town the size of Port Townsend. In all cases, rats had been to blame for the spread of the disease.

I sent Tom a gushing email about how much I appreciated his sleuthing. I promised him more information soon and hoped he'd continue digging into the past. My eyes were blurring as I turned off the computer. I knew it was time for me to go to bed but I still felt betrayed by James and couldn't fathom being next to him in our bed. I made my way up to Willa's room instead.

The steps were cold on my bare feet. As I pushed open her door, I thought I saw the outline of her body in her bed, but it was just a shadow. This had been my room growing up and it held a special place in my heart. I felt safe here. I climbed in under the covers as a rumble sounded above the house. The thunder was closer and with it came the light tapping of rain on the old window. With my head on Willa's pillow, I breathed in her smell. It wasn't the nauseating aroma of rotting peaches that met my senses, but rather her own distinct perfume. A combination of blackberries and summer rain lingered on the bedclothes. I pulled the quilt around me and pictured myself holding her as a baby. Safe and warm, she was snuggled next to my heart. I tried to convince myself that nothing could harm her if I kept her close to me, but I knew that was no longer true.

Here I was in her empty room as she lay in the hospital with a broken wing and a monster intent on plucking all of her feathers until she was nothing more than an empty carcass. The branches from the willow tree tapped on the window along with the rain. Was it telling me to take heart? That it was still watching over us even though evil was gnawing at its roots? As I pulled my legs up to my chest, wrapping myself in the cool blankets, I sent out a silent prayer to the beings of light and all the Winships who had come before me. If I had to face the vampires to save my own that was perfectly fine with me, but I couldn't bear to lose a single loved one. I sent out an offer to the heavens to take me instead if they needed a sacrifice. I would give my body if it meant saving my family because without them, I would never survive.

Tears finally began to wet my cheeks as the rain outside went from a drizzle to a downpour. Exhausted, I cried myself to sleep only to become lost in a dream. I was standing in an old-fashioned barber shop. Men were having their beards trimmed and their mustaches waxed into extravagant curlicues. The proprietor was a handsome man with a soft English accent. It was Dennis Morrison. There in the corner was his wife, Anita, loading a camera on a large wooden tripod with a glass slide. I looked to my right into one of the many mirrors that lined the shop. The reflection that stared back at me was that of Magdalene Winship. I was seeing this moment through her eyes. I was holding a woman's hand as she led me to sit on a small red velvet settee that was part of the photographer's props. I sat quietly with my hands in my lap. I wanted to observe all the people in the barber's shop. They were fascinating to me with their gold pocket watches and exuberant laughter.

Anita smoothed my dress out around my legs into a perfect semi-circle. I had on my favorite white lace gloves that had tiny clovers hidden in the delicate weave. Clovers were lucky, this I knew well. But I also knew that something very unnatural was about to happen. The smell of peaches and dead rats mingled in my nostrils as Anita finished primping my hair. The smell was everywhere as if the sweetness of the fruit could hide the decay beneath. My nose told me otherwise. The decay would soon be everywhere. I watched as the white lace of my gloves shifted and became a squirming mass of maggots burrowing into the pure flesh of my tiny hands. And yet I could not move, frozen in time as the photographer prepared to take his picture. I listened close as Anita leaned over to whisper in the photographer's ear. Her words implored him to "make sure and capture them all." Dennis Morrison quickly ducked under the cape that protected the lens and in his formal voice told me to smile as he clicked a handle to release the shutter. A blinding flash was followed by a loud bang.

I woke with the flash from the dream camera still in my eyes as the early morning sun was pouring through the nearby window. I heard James' feet on the stairs climbing to the turret room to find me. It was a rare thing when we slept apart. I was sure that he had come to take me back to our own bed. He pushed the door open and I was tempted to feign sleep. I was still angry with him. Without saying a word, he gently lifted me from the bed and carried me in his arms back down to our bedroom. The clock read 7:00 a.m., which was far too early to wake up after such a horrific night. He carefully tucked me under the covers and when he climbed in next to me we both fell into a deep sleep wrapped in each other's weary arms. The last thing I remember as I drifted into slumber was the smell of lilacs rising up from his warm skin.

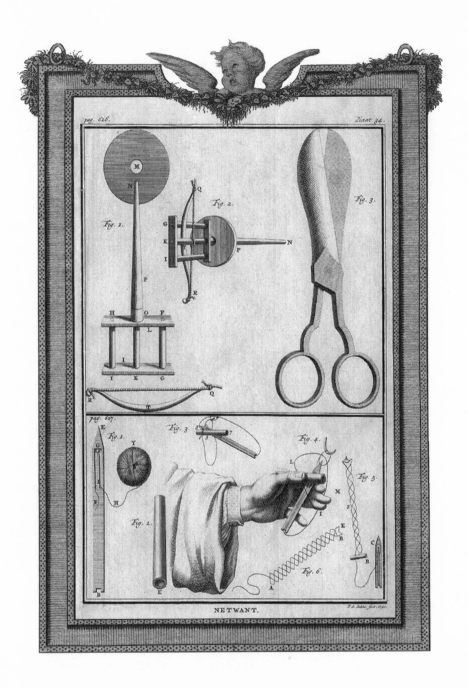

Fig. 1.

Fig. 2.

Fig. 3.

pag. 627.

Fig. 1.

Fig. 3.

Fig. 4.

Fig. 5.

Fig. 2.

Fig. 6.

NETWANT.

F. de Bakker sculp. 1740.

CHAPTER 33

As soon as James and I awoke, we dressed quickly and headed to the hospital. Margot had called saying she and Felix would meet us there. He wanted to see if he could visit Cody. It weighed heavily on his young soul that his best friend was ill and alone in a cold hospital room.

James and I moved around each other in awkward silence. I was a stubborn creature by nature but this was a subject I was more apt to understand than he. There was no way I'd give in to his idea that the Renards were innocent newcomers. I knew better. But I also didn't have the energy to try and convince him of their inherent evil. It would be too complex to put into words for someone who simply wasn't aware of the layers of the hidden world. For now, I would move stealthily to try to find the talisman dolls without James being any the wiser.

We arrived at the hospital an hour before Willa was to be released. Stepping into the room, I expected to see Margot and Felix and was instead greeted by the Renards. Daniel was sitting by Willa, holding her hand while Sophie and Thomas stood near the window. A bouquet of white roses sat by her bedside yet the room reeked of peaches with an underlying odor of death. The smell from my dream of Magdalene still lingered on the periphery of my senses. The overpowering sweet smell of the Renards was all the more revolting as it was now mixed with the unmistakable odor of dead rats. I almost gagged when I walked in the room. I was obviously the only one who could smell the stench. Willa looked exhausted and pale. The dark circles that had faded the night before during our time together were present again.

James greeted the Renards with warm thanks for visiting Willa as well as for the prior evening's revelries. I scanned the room trying to take in every detail. A little bolt of surprise rushed through me when Sophie touched James' arm. He gave a small jump as if he had been shocked. There was a ripple of consternation that flashed across his face. Had he finally opened his eyes? It was only a fleeting change and he was back to his usual charming self. He gave Willa a long hug. Daniel had clasped one of her hands so jealously she was hardly able to hug her own father. A look of relief and pain mingled in James' eyes as he pulled up an empty chair on the opposite side of Willa's hospital bed. The white bandage and cast on her arm reminded me of a dove's tender wing.

"I guess you'll have to take a rain check on softball this year," James said to Willa. This had been one of their favorite conversation points. When she was seven, they'd spent hours in the backyard pitching softballs until the light left the sky. I think it was their way of discussing life in their own secret language. Sports were something completely foreign to me. I loved that father and daughter had this as one of their connections.

"There is always next year," she said, almost breathless with fatigue. "I just hope Lily is ok," she said, choking back tears. Willa was proud and didn't easily cry, especially in front of other people, but she was on the edge of emotional and physical collapse. I looked at Sophie and Thomas hoping they would take this as their cue to exit. Instead Thomas had a glint in his eye as he looked at Willa that made me more than uncomfortable. He was looking at her the same way he had looked at the photographs of the ghost children. Her pain was giving him pleasure; I was sure of it. Sophie on the other hand seemed apathetic. She glanced from Daniel to Willa with a stare so icy and indifferent I wondered how she could ever have been a mother. Daniel, on the other hand, was leaning closer, devouring Willa's every movement with a fiery emotional intensity that was smothering.

"We need to get Willa ready to go home. I hate to be rude, but you should be on your way, please," I said, trying to be as polite as possible when I really wanted to shout "Get out!" I thought James would be irritated with me, but instead he thanked the Renards for their flowers and attentions signaling that he, too, thought they should leave. Thomas licked his lips in a repulsive gesture as he tore his eyes from Willa and led Daniel out of the room. They wished Willa a speedy recovery, which felt empty and hollow, considering the accident had been their fault. Sophie gave me a subtle glare as they left, taking their unbearable stench with them. They were nearly out the door when Sophie leaned back in for a quick word with James.

"Last night when it rained, the skylight in the ballroom leaked heavily. Please come take a look at it soon; we need to put our heads together and find a better solution to repair it," she said with an air of innocence, though I hoped James would see through it. He gave a quick nod and said he would send someone by to take a look. Sophie was visibly irritated with his response. A week ago, James would have jumped and assured her he'd be there in person to follow up on her request. But something had changed. I could only hope he was beginning to see the Renards for what they truly were.

When the door closed behind them, I immediately opened the window to let in the cool, damp air of the Spring afternoon. I heard Willa let out a lovely sigh as the breeze rushed into the sterile room. James began to gently ask her about the crash. Even though I'd told him about it, he needed to hear it in her own words. I knew this would be good for both of them. I kissed Willa on the forehead and told them I was going to check on Lily, leaving them to talk alone.

In the long corridors, the sickness demons peered from behind half-opened doors and pristine curtains. They cleared a path before me as I walked down the darkened hallway, sending light radiating ahead of me. The sound of beeping machines echoed in my ears as I passed each doorway and made my way to the ICU. As I turned the corner, I heard the faint sound of choked sobs. I knew it was Kat making those heartbreaking gasps. She sat in one of the hallway chairs with her elbows on her knees and her head in her hands. Gavin was next to her, his hand rubbing her back, comforting her. He, too, had tears streaming down his face and I immediately sensed that Lily had taken a turn for the worse. As I moved closer, Gavin gave me a weary smile. I was about to take Kat in my arms, when I noticed that Margot, Felix and Morgan were standing inside Lily's room.

Confused, I moved silently into the room and stood behind them. Lily was still unconscious. Morgan stood at the end of the bed with his eyes closed, his hands outstretched at his sides. Margot held the same position on the left side of the bed. Morgan was whispering a series of prayers under his breath and I immediately felt a rush of power emanating from them. I knew this pose as it was the same one I'd taken many years before with Deidre and Margot to free Morgan from the dark entity. They were creating a circle of healing; all their energy was being funneled into Lily. Her breathing was steadier and the contusions that had scarred her beautiful face just last night seemed to have faded some. She almost looked herself, but she wasn't out of the woods yet. Her eyes were still closed and her body flooded with poison.

I watched as they held their positions, unselfconscious in their efforts to jointly remove the Renards' evil intentions from Lily's body. Then in one simultaneous motion, their hands fell to their sides and they released a unified breath of air. In that same moment Lily's eyes fluttered open. She was obviously medicated, but she was also present. I felt her mind clicking as she gave a weak smile first to Felix, then to Margot and finally to Morgan. She knew who everyone was and where she was. Kat instinctively rushed into the room. Lily started to cry. Her tears mingled with Kat's as mother and daughter held hands. Kat kissed Lily's hands fiercely, holding them to her face, as she smiled in relief.

I stepped out of the room and back into the hallway. Gavin was leaning against the wall wearing a look of deep consternation. There was no joking in his eyes. Instead, I found smoldering anger. Kat and Lily were his family as much as the Winships. We were the only people left in his life as his family was all dead. If something happened to us, it would be the end of Gavin. I often thought this was why he never allowed himself to get too close to any one woman. In a way it was self-preservation. To Gavin, giving his heart meant doing so without reservation, which also meant taking the risk of complete devastation in the event of loss. He had lived through it with the death of his parents when he was just a boy and later the death of his Great Aunt. We were his last source of weakness and if anything happened to us, he might very well never recover.

"I want to put an end to them, Charlotte," he said in a hushed tone filled with rage. I knew he meant the Renards. Margot, Morgan and Felix were hovering around Kat and Lily out of earshot but still we kept our voices low.

"So do I, but I'm still not sure how," I said, feeling his anger well up inside me along with my own frustration. "I'm trying to find where they keep those talisman dolls. I think I know where, but I'm not sure I can find them soon enough to stop them."

"Just be careful," he said, his eyes staring into Lily's room. "I bought this for you, kind of as a joke, but now I think it may be useful if all the things I have read about vampires are true," he said with a smirk as he handed me a small bag of sunflower seeds. I looked at him not understanding what sunflower seeds had to do with vampires. He let out a strained chuckle when he saw the incredulous look I was giving the transparent bag.

"In case they really *are* obsessive-compulsive," he said with a weak smile, "Tear open that bag and throw them in the vampire's path. They will have to pick them up." His voice trailed off and I thought I heard him whisper under his breath as he turned to leave, "Saved many a maiden." As I watched his lanky form turn the corner, I felt a sharp pain in my chest as yet another member of my family was feeling the ill effects of the Renards so deeply. I tucked the bag of seeds into my purse and joined everyone in Lily's room. She and Kat were talking about the accident. While Lily's words were slow to form, it was obvious that her mind wasn't damaged.

Soon it was time to take Willa home and leave Lily to rest. The doctors were thrilled by Lily's miraculous improvement, patting each other on the back for a job well done. They insisted that Lily would need to stay in the hospital for at least two weeks as they monitored her improvement and make sure she didn't develop sepsis. But the blessing was that her brain was unharmed. Morgan and Margot planned to come back once a day on alternating shifts to make sure Lily was getting an energetic boost. Kat hugged us all, refusing to leave Lily's side until she was home again. The nurses were preparing a cot next to Lily where Kat could sleep.

As we made our way back to Willa's room, Margot told me in a hushed tone that they hadn't been able to see Cody. Morgan and Felix walked ahead of us, so we slowed our pace to speak without Felix overhearing. She explained that his fever was getting steadily worse and the doctors had no idea what was causing it. He was isolated in a special room in the hospital much like Morgan had been so many years ago.

"Charlotte, he will be the first in a long list if we don't end this quickly," she said. I condensed all the new information I had learned in the last twenty four hours. She listened intently as I told her I wanted to find the talismans and from there destroy them in a ceremonial fire to hopefully set the souls free and weaken the Renards. She nodded in agreement, but neither of us knew what would happen after that.

"Tomorrow afternoon when the workers leave the Cliffside Chapel, I'm going to sneak in and try to access the tunnels and look for other hiding places," I said in a conspiratorial whisper as we reached Willa's door.

"Be careful," she said, and then with a stern look added, "...and take your damn phone!" Then she turned into the hospital room where Willa sat dressed and ready to go home. We parted company with Morgan and Margot returning to their homes and James, Willa, Felix and I to ours. We walked into the rainy afternoon, exhausted, but relieved at having our family reunited. As we made our way back to the Winship house, I knew that the loss of my husband or child would feel like an amputation of the soul. This family body needed to remain whole for each of its members to survive and I wouldn't allow anything — or anyone — to tear us limb from limb. For tonight, I would cherish my family and bestow love upon them. Tomorrow, I would begin the hunt for the enemy's weakness.

Mulier sine verecundia, lampas sine lumine.

Mulier inverecunda lampas
sive lumine

CHAPTER 34

Monday arrived with dark clouds and louder, more persistent thunder. Willa insisted on going to school despite her recent injury and I was sure it was because Daniel would be there. Felix had been harder to get out of the house. Since we'd brought Willa home from the hospital, he had lingered close to James and me, worried we'd suddenly disappear. He was pensive. This morning I could tell he didn't want to go to school. I wouldn't have been surprised if he'd feigned an imaginary illness to stay home. Instead, he dragged his feet out the front door, clinging to James and me as we tried to hustle him off to school. He would have to make the walk to school alone since Cody was still in the hospital. He stood for several minutes unable to take the first step off the Winship porch. I convinced James to give him a ride. It was only three blocks, but I could tell it was weighing on Felix.

Once everyone was out of the house, I quickly caught up on the work that had accumulated into precarious piles on my desk. My mind had been elsewhere the past several weeks and work felt arbitrary compared to my next task. Adrenaline began building inside of me as the thunder moved closer to Port Townsend; ocean winds pushing in from the northwest. Despite the clinging humidity that had settled over the town, there was no sun. Everything turned a sepia tone the day the lilacs and other trees had died. The grass was a sickly yellow; the trees were tinged brown. Only our willow tree remained a vibrant green, but I could see it was only alive due to sheer stubbornness, much like all Winships.

Before long the grandfather clock struck four o'clock. It was time to begin my search for the talismans. The workmen would be packing up soon and James would still be at his office. Margot and Morgan would be at the house at five o'clock to stay with Felix and Willa after school, although they would really be waiting for me to return. If I found the talismans, we would have to perform the unbinding quickly before the Renards knew what was happening. Surprise was our only tactic, besides what I hoped would be a bit of blind luck.

Unbinding would be simple. The souls wanted to be free and setting that into motion with the proper tools would work naturally. What the Renards had done by using the energy from the children's' souls was to preserve their own existence, and it went against the natural order of things. In the end, nature would strive to follow its intended course. Once the impediments were removed, our hope was that the Renards would then be weakened to the point where we could bind them forever. Morgan had assured me that he'd find a way to do this and I trusted him. When he said that, I knew he might call on dark forces for help with the binding, and this made me fearful. I hoped there would be another way, but if not, I was prepared to cross that line to stop the Renards.

I donned all black attire, although today it was for stealth as well as comfort. I packed a flashlight in my purse and folded a large shopping bag inside, hoping I'd need it to carry the 130 dolls. My fingers reached under the desk to the secret compartment where I'd hidden the keys and Dennis Morrison's photographs. The latch clicked and I found the keys quickly tucked back into the farthest corner where I had stashed them. Feeling around to make sure the pictures were still safe, I was flooded with panic. The photos were gone. I crawled under the desk and let my flashlight illuminate the compartment but it was empty. I sat at my desk completely dumbfounded. I had been alone when I'd stashed those pictures. It had been late at night when no one was awake. How could they be gone?

As if in answer I heard a scratchy caw from the window. It was the night heron, staring at me in the fading afternoon light. This wretched bird had seen me stash those photos away in my own nest. And like any familiar, it had flown home to the Renards to tell them where the children were hidden. I ran to the window and slammed my hand on the glass where the bird's red eye peered at me defiantly. It ruffled its feathers and flew back to its hideous perch high in the willow. I wanted to climb after it and wring its ugly neck. The realization that one of the Renards had been in this room and stolen the photos struck me. They had dared to come into my home and take what was not theirs. Daniel had stopped by to see Willa last night even though we had forbidden any visitors. I was sure he'd been the one to slither into the library and unlatch the secret compartment before I had asked him to leave.

Fury suddenly replaced my shock. It was my turn to break into **their** house and steal **their** treasures. I shoved the keys into my pocket and stormed out of the house with a determined gait. The sky was dark; tiny rain drops fell, though the air was stiflingly hot. Thankfully, the rain acted as my cover. I wanted to remain unseen heading to the Cliffside Chapel. It was a sleepy Monday; there were few cars on the road. I imagined people were still recovering from Saturday night's decadence.

The world felt quiet and heavy with foreboding as I reached the Cliffside Chapel. I had been right; the crew had packed up for the day; things looked quiet. I decided to slip in using the key for the downstairs entrance. The white clapboard building sat stoically on the far edge of the cliffs where it had been battered by winter tempests for over a hundred years. The building itself was humble compared to the Bell Tower House and yet it had a certain purity that other local structures lacked. The upstairs was one large room lined with windows where I could be seen by anyone from the outside. Downstairs was a simple room that had once been a basement with windows that overlooked the cliff. The key turned in the lock and I rushed inside closing the door quietly behind me. I was definitely alone. Paint buckets lined one wall and a makeshift work table was against another. I let my eyes adjust to the darkened room, which was still being renovated so was all but empty. A staircase to my right led up to the chapel and a wood-paneled wall stood opposite me. There were no doors. Was the tunnel hidden under the floor boards? Just as I was about to start searching, I felt a rush of air enter the room. It was Mario Cabral, standing in the shadows across from me. His grey silhouette had once again come to my aid. He motioned to a board on the paneled wall. I made my way to it and ran my fingers along the wooden edge feeling for a latch but there was nothing. It was solid. He watched me patiently, a ghost has nothing but time, until I finally noticed a small knot in the board that was obviously manmade. As I pushed it, a click sounded from behind the wood and the beautifully concealed door popped open. The way to the tunnels lay before me.

I expected nothing more than a glorified rat hole, but this was not what I found. The floor was hard packed dirt mixed with some type of concrete. The walls were covered with mysterious clumps of hardened clay held up by beams of wood that formed archways across the ceiling. It was like walking inside a hollowed out snake. I closed the door behind me, hearing it click and then felt an immediate rush of panic. Had I just locked myself inside with no way to escape? I fumbled in my purse for the flashlight as I was now in complete darkness. Relief flooded me as I illuminated the tunnel and saw a small latch on the inside of the wooden panel. It would be easy to open and find my way out again.

I moved down the tunnel to my left, which seemed most likely to head down the cliff towards the Haller Fountain. I moved swiftly, careful to alternate between shining the light on my feet and the tunnel ahead of me. It moved downwards at a steep slope, but nothing seemed out of the ordinary. I didn't find any hollowed out sections where something could be hidden. There were just smooth walls and the wood vertebrae that kept the structure from caving in. Just as the thought of a cave-in crossed my mind, I found one directly in my path. A section of the tunnel had crumbled into nothing and dirt blocked my way entirely. There was nowhere to go but back up.

It was more difficult making my way back to the entrance. With each step, the air grew heavier. I was beginning to feel faint. This reminded me of being in the Bell Tower House and the dizziness I'd felt there; that lack of air that had been incapacitating. I raced to get out of the dirt catacomb; longing to reach the door so much that I nearly abandoned the search. But then Mario appeared again and silently pointed for me to carry on to the other side of the tunnel. This path led up to the Bell Tower House. My heart was pounding as I forced myself to continue, leaving the safety of the exit behind me.

The walls on this side of the tunnel were smaller and a feeling of claustrophobia set in. The ceiling was only a few feet above me and the walls drew closer on both sides, but I pushed forward. As I rounded a tight corner, I saw the glow of light up ahead. I quickly switched off my flashlight and moved forward in the darkness following the soft flicker of illumination. I tried to breathe quietly as I inched closer to what was surely candlelight. I was nearly gasping for breath by the time I discovered what I'd been searching for – the dreadful altar.

Set into the wall of the tunnel was a carved opening leading into a small alcove. If I'd been in Europe, I would have instantly expected to see the statue of a saint before me, but there was nothing holy about this altar. There were thirteen shelves formed out of the clay. On either end of each shelf was a black candle burning brightly, giving a horrible glow to the 130 small peach wood statues that were arranged in perfect rows of ten. I held my breath as I moved closer to them. They were all here. Trapped in this tunnel for the past 100 years, these small effigies were far more than just symbols. They held the souls of the dead children and would soon be replaced with new sacrifices. Standing directly before them I saw that behind each statue stood one of Dennis Morrison's pictures, giving a face to each victim.

I pulled the sack from my purse. I had to take every last one of the statues and the photographs and get out of there as fast as possible. But it felt like my feet were glued in place. And, it was getting harder to breath. The dizziness threatened to overcome me again. I tried to clear my mind. I stepped forward and reached for the talismans but I couldn't move. The smell of peaches grew stronger in the small, cramped space and the candles were burning in long, thin flames. I wondered if there was a spell working to keep intruders away, but couldn't detect anything but an increased difficulty in my breathing.

I reached up with a shaky hand to the first statue that caught my eye. It had Magdalene's picture behind it. The same picture I had dreamt of with her eyes staring forward in haunting defiance. I still didn't know what power the pictures held or if Dennis Morrison had been a friend or a foe. Seeing these pictures combined with the statues made me feel increasingly anxious about his role in this tragedy. As my fingers grazed the edge of the statue, fear overtook me. Being in this tunnel was like being held underwater. I felt myself gasping for air. I was disoriented — like being dragged into an undertow where up was down and light was not always one's savior.

I pulled my hand away from the statue, but air wouldn't fill my lungs. I reached for the statue again, and heard something moving in the tunnel. Instinctively, I retreated from the altar and went farther into the darkness, away from whatever was moving towards me. It was a scuffling sound coming from the direction of the entrance I had used. As it approached, it sounded more like footsteps. It wasn't until the sound was about to round the corner that I knew what it was. It was the familiar grunting noise unique to Thomas Renard. Fear and revulsion mixed together. I tried to blend into the shadows as he walked straight towards the altar. He passed within a few feet of where I was standing, but blending into the darkness had always been one of my tricks and I remained hidden.

I watched as he stood before the statues. His outfit of khaki pants and polo shirt was an absurd contrast to the black altar before him. I would have laughed under different circumstances. I breathed in small, shallow gulps of air trying to be as silent as the grave. The smell of peaches had been replaced with the stench of dead rats. It radiated from Thomas as he lifted his fingers to caress each of the statues with his repulsive fingers. From where I was standing, I saw a look of illicit pleasure fill his face as he fondled the objects that had captured all the innocent souls. The loathing that I felt for him almost surpassed the fear I'd felt. I heard my heartbeat thudding in my ears so loudly I was sure he'd heard it, too.

His eyes licked across the photographs with a lascivious gleam and bile began to rise into my throat. At this moment, when he thought he was alone, his lack of soul was completely revealed. I was sure that if there had been a mirror in this dark tunnel the only reflection he would have cast would have been that of a putrid corpse in the final throes of decomposition. I don't know how long I stood frozen in the shadows, holding my breath while I observed Thomas. It felt like years, but it was probably no more than a few minutes.

To my relief, he turned and moved away from me back down the tunnel towards the Cliffside Chapel. My heartbeat slowly began to find its usual rhythm as his steps moved away from me. It was still hard to breathe, but I managed to let out a small exhale as he neared the corner. Just then, the stillness was shattered by the sound of my cell phone. The chirping ring was deafening in the hollow tunnel as each tone ricocheted off the clay walls. Renard froze, then slowly turned and in an instant our eyes connected through the darkness in the soft candlelight. The shadows couldn't conceal me any longer as the traitorous ringing revealed my location. Our eyes locked as he slowly moved towards me. I was frozen in place, my feet mired to the spot as if in quicksand. As he inched closer the only thing that registered was the expression of unbridled rage on his face. I felt like a fly caught in the spider's web as it moved in to devour its prey with deadly purpose. The ringing stopped just as he stood a few feet from me. I realized I might never leave this catacomb alive.

Armurier.

Chapter 35

Our eyes were locked, but neither of us spoke a word. Thomas knew he had me trapped in this stifling tunnel. The smell of candle wax mingled with the heavy odor of decay surrounding him. He paced slowly back and forth, just a few steps to the right and then back to the left, his eyes never leaving mine. What was he contemplating? What did he want to do with me? Would I be his next victim? He had an obvious fetish for children, yet I knew he wouldn't hesitate to subdue me to keep his secrets safe.

Stealthily, I moved my hand into my purse. I always carried a utility knife with me, a habit for any antique dealer. It was a short blade, but deadly sharp. I hoped it might give me the element of surprise. Could I distract him and somehow manage to escape? My purse was slung over my shoulder behind my back, my hand's actions obscured from his eyes. He watched me, seemingly unable to speak. There was nothing to say after all. I knew what he was and he most certainly knew what I was: a witch, trapped in his hidey hole.

The moment he stopped pacing my heart began racing faster than the million thumps a second it was already beating. A shiver ran through my body as his lips curled into a menacing grin. My hand fumbled more frantically in my purse and instead of finding the knife it uncovered the bag of sunflower seeds Gavin had given me yesterday. At this point I was ready to try anything. I ripped open the package containing the thousands of tiny seeds in one violent tear and threw it into the air at Renard. The seeds showered down around us like rice at a wedding, their black and white shells littering the floor of the tunnel.

I didn't think it would work and was relieved when my hand closed around the knife in my bag. I steadied myself for an attack. Instead I was shocked to see Renard drop to his knees. He let out the most terrifying scream I'd ever heard. A retched sound bubbled up from his gut and echoed through the tunnel. The combined expression of rage and frustration was so palpable it left me frozen in place until I saw him drop to all fours and obsessively begin picking up the seeds one by one. With every few seeds recovered, he looked at me with such loathing I knew I had to get out of there fast. But first I rushed back to the altar and, rapidly swept every statue and corresponding picture into the bag I'd brought with me.

Renard was on the floor making undecipherable sounds of fury as he watched me steal his altar while he continued to compulsively search for seeds on the tunnel's dark floor. He alternated between whimpers of distress and growls of rage. Now the only obstacle to my exit was his body blocking the passageway. He may have been occupied by picking up the seeds, but there was no way he was simply going to step aside and let me pass. I had no choice but to turn and run into the darkness that led to the Bell Tower House. I just hoped there was an exit that wasn't caved in like it had been in the other tunnel. If so, I'd be at his mercy, which meant certain death.

As I turned to run, flashlight in hand, I heard Renard bellow the words "sobolani de moarte!" behind me, his furious screams filled with hate. He was sending a curse. I knew instantly that his words were in his native tongue. For whatever reason, each of the Renards had taken on French personas. But the words that lingered in the air, chasing after me, were Romanian. Morgan had spent his life collecting books of rare spells from Romania. I was familiar with the language because he'd spoken the spells to me whenever we talked of magic. It was a language I'd found beautiful and comforting; almost maternal to my ears. There had even been occasions when I'd dreamt in Romanian, waking to write down the mysterious words only to discover they were part of some ancient spell. This was the first time the language had filled me with mortal fear. The spell he was casting was for "the rats' death."

The tunnel got smaller as it climbed upwards. I could still hear Renard screaming in his mother tongue from behind me. I was fast putting distance between us, but eventually he'd find every last seed. When that moment came, I wanted to be as far away from him as physically possible. My breathing was short. I felt a stabbing pain in my chest. The air was tight in the tunnel and while the raging voice moved further away from me, I began to hear another sound echoing through the dirt and clay chamber. It was the scampering sound of not one, but many feet — rat feet — coming straight for me. I stumbled as I tried to run faster. Maneuvering with the heavy bag of statues and my purse on one arm was no easy task, made more difficult by the stifling air. I dropped my purse and held on tight to the bag of statues. My flashlight gave only a dim light.

The scuffling rats began to bear down on me. By the sound, there were hundreds of them closing in on me in the darkness. I had nothing to defend myself with but a single utility knife, which would be of little or no use. I turned a sharp corner and found a small door at the end of the tunnel that was waist high. I gave it a firm push, leaning on it with all of my weight. To my relief, it began to open. This door wasn't like the one below; it had metal hinges and workings instead of wood. It must have been a hundred years since it had been oiled. With my last breaths, I forced the door frantically open as the first set of red eyes rounded the corner behind me. I crawled through quickly pulling my bag of talismans behind me. As soon as I was through the door I pushed it closed just as a huge rat thrust its face through the crack. Its head thrashed back and forth as it snapped at me and tried to bite my hands. I didn't care if I decapitated the vile creature to make it stop. I gave the door one last heave and the rat wriggled back into the tunnel in order to keep its head.

As the door shut, I was shocked to see my own face staring back at me. The door was a mirrored panel of some kind. I looked wild with fear and determination. My long black hair was a massive tangle and my black clothes were smudged with grey clay and dirt. A swath of dirt slashed across one cheek. I stood clutching the bag, my chest heaving from the effort of escape. I was in the mirrored ballroom of the Bell Tower House. The panel that had opened into the tunnels was the same one Magdalene had been motioning to the night of the masquerade ball.

The room was entirely empty. The walls and floor were spotless. The only remnants from the party were the white lights that still hung in a gorgeous web from the skylight above. They were splayed across the room attached to the tops of the mirrors. Other than that, there was no evidence this room had been used a few nights ago.

It was cold and damp despite the unseasonably warm weather. That was when I noticed another reflection in the very center of the room underneath the skylight. It was a huge puddle of water. I heard the tapping of rain on the glass above. Then I heard the telltale signal of a leak; the persistent plunking of droplets hitting standing water.

There was a shimmer across the water that drew me closer. I had become accustomed to seeing the children in the mirrors, but this was something different. The floor was made with exquisitely inlaid white marble with natural veins of grey and black. Suddenly, I thought I saw the image of Dennis Morrison flicker across the puddle like a black and white photograph. It was gone in an instant. I looked around, but it was obvious I was alone. Remembering that Renard was most likely after me at this very moment, I rushed to the exit of the ballroom. The double doors were closed unlike at the party. With near silent movements, I slipped out of the ballroom and into the long hallway. Just as I was about to reach the front door, I heard a disconcertingly familiar voice coming from the opposite direction.

The voice was James' deep tone sounding through the silent house. It was followed by Sophie giggling with girlish delight. My heart was beating fast again and my mouth had gone dry. I knew he would come to inspect the leaking skylight, but thought he would have done that with one of his crew. Instead, he was alone here with her. All my instincts told me to run out of the house and get the talismans back to the Winship house before Renard found me. But for some reason, the voices drew me to them, like a moth to a flame.

I tiptoed towards the muffled sounds, knowing I'd probably find a scene that would burn my wings forever, yet I inched closer. The door was slightly ajar to the kitchen. James was leaning against the countertop with a casual stance that made me think he'd been in this same position before. He was drinking a glass of water and Sophie was flitting around the room. She was wearing a dress that was no more than a summer slip. It clung to her body showing her every curve. Her bare feet moved softly around the room as she told him all the things that she thought were too provincial about Port Townsend. James was agreeing with her assessment, joining in with his own mocking appraisals of country life compared to city living.

It wasn't the conversation that made me feel belittled, but rather the fact that he was trying to please her — at my expense. Just as I was about to turn away, the room became abnormally silent. I heard James' water glass clink as it hit the countertop. In the stillness, I thought I heard him gulp nervously. Then I saw how close Sophie was standing to James. She was leaning in, her breast brushing against his arm as she put her hand on his cheek. That was when she kissed him on his lips. It was a lingering kiss and James did nothing to pull away. He seemed startled, yet he did nothing to stop her. I gasped, shattering the silence.

James jerked away from Sophie and looked straight at me. I was covered with dirt and clay and looked like a wild woman. Sophie smirked at me with a look of pity and loathing that made me want to rake the utility knife across her perfect face. Instead, I ran. I didn't look back when I heard James call my name. His voiced cracked with panic, pleading for me to stop, which made me run even faster. I burst through the front door, down the steps and out the driveway. I was running down the street in only a few seconds.

I don't recall running the blocks back to the Winship house. My mind was in a state of shock; the ache in my chest was unbearable. I still clutched the talismans to my breast, as if they were living children left in my care. Clouds rushed overhead as the wind rose ominously. I heard the wind chimes on the back porch clanging their reassuring jingle that had always been a part of my life. I couldn't wrap my mind around what I had just witnessed. I wanted to ignore that scene in the Renards' kitchen. I shifted my focus to destroying them, even though my heart was broken.

All I could do now was funnel that pain into the act of unbinding the statutes. Morgan, Margot and Felix were in the backyard standing around a blazing fire. Like the traditional flames of St. John, the fire was a perfect circle of vivid red. I ran to them, letting Margot fold me into her aging arms. This was no time to give in to my emotions, yet the lump in my throat threatened to choke me with tears. Instead, I breathed in her familiar scent of roses and handed Morgan the bag of statues and photographs.

"I don't know what the photographs do, but they were stolen

from my desk and I found them with the statues on a black altar," I gasped, keeping my emotions at bay. I didn't want Felix to see me upset. In fact, I didn't want Felix to see any of this at all! At the same time, I felt he had a right to know we were fighting to stop evil incarnate – the Renards.

"We have to begin, now!" said Morgan, his voice grave as the rain continued to drizzle and thunder rumbled closer. There would soon be a downpour which would make keeping the fire going a much harder task.

"Where is Willa?" I asked, wanting to make sure she was safe at home when we began to destroy the Renards. I knew she had fallen in love with Daniel. I had no idea how she would ever be able to forgive us for what we were about to do. And yet there was no other way. They had to be stopped. I told them to begin as I rushed into the house. I had a nagging sensation that something was wrong with Willa. As I bounded up the steps towards the turret room I heard Willa raise her voice to a scream that was followed by a loud thud. I burst through the door and found Daniel standing over Willa's unconscious body. She had a bruise blossoming across her pale cheek. Daniel had struck her. Before I could stop him he reached down and lifted her body in his arms. I though he was going to push past me. I was prepared to stand my ground, but instead he headed straight for the window.

Daniel opened it with one arm while holding Willa. Her legs were folded over his left arm and her back draped over his right. In the two seconds it took me to move across the room, he gave me a horrifying sneer and jumped out of the window with Willa in his arms. It was three tall stories down from the turret. I let out a blood curdling scream as I heard a cracking thud sound below. A rustle of leaves and feathers whooshed onto the window sill as the night heron landed on its edge. It mocked me, one red eye fixed on the precious treasure that most certainly lay broken on the dying grass. It took all my will to rush at the bird, scaring it into a frenzy of flapping wings, so I could look on the tragedy that waited below.

SEMELÉ, CONSUMÉE PAR LA FOUDRE DE JUPITER.   Semele durch den blitz von Jupiter verzehret.

Semele is consum'd by Jupiter's thunder.   Semele door den blixem van Jupiter verteert.

CHAPTER 36

I held my breath as I leaned over the windowsill, expecting to see Willa's broken body on the ground like a smashed china doll. Instead, I saw James staring up at the window with what could only be described as astonishment on his usually calm face. There was no sign of either Willa or Daniel. I ran downstairs and out into the yard. Perhaps the jump was nothing dangerous for a vampire. I wasn't sure which was worse in this moment: Willa's broken body on the ground or Willa being kidnapped.

The back door crashed open and slammed loudly behind me as I ran to where James was standing. I wanted to slap him as hard as I could. I felt angry and betrayed by him. Yet I knew I needed him right in this moment if we were going to survive what was to come next. He hadn't moved an inch. I could tell he was about to hyperventilate.

"He jumped, Charlotte," James said in gasping breaths and he look at me with wild eyes. "It's not possible, how could he survive that jump?"

"Where did he go?" I screamed in a voice so full of rage that James actually shrunk back from me.

"Towards the Bell Tower House," he stuttered, reeling from what he had seen. He would have had a heart attack by now if he had seen half the things I'd witnessed on a daily basis. All the same, I was glad he was finally starting to look past the illusions. Even though I was furious with him, there was still a part of me that knew he was also in harm's way. He grabbed me by the shoulders, forcing me to look at him.

"Is this real, Charlotte?" he asked, his eyes slightly glazed with shock. Underneath was the glimmer of a spellbound mind. Logically, I knew he was not to blame for Sophie any more than Willa was to blame for Daniel. But my heart stung all the same.

"It is very real, James," I replied through gritted teeth, breaking free of his grip. I grabbed his hand and pulled him towards the side of the house where my family was getting ready to destroy the talismans.

Margot, Morgan and Felix were busily preparing the sacred fire. I knew that my first priority was to save Willa. They had not seen Daniel steal her away from the back of the house. James and I quickly told them in a rush of panic. I hadn't wanted to frighten Felix, but had no choice. We had run out of time. Our element of surprise was no longer going to work in our favor.

"We will do the ritual," Morgan said in a reassuring voice. "You two need to get Willa, now. If we work fast, by the time you find her we will have released the souls from the Renards' control. They will be weakened."

"Go to the Bell Tower House," said Margot, pulling Felix close to her side, "They will do what is natural to them. They'll run. Don't let them take Willa with them or we will never get her back."

James was struggling to make sense of the scene before him. The fire was burning high and the sacred statues were laid out on the ground like abandoned dolls. Felix held the stack of Dennis Morrison's pictures protectively in his hands. They would burn the images, along with the dolls, in case he had managed to capture the children's souls within them.

"What is all this?" James asked in a terrified voice. He looked horrified as Felix moved with confidence around the fire watching Morgan and Margot for cues to act. Felix was a natural sorcerer and for a brief second I could see something of Elsiba in his ways. There was no time to explain everything to James. I needed him to help me save our daughter. Regardless of how furious I was with him, at this moment, we needed to come together as one to save Willa.

"Later," I shouted, then added, "We need to get Willa — now, James! I need you with me in this!"

"Of course I'm with you," he answered quickly. Had he forgotten that I'd just seen him kissing Sophie? Or that he had suggested I get psychological help for thinking the Renards were vampires? I had to put all that aside, but my blood was boiling nonetheless.

We ran to the car and sped down the driveway back towards the Bell Tower House. This was the last place I wanted to set foot considering I had just escaped from it and its collection of horrors. I hoped that Daniel had taken her here, if not she would be lost to me forever. The car skidded when we turned down the long driveway lined with peach trees. James gunned the engine as we barreled down the one lane drive. I screamed for him to stop as we neared the entrance to the large circular drive. I wanted our car to block the exit.

"Leave the car parked here so they can't get out!" I shouted, as James brought the car to a sudden halt. As we sprinted towards the front door, the sky rumbled ominously. The air was oppressively hot, even with the drizzle. All movement was exhausting. Looking at the dark thunder clouds that had finally reached land, I knew the drizzle was about to turn into a downpour. As James and I set foot on the porch, the sky lit up with a blinding flash followed almost simultaneously by a deafening crack of thunder. The storm was just overhead. Rain burst through the clouds driving so hard I prayed that Morgan would be able to keep the ritual fire burning using his elemental gift. Real fire wouldn't stand a chance in this deluge.

James burst through the unlocked door. Even though he was still in a combination of shock and denial, he knew in his heart that Willa needed him. It was the one thing that might keep Sophie's power over him at bay. His love for me had not been enough, but the love of a child carried a sacred bond I prayed no vampire could break. As we pushed into the long hallway, I saw a stack of neatly packed luggage waiting by the doorway. Margot was right; they were going to run now that we had the effigies and knew exactly what they were. In their core, vampires are cowards. All people fear death, but most wouldn't trade the lives of countless others to remain esthetically intact. The Renards were aberrations filled with a combination of cowardice and lust that had eventually turned them into monsters.

James immediately bolted upstairs, skipping steps with his long legs. I kicked open all the doors along the hallway, searching the downstairs of the old manor. The house was eerily silent. I felt them lurking somewhere in the colossal building like spiders in the shadows. As I checked each room I found them all empty. James rushed down the main staircase and shook his head signaling they were nowhere to be found. The only place we had not looked was the ballroom.

Together we rushed towards the double doors pushing them both open wide.

The first thing that registered in my mind was relief; Willa was lying on the floor in the right hand corner. Her clothes were disheveled and she was still unconscious. James reached her first. He slid on his knees to her side checking for wounds and gently speaking to her in the hope she'd awaken. She let out a small groan as she began to regain consciousness.

The small door to the tunnel had been left ajar. I swallowed hard and gathered my power from the ground into my body. I was ready to chase the Renards into the tunnels. Just as I was preparing to delve back into the rat-infested darkness, Thomas Renard emerged from the secret door followed by Sophie and Daniel. Their faces were insane with fury that their precious plans had been destroyed. Apparently nothing irritates an obsessive-compulsive vampire like messing with their ritual. The fact that the Winships were about to light theirs on fire gave me just the tiniest of pleasures. It was fleeting, however, as I still had no idea how to stop them definitively.

James was cradling Willa in his arms as he had when she was a baby. She was still reeling; unable to stand. He hadn't yet noticed the Renards. As they stood next to each other, glaring at me with unbridled hatred, I noticed a flicker of light above us. The mirrors were shimmering as the thunder rumbled loudly above our heads.

"Where are they?" snarled Sophie, as she began to walk purposefully towards me. "Tell me or I will take your children with us and make sure you suffer for the rest of eternity!" Her voice keened, echoing off the empty mirrored walls and marble floors. She was grasping at straws. My children would be going nowhere with these corpses, of that I was sure. Thomas was furious as he repeatedly tried to brush dirt from his clothes. Apparently vampires are also quite particular about their attire not being sullied. Their power was in their illusion of perfection and beauty. In reality, what was beneath would repulse any living human, if they looked closely.

"James, we have to get out of here now," I said under my breath not taking my eyes off of the Renards. Daniel had his eyes fixed on Willa; a beast locked onto its prey. He wanted her and we were standing in his way. A flash lit the room as lighting illuminated the sky followed by another crash of thunder and the pounding of rain on the glass roof. Water was rushing through the cracks in the skylight above, adding to the puddle that was quickly becoming a small lake. In a way, the water that separated us from the Renards gave me an odd sense of security, as if it was a barrier.

Sophie and Thomas began speaking to each other in Romanian. The words floated in the space between them as they abandoned their façade entirely. Daniel listened with only half his attention. He was still watching Willa. I knew he was calculating how quickly he could get to her, overpower James, and snatch her from us once again. I had no words. Instead I inched closer to James and Willa. We would need to make a run for it, but I wasn't sure we'd make it out before they caught us. I still had no sense of how to fight them off unless the sheer will to survive and protect could become a supernatural force.

Just as Daniel was about to rush across the room towards us, an eerie wail filled the room stopping him in his tracks. At first I thought it was Willa, but the voice was too high pitched. It was the haunting sound of a dead child, screaming. The noise began to grow louder filling the room completely. The Renards looked as startled as I was. James was terrified as he looked in all directions trying to identify where the noise was coming from. Another flash of lighting lit the room and in doing so revealed the figures of the 130 children standing inside the mirrored panels. It was Magdalene who was making the noise. Eva and Colette were standing at her side. All the children had their eyes fixed on the Renards. A ripple shuddered across the glass. In one united movement, the children stepped from their mirrored prisons.

I knew the moment the ghosts set foot on the marble floor that Morgan, Margot and Felix had destroyed the cursed peach wood dolls. The souls were no longer being used as an energy source for the Renards. The children's souls were now free. Another flash of lightning lit the room, revealing what lay beneath the skin of the Renards. I heard James gasp and Willa let out a heartbreaking whimper. Sophie was no longer the lovely woman she had been only moments before. Rather, she more closely resembled a decrepit corpse with hideously vibrant eyes. Thomas' flesh was rotting on one side of his face revealing bone and tendon. Daniel's once sixteen-year old body looked more like the bent, sagging body of an old man.

The ghost children surrounded the Renards, corralling them into the center of the room. The mirrors created a dizzying mix of movement as they inched closer to the monsters who had held them captive for a hundred years. Magdalene was still screaming a continuous cry that bounced off of the walls. I rushed to James and Willa feeling an unbearable urgency to flee this place. James lifted Willa into his arms ready to carry her injured body. As we were getting ready to make a run for the door, a sound as loud as a gunshot filled the room. The mirrors filled instantly with a flash of light so radiant I was sure we'd be blinded. The sound of shattering glass filled the room as the skylights exploded. Even Magdalene's glorious scream was drowned out by the earsplitting crashing sound that filled the space.

James, Willa and I froze in place as we watched the lightning bolt that had struck the metal of the skylight travel through the mirrors. The room buzzed dangerously with the current. I realized that the Renards were standing in the puddle of water just as the lightning bolt traveled from the mirrored walls across the marble floor to the conductive pool.

Magdalene's scream had been as lovely as a lark compared to the horrific noise that came from the mouths of the Renards as they were electrocuted. Their bodies lifted from the floor creating a massive electrical arc. Blue and white lightning crackled in the air as the rain fell into the now gaping hole of the skylight. The smell of rotting flesh burning to the bone filled the space. I couldn't tear my eyes away from the sight of their bodies suspended in the air. The lightning had them in its clawed grasp; twisting around them with ropes of silver light. I could feel the charge everywhere around us in the room but the lightning only had eyes for the Renards. James retched as we watched with horrified fascination as the three vampires were reduced to nothing more than a pile of gore and ash. If it hadn't been for the horror of the situation, the shimmering light of the electricity combined with the mirrors, water and marble would have been a thing of pure beauty. I should have been terrified. Instead, I knew it had come for them alone. The current sparked and swirled until the Renards were no more and we were left unharmed.

The room was alive with an electrical pulse. The ghost children watched as their capturers were reduced to a pile of dust and the lightning began to recede. The rumble above lessened as the rain slowed. James stood next to me with eyes as round as silver dollars. I knew he was not only seeing what remained of the Renards, but he was also looking upon the ghost children. He could see them as clearly as I could. Willa was sobbing in James' arms. For the first time I felt a tug of regret, not that Daniel was no more, but for the hurt that his death would cause my Willa. It was only a small consolation when, as I looked at the smoldering pile of ash, I remembered that on one of Gavin's lists of "ways to kill a vampire" had been the word: electrocution.

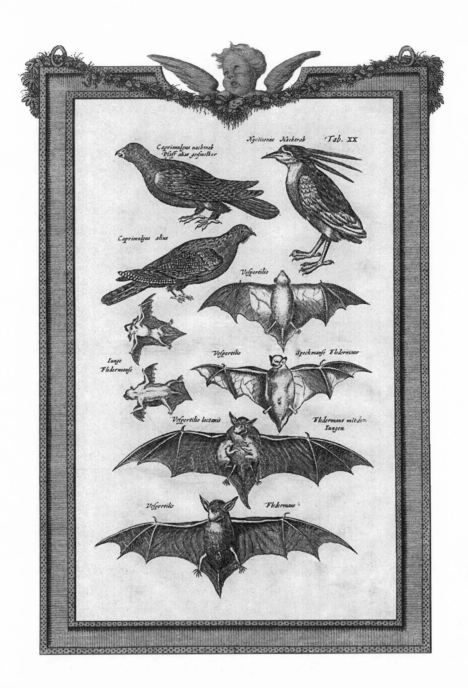

Chapter 37

I carefully inched my way closer to the pool of electrified water. James continued to hold Willa in his arms; she was still coming in and out of consciousness. As I moved forward, I noticed another bruise on Willa's arm. It was a fresh blue with a tiny red dot at its center. She had been drugged. With what, I wasn't sure, but she was trying to fight it, coming in and out of lucidity. As if reading my mind, Magdalene whispered "it's poppies." I nodded to her, swallowing hard, imagining already the devastation that had been dealt to my innocent girl.

The air was still crackling with electricity. I dared not touch the water; the current might still be live. The ghost children had made a large circle around the water's edge. Even though they were now free, it didn't change the fact that their lives had been taken. All of their lives in exchange for a now smoldering pile of ash. From where I stood, there wasn't much left of the Renards. The ash was mixed with shards of bone and lying neatly on top of each pile sat their perfect sets of white teeth. These were the vestiges of greedy soul-less beings intent on devouring all. A dark part of me wanted the teeth for myself. It would be a grisly reminder they were truly gone. But then I remembered the look on Thomas' face as he caressed Dennis Morrison's pictures and I felt a wave of revulsion. This was not a souvenir I wanted to bring into my home. I would not become like them in any way.

The ghost children stood motionless. I felt their grief ripple through the room. James stood beside me with Willa's drugged body still in his strong arms. He carried her as if she was a feather and yet I knew his heart was heavy. Tears threatened to overflow from his eyes as he looked at the solemn ghosts, lost so young, and at our own daughter abused at such a tender moment in her young life. He touched my arm lightly with the back of his hand as he shifted Willa in his arms.

"We should go," he said in a tense tone. This was all very new to him and I was surprised at how well he was taking it. I didn't know what to do next. The children stood there, seemingly lost. I needed to get Willa back to the Winship house and yet I felt as if I could not leave the ghost children alone. The rumbling outside the house continued, although the rain had nearly stopped. I took in each of their grey faces as they peered at me with stern eyes. Then it dawned on me, they too needed to know this would never again happen in this town. Ever since the first visit from Eva and Colette, the ghost children had sent me warnings hoping to avoid another vampire plague among their descendants.

"You can leave now," I said to the room, feeling their attention fixed on us, "We will never let this happen here again." James moved closer to me trying to get me to leave. We turned together and made our way carefully to the open doors. The acrid odor of electrical destruction filled the air. As we reached the door, we heard the sound of hundreds of flapping wings. The children were gone and in their place 130 swallows funneled through the gaping hole in the roof, where the skylight had been. Despite their escape and the Renards' destruction, I still found it hard to breathe. The air in the room was heavy and my lungs burned from the ash in the air. James led the way out of the Bell Tower House. He moved swiftly, placing Willa's small body gently on the back seat of our car. The sky was still grey and the town remained a sepia tone as we sped towards the Winship house. In my heart I knew something was still dramatically wrong.

As we pulled into our own driveway we saw Morgan, Margot and Felix picking through what was left of the fire. James carried Willa into the house and up to her room as Margot rushed in behind him. My adrenaline had kept me going up to this point, but now I felt the strain of fatigue. Felix was squatting next to the fire with a pile of soot smudged objects at his side. Morgan continued to pull things from the embers. It wasn't until I was standing next to them that I realized they were Dennis Morrison's pictures.

"They didn't burn," said Felix with obvious concern. "No matter what we did they wouldn't budge."

"It worked," I said to them, explaining that we had been extremely lucky when lightning struck the Bell Tower House, reducing the Renards to nothing more than ash and teeth. Morgan gave me one of his usual smirks.

"Luck had nothing to do with it," he said, punctuating his words with a laugh, "That was an act of God. Nature will only let things move against it for so long before it takes matters into its own hands. We, the Winships and others like us, tend to amplify the will of nature. Help focus it in a way." Just as he said this, the flock of swallows landed in our willow tree. These psychopomps of the lost children, souls in the guise of birds, still hadn't left us for the other side. I had the lingering feeling that this episode wasn't yet completely over. Something still felt terribly wrong.

"I don't know what to do for Willa," I said, feeling my throat tighten as I thought of her upstairs in the turret room. She had been struck, drugged and had watched as her first love had been electrocuted. Regardless of how evil Daniel was I knew this would be devastating for her. I felt helpless. I knew James and Margot would tend her physical wounds and make sure she was safe, but it was her emotional wounds that worried me the most. Morgan didn't reply. He knew all too well what the darkness could do once it entered the soul. Willa's return to the normal world would be a difficult one. In many ways I had failed to protect her.

The swallows sat patiently in the willow tree watching over us. A loud thud sounded from one of the branches as the heron's nest was pushed from its perch. It crashed through the massive tree until it hit the ground with a sickening crunch. I approached it with caution. The heron had been one of the Renards' familiars. I had no idea if it had died with them or was waiting to pluck my eyes out when I least expected it. The nest was surprisingly large up close. It was an odd combination of moss, twigs and other debris carefully woven into half of a sphere. I pushed it over with my shoe and found three crushed eggs. Blood oozed from the white shells, reminding me of the teeth sitting atop the gory piles of what remained of the Renards. The swallows above were silent as they watched me examine the remains of the night heron's nest.

The next contained nothing but the broken eggs, bits of Willa's hair woven into the moss and the smell of peaches and death. Then I noticed two small red eyes peering from one of the rat holes at the base of the willow. Then another pair of red eyes appeared from under the rose bushes. Before long, the red eyes were gathering together, creating a small army. They zipped under the gate towards the house, scurrying from their dark holes. I backed up slowly towards Morgan and Felix who were standing by the fire pit. Felix was wiping the last of Dennis Morrison's photos clean with his shirt sleeve. They were smudged with a bit of soot, but no other harm had been done to them in the flames.

"Morgan, the rats are gathering," I said in a voice edged in panic. He looked at the exact spot where hundreds of rats were congregating by the base of the willow tree. I looked out onto the street and saw dozens more of them, some as big as cats, rushing towards the Winship house. If the familiars were still alive, then the Renards might not be gone either! Quickly, I rushed to Morgan and Felix's side. The rats came at us through the front gates and out from under the dead lilac bushes. They spilled from under the foundation of the house and formed a circle around us. We were trapped!

They stared at us, as their circle grew. It was impossible to know how many of the filthy creatures waited to attack us. Just their organizing into a disciplined formation, like a regiment of soldiers, made my skin crawl. Who was giving them orders if the Renards were nothing more than disembodied teeth? Felix tucked Dennis Morrison's photographs into his shirt pocket and grabbed Morgan's and my hands. I felt his power and energy crackling through the three of us. But there was also uncertainty about how to crush these creatures once and for all.

The rats were six feet from us on all sides, pacing and snapping their jaws. Some hissed with fury; others squeaked impatiently. Their long, dark fur glistened and their long hairless tails thrashed like worms in the mud. The dark sky overhead menaced with thunder clouds. I knew there was no chance of a second lightning strike to destroy the rats – what were we going to do?

The window of the turret room opened with a creak as Margot and James looked down at the horror. James looked terrified and conflicted. I knew he wanted to rush to our aid, but something held him back. He must still have been under Sophie's spell! I could almost feel him straining against it, fighting the darkness within. Margot was calculating. I could see the wheels turning as her dark eyes peered down at the sea of rats surrounding us. She looked up at the sky and a massive thundercloud burst open sending driving rain down upon us. Her thought must have been to drown them. But these were hearty beasts. They merely became more agitated as they paced in the thickening mud. We were soaking wet, shivering as we gathered our energy to ourselves in the hope that we could create an energy shield.

The rain continued falling, though it lessened as Margot realized it was doing more harm to us than to the rats. Felix, who had been so brave up until this moment, began to panic. He pointed at one of the largest rats directly in front of us. It bared its sharp teeth in response to Felix's gesture.

"Mom, that's the one that bit Cody!" he said with a high trembling voice. "It's the one that was looking at me by the school." I let my eyes burrow into the creature as it swiveled to look straight at me. I recognized something about it that felt unnatural. Then I realized — its greedy eyes looked exactly like Thomas Renard's. Had he shape shifted into one of his familiars? I didn't know if it was just his messenger or if he had been able to actually transform into the vermin that stood threateningly before me.

At that moment, the night heron erupted from under the eaves of the house and flew straight at us. As it swooped overhead, it let out a horrific caw at the sight of its destroyed nest. Like a commander telling its troops to charge, it screeched again and in a second the rats were upon us. They pinched and tore at us, their teeth clamping onto our skin. Morgan had Felix hanging over his shoulder as he tried desperately to keep him safe. He was wringing the rats' necks as hundreds of them clawed our delicate flesh. James and Margot let out terrible screams from above as they watched us being torn apart by the angry rodents. Even if we had been able to run, it would have been straight into the fray as we were surrounded. And now, we were overpowered by them. Streams of blood flowed from the multiplying gashes all over my body. Felix was throwing them off Morgan's back as they climbed higher onto his uncle's body biting and gnawing their way to reach Felix's small hands. That was when I stumbled. My body hit the ground hard. I knew it was over when my face landed in the mud. I felt a rush of their feet climb across my hair to bite at my neck. Their weight was too great; I couldn't raise myself up without being pushed back into the muddy ground.

Then I heard a roar so loud I thought it was thunder closing in again. The ground beneath me began to vibrate and emitted a low, rumbling, thumping sound. Somehow I lifted myself out of the mud, and climbed to my feet again. The rats were still writhing all around us, but they were suddenly mesmerized by the noise coming from beneath us. As I listened, it became clear it wasn't thunder. The noise was a consistent series of thuds that echoed through the wet air as Morgan pulled me close to him with one arm. I shivered uncontrollably, holding Morgan for support. The rats were still surrounding us, but instead of attacking as they had moments before, they were actually swaying from side to side. They stood on their hind legs, noses pointed up in the air, frantically searching for the source of the noise.

That was when I saw them walking in a single line down the street towards the Winship house. It was Pat Savage and his coven from the Beltane Lavender Farm. Each member of the coven carried a drum. There were percussion instruments of various shapes and sizes and one, massive drum held by two members walking at the back of the line. As they moved closer the loud throm, throm, throm became more melodious. The small drums held by the women of the coven beat in intricate harmonies, while the largest one created a primal base. The wind carried their chanting along with the music. More shocking still was the sight of the rats moving into a perfect line behind them.

Chapter 38

As Pat and his coven arrived at the iron gates of the Winship house, I saw that each of their faces was in deep concentration. The words they spoke had the same rhythms I'd heard Thomas and Sophie speaking to one another. It was Romanian. It was the Pied Piper's tune transformed to lead the rats away from the town! How they had known that we needed them in this precise moment was a mystery, but the drums they held were undoubtedly those made from the skins I'd seen them stretching when I visited the farm days before.

Pat made a ceremonious bow as he passed us, without breaking his chanting or drumming. The line moved past the house towards Chetzemoka Park. The rats seemed enthralled by the haunting song; they followed behind the coven in step with the drum beats. Margot and James crashed through the back door and ran frantically to our sides. James took me and Felix in his arms despite the fact that I was covered with mud and blood. He squeezed us so hard that Felix began gasping for breath before James loosened his grip.

I looked up at the turret window and saw Willa looking down at the broken night heron's nest. Her face was drawn and dark as the shadows from the grey clouds overhead moved above her, little snippets of light peeking through. She was alone in her tower, too far for us to reach her. The rats continued gathering into lines and funneled out the main gates of the house behind the beating drums. I was drawn to the rhythms. Unable to resist, I began following behind the rats. Morgan, James, Felix and Margot were compelled as well. Together we joined Pat's procession. Inside I felt a new-found sense of hope that this would finally be the end of the Renards.

I glanced desperately back up at Willa. She looked like a tragic princess held captive in a castle fortress. Her auburn hair hung over the windowsill in tangled curls; her bruised cheek a painful shade of purple. The swallows still perched in the willow tree. They had no song for us as they watched the rats tremble and sway with the drums.

I wanted to stay with Willa, yet I was pulled into the music.

As we moved down the street, following the chant, people opened their screen doors and peered out their windows at the shocking scene. Thousands of rats were now in the procession. They came from the sewers, abandoning their hiding places. The rats were a black, furry, undulating mass heading toward the park behind the coven. People eventually began to follow as well, fascinated by the sight and the sound of the drums. The words of the coven's song filled every corner of my mind. I, too, joined in, repeating the words. Morgan, Felix and James did the same. Families abandoned their homes, doors left wide open, to march along to the curious beat. Soon much of the town had joined the procession of rats.

Reaching the park, Felix took my hand as we passed our favorite swings. The coven was leading the rats down the steep dirt path that ended on the beach. It was early evening. The tide would be coming in soon, creating an undertow that would pull the sand and any debris on the beach out to sea. We stopped at the cliffs' edge, as did the others who had followed. We watched as Pat and his coven arrived at the water's edge. The rats, however, did not stop. They reached the waves and continued marching — straight into the treacherous waters. One by one, they drowned. In a matter of minutes, thousands of their corpses floated on the ocean's surface like pieces of black coal bobbing in the waves.

The coven continued to chant and drum, with the town watching from above on the cliffs, until the last rat was swept out to sea. We were all connected in this moment. As we chanted together, we ensured that the dangers of pestilence were eliminated from our midst. Only my family and my close friends would ever know what the Renards had really been. But the story of Pat's coven emptying the town of the plague-ridden rats would become a part of our town history. And the coven would finally, later be accepted by locals.

As we slowly made our way back to the Winship house, weak from blood loss and exhaustion, the iron gates were a welcome sight. As we walked towards the house, the sound of fire engines and ambulances were heard rushing down the street. They were headed in the direction of the Bell Tower House. The lightning strike had been noted by neighbors; I wondered if a fire had started in the ballroom. In a way I wished that the house, with its tunnels, would burn to the ground, taking the teeth and the ashes with it.

Back at the Winship house, the swallows silently waited in the willow tree watching over us. I dragged myself up the stairs to the turret room leaving James, Felix, Margot and Morgan at the kitchen table, deep in shock and exhausted from their efforts. For the first time in the many years that James and I had been a couple, he was truly one of us. The moment the rats became submerged, I felt him come back to me. The vampire allure had been lifted and his heart was his own once again.

When I reached the third floor hallway, I walked quietly to Willa's bedroom door. As I reached for the white porcelain knob, I realized just how filthy I was. My hands were covered with dirt and blood. I turned the knob and found Willa deep in sleep, wrapped in the protective covers of her bed. She looked so small, like a tiny fairy in a world too big for something so delicate. I had kept the tears inside for weeks now as I worried and fought and did what I could to save her. I hoped I wasn't too late. The tears that streamed down my face cut streaks through the caked mud on my cheeks. I looked like a wild creature; some type of golem formed from clay to do its master's bidding.

I quietly left her room not wanting to wake her. The sight of me would have terrified most. Considering all she'd been through, I didn't want to add further trauma. Somehow I made it to our bedroom and into the shower. I stood under scalding hot water washing away the filth, letting the drops cleanse my wounds. Tiny bite marks covered my legs and arms. My body ached. I rubbed shampoo into my tangled, matted hair. But no matter how much I scrubbed, I still couldn't get the smell of death from my nostrils. The sickly sweet aroma mingled with the smell of soap and refused to be removed entirely. Eventually I gave up and stepped from the shower onto a clean towel.

As I dried my body and wrapped my hair into a messy bun, I noticed something odd in the mirror behind me. A shimmer, like the one I had seen in the puddle at the Renard house. An image of Dennis Morrison wobbled in the steamed reflection. I had a full-length mirror that reflected off of the mirror over the sink on the other side of the room. There was a word clearly smudged onto the mirror: RENARD. A chill ran through my body despite the heat in the room. Dennis was giving me a message. That was when the reflection of the word in the full-length mirror made me shudder. I hadn't noticed it until this moment but RENARD was DRANER written backwards!

There is much that can be held in a name. The Winships knew this better than most. Was Dennis Morrison showing me the Renards had chosen this name for a reason? What was so important about their name? I was already certain they were the same family who had come to town in 1912. I didn't need any more convincing on that front. I was still missing something. I could feel it hovering in the corners of my mind, yet I was too exhausted to locate it amid the many volumes.

I put on a nightgown and crawled into bed, exhausted. I didn't even bother to turn off the light. The name went into dreamland with me as I drifted into a dead sleep filled with visions of rats and lightning. No ghost children came to me. They slept in their bird forms tucked in the willow tree outside, refusing to leave. Instead, I dreamt of the photographs that would not burn through the eyes of the man who had taken them. Dennis Morrison was cleaning the lenses of his camera in the empty barber shop. The finished photographs of the 130 children had been sent to Boston that morning. He wanted them far from this place where the last child had just died. A bell rang and the door to the barber shop opened and closed with a thud. He was about to say that they were closed for the night, when he saw Mr. Draner standing in the doorway.

"I would like to invite you and Anita to our home for an informal meal. We are the newest members of town, after all, and both of us from the Old Country," he said politely, although there was an underlying menace to his words. "Will seven this evening do for you and your lovely wife?" Mr. Draner asked. Dennis Morrison agreed, but his heart began to sink. He knew what this man was and he also knew that he had failed once again to stop him. They were at the apex of their power, having restored their energy from Port Townsend's most innocent citizens. Morrison had no idea how to stop them. Dennis began gasping for air. Everything went dark and he suddenly couldn't breathe. I heard Mr. Draner, (in the more familiar voice of Thomas Renard) comment on the usefulness of a traditional English name. Then the dream vanished in a flash of black and white.

I awakened gasping for air in the dark and sat up in bed immediately. James was sleeping next to me; the room was filled with shadows. The town was silent with an occasional rumble of thunder overhead. I made my way to Felix's room. His door was ajar; he was fast asleep, his owl night light burning bright. Dennis Morrison's photographs were stacked neatly by his bedside table. A shiver ran through my body looking at them. I climbed the stairs to the turret room to check on Willa. She was still asleep. Her breathing was steady; I saw the swallows still sitting patiently in the branches outside the window standing guard. Tonight, the house felt safe for the first time since the arrival of the Renards.

Just thinking of their name brought back the stifling feeling of the dream. I went back downstairs and slipped quietly back into bed. James shifted in his sleep and before I knew it, I was wrapped in his arms. His warmth next to me was comforting. If ever a man deserved forgiveness for his trespasses, this was one of those moments. It wasn't every day that a manipulative vampire set its sights on one's husband. Exhausted, I succumbed to sleep. This time the world went black as I tried to remember what was so important about the vampires' name.

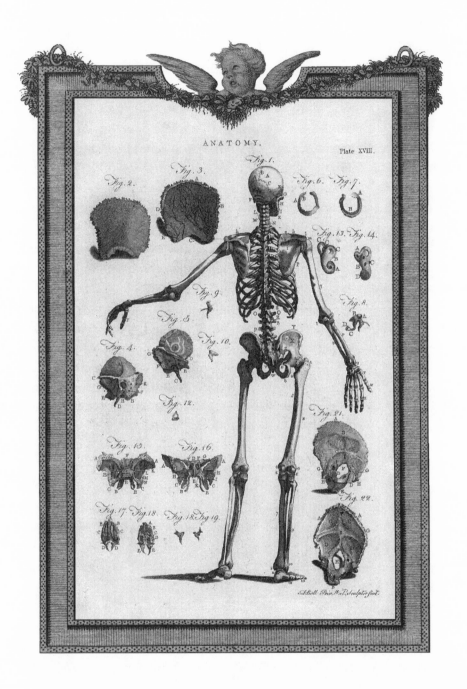

ANATOMY.

Plate XVIII.

CHAPTER 39

Morning arrived with a rush of cool air typical for a mid-March day. It washed through the open windows of the Winship house. The stifling heat of the past several weeks abated, leaving a crisp breeze in its place. When I was a child and had difficulties resolving a problem, I would ask the dream gods to help me find the answer in the Land of Nod. Almost without exception I would awake the next morning with a solution waiting on the edge of sleep. Last night I had asked them for help in finding what was so important about the Renard's name. I woke with what I thought might be the answer. It was a hunch more than a certainty, and a crazy one at that.

I walked into the kitchen and found James and Felix eating their breakfast. James had a cup of coffee waiting for me by my chair. Willa was still sleeping, which left me feeling a deep wave of worry and sadness. The same look was spread across James' face as he greeted me with a tentative kiss. Felix had a glow to his skin that looked healthy. I was relieved when he told me he hadn't been bitten by the rats. Morgan and Margot had gone home exhausted last night. Both felt confident that with the destruction of the rats, the Renards would have no way to return. Morgan promised to bring me something from his garden for the rat bites that we both had all over our bodies.

The smell of coffee helped me feel somewhat centered again. I waited until Felix left the room before speaking to James. The truth was, I needed his help in what was to come next and I had no idea how he was handling all that he had witnessed yesterday. One thing was obvious, he wasn't his usual chatty self. Granted there was much to talk about; I just wasn't sure where to start. I had no desire to speak of Sophie Renard and what may have gone on between them. I was too exhausted to open that door, especially now that any connection between them had been lifted with Sophie's destruction. But I still needed to know how he felt about ghosts and my connection with them. Did he finally believe me? Or had he retreated back into doubt in order to preserve his safe version of reality?

"James," I said with a bit of a sigh as I sipped my coffee, "I need your help with something that I don't want to do alone. It has to do with the Renards." I could see his body tense and his head drop when I mentioned their name.

"Ok, I'll do whatever you need me to do," he said with a slight crack in his usually deep voice.

"Do you remember those ghost children that we saw last night and how they came out of the mirrors?" I asked, waiting to gauge his response. He simply nodded in affirmation and waited for me to continue. I felt a sense of sudden hope that he was acknowledging them. "We freed them. But there is still someone else who we need to help and it means going back to the Bell Tower House." He shuddered slightly as I mentioned the house he had loved for so many years. It was ruined for him forever after what he had experienced inside. Even so, I was feeling a tiny victory that he was acknowledging the paranormal aspects.

"I want Gavin to come with us. I need to call him and tell him what has happened. It's important that he knows. He has been helping with all of this. Without him, I probably wouldn't be alive." The last phrase brought James' eyes to mine. They were glassy with tears. This was a rare occurrence for him; I could count on one hand the number of times I had seen him cry.

"Call Gavin," he said as he swallowed hard, trying to fight back his emotions. I wasn't sure if he was upset because I had been in peril and he had been none the wiser. Little did he know, it had been at the exact moment when Sophie was entangling him in her web that I had been in mortal danger below in the tunnels. If I hadn't had Gavin's bag of sunflower seeds to distract Thomas, yesterday's events would have ended quite differently. Or maybe it was simply because he hadn't believed me when I'd come to him with the truth about the Renards. Whatever it was, there had been evil at work within him. Now that he could more clearly see the Renards for what they were, I hoped it would bring him a deeper sense of understanding. But first, there were things that needed to be resolved in order to set old wrongs to right.

"I need you to get three shovels from the garage." He looked at me with a sudden flash of fear. There were things hidden in the dirt of the tunnels that needed to be revealed and I didn't want to do it alone this time. I left him in the kitchen taking my coffee with me to my workroom. The old Winship library was my safe haven. I had loved this room from an early age. Surrounded by ancient books and jars filled with all my precious stones, it was mine alone. I dialed Gavin's number and was relieved when I heard his voice, thick with the vestiges of sleep, on the other end of the line. Once I began telling him all that had happened the day before, he was immediately alert.

"I missed the fireworks again didn't I?" he asked with a tense laugh. This wasn't the first time that I'd been caught up in the action of fighting demons, only to tell him the morning after what had transpired. He teased, but I knew underneath he was hurt I hadn't called for help when the sky was falling. When I told him about the lightning and the final march of the rats into the sea, it only increased his irritation. The only condolence was when I told him that the sunflower seeds had most likely saved my life.

"Saved by a bag of seeds against a vampire," he sighed mockingly. "It's official. I will never again be able to read another vampire book. Ridiculous, really. The only thing worse would have been to stake them with a toilet plunger or something. Monsters just aren't what they used to be." Despite my fatigue and worry, Gavin managed to get a laugh out of me before I told him about my plan. He wasn't laughing anymore after I relayed my suspicions. Instead, he said he'd get dressed and come over to the house in ten minutes.

I hung up feeling the heaviness in my heart begin to lift if only for a brief moment. I quickly dressed in jeans and an old t-shirt before heading up to the turret room to check on Willa. When I opened the door I expected her to be asleep. The room was completely silent. Instead I found her, eyes wide open, staring at the ceiling. Her lashes fluttered as she turned her head to me. The bruise on her face was still a vibrant purple and the pinprick on her arm was a livid red surrounded by blue tinged skin. Her other arm was still in a cast held tightly to her small chest. If ever she had looked like a wounded dove, it was at this moment. I moved to the side of her bed and sat close to her. My hand moved instinctively to her head as I brushed the tangle of auburn hair from her eyes. A small smile lit her face for a brief moment only to be followed by a shudder of pain.

Pain was a deceitful enemy. I knew all too well that it could claim its place in one's heart only to defer the sensation to the flesh and bones. Willa's pain was undoubtedly of the physical variety in this moment, but below the surface was the dark pain that bloomed into thorny vines. Those weeds of desolation needed to be pulled at the root before they were able to thrust themselves into her very being. I worried that what had been put into her veins by the Renards would be her undoing. Magdalene had called it 'the poppies' and I knew all too well the destruction those delicate red petals contained in their juice. Our shores had been rife with opium from the founding days to the present. I had the foreboding sense that their alluring numbness would soon call for Willa. I would need to watch her very closely in the days and months ahead.

"Are you ok watching Felix for a little bit?" I asked, hoping that being responsible for him would take her mind off of things for a short time. "He's reading in his room." She nodded a yes and carefully pulled the covers back. Her body looked shockingly thin in her favorite dark purple pajamas. They hung on her fragile frame. "I have coffee downstairs and we'll be home soon. You don't have to get up."

"I need to get up," she said in a soft voice. How we would ever breach the subject of Daniel was beyond me. I had no idea where to start and felt it was far too soon to speak of such things. Instead, I took her in my arms and held her. Her body was stiff in my embrace but she didn't pull away, which felt like a small victory. I reluctantly left her as I heard Gavin's familiar knock on the front door. As I made my way past the grandfather clock down to the first floor I saw James let Gavin inside. There were three shovels leaning by the front door. I gave Gavin a quick hug as I reached the landing and quickly put my boots on.

Together we drove to the Bell Tower House. James had received a phone call from the fire department about the lightning strike the previous night. The police explained that they'd found the remains of the Renards in horrible circumstances. He was given the green light to inspect the structure for damages. The Renards' remains had been removed from the premises. It seemed that every time I closed my eyes I saw their gory piles of dust and teeth still smoking on the marble floor of the ballroom. To go back into that room would have been unbearable if James and Gavin hadn't been with me. I wasn't normally faint of heart by nature, but these were extreme circumstances.

As James pulled up to the Bell Tower House's massive front porch, the sun drifted behind a cloud. The world went grey for a brief moment. The three of us strode to the front door, which we found unlocked. James had his keys in hand, but one turn of the handle proved the house had been left open by the firemen. The odor of peaches still lingered in the hallways, though it was the stronger smell of burnt flesh that permeated the home. Gavin followed us wearing a look of dread. There was no room for jokes; the reality of yesterday's events was nauseatingly present.

James pushed open the double doors to the ballroom. Nothing had been cleaned with the exception of the remains. There were red and grey smears across the white marble floor where what was left of the Renards had been found. Shattered glass from the skylight was littered everywhere creating an odd glimmer in the silver mirrors that lined the room. I put my hand gently on James' arm. He was shaking slightly under all that muscle and manly composure. I could only imagine how everything last night had looked through his eyes. Mine were used to visions of ghosts and things that went bump in the night, but he had only had inklings of what lies behind the veil. It would take time for him to sort through the layers of what he had witnessed before he could find a place for it in his reality. Gavin, on the other hand, was silent and stoic as he took in the lavish room that was now a shambles.

I took a deep breath and walked towards the hidden door that led to the tunnels. James and Gavin followed me as I turned on my flashlight and slipped inside the dirt enclave. The tunnel was tight as we filed in and headed downwards in darkness. Only the bobbing white circle of the flashlight lit the way. James and Gavin both had to stoop to fit inside being a head taller. I heard their quickened breathing behind me as we made our way down into the earth. James was carrying the shovels. A growing sense of panic began to rise in me as we grew closer to the altar. It was harder to breathe with each step downwards. I banished the thought of the rats from my mind. I knew they were all at the bottom of the sea by now, but it didn't alter the fact that less than 24 hours earlier a horde of them had chased me through this very tunnel.

I was gasping for air when my flashlight landed on a perfect pile of neatly arranged sunflower seeds on the ground. This marked the site of the altar. The place where Thomas had been thwarted by Gavin's addiction to reading all things monster related. It had been unnerving to see Thomas sitting on the ground carefully picking up each of the tiny seeds; unable to chase after me as I stole the objects that insured his survival. I thanked the universe that he had been a slave to order as it had ensured my life and his demise.

The altar was dark. I had brought a lighter along hoping the candles were still intact as it would give us a way to see our gruesome work. I quickly lit the black candles that were lined up in perfect rows. It gave the dirt tunnel instant illumination, even if it was in the form of an eerie flicker. I stood on the packed dirt directly before the shelves where the peach wood dolls had been. My breathing was labored as I took a shovel from James and scooped out the first clump of dirt from the floor.

"This is where we need to dig," I said. James directed us to put the dirt further down into the tunnel. He wanted to make sure we were safe in what we were attempting to do. Gavin and I followed his lead as we removed the dirt that had been packed down for a hundred years. I had to stop several times as it became increasingly harder to breathe. James and Gavin weren't having any trouble with their respiration. The fact that I found it so hard to breathe in the Bell Tower House from the very first time I stepped inside had been one of the clues that made me suspect someone had died here. It wasn't until I had dreamt of Dennis Morrison being invited to dine with the Draners that I was able to put my finger on who may have died in these tunnels.

Just as the memory of him in the dream came to mind, my shovel hit something solid. I quickly told James and Gavin to stop digging. James grabbed one of the candles from the shelf and held it closer so we could see what lay beneath. I crouched down in the three-foot deep trench we had dug and carefully dusted the dirt away. Something sharp grazed my finger as I dug. A few more swipes across the surface revealed a perfect set of screaming teeth attached to the full skeleton of the late Dennis Morrison.

1. L'Hirondelle de cheminée.___2. Id À croupion blanc.

3. L'Hiroxdelle de rivage.

Chapter 40

To be buried alive is a horrific death. It was obvious looking at the remains that Dennis Morrison had been dumped in this shallow grave and buried while he still had breath in his lungs. James and Gavin were stupefied as they leaned in close to see what was left of the old photographer. I crouched next to him, slowly feeling my breath come back to me in normal rhythms. Standing in the corner, finally freed from the binding of his unofficial grave, the grey figure of Dennis Morrison stood tall in the candle light. As my fingers continued to uncover his bones, I began to see glimpses of Dennis Morrison and his wife in the last moments of their lives.

This unusual contact gave me a way to see the world through his eyes. This man had looked through the camera lens hoping to capture a piece of a child's soul — not to use them but to protect them. Protect them from the Draners. Dennis whispered to me in the darkness, as the dirt fell away, about how he had been a scientific man. He had hoped that maybe something about this new technology would somehow make the souls incomplete for the likes of the Draners and therefore unusable. They had met the Draners at a masquerade ball in one of the glamorous homes of a dear friend. Thomas Draner had reached out to shake his hand in welcome only the once. Anita had instantly known what he was. She had whispered under her breath in her husband's ear the terrifying word: vampire. At first he ignored her, but then when Mr. Draner licked his lips in an unsavory manner and asked if he had any children, Dennis knew the truth about them as well. His son had died on a cold winter morning in England, only a week after meeting the vampires at the ball. It had been a ravishing fever that had struck all those dear to him. He could never forgive himself after that moment for having allowed all of those children to be led like sheep to the slaughter.

That was when he started to plan. He followed the family when they made a swift escape to the New World after the last child died.

People had become suspicious. They set up a home in Boston; Dennis and his wife did the same. With the loss of their only son they had nothing to keep them in England and nothing to lose other than their own lives. Their obsession with the Draners mounted and yet they were unable to find a way to stop the loss of life in the upper echelons of Boston. Yet again, 130 children perished and they were powerless to stop them.

As I brushed the dirt from his boney fingers, an image of him pulling the cape over his head and pressing the small button to release the shutter, danced in my mind's eye. A flash of light and he had hoped a tiny piece of the child's soul would be safely hidden within the box. When the Draners moved west, Dennis and his wife were more prepared for what was about to happen when they reached Port Townsend. They had stayed on the periphery in Boston, never revealing their presence to the Draners. But it had been considerably harder to do in such an isolated place like Port Townsend. Why the Draners had chosen this far off place seemed odd. It didn't provide the anonymity of a city and the native tribes had sensed what they were immediately. None the less, the Draners set the plague in motion and once again began to capture souls. Dennis Morrison worked tirelessly taking photographs of all the children in town hoping that somehow it would save a piece of them, allow them to at least fight back when the time came. I wondered if this was why they had come to me in the mirrors. Dennis didn't seem to know, except that he had been trapped here unable to leave and unable to die. Until now.

As I carefully removed the dirt blanket that enveloped his legs and feet, he told me about the night he had died. He and Anita arrived at the Draners' home in the hope of finding a way to stop them. Anita was nervously twisting her gloves in her hands, wishing they could be anywhere else but on the front steps of a vampire's home. Dennis tried to calm her saying they were in no danger and hopefully they would be able to figure out how the children had been trapped. If they knew how, then they would be able to figure out a way to stop them before they moved on to more victims. When they arrived, the Draners had bags packed, waiting in the hallway. The last child had died that very morning. They had to move on. Dennis had sent the photographs to a trusted friend in Boston. He had hoped that someday he, or someone else, could free the children using the black and white reflections of their souls.

They ate a rich meal in the dining room where Sophie Draner served endless plates of delicacies. As the night rolled on, Thomas Draner became increasingly drunk. Dennis had sipped little of his wine wanting to keep a clear head to pry information from the Draners. That was until he began to feel light-headed. The room was spinning as he fell from his chair. The last thing he remembered was seeing Sophie grab Anita by the hair and inject a dark substance into her neck. The room had smelled of poppies and blood as Anita fell to the floor like a broken doll.

Laid together side-by-side in the shallow graves, Thomas shoveled dirt as Sophie, Daniel and Violet Draner watched impassively. Only Violet shed a tear for Dennis and his wife. Violet had been taken by the Draners in Boston as a companion for Daniel. There had been another young woman taken in London, but she hadn't survived the stormy seas. It seemed that Daniel was more partial to budding ladies than children as a source of life and energy. As Morrison's memories flashed through my mind, I saw that Violet was almost the mirror image of my Willa.

I pulled my hand away, suddenly fearful of what more Dennis would show me. I was overwhelmed with piercing sadness that threatened to submerge me. Then I felt a warm hand rest on my back. It was James. With his palm touching me protectively, I continued to reveal the skeletal remains of Dennis Morrison and with them, his story.

The last thing he heard, as the dirt covered his still-breathing body, was that the Draners would be taking his name when they moved to the next town. They laughed that a good English name was hard to come by and that being Romanian had grown stale. They immediately began to speak in perfect English accents, laughing at their own cunningness. Then Dennis was in the dirt. Everything was dark and he couldn't breathe. The weight of the soil on his chest was unbearable and the only sound was that of rodents scratching at the surface. He would stay this way until today, unable to leave and unable to rest. The Draners had bound both him and his wife in the dirt; forcing them to take their secrets to the grave.

I pulled my hand away from the fully uncovered skeleton. To his left were Anita's remains. Gavin was leaning against the tunnel wall, pale as any ghost. James was crouched beside me watching my every move, wearing an expression of deep concern. It was a relief when I told them both what I had learned from touching the bones. Gavin nodded his head as tears rolled down his cheeks. James held my dirt covered hand in his own and asked what he could do to help. There was no doubt in his voice, only concern which made my heart flutter in my chest. I worried that what had happened in the past few weeks might have signaled the end of our relationship. The issue had been far more than an unimportant kiss; it was the refusal to acknowledge my gift at the expense of our family and all that we had built together. We had been dancing around it for nearly two decades and finally it seemed we might be beginning to understand one another.

"I need to get some air," I said to James, and he nodded while helping me up. My legs had pins and needles prickling in the muscles. We agreed that the bodies would need to be removed by the police. As we started to move up the tunnel, Gavin stopped.

"I want to stay with them until the police get here," he said in a voice full of raw emotion. I gave him a quick hug as I felt his body choke back tears. James and I made our way out of the tunnel and back into the ballroom. For the first time since coming into this house I was able to breathe. As soon as we were upstairs, James called the sheriff and told her about our gruesome discovery.

Sheriff Joy Hanley and I had gone to school together. When we were twelve her twin sister Jewel died of a rare birth defect in her heart. It seemed that Joy would die along with her as her own heart broke into tiny piercing slivers. Three days after the funeral, Jewel came to me in the night with a message for Joy. There was a journal in a secret hiding place with a list of cities she wanted to go to someday. She wanted Joy to go there for her so she could move on in peace. Jewel had also made me promise to tell Joy that she should protect others because that was her gift. The following morning, I made my way dutifully to Joy's house, feeling awkward with fear at being unwelcomed. Instead, I had found Joy sitting on her front porch looking devastated until she saw me turn the corner. Her face suddenly lit with emotion that was true to her name as I sat next to her. All she said was "I was hoping you would come see me," as she waited excitedly to hear what Jewel wanted her to do. It was one of the few times I was ever greeted with such a warm welcome when I brought news from the deceased.

Today, as she pulled up to the Bell Tower House in her truck marked "Sheriff," it was I who sat on the front porch looking devastated. There was no need to explain how I had known to look in the tunnels for two, one-hundred-year-old, skeletons. Joy knew it was my gift. She and her team would take care of the rest from here. I sat there with James' arm wrapped around my shoulder, watching the sky lighten into blue as the dawn arrived. The clouds had moved out to sea with the rats and the world was getting its color back. The nearly dead trees had little green sprouts where their leaves had withered.

The flock of swallows was watching from the largest of the peach trees on the Bell Tower House property. As the two skeletons were wheeled out on gurneys covered in white sheets, the swallows took flight together. There was a whisper on the wind as all one hundred and thirty birds made a rapid retreat in the direction of the cemetery. Many of the townsfolk saw the flock land in the old Laurel Grove graveyard, but none witnessed the flock depart. The children had finally been laid to rest and along with them my own ancestor, Magdalene Winship.

As Gavin stumbled out of the Renard house after the bodies of Dennis and Anita Morrison had been removed, he collapsed on the stairs next to us. The three of us were covered in dirt and filth. There was a stillness in the air that had been missing since the day of the red tide. Together we threw the shovels in the car and silently made our way back to the Winship house. I could tell this had taken its toll on Gavin as he sat in our kitchen drinking a beer with James. The two of them looked like soldiers returning from battle; weary and shell-shocked. As I left the kitchen to make my way upstairs, I heard James ask Gavin about ghosts. It brought a smile to my exhausted face. If

James was asking the one person who had always believed everything I said about the unseen world, then that meant he wanted to be let in on the secrets as well.

I climbed the old Winship stairwell, dragging my feet up the first flight to look in on Felix. I must have looked like a ghoul with dirt smeared all over my clothes. I had washed my hands but there was still filth lingering in the crevices. I pushed open the door to Felix's room and found him stretched out on his bed reading the old book I had seen him toting around the past few weeks. It was what looked to be an old volume on botany.

"Hey there little man," I said in a tired voice, "What are you reading?"

"This book by Elsiba, it is fascinating," he said with an eager lilt in his young voice. I froze in place. This was definitely not the book I thought it had been. My Grandfather George's books about plants had similar covers but looking more closely I saw that this book was all hand written.

"Where did you find that?" I asked, remembering that Margot had misplaced Elsiba's grimoire years ago when she had moved. Could this be it, I wondered?

"That girl, Magdalene, left it for me weeks ago," he said with an innocence that made my heart tighten. "She told me to keep it near and not to show it to anyone until the rats were gone." My mouth fell open and I almost swallowed a bug in the time it took my mind to register what he was saying.

"Can I see it?" I asked, almost feeling like an intruder. He gave a slight shrug of his shoulders.

"I guess so. The rats are gone now so it should be ok," he said as he pushed the book towards me. It was filled with pages of journal entries. This was not Elsiba's grimoire but something else entirely. It was her travel journal. The first set of pages were marked Portland and the name Draner and Morrison were strewn everywhere through the thick pages. She had been hunting them both.

"She got really close to getting them once," Felix said in a quiet voice. "But they got away and she had to come home because she was going to have Great Grandma Margot." His tiny voice was so filled with passion as he talked about the contents of the book, it lifted my heart. There was no doubt that Felix would use his Winship gifts for the better of the world. It was in his nature.

I kissed his tiny head and handed him back Elsiba's book. Magdalene had wanted him to see it, not me, and I would respect that. This would be his secret. I had seen enough of the Draners/Renards to last me a lifetime. As I left his room, worry returned to its usual spot in the pit of my stomach. My sweet Willa was nursing a broken heart the likes of which I could hardly fathom. I felt lost around her, not knowing what to say or do to make any of this tragedy better.

I climbed the steps to the turret room and saw that her door was slightly ajar. The hallway was quiet as I moved towards her room. I silently opened the door, thinking she might be deep in sleep again. I was shocked to find her standing at her open window. She was still in her purple pajamas which hung loose on her frail body. She spun towards me as a look of guilt crept over her face. There on the window sill was the night heron peering at me with its red eye. It let out a defiant caw and then quickly took flight into the March sky.

"He won't come back," she said, the words stumbling from her numb lips in a panic. The night heron had been Daniel's familiar, of that I was sure, which meant that he might still find a way to return. Thomas and Sophie were gone for good, but Daniel could still peer in windows as he tried to build a dark nest for his soul in a young maiden's heart. I turned, leaving her without a word. I heard her call after me in a frantic voice trying to explain her love for him but I kept walking down the stairs. I rushed into my bedroom and locked myself in the bathroom. I slipped down onto the tiled floor and let the tears flow from my eyes with impunity. The one thought that hovered at the forefront of my mind was that I had utterly failed her.

PAVOT.

Turpin. P.   Lanciere S.t sculp.

CHAPTER 41

Willa's birthday arrived on a rush of spring air that signaled the world was returning to normal. In the week separating the destruction of the vampires and my daughter's sixteenth birthday, the dead plants were resurrected. Where sepia tones had once been, new leaves rapidly took their place. Rat holes were filled by town members until nothing remained of their ghastly maws. Dead flowers were removed allowing fresh blossoms to push forth. And on the morning of Willa's birthday, the lilacs all bloomed for a second time, at what would have been their normal moment to flower. Primroses and crocuses popped their heads up surprised to see the world twice in one spring. Soon the tulips and daffodils would follow, all in their own orderly way.

The morning of her birthday, I woke her with a tray of coffee and pastries in bed. She had been drawn and pale the past week as she dutifully went to school and came home. A phone call that morning had given me the good news I had been hoping to hear. Lily was on her way home after a miraculous recovery. Felix had been standing next to me as the phone had rung a second time to announce that Cody's fever had broken and he was expected to return home in a few days. The doctors still hadn't found the source of his illness and were astonished at his sudden recovery. Unsurprisingly to me, his turnaround coincided with the parade of rats. Felix was overjoyed when I told him. He even did his happy dance. I had expected the same from Willa. Instead she met me with a hollow smile, the smell of poppies somewhere on her skin.

I subtly inspected her arms for any other needle pricks and found nothing. But there was a lingering anxiety within me. Was she in the process of losing herself in the search for numbness? We had originally planned on buying her a car, but she had refused, saying the accident had left her too shaken. Instead, she wanted a darkroom. She had found an old camera in the attic of the Winship house and had been using film to capture the return of spring to our garden. The local grocery store took weeks to develop film and she wanted to learn how to do this on her own. James built it in less than a week in one of the Victorian carriage houses in the backyard. The plumbing was already in place but he made it state-of-the-art. By the morning of her birthday, he had managed to find a huge piece of ribbon to wrap around the entire studio. It had done him good to work on a project as an expression of his devotion to us.

Willa exhibited excitement for the first time in weeks as James and I brought her to see her present. For a moment a glimmer of her light and energy burst through the veil of lethargy. Her arm was still bound tightly to her chest, but she managed to wield her new camera with her other arm as if it was attached to her hand. Her hair was pulled back into two long braids and she was dressed all in black. For a moment I pictured her in Paris, snapping photographs of buildings and people. She looked happy. But then the cloud returned again as she silently inspected her new dark room. Willa was with us, but also in a very far-off place I could no longer access. It had all happened so quickly. Like the fading petals of a wild poppy, her innocence had been taken from her in an instant.

The family gathered in the rose garden under the willow tree for a leisurely Sunday lunch to celebrate Willa's birthday. Morgan and Astrid arrived with Margot. Gavin and Kat brought Lily straight from the hospital to our house as she refused to lay in bed another second. James, Felix and I rushed in and out of the back door carrying trays of food and drink laden with the taste of Spring.

Astrid made rosemary bread so fragrant that each bite brought waves of joy. She explained it was meant to solidify family ties. I had told no one about Sophie's attempted seduction of James. That tie had been crushed entirely the moment the rats were washed to sea. James was himself again entirely; no darkness lingered around his soul. I was more concerned with my daughter's heart. First love is rife with pain under normal circumstances, but the fact that it had been with a vampire would destroy most people. I cut extra pieces of the rosemary bread and slipped it onto Willa's plate but she barely touched her food all afternoon.

Lily was exuberant when she and Kat walked through the garden gate. Gavin unhooked the tedious latch to let them in, allowing Lily to rush to Willa. For a fleeting moment, it seemed all would be well. Willa and Lily chattered away, thrilled she'd been released from the hospital. There were still bruises on her face and an overall look of fatigue, but her mind and soul were intact. The same could not be said for my Willa as I compared their light from afar. Lily had vibrant orange halos circling around her much like her mother, Kat. But Willa was a greyish purple. It was as if the pigment had been sucked out of her, leaving her a wilted, ashen color. There was only a hint of violet underneath desperately trying to seep through the pain.

As the day wore on there were many visits to the house from neighbors and friends. They all wished Willa a happy birthday while gently leaving gifts. No one dared to mention the Renards and the tragedy that had befallen them as everyone in town had known that Willa and Daniel had been a couple. Her mourning was respected by all until Pat Savage and his wife arrived with a huge bouquet of lavender. I could tell by the way that he looked at her that he was seeing the grey as well. If you knew how to look for these things it was hard to miss. I had called the coven the day after they saved both the Winships as well as the rest of the town from Sophie and Thomas' rats. It was awkward at first as my appreciation gushed into a random mix of thanks and praise. I knew it hadn't been an easy choice for them to make. He had assured me that it had been in the works when I had visited them after the Renards had arrived in town, but I could tell there was still a bit of hesitation in his voice. Now, watching Pat and his wife move around the family table talking casually with everyone, I saw that his furtive glances at Willa were more than just concern. Part of me feared she had perhaps been infected by the Renards in a way that was irreversible. James glowed in the same way he had been before the vampires had come to town. I knew he was unfettered by whatever had occurred between him and Sophie. I also knew that unlike Sophie Renard, Daniel might not be entirely dead. The night heron hadn't reappeared since the evening we uncovered Dennis and Anita Morrison's shallow tombs. And yet Willa could be found gazing out her bedroom window without fail, every night at dusk.

As the day wore on, Margot and Morgan showered Willa with protective gifts. Margot gave her a holy water font to keep by her bedside that had an exquisite French porcelain image of the Madonna painted on it. She also gave her a rosary that had been blessed at the cathedral of Notre Dame in Paris, France. Morgan gave her a book on holy sites throughout Europe and an amulet to carry on her person at all times. I had the feeling that Willa would soon be leaving our cocoon for faraway places and these gifts didn't help my peace of mind. I wanted her close where I could keep an eye out for her and yet I didn't want to smother my girl who would soon be a woman.

When Felix gave her a travel journal with a picture of the Eiffel Tower on the front, I knew she would soon be making her way to France. My heart filled with dread. Would Daniel return and steal her away? I didn't think so, but that was my worst fear. The only thing that gave me even the slightest bit of hope was that Felix seemed happy as he and Willa looked through the book Morgan had given her. They had their heads together as they flipped through the pages, pointing excitedly at the names and places in France and England. If he had had a premonition of his sister being in France with a vampire, I was sure he wouldn't be so effusively contented.

By evening, the world seemed to have returned to its natural order. The late March air was cool as the sun began to set and James and I cleaned the tables and stacked the chairs in the garage. He held me in his arms under the willow tree after we had finished setting the house in order. It was just a brief moment, but it spoke volumes to my heart. The hint of betrayal was already gone as he leaned down and gave me a lingering kiss. I was his forever and he was mine; through the good and the bad we would do our best to mend the missteps of life. In the end, we all have a bit of vampire in us, pulling energy from those around us when we are weak. But the one difference is that, unlike the Renards, when we are strong, we give the energy back in the form of love. I loved my family and I loved James. If this was his one moment of weakness, I was sure that somewhere down the line my own fragility would appear and he would be the strong one. Such is the way of nature; the flower wilts and gives its body to nourish the earth and the earth gives it back to grow the new flower.

As we entered the kitchen, we heard the sounds of zombies moaning for brains coming from the parlor. Willa, Lily and Aaron were having a zombie movie marathon for Willa's birthday. All three were still in various stages of healing from the car accident and a night in with junk food and bad movies had been their choice of celebration. Aaron was sprawled out on the floor with a stack of pillows, while the girls each had one of the couches for their own. The light of the TV flickered across the dark room as they gasped and laughed at their first movie of the evening. As the night progressed, they planned to increase the fear factor by watching a movie that was scarier than the last. I was sure that by the early morning hours I would find them all asleep, dreaming of the walking dead, and hung over from sugar. It would be a relief after the close calls with death the three of them had had with the Renards.

Gavin and Kat had gone home earlier in the evening as they had a business to tend to now that everyone was safe. Much of the town was in need of strong beer and conversation, as the subject of lightning killing the Renards and the coven performing a rather unusual rat extermination were still big news. When the discovery of Dennis and Anita Morrison's bodies began to buzz through town, people could hardly wait to get to the Waterside Brewery to talk about a new mystery. There was one person, besides my immediate circle, who I had called first before the news began to circulate.

Tom Caldwell actually dropped his glass when I called him and revealed that Dennis and Anita Morrison had spent the last hundred years buried under the Bell Tower House. He had been searching endlessly for a lead on where the Draners had gone after Port Townsend and had come up with nothing. When I explained that the Draners/Renards had murdered the Morrisons and stolen their identity to start a new trail of death, he could hardly speak. We decided that the photographs, which had been untouched by fire, would be given to Evelyn Pettygrove of the Historical Society, but only on the condition that she create a memorial show in their honor. With all the news going around, it would end up being the most visited photography exhibition the town had ever seen. Evelyn spent weeks organizing a truly spectacular show of all the haunting children who had perished. In a way, Dennis and Anita Morrison had captured tiny pieces of those children's souls in black and white; now their existence would never be forgotten. People came from across the country to see the exhibit as news of the mystery made it to syndicated television shows and newspapers. The exhibit remained on permanent display in the Historical Society Museum creating a shrine to the lost. Dennis and Anita Morrison were laid to rest in Laurel Grove Cemetery with the proceeds of the exhibit, as the town adopted them as an official son and daughter of Port Townsend.

As for the Renards, all that was left of them, their teeth and ashes, would remain forever unclaimed in police custody. The town would always be ignorant to the tragedy they had missed. Only our small circle knew what had really happened to the Renards. In truth, I would always feel haunted by them in a less obvious way than my usual ghosts. An innocent rat or night heron would make an appearance and I would freeze with fear.

It was with Willa in mind that I left the house on the night of her birthday to visit Tom Caldwell. Gavin and James had been by my side when we uncovered the Morrisons' graves, and if it hadn't been for Tom's advanced age, he would have been there as well. I kissed James and headed into the dark night as he made sure the children were safe in the Winship house. The dusk air smelled of lilacs again as I drove up to the lemon meringue-colored house. Tom answered the door with a crooked smile, unable to hide his excitement of hearing the details of the past few weeks. Little did he know, I was about to bombard him with a new round of questions about our collective town history.

We walked back to his study where he offered me one of his lounge chairs amid the precarious piles of books. As I sat in the worn out leather with the fragrance of lilacs and pipe smoke mixing together in the room, I asked him a simple question.

"Tom, what do you know about opium?" My words rose into the air like a djinn escaping from a forgotten lamp. I had a foreboding this treacherous elixir was to be my daughter's new enemy. This meant it would also be mine. All my instincts told me that Willa had been damaged by Daniel. Her soul struggled against the darkness, fluttering with clipped wings. When I looked at her, dark poppies bloomed beneath her pale skin.

"You're going to need more than one of these," was his response as he shot me a wrinkled grin, pointing to his glass of whiskey. I let out the first unhindered laugh to escape my lips since the grim discovery of the Morrisons. If anything, the last few weeks had shown me the past could mirror the future. If the poppy omens were a sign of things to come for my Willa, then I wanted to know everything about their dark allure. This time I would be prepared for the arrival of monsters, whatever their form. I gratefully held out my hand for a very full glass of moonshine, as Tom's portentous stories began to unfold.

ACKNOWLEDGEMENTS

The idea for the second book came quickly on the heels of finishing the first novel in the series. I wrote the draft in three months and then began the process of releasing the first book into the world. I had no clue if anyone would even read the first book, let alone the second! For this I am grateful to everyone who picked up a copy of my first book and gave my self-published words a chance. It means the world to me to write stories but what use is it if there is no one to read them? So to all of you, I am forever thankful.

To Lynn Smith Grigsby for not only taking the time to edit the first book but for digging into the second with an enthusiasm that kept me on my toes! I trusted you with my stories and you gave them a newly polished shine. To Carla Haddow and Merideth Tall for reading the first book, at least twice, in search of pesky typos. I am grateful for your keen proofreading eyes on the second as well! Most of all, I am thankful for your steadfast encouragement of the Winships. To Jennifer Jahahn for always being my buddy (fastest reader I know) and for traveling with me to Port Townsend for the best book signing day EVER. The "mermaid day" bears repeating, as does a trip to Sirens but with the menfolk next time. To Crackerjack, Art Beat Foundation and Wynwood's Gallery for promoting my first book with so much enthusiasm!

To my family and friends for always encouraging me to create. To Laura and Bella Carriker for always cheering on the Winships! To Leta Rose Scott for seeing through the veil, into the source of the stories, with profound clarity. To my old friend, Beau Longwell, for understanding the magic in the world and to my new friend, Kim Dehuff-Longwell, for making me smile with the perfect sarcastic quip! And to you both for sharing the lilacs to make the first batch of Elsiba's potion; can't wait to start again next spring. To Wendy Thomas for being a loyal and true friend, always. To the Gorochs for being my other family, I love sharing hopes and dreams with each of you! To all my French friends and family who braved English and read the first book! Maybe someday it will be translated but until then, I miss you all and you are going to love the third book in the series. Most of all to my husband, Laurent Gallego, for being my fiercest advocate, my best friend, my confidant, my "computer alchemist" and my soul mate. The third book is all for you!

ILLUSTRATION INDEX

Frame used on the cover by Darkrose42.

All chapter borders are from "Natural History, General and Particular" by Buffon, engraved by A. Bell, published by Strahan & Cadell in London, 1785.

Title: "A Mask Held by Two Genii" by Hans Sebald Beham, 1544.

Acknowledgement: "Afbeeldinghe van d'eerste eeuwe ..." by Jean Bolland, Antwerp, 1640.

Chapter 1: "Dictionnaire Universel d'Histoire Naturelle" by d'Orbigny, 1849.

Chapter 2,13 : "Natural History, General and Particular" by Buffon, engraved by A. Bell, published by Strahan & Cadell in London, 1785.

Chapter 3: "Autel d'Or des Parfums" by Lanvin, engraved by Lecerf, 1859.

Chapter 4: "Polygraphice" by Salmon, Fabre, Churchill and Nicholson, 1701.

Chapter 5: "Liber de arte Distillandi de Compositis" by Hieronymus Brunschwig published in Strasbourg in 1512.

Chapter 6: "Horologium sacerdotale" by Jean Dirckinck, 1700.

Chapter 7: "De Europische Insecten" by Maria Sibylla Merian, published by J.F. Bernard in Amsterdam, 1730.

Chapter 8,21,35: "L'Encyclopédie ou Dictionnaire raisonné des sciences, des arts et des métiers, par une Société de Gens de lettres" under the direction of Diderot and d'Alembert, 1751-1772.

Chapter 9: "Erasmus of Rotterdam" by Albrecht Dürer, 1526.

Chapter10: "Academicarum annotationum" by Bernhard Siegfried ALBINUS, 1754.

Chapter 11,20,23,24,29,41: "Flore Médicale" by Chaumeton, Poiret & Chambert, painted by Turpin & Panckoucke, 1833.

Chapter 12: "Die Gartenlaube", Germany, 1875.

Chapter 14: Allain Manesson Mallet, Frankfurt, 1719.

Chapter 15: "Das Buch der Welt", 1843.

Chapter 16: "Cacenten Pati" by Louis Constant Lorichon, ca.1800.

Chapter 17: "Encyclopédie Méthodique ou par ordre de matières" published by Panckoucke, between 1782-1832.

Chapter 18,37: "Historiae Naturalis De Avibus Libri VI" by Johnston, published by Merian in 1657.

Chapter 19,28,31: "Histoire Naturelle Générale et Particulière" by Buffon, engraved by C.F. Fritzsch, Amsterdam, 1767.

Chapter 22: "Physica Sacra" by Johann Jakob Scheuchzer, Augsburg und Ulm, 1731-1735.

Chapter 25: "Fables de la Fontaine" by Jean Baptiste OUDRY, engraved by Gallimart, 1700's.

Chapter 26: "L`Antiquité Expliquée", published in France between 1719-1724.

Chapter 27: "Bibliograph Institut", Leipzig, printed in Germany, 1894.

Chapter 30: "Ball in the Ducal Palace in Honour of a Visiting Prince by Giacomo Franco", Museo Civico Correr, Venice, Italy, ca. 1590.

Chapter 32: "Afbeelding der Artseny-Gewassen" by J. Zorn, Nurnberg, Germany, 1780.

Chapter 33: "Huishoudelyk Woordboek" by M. Noel Chomel, published in Leyden and Amsterdam by S. Luchtmans & H. Uytwerf, 1743.

Chapter 34: "Alle de Wercken van den heere Jacob Cats", 1726.

Chapter 36: "Tafereel, of Beschryving van den prachtigen Tempel der Zang-Godinnen" by Bernard Picart Le Romain, published by H. Chatelain in Amsterdam, 1733.

Chapter 38: "Les Travaux de Mars, ou l'Art de la Guerre" by Allain Manesson-Mallet, Paris – chez D. Thierry, 1684.

Chapter 39: "Encyclopaedia Britannica", published by Bell and MacFarquhar, Edinburgh, 1797.

Chapter 40: "Œuvres Complètes de Buffon" by Edouard Traviès, 1860.

THE CURIOUS VOYAGE OF A LOST SOUL

In the third Winship novel, Wilhelmina Winship dusts off her wings and learns to fly. Hoping to restore her fragmented soul, Willa jumps at the chance to be a photographer's assistant in Paris. All goes well until an unexpected project sends her to the Alps and headlong into a thousand-year-old magical feud. While there, Willa becomes ensnared between visions of an ancient woman clad in blue veils and her ever-growing attraction to a wolfish young Frenchman. Willa's adventure in the mountains quickly becomes a quest to uncover the elixir that will make her whole again.

Made in the USA
San Bernardino, CA
03 May 2014